MURDER

IN

MIXTECA

MURDER

IN

MIXTECA

BY J. ROYAL HORTON

SUNLIGHT
PUBLISHING

The author wishes to acknowledge the following:

Thanks to my family, of course, and to Kay & Judy and Jac, all angels. Special thanks, again, to Malcolm for the cover art, Larry for the legal advice and special friendship, and Heather, Dan and Kristin for their editing expertise. Those anonymous folks and God are still in Wilson and I still go to them for love and acceptance. Help arrived in the friendship of Bruce in both Wyoming and Mexico, where he risked his life for me. Anita, Chano and Marcos, "Jeemy" and Cristina also gave me shelter. Stormy and Shane have done the hard stuff and had none of the fun or adventure. Thank you. But, most of all, I want to thank the still suffering Cloud People of the Mixteca Alta for their example of genuine humility. God bless you all.

ISBN 0-9643978-1-1

Printed in the United States of America

Published by
SUNLIGHT PUBLISHING
Colorado Springs, Colorado USA

Cover art by Malcolm Furlow,
represented by the Center Street Gallery
Jackson Hole, Wyoming

First Edition

This story is dedicated to Pastor James O'Neal and Pastor Michael Atkins, whence came the help when I needed it so badly. To the little saints of Piña Palmera and to Willie LeClair, who introduced me to the pipe and the redemptive pain of the Shoshone sweat lodge — and to *Tam Apo* and "all my relations."

To God, in his many manifestations,
and all His loving helpers here on this wonderful, pitiful planet.

MURDER IN MIXTECA

Prologue

Lauro Osorio Cruz picked his way carefully over the rocky path. A crescent moon hung overhead and a bright star appeared almost cupped in it. The thin moon was an angry orange. The dry season had continued far into June, when it should be raining. Lauro was a young Indigeno boy – he didn't understand that the orange color came from the smoke of the fires that were burning on the hills above him. Burning because they were so dry. All Lauro knew was that he had fallen asleep in the late afternoon because of a sickness in his stomach and wakened in the dark. He had no way to start a fire and wait out the night, so he had set out for home full of fear. In the Mixteca Alta of southern Mexico the night is full of things that one should fear. Flying people most of all. El hombre volador.

Lauro made his panicky way through the smoky night until he finally reached the dry riverbed. His huaraches crunched in the rock. His steps whispered in slight echoes as he neared the other side. He whimpered with fear as he entered the narrow barranca that led up the hill toward his father's rancho. He glanced over his shoulder. The dome of a sixteenth-century convent's nave barely whispered of moonlight. It sat on the hill high above him, on the site of the ancient city of Achiutla. And above it was the mysterious ruined mound that had once been the pyramid city of his ancestors. But Lauro knew little of this. The Spanish Capitanes had superimposed their influence on his ancient culture for four hundred years, but only superficially. Lauro Osorio believed in God, but mostly Lauro believed in the beings and things that populated the nights of San Miguel Achiutla. The flying people, hombres lobos, and others.

Lauro was a goatherd. For many of his fourteen years he had moved his father's goats along the barranca he was about to enter. It was part of his home territory and he knew it by feel, by second nature. But only during the day. He crossed himself and kissed his fingers, just for luck. Sweating, he entered the thinning willow grove at the mouth of the barranca. The springs above were only trickles this dry year and the willows suffered too. He felt better after a few minutes as his feet began to pick up familiar messages from the ground. He kept his head down and walked with determination, moving closer to his house by the moment. Dreading the sound of wings. Wings big enough to carry a man.

He turned right up a branch of the gully. His head was still down, his eyes on the ground to pick up the faint light reflected by the white limestone rock that marked the deeply worn footpath. He hardly noticed that the white rocks were growing gradually brighter, taking on the smoky orange color of the sliver moon above. He didn't look up until he was stopped in his tracks by the wet smack of a whip and a man's scream.

Lauro started to run away in the dark, run back down the arroyo. But after a few stumbling steps, his fears of the dark returned. And after the first shock, he was curious. Whipping was a common enough punishment in San Miguel, meted out for serious breaches of the local laws. But why this night in the barranca? Lauro's curiosity drew him closer to the circle of flash and torch light which illuminated the scene.

Marcos Albino was being whipped. Each time the anciano brought the vinza down on Marcos' bare back the young man screamed. In between the strokes he cried out for mercy. And help.

The whips of the ancianos are made by tightly twisting the split penis of a slaughtered bull. When dry it makes a whip about two feet long. The whip is very hard and the exaggerated twists have a terrible effect on human flesh.

The men had laid Marcos face down on the ground. A man held each arm. Two men restrained each leg. At first, every time the whipper brought the vinza down the men had to exert all their effort. After a dozen strokes, however, Marcos no longer screamed and the men no longer had to struggle to hold him down. He had either fainted or died of shock. Still, the man with the whip threw all his weight into the work he'd been given. The men who held the arms and legs turned their faces at each stroke. Not because they were squeamish but to avoid the sprays of blood. After twenty-five strokes it was over.

The anciano who had wielded the whip took it from his wrist. Lauro had crept forward during the lashing and now, in the flickering light, he could see the face of the man, wet with tears. It was Marcos' father, Venustiano.

The man knelt, turned his son's face to his own, and bent to kiss it. Then he said a few quiet words to the men who held the young man. They dragged the limp figure a few feet to the spring which trickled from the small limestone grotto rimmed with fern. They took clean white cloths and, dipping them in the scant water, bathed the ravaged back. Marcos moaned.

Venustiano took off his hat and raised his wet face to the smoky sky, to the crescent sliver the color of dried blood. He said, "This man has paid for his sin against the rain. He has redeemed himself. Our crops lie waiting in the ground for your mercy and without your mercy we will starve. Forgive us, Dzaui. Please. Bring us rain."

The powerful old man put his hat back on and motioned to the other men who had put Marcos on a rough stretcher. He then led them up the arroyo and through the dusty fields toward their casitas which squatted in the hot, smoky night.

To the north, above the mountain called El Carbonero, there was another flash of dry lightning. There would be no rain this night.

Chapter 1

In Riverside, California a big, faded green 1974 Chevrolet sedan parked in front of a Spanish Colonial style house. After a few minutes two people got out. The man was small, an inch or so over five feet. The woman was even smaller.

"Seguro?" the man asked, nervously.

"Si, aqui... seguro." And then she said to herself, in English, 'Yes, I am sure this is the place.'

She went to the front door while the man waited on the lawn. He shrugged his shoulders helplessly and took off the battered bill cap with Raiders embroidered on the front.

The little woman rapped on the door. In a moment it opened. A tall woman with graying hair and half-glasses perched on her nose looked at the couple and said, "Buenos dias."

"Buenos dias, Señora. Soy Concha Osorio," the small Mexican woman answered, identifying herself. "Usted Profesora Roberts?"

"Si, si, soy Señora Roberts." The woman motioned to the man on the lawn, then stepped back, waved them in, and said, "Por favor, mi casa es su casa — y el otro?" inquiring about the man in the car.

The little Mexican woman, switching to English, said "We cannot stay so very long. But perhaps he could have some water for drinking?"

"Of course, of course, let me get him something." She turned and called toward the kitchen, "Maria?"

A woman wearing an apron, came out, wiping her hands.

"Si, Señora?"

"Por favor, agua de limon para todos."

"Si, Señora," she said and disappeared into the kitchen.

The woman went to a table and picked up an envelope. She returned and handed it to the little Mexican woman. "Here is the money that Señor Garcia asked me to give you, Concha. Is there anything else I can do?"

"No, Señora, I am very thankful that you could do this for us. Now we can return home and save our world."

"I am always glad to help any of the Mixtec people who need me."

"You are famous for your generosity, Señora. Everyone says that you are a saint."

The woman tilted her head back and laughed. "Hardly a saint, Concha, just an old professor who loves the Mixteca."

"The money will be paid back. I will get it from the ejido elders when I am home in San Miguel Achiutla. Do not fear for this, Señora."

"There is no hurry. Ah, here is the lemonade."

Maria had come from the kitchen with a gallon jar of ice and lemonade. She was also carrying a bulging brown paper sack.

"Tamales, frijoles negritos y tortillas gorditas. Salsa tambien," she said, describing the contents.

The little man smiled broadly, his eyes disappearing into his moon face. "Bien, bien, muchas gracias a usted, Señora."

"Gracias a Dios," the woman returned.

"Yes, yes, thanks go to God," he said and took the food.

Concha went back to the door and Maria opened it.

The tall woman followed them to the lawn and waited until they were in the car. Then she waved and said, "Buen viaje!" as they pulled out of the drive.

When they were gone she added, to herself, "And luck . . . suerte."

"Si," said Maria from the front step, "suerte." She crossed herself and kissed her fingers before she went back into the house.

———

Up the coast, in Berkeley, California, Milton Ozro "Oz" Gardner was signing books at the Shambhala bookstore. He was a big man with a long silver ponytail. Dressed in sandals, homespun white pants and a light, homespun white poncho secured by a wide brown belt, he was an impressive figure. But his eyes were even more impressive. They were a rainy gray to match the rainy gray day outside. But there was something else about them—a profundity, like looking down twin wells to the pinpoints of black water far below.

He signed the book in front of him and underlined the signature with a delicate flourish.

The beautiful, and expensive, older woman for whom he was signing protested mildly. "I was hoping you'd address it to me personally."

"The jaguar has no ego. You do not need one either. Let your life be ego-less and powerful!" Oz said, emphasizing the last word with a verbal flourish.

'Let your life be stoned to the max, you mean.' Detective Sergeant Pete Villareal was in an ironic mood as he waited in line to have the police department's book signed.

He observed the others in line. They were almost all well-to-do people in their forties and fifties, maybe a few in their late thirties. Mostly vets of the 1960s and 1970s, he thought. People like himself. Except he hadn't gone off on a vision quest on his Diner's Club card and been ripped off, as some very rich and influential people were complaining they had been. Oz had "conducted" on a couple of the rips. Pete had been assigned to find out more about the folks who were taking the ricos to some remote place, getting them stoned on various substances, then letting them run around panicked when their "trip" turned into a "bummer." It was more of the same sort of thing Pete had seen for himself twenty-five years earlier. Only now it was upscale boutique freakouts instead of those raunchy kids in Hashbury living on brown rice, dope, and what they could find in their noses.

Villareal had been raised in South San Francisco. He'd been a student radical at San Francisco State at the time of the Free Speech Movement in Berkeley. He'd been a real part of it. In fact, he had witnessed the riots around the People's Park — even been one of the students running from the tear gas and buckshot. Now part of his job was infiltrating the action that took place in that same park, plus student housing and just about everywhere else in town. Pete worked undercover and did it well. His cover had never been broken and was one of the street intellectuals who orbited the huge university campus. He hung at the Cafe Med, Cody's Books and the other little shops which line Telegraph Avenue. He did little deals in the back rooms of the trinket shops, ethnic restaurants, and other interesting corners of the city. He knew the scene. And its history.

Oz had been a part of the scene since the late fifties. He was a minor figure in the literary crowd, had known Kerouac, Casady, Ginsberg — was supposedly alluded to in the poem Howl!, even.

He was also a historical figure in the drug underground of Berkeley. By reputation, he'd been a source of the best Mexican dope in the fifties. In the sixties he'd moved LSD for the legendary

Owsley. A friend forever of the Grateful Dead and the other legendary Bay Area bands, he was a paterfamilias to the most exclusive part of the region's boutique drug world. And now he was back on the cutting edge of the scene, a conductor of souls to the underworld. Pluto and Charon's buddy.

Pete put his copy of *Power Places of the Americas* down on the table and said, "Hey, Oz."

"Hey, Pedro," Oz said in his husky whisper, "How goes?"

"Beautiful. Thanks."

"There you go, my man," he said as he signed in his florid but meticulous hand.

"Can I buy you some coffee at the Med when you're done?"

"Gotta go. Got some people to see at seven. Soul tourists."

"Where you going this trip?"

"Mexico, man. There's a power place in the Oaxacan Sierra that you wouldn't believe. We're going there for the solstice. Ancient Mixtec astronomical observatory. One of the most powerful places on the planet."

"Sounds trippy."

"Blow your mind. You goin' with us on this one?"

"Still saving my money. Maybe on the next one. Hey, thanks for the autograph."

"Pleasure. See you 'round the campus."

Pete put the book under his poncho, pulled up the hood and walked out onto the rainy avenue. He looked at his watch. Four-twenty. He was due to make a buy at six. Time for a cup of coffee and smart talk at the Med.

"What a job," he said to himself and grinned. He was getting paid a lot of money for doing exactly what he had been doing when he was twenty years old.

———

The ax came down directly into the center of the Doug fir round. The blade drove through the sinewy pink wood and it fell into two near-perfect halves. Tommy Thompson stooped to turn a half and then rose again and cut it into a quarter with another quick slash of the ax. The summer morning sun shone on his back and he felt good from the hour's exercise.

He split the second half and threw the four pieces onto the growing pile of redolent wood. He and his son, Jackie, had felled the trees and bucked them into eight-foot lengths. Working together they had loaded and hauled the logs to Tom's place in the mountains west of Jackson Hole. There they had blocked them into sixteen-inch rounds for the wood stove.

4

Tom took out a blue bandanna, mopped his face, and smiled. The memory of his son's slim, sinewy strength as they'd worked the wood made him feel good. The boy was growing. In more ways than one. The two had joked and laughed easily as they worked and it was a miracle. One year earlier most of their time together had been consumed by painful silences and scant conversations.

He bent, rolled the last round into place, split it. Then he put those pieces on the pile and drove the ax into the chopping block. It had been a perfect morning. On the way down the wooden walk to the house he paused for a moment and said, "Thank you, Lord." And he meant it. He was thankful for many things but this morning he was most thankful for his feelings. For twenty years he had felt mostly nothing, spiced only occasionally with flashes of anger and blossoms of violence. Being a cop had given him an excuse for indulging in the perverse pleasure of the violence. Being happy was something fairly new to Tom.

After showering and changing, Tom went to the kitchen and mixed a bowl of tuna salad. It was four in the afternoon, Pacific time. He could probably catch Polly at home.

Sugarbritches. It still made him pulse with happiness when he thought about her. She'd reappeared in his life the previous summer after twenty years. And nothing had cooled. The thought of her hot body and clean mind made him flush all over. Shivers ran over his shoulders and he shrugged them away. He was waiting for her to phone. "Zowie," he said, and smiled at the feelings she raised in him, even at long distance.

He was spreading the tuna salad on a slice of bread when the phone rang. A thrill ran through him as he picked it up.

"Hi, Sugarbritches," he said breathily.

After a pause a male voice said, "Gee, Tom, the last time I looked, there was only a brown streak there."

Tom looked out the window and said, "Well, shit!"

"Embarrassed, huh?" It was Sam Harlan, the Teton county sheriff and Tom's boss.

"Yeah . . . what's happening?"

"I just got a call from the other side of the mountains. They've found a dead guy in a cave above Alta. I need you to run over there and investigate."

"Dammit. This is a comp day for me, Sam."

"Sorry but this is a strange one. I don't want it messed up."

Tom sighed. "Tell me about it."

5

"Some local hikers were messing around in the woods and smelled something dead. They thought that it might be a bull elk or something they could get some horns or ivory off of. Poked around until they found some rocks piled up in front of a cave. That was odd enough that they pulled the rocks down and found the body."

"That sounds more like a burial than anything else."

"Bingo. That's good, Tom. It was a burial."

"Weird."

"Weirder than you think. This guy was buried in all kinds of strange clothing. He even had dealies braided in his hair and strange things piled around him. I'm afraid that it might have something to do with the Satanism that we hear about over there every once in a while."

"Hell, I hope not. You say he had dealies braided in his hair? What kind of dealies?"

"They tried to explain them to me but it didn't make any sense. Get over there and take a look. It's on the forest so there will be some rangers involved. They're waiting for you at the district ranger's office and will take you up Teton Canyon where Nolan Jensen is doing the preliminary investigation. I haven't been able to raise the coroner yet so take a look around and wait until he gets there before you move anything."

"OK." Tom looked at the clock. "Tell them I'll be there in about an hour."

"Take your camera."

"Will do. Bye."

The drive over Teton Pass is steep and beautiful. It winds over the south rampart of the Teton range and then drops down into the Teton valley, which the mountain men called Pierre's Hole. Holes were what they called circular valleys. Jackson's Hole was named for its discoverer, Davey Jackson. Pierre's Hole was name for an early French-Canadian mountain man who simply called it "the big hole," a name that stuck to the Big Hole Mountains, which rose on the west side of the valley.

Tom entered Idaho at the bottom of the pass. The highway gradually swung north to pass through Victor and continue up the middle of the broad green valley and into Driggs.

It was a whole different world on this side of the mountains. This was Mormon country with ranches and dry farms rather than the federal land and condominiums of Jackson Hole. A different mentality ruled here. Jackson was yuppie country where the environment as a lifestyle held sway. On this side it was still bucolic, loved in the nineteenth-century way simply as "good country." A T-shirt seen often in this valley read: "Dogpatch of the West." They liked to get down and wallow in the disdain of the upscale folk from the other side of the hill.

In Driggs he went to the U.S. Forest Service office. There were two rangers waiting in the morning sun.

"Hi," he said when he got out of his car, "I'm Tom Thompson with the sheriff's office in Jackson."

They introduced themselves and the three men got into a government 4x4. As they drove east through Driggs and started toward the mountains Tom thought through the agreement which Teton County, Wyoming, had with the governmental agencies in the area.

Because the county shared its geography with national forests and parks, a protocol had been worked out between the agencies in which criminal investigations were divvied up among the several parties. In homicide cases the county reserved primary investigative and prosecutorial powers. Others fell under federal purview and were handled by officers of the Forest and Park services. This protocol was in force with all the Wyoming, Idaho, and Montana counties which bordered Yellowstone National Park. Sometimes it got complicated but, for the most part, the federal agencies were cooperative with local jurisdictions and things went smoothly.

The state line which divides Idaho from Wyoming runs straight north and south, following the apron of the Teton Mountains. The unincorporated area called Alta-Leigh Canyon is cupped in Wyoming and accessible only through Idaho, except for a trip by foot over the rugged and spectacular range.

Tom ran the local geology through his mind. The Teton Range was the surfacial expression of a massive granite block which had been shoved up through the earth's crust. It was some ten by forty miles square and had come up at an angle. Breaking in half at a thrust fault, the western section reared into the sky while the eastern half represented the valley floor in Jackson Hole. This western half dropped down at a fairly shallow angle to the valley floor but the eroded eastern edge of the granite block was distinguished by the world-famous Tetons. Here on the Idaho side the geology was characterized by sedimentary rocks which had been carried up on the back of the basal rock thrust. On this side the country was ramped, leading up at a gradual angle to the base of the spires.

This area was known for its caves. Karst limestone had been carried up from below and exposed to ground water and runoff. Those water sources enter cracks in the limestone and precipitate it to make cave and tunnel systems underground. And surface caves are formed where the limestone is exposed to weather. The guy had probably been buried in one of thousands of such caves.

When they reached the head of Teton Canyon Tom saw the white Teton County sheriff's vehicle parked on the side of the road. He leaned out the window and followed the pointing finger of the ranger who was driving.

"Those buttresses up there are called 'The Ten Sentinels,' supposedly named by the local Indians a long time go. The cave is at the base of them."

They parked the vehicle, put on their backpacks, and started up the hill. When they neared the base of the buttresses Tom saw four men sitting under a tree, digging their lunches out of backpacks. Two of them were still wiping their upper lips clean of Mentholatum. A bad sign. Tom's stomach had always been sensitive to corpse smells. He sighed inside.

"Hi, Tom." The local deputy, Nolan Jensen, was lying down in the shade of a large pine, eating a sandwich. He didn't look happy.

"Hello, Nolan. What ya got?"

"A friend of mine."

"Sorry. Who is he?"

"Doc Ward. He was a caving buddy of mine."

Nolan was a local and a mountain climber, spelunker, skier, search-and-rescue expert and general back-country person. It was why he'd gotten the job. Over here, a lot of what went wrong happened in the huge back country.

"What happened to him?"

"Head trauma, depressed right-rear quadrant. Maybe other trauma to the body, going by some staining of the burial clothing. We haven't moved him very much, been waiting for you and the coroner."

"What do you know about the subject?"

"Nice guy. Hell of an athlete — expert climber, caver, skier. Loner, pretty much, but good company for someone who doesn't like a lot of talk. Had money. Inherited his bucks."

"Married? Family?"

"No. He had a housekeeper, a little Mexican gal. But she's gone."

"Gone for the day or just plain gone?"

"I don't know for sure. I asked one of the Idaho deputies to go to the house and he said that there was no one around."

"How about other family, like parents? Where was he from?"

"Maryland, I think. But I don't know where."

"What's with the burial? The sheriff said that it might be something satanic."

Nolan nodded his head at one of the Forest Service officers eating his lunch under the next tree. "Kelly, here, says that it's nothing like that."

The other man said, "My degree is in archaeology. I worked a couple of digs in Central America and this guy is buried with some world-class artifacts, as near as I can tell."

"Artifacts?"

"Yeah. The hair decorations are a fairly common practice among the indigenous people of the older American civilizations and he's wearing an interesting gorget. There's a couple of pots whose decorative style looks real familiar and the textiles will be fairly easy to identify, I'm sure. Very distinctive needlework. He's also wearing white cotton peasant clothing and the style, if I'm not mistaken, is Mexican."

"South American and Mexican stuff as well?"

"I'm no expert."

"Where do I find an expert?"

"I went to school at the University of Idaho. They have a real good grad school up there. It'd be easy to get someone down here to take a look and give us some opinions."

"That sounds like a good idea. Would you give me some names?"

"Be glad to."

"Thanks." Tom took a deep breath and opened the top of his backpack to dig out his jar of Mentholatum. It was hot and the guy was sure to be real ripe. "Where is he?"

Nolan stood up. "About a hundred yards up the slope, there's a small cave in the base of that limestone outcrop. I'll take you there."

Chapter 2

"Ritual strangulation?" Tom asked.

"Yeah," said Bill Hoskins, the coroner. "He was knocked unconscious, or into a coma, and then he died of suffocation.

"This is not just your everyday twine, see this decorative knotting? And it also has a clever one-way slipping knot. It was designed for strangulation."

"I don't want to have to deal with any ritual stuff. It's evil."

"I know," said Hoskins. "In this time of space shuttles and space travel people have a hard time believing in a literal Satan. Evil, for many Americans, doesn't exist anymore."

"If they ever got to see the things we see it'd make believers of them," said Tom.

Bill nodded. "It gets me down sometimes."

"Me too," Tom said and the old sadness began to creep into his heart. This was his job and it had been put before him as his portion. Someone had to do it. But he had a hard time not turning his heart off when things like this were handed to him.

Hoskins shook his head and said, "The heart is deceitful above all things, and desperately wicked: Who can know it?"

"Is that from the Bible?" Tom asked. He knew that Bill was an elder in his church.

"Yes. Jeremiah 17:9. C'mon, let's zip him in, get him in the Stokes litter, and back to town where I can cool him down."

Tom turned to the Forest Service people who were standing at a distance. "Would a couple of you come over and give us a hand getting this guy down to the ambulance?"

When the litter carriers started down Tom turned to the archaeologist ranger. "Let's get this stuff tagged and put in boxes. I will need you to give me a brief description of each item, the more descriptive the better."

———

10

Another Teton County deputy, Jeff, had come over with the order from Judge Herschler to enter Doc Ward's house. Tom used his burglar set to slip the locks and they went inside the big log house. Huge picture windows filled most of the east end of the big room, framing the Tetons. The view was magnificent, but the mountains were a mirror image of the ones Tom had grown used to, as a native of the other side of the range.

The living room was decorated in tasteful western decor. Tom's eye fell on a museum-quality Navajo chief's blanket, a ditto Teec Nos Pos, a glass case full of antique kachina dolls, and, as he observed on close examination, an original oil by Charlie Russell. That probably meant that the framed Frederic Remington drawings were originals as well. He let out a low whistle. "This guy had very serious money."

Tom knew a little about kachina dolls, so he went to the case and examined its contents. They appeared to be authentic dolls, some of them retaining a little of the original paint and feathers. He had a dozen of them himself, inherited from a grandfather who had served a Mormon mission in the southwest among the Pueblo Indians. The only two dolls he recognized were a shalako and a bear kachina. He remembered that the bear doll represented a powerful healing spirit.

Tom had begun a collection of Zuni fetishes as an affordable offshoot of his grandfather's kachinas. He had also approached his brother and sister about putting all the dolls in one place and they had agreed that it would be a real good idea. Their ideas had diverged, however, on the question of who should hold the collection — neither had agreed with him that he should be the conservator.

He turned his attention away from the glass case. This part of the house was immaculate. No signs of struggle, no obvious staining.

"You say he had a full-time housekeeper?"

"Yeah, a little woman from Mexico. Real cute."

"Think there was anything going on between them?"

"Like what? Sex?"

"Something to do with passion."

"Looking for a crime of passion? I thought we had a ritual murder here."

"Just running all the possibilities around in my mind."

"I don't know if there was anything going on between them, but you know how it is — a good-looking woman a long way from home in the house of a good-looking guy. And the winters get long out here." Nolan shrugged his shoulders. "Who knows. I always try to give 'em the benefit of the doubt."

Tom sighed. "And I'm a suspicious prick. Can't help it." Another one of the character defects he was trying to work on.

Tom was a card-carrying alcoholic. The card was in his wallet and had the Twelve Steps and Twelve Traditions on it. A talisman against his own bad side.

The upstairs included two large bedrooms and bathrooms as well as an entertainment center. The man had an impressive collection of jazz and classical music as well. There was another glass case holding old seventy-eights, some dating from the 1920s. Tom whistled again. "Good grief, here are some original recordings of Caruso."

"Scott Joplin over here." Nolan shook his head.

Tom went to another large case. "Video freak too."

"Yeah, he always had a camcorder with him. He videoed a lot of our explorations and grotto functions in Idaho Falls."

Tom saw an unlabeled videotape sticking out of the VCR. Almost absentmindedly he turned the TV and machine on. After a moment of confetti static the picture clarified and a naked, sweating woman appeared. Her mouth was open and her eyes wide and unfocused. Moving her hips and gasping audibly, she was sitting on the pelvis of a naked bearded man. He was open-mouthed and sweating too. Near his hand was a remote control, probably for the camera.

Tom pushed the stop button on the VCR and turned off the TV. "Well, that certainly answers my question, I think."

The woman had been small and Latin. "Was that the housekeeper?"

Nolan smiled self-consciously. "I don't remember ever seeing her like that but yeah, that was her."

Suddenly they heard a holler from downstairs. It was the other deputy.

"Sounds like Jeff found something," Nolan said.

They went to the landing and saw the tall blond deputy in the basement doorway .

"You won't believe what I found down here," he said.

They all went down the stairs. Jeff led them to a door hidden behind the large gas furnace and air conditioner. The door opened into a small foyer. In the foyer was a formidable bank-type vault, complete with spoked hand wheel to drive the tumblers and florid 19th century script which read "First State Bank ~ Sydney, Montana."

An hour later, outside, they found what they were looking for. Tom stepped around the side of the house and saw two magpies take a couple of hops and look over their shoulders before reluctantly flapping away.

Tom found a sizeable patch of dry blood where the birds had been tugging at the grass. Not too far from the blood was a piece of firewood. It also had blood on it and what he would bet was human hair and scalp tissue.

"Hey, Nolan!" he hollered.

Nolan came around the side of the house and said, "What?"

"Bring me a big plastic bag."

"Whatcha got?"

"Looks like the classic 'blunt object' — piece of firewood with boogers on it."

"Bingo! I'll be right there. Just a sec'."

Tom sighed and looked up at the mountain spires. They were lit by the afternoon sun and the light shone through the long reds of the light spectrum. It made the residual summer snows turn a soft pink and lightened the dark granite to purples and lavender. The soft pastels of afternoon, shading into the fragrant cools of the coming evening ordinarily calmed him. He purposely kept his eyes from the weapon and waited for Nolan to return. He kept his eyes on the mountains and the hills. A small meditation. Turn it over for a second and let someone else have the control and the power. He was just a medium, a second, a supernumerary. None of this had much to do with him, finally. His responsibility was to do what was put in front of him at that moment and leave the outcome to God. Turn it over. His stomach was flaring.

"Here ya go," Nolan said as he walked up. Jeff was with him.

"You secure it, please." Tom turned to Jeff. "Let's do a careful search of this area and see what else we can find. The grass hasn't been mowed for a while so let's take our time so we don't miss anything."

"Rog," the tall man said.

In about ten minutes Jeff hollered, "Come take a look at this!"

When Tom and Nolan reached the front of the big house they saw Jeff pointing down into the grass at the edge of the driveway.

"Got a license plate — Oregon." He pointed at the garage. "If you look you can see where the garage was banged into. Looks like someone knocked the plate loose and then lost it when he cut the corner on the driveway and bounced over these rocks in the weeds."

"Good work, Jeff. Why don't you go run the plate and see who it belongs to."

"Already have." He handed Tom a slip of paper.

"Cenovio Osorio Espinoza. Wilsonville, Oregon."

"Whoa," Nolan said. "I think that was the housekeeper's name — Osorio."

"You positive?"

"No. But I've seen it . . . Yeah. She ran the stop sign at the Targhee road and banged into the Capellen's car. She had a driver's license and the name, I'm sure, was Osorio. I remember it because it was so different from the Sanchezes, Hernandezes, Garcias — the usual Latin surnames."

"Was it a Wyoming license or an Idaho?"

"Uh, Idaho."

"Jeff, run Osorio in Boise. Ask for a last name sort. I'll bet it's a box number in Driggs."

Nolan nodded. "Yeah. Mail here is a mess because they make the Alta post office use an Idaho zip. You get your mail sooner having it delivered to a box in Driggs and driving down to pick it up."

Jeff touched Tom's arm. "Here comes the boss." Sheriff Harlan's car was moving up the lane toward the house.

When the car reached the wide yellow perimeter tape it stopped and Big Sam uncoiled himself from the driver's side. Bob Bilyeux got out the other door.

"Good afternoon, gentlemen."

"Hi, Sheriff," Nolan said.

"Whatcha got? I talked to the coroner when he got to town and it sounded like this is going to make a bunch of noise in the media. Figured I'd better get Bob over here." Bilyeux handled the press relations for the department.

Tom took out his notebook.

"The man's name is Amos Nathaniel Ward, 42 YOA. Originally from Owings Mills, Maryland, with degrees from William and Mary and a Ph.D. in Anthropology from Vanderbilt. That's according to the framed certificates on the walls in his office. Looks like he came to Wyoming with the National Outdoor Leadership School because he has all his graduation certificates hanging on the wall with the other stuff. Probably another protégé of Paul Petzoldt or Tap Tapley. His age is about right.

14

"Also, he has one which says he was a vet. Army Rangers. Expert outdoorsman — climber, kayaker, caver and who-knows-what-else. Has an equipment room chock full of outdoor gear and Nolan knows him personally as an expert in climbing and caving. "This man has major money. We fired up his computer and took a brief look at what was on the desktop display. The numbers in his portfolio make your mouth water. We also got his address book off the machine. His parents are in there so maybe you'll want to notify them ASAP..."

"What about the MO?" Bilyeaux cut in.

"You mean, how was he killed?" Tom asked. Bilyeaux misapplied a lot of official terminology. He had a degree in PR and thought like a journalist. Always looking for a buzzword or a sound bite. He made Tommy's ass work buttonholes.

"Yes. How was he killed, how was he buried?" Bilyeux had his pencil poised over a journalist's notepad.

"Uh, let's go take a look inside," said Sheriff Harlan. He had seen the disgusted look on Tom's face. "You said on the radio that you'd found something real interesting in the basement."

"Yes. Also, we found what appears to be a bludgeon. Also, Jeff just found an Oregon license plate and has run it. The registered owner may be related to the housekeeper, who seems to have disappeared."

"Good. You guys have done a real good job for such a short time. I know you're following up on all that."

"Yes. Nolan and Jeff have done some real class work."

When they reached the basement Sheriff Harlan took one look at the vault and said "Phone Daddy-O at Teton Locksmiths and get him over here." He then bent over a plate which was fixed to the front of the safe. "Write this down: Schwab Model 7840-6, serial number 2411617, relocking device number 7514." He turned to Tommy. "I'm going to get the judge to meet me at the courthouse and get an order to have this thing opened, one way or another. If we can't get a registered combination from the manufacturer we can try to coax or force it. We'll meet here at eight o'clock tomorrow morning and see if Daddy-O can open this thing."

———

When Tommy got home it was dark. He went into the dark house and turned on the kitchen light. His dog, Millie, came into the kitchen and stretched then went to Tom's feet and sat. She smiled up at him.

"Hi, Mil. Glad to see me?" He scratched under her collar. "You're a good girl."

Tom went to his answering machine and saw the light blinking. Both messages were from Polly.

He dialed her number When she answered the phone Tom felt a great sense of relief. He sat down on one of the stools at the breakfast bar and said, "Polly, I love you."

"You sound tired."

He stretched one over his head. "I've got another murder investigation going."

"Oh no. I'm sorry." She knew what a toll murder took on his emotional life. They had been through a lot of this together. The past winter had been a mess for both of them.

"This is going to be a sick one, I'm afraid."

"Sick?"

"Ritual stuff, maybe satanic."

"Oh, Thomas."

He swiveled the stool and looked out the glass doors at the night lights in South Park, far below in the valley. It was beautiful.

"I'll be OK. How are you doing?"

"A lot better, now that the divorce is going to be finalized at some real point in time. August first." She sighed.

"I still don't understand why it's taken so long."

"If you had ever lived in California and knew about real estate, state taxes, and the court system down here you would understand, believe me. We have the most intrusive legal system in the civilized world."

"You'll like Wyoming a lot better. Life is still livable here."

"There are a lot of things I love about Southern California."

"Like what?" Tom couldn't think of anything. Except the ocean. He loved the ocean, especially the sight of large ships sailing along the coast. It touched some romantic part of him and his imagination.

"Well, for one thing, it has 171 museums . . . and Disneyland – ask Jackie about that one! And, it's one of the most spiritual places in the world."

"It's also one of the sickest, most murderous places in the world." He had murder on his mind for some reason.

"I also love the contradictions of the place. It may be why oriental philosophies and religions flourish here. Yin and yang are part of everyday life — you have to be able to accept the tensions."

"You're really saying it's a place only a philosopher could love."

She laughed. "Maybe that's true. It's sure hell on cowboys."

It was his turn to laugh. He had taken his son, Jackie, to California the previous spring and the traffic, among other things, had driven Tommy crazy. Too many people.

"If it hadn't been for the AA meetings I'd have gone nuts."

"Now, there's an example of the spirituality. You forget too easily."

She was right. In California there were five times the national ratio of people kicking addictions, meeting their personal monsters head-on. Churches were sprouting like mushrooms in a wet summer.

"Are you sure you're going to marry me? How are we going to have a life if you live in California and I live in Wyoming?"

"Yes, I'm going to marry you. We'll see what happens with the second part."

"That's why you want to be married at Christmas."

"No. It's because you're such a sentimental sap that if we marry at Christmas you'll feel indebted, obligated, and be so saturated with the romance of it that you'll never be able to say a cross word to me — the guilt will keep you in line."

"I'm so glad that we're both so manipulative and dishonest. It makes things so much easier." He was smiling. He tickled Millie under the chin with his toe.

"Thank God for alcohol." There was a smile in her voice. "If our parents hadn't decided to drink we'd be so bored and boring we'd have to live in front of the TV set to get a life."

"I love dirty talk!"

"Then: television, television, television! Maury Povich, Geraldo, Donahue . . . Sam Donaldson!"

"Whoa. That's a little too dirty, even for my sick mind."

She giggled and he closed his eyes. He could see her little blonde head, hair falling forward and her pulling it up with her free hand as she talked. "God, Polly, I love you so much." A quaver of emotion slipped into his voice.

"Oh, Thomas, I wish I were there. I can tell you're hurting."

He took a deep breath. "I'd give anything for you to be here. This one is going to get me down. I'm afraid of this satanic stuff."

There was a silence. "I'm going to fly out."

"You can't do that."

"Yes I can." It was a statement. "I can come out for a few days, Christina can handle things for me here." Christina, their daughter through youthful abandon, was a real estate agent in the family brokerage.

"Are you sure?"

"I'm sure about everything I do."

And she was. It was one of the reasons Tom loved her. In some ways they were complete opposites.

Chapter 3

At eight o'clock in the morning the locksmith was unloading his equipment and a deputy was helping to carry it downstairs. They had to make way through a crowd of investigators, including people from the Wyoming, U.S. Customs, the FBI, plus curious local jurisdictions.

Tommy followed Daddy-O, nickname for the locksmith, Mark D'Addario, to the vault and watched as he looked it over.

"Uh oh, this came from a bank." Daddy-O observed. "It's going to be a tough one, especially if it's a retrofit."

"Retrofit?"

"Yeah, you can have the wheel pack modified to work around your schedule. For instance, this type has a mechanical clock mechanism as original equipment. See where the key goes in? Well, it looks like it hasn't been used for a long time so that means they could have put a battery-driven wheel pack on this one."

"Why would they do that?"

"Well, when the wind-up mechanism winds down, the door opens, and that could be, oh, seventy-two hours maybe. With a battery pack it could take months. All depends on the guy's schedule."

"So chances are you're going to have to force it?"

Mark smiled and gestured toward the door. The massive structure answered Tom's question.

"I'd rather try to manipulate it."

"How can you manipulate it?"

"Yeah. If it's a group two lock I may be able to listen to the mechanism with a stethoscope and try to get the tumblers to fall. If it's a group one, which is most likely, I'll have to do something else." He waved at the dozen or so men who were now standing in the foyer. "But I'm going to need dead silence right now."

Tom turned and saw that Sheriff Harlan was in the group. "Sheriff, Mark needs dead silence while he tries to manipulate this lock."

"OK, guys, let's give the man some quiet," Sam said and herded the onlookers out of the basement.

Tom watched as Mark worked for an hour or more, holding the stethoscope next to the lock as he moved the dial slowly and methodically back and forth. He finally sat back in his chair and said, "I'm going to have to try something else."

Tom looked at the big variable speed drill with its magnetic mount that lay on the floor. "Like drilling into it?"

"Well, it's not that simple. Let's get the sheriff down here and talk it over a little before I start that."

Sheriff Harlan and two of the federal people entered the foyer. "What's happening?" asked the sheriff.

"I'm going to have to drill, it looks like."

"OK, so drill."

"First let me run through some of the back-up or re-lock mechanisms that this guy could have in this door."

"OK."

"First, there are lead linkages and they're fairly common in older doors like this one. If you try to burn through the door the lead melts, at a real low temperature, and the re-locks pop into place. In case of a relock you'll have to go into the vault through a wall."

"But you're not going to try to burn into it, are you?"

"No, I thought I'd try to drill but we might have a glass plate backup which can shatter and do a re-lock too."

"Will drilling break the glass if you're real careful?"

"Well, I'm familiar with this kind of door. They had one at the school I graduated from, as an example of things we could run into. If they are the same, this one is magnesium/cobalt with carbide chips embedded in the matrix. The only way to get through is to drill until you get to a chip and then pound on the carbide, which is brittle, blow the carbide chips out and drill some more. It means a lot of drilling 'n' pounding and that could break the glass and trip the relock."

The sheriff nodded and said, "Go to it. If we have to go in through a wall we'll go in through a wall. Are you going to have to drill the whole lock out? How long will that take?"

"No, no. I drill through and then use my orthoscopic borescope and a dental mirror to look at the slots in the wheel pack. I put one slot where it belongs and then extrapolate the other numbers to get the combination."

"How long is it going to take?"

"I don't know. Could take hours."

"Well, go for it. Do you need any help?"

"I could use one man."

"I'll get Nolan or Jeff down here to give you a hand."

"Thanks. I'm going to seal this door with tape and I want you to initial it. That way you'll be sure that I didn't go into the vault before you got here."

The man sealed the vault door on all four corners and Sheriff Harlan initialed it with a Magic Marker. Then Mark and Nolan mounted the drill next to the dial and Mark started the process. The noise was incredible. Tom leaned over and pulled the ear protection away from Nolan's ear and said, "Let me know when you're getting close."

He gave Tom a thumbs-up and returned to the drill. Tom left the racket in the basement.

Upstairs he wandered around the house, watching the various investigators as they went conducted an inch by inch search of the house.

He went outside and checked the progress of the search for other objects in the tall grass behind the house and then went back inside.

When he entered the front room he saw the Forest Service archaeologist, Kelly Dittus, making annotated drawings of the kachina dolls.

"Pretty interesting, huh?" Tom said as he walked up to the man's elbow. The drawings were excellent.

"More than interesting. I worked in the Taos, New Mexico, district office for four years and got to know a lot about kachina dolls from a man who owned a gallery there. These things were his passion and he passed it on to me."

"I have a few antique dolls that my grandpa collected back in the late twenties, in Arizona and New Mexico," Tom said.

The man looked at Tommy and smiled. "I'd love to see them sometime."

"Any time."

"Thanks. Maybe you have some unknown ones too. Wouldn't that be something."

"Unknown ones?"

Kelly pointed at two dolls on one of the shelves. "I have all the published research materials on kachina dolls and neither of those two appear anywhere in the literature. They are priceless."

"Really?"

"Yeah. And almost all the rest of them are known only from late nineteenth-century or earliest twentieth-century collections." He pointed. "That one is Tuma-oi, White Chin Kachina. The last known collection of that one was in 1895." He pointed at another. "That's Chowilawu, Terrific Power. It's known from a collection dated 1901. Those three up there are Owa-ngaroro, Stone Eater Kachinas and the last years their dances were danced was in 1909 and 1910." His voice trailed off in awe.

"You know a lot about these."

"I fell in love with the whole kachina thing when I was down there. I hated to leave and come up here but they transferred me and I didn't have any real choice." He shrugged.

"But then, if I hadn't been here I would never have seen these." He smiled. "These dolls were very important in the education of the people. The kids learn to recognize the spirits through the dolls and later they learn the oral history and medicine ways that match the dolls they played with. It's a wonderful way to teach.

"The men make them from the dry roots of cottonwood trees, the wood is real easy to work. The paint scheme is pretty simple — there are six compass directions and a color to represent each one. Yellow is north, blue-green is the west, red is the south, white is east, all those colors combined is up and black is down.

"Distinguishing decorative symbols fall into six classes too: animal and bird tracks; celestials like clouds, lightning, sun, moon and stars; vegetable—corn, flowers, cactus and the like; phallic symbols for fertility. Inverted Vs are for kachina officials and pairs of vertical lines under the eyes represent the footprints of a warrior.

"There are thirteen costume classes ... and there's a lot more to it too. It goes on and on. It's fascinating stuff."

Tom said, "I'd really like you to take a look at my dolls. There are almost forty more that my brother and sister have. Maybe we could get them all together and let you look at them."

"I'd love it. Maybe I could get another monograph out of it."

"Another?"

"Yes. Those unidentified dolls are going to get me published, no doubt about it."

"Great. I don't hear any drilling or pounding, maybe they're into the vault."

He went downstairs and saw the locksmith looking into his borescope and manipulating the dials.

Nolan looked at Tommy and gave him a thumbs up. Tommy went upstairs and told one of the deputies to get the sheriff, then returned to the basement just in time to see Mark spin the spoked handle and gently tug the door until the tape seals deformed but didn't break.

Tommy waited for the sheriff and the others. When he pulled the vault door open he was surprised. The room behind the door was large, much larger than he had anticipated. He stepped inside and slid his hand along the wall until he found a switch plate. He flicked up the two buttons and filled the room with light.

The first man to follow Tom into the room was Kelly, the archaeologist. He drew in a sharp breath at what he saw. After a moment he said, "Man, this son of a bitch deserved to die."

Chapter 4

The back of the room was a library, including filing cabinets, and a computer workstation with its own collection of software reference works. From the ceiling, Tom saw, hung a Halon fire extinguishing system usually found only in museums. On the sides of the room were custom shelves and on the shelves were artifacts. They looked exotic to Tom, maybe Mexican and South American. He subscribed to National Geographic magazine and that was about it for him.

But Kelly was shaking his head in awe. He finally stopped at the center of the room in front of a glass case. In it was a mummy, obviously the showpiece of the collection from the way it was presented, with special lighting in the ceiling and inside the case.

The mummy was in a sitting position with his knees drawn to his chin. He was wearing a wrapped headdress made of a wonderfully woven cloth. Many bird plumes, an iridescent midnight blue, were stuck into the headdress. He was wearing a magnificent cape made of small bird feathers, probably breast feathers. The top third was a checkerboard design of showier feathers, jungle bird feathers, a shimmering yellow and green. The bottom two thirds of the cape was a field of white feathers with a broad stripe of orange, occasional yellow checks running through it just above the hem. The feathers looked as though they'd been taken from the birds within the month.

In front of the mummy were ceramic boxes and little sacks. At his side was a leather pouch from which protruded bone and stone instruments.

Dittus's voice was awestruck when he began to speak, "This was the archaeological scandal of the century about five years ago. A box bound for Washington University was supposedly lost by a local guy who ran the government warehouse in Peru. He was a former grave robber so everyone knew he'd probably sold it. The shipment included this shaman mummy which was being sent north to be studied, curated and returned to Peru. Paula Clark, the woman who is on her way down here to look at the textiles in which Ward was buried, was on that dig. She is going to die when she sees this."

He sighed and turned to point to a shelf. "That is a world-class turquoise mask. It looks real familiar to me and it may be another stolen piece. Those jade hachas, axeheads, are also the kind that you find on display only in Mexico City or Berlin or the Smithsonian."

Leaning over the sample cabinet, Kelly pulled a shallow drawer from the wall and examined the ceramic pieces inside. "Adornas — earplugs. My God, this one still has Quetzal feathers sticking out of it! I've never seen any in this condition before. They look like the owner just took them out of his ears and set them here."

He opened another drawer and straightened up in shock. Tommy peered around him and saw bracelets, armbands, pectorals, and other, smaller pieces. Solid gold.

By this time all the investigators had crowded into the room and Tommy realized that, even though they were all professionals, something could get seriously screwed up with everyone opening drawers and whatnot.

"Sheriff, we need to get this thing organized."

Sheriff Harlan said, "OK everybody. Outside until we decide who is going to do what!" He motioned to the head of the FBI detail and said. "Let's all go upstairs and sort this damn thing out."

The man nodded and said, "Right."

As Dittus was getting ready to leave Tommy pinched his shirtsleeve. "When did you say your friend was going to get here?"

"She should be here today but I'm going to phone and make sure she's left. And if she hasn't, I want her to know what she's in for. She may want to bring down someone else down with her to help."

"I heard the U.S. Customs guy mention phoning the Smithsonian for someone to fly out, too."

"No doubt. Everyone is going to be interested in this and I'm sure that the Smith will end up being the primary curator." He returned to the mummy and stared at it again. "Everyone in the academic world was interested in this guy. He was buried with his medical instruments, as well as his whole pharmacopoeia."

He pointed at the leather sack at the mummy's side. "He had llama leg bones which he used for giving drug enemas too potent to be taken orally—he was buried with over sixty different kinds of drugs which were in all the little boxes and sacks there. He even had trepanning instruments used to do brain surgery." He stared at the dried little man for a long moment and added, "This guy was a brain surgeon." He shook his head in wonder. "They were more advanced in their knowledge than we will ever dream."

———

Tom was late meeting Polly's plane but she didn't seem to mind. She was sitting in the airport snack shop with a soft drink, sunglasses, and a Mirabella magazine in front of her. She had on a chocolate-colored cowboy hat but the rest of her clothes said that it was a fashion accent. Her clothing was simple — Wrangler jeans, a khaki safari shirt, expensive brown cowboy boots. But the Hopi silver button earrings and the authentic concho belt set them off perfectly. This woman had class, something which had not escaped the notice of the men in the room. A couple of them were frankly staring at her.

And so was Tom. Polly glanced up with a neutral look in her eyes which was meant to discourage his stare but when she recognized him a slow smile spread over her face. She was happy to see him. He was more than happy to see her. She was perfect.

He walked to the table and said, "Hi."

She just maintained the loving look and took his hand. Not saying anything just looking up at him.

Finally she said, "Sit down."

He sat and put his hat on a chair. "You...are one beautiful woman."

"Thank you. You are one tired man."

"Huh? Don't feel tired."

"I can see the stress in the lines around your eyes. Sure you're not tired?"

He shrugged. "No. Not really."

She stood. "Good," she said and smiled a languorous smile.

Tom saw the look in her eyes that he remembered from the first time, years and years ago, when she had cut in on a girl he was dancing with and whirled him away. Back then he thought that she was just intent on having a good time. He had learned that it meant exactly that. It also meant that she was hungry.

"Damn," he said and looked around the room. Seeing that everyone else in the room's attention was on something else he retrieved his hat, put it over his lap and stood up from the table.

"You're gonna have to carry one of them suitcases your own self, Lady," he said.

When she looked down and saw that Tom was hiding the front of his pants she said, "It seems like the very least I could do. My, my, but aren't you an excitable man." She put on her sunglasses and giggled.

"Excitable ain't the word."

"I hope that doesn't go bad before we get it to the house, Thomas."

"Don't worry, Britches. Blue steel doesn't go bad. It may get a little rust on it, but it never ever goes bad."

———

They had passed safely through Culiacan when in the distance, a hundred meters ahead, a soldier with a slung rifle walked out into the roadway and held up his hand for their vehicle to stop. When the car was near enough to identify the license plate, the soldier turned and called to another soldier who was sitting in the front seat of a battered olive-drab pickup truck. A sign made of tattered plywood and crudely hand lettered Policia Judicial was propped against the side of the truck.

The young soldier in the truck put on an officer's garrison hat and walked toward the car. He was grinning. He said something to the man with the rifle and that man grinned also.

"Buenas tardes," he said as he walked to the driver's side of the vehicle. He bent a bit to look at the other occupants. Encouraged by the submissive demeanor of the three occupants, and recognizing them as indigenos, his face took on an arrogant look.

"Get out of the car and open the trunk," he said to the driver. Then he looked inside again and said, "Everybody out."

The occupants looked at one another and the driver nodded, almost imperceptibly. He went to the trunk and opened it. The officer nodded and the soldier began to take out the boxes inside, which were secured with twine. Once they were on the ground he leaned his rifle on the bumper and took out a knife. He cut the twine on the first box and threw the contents, women's clothing, on the ground. He cut open the second box and took out a flat object wrapped in cloth.

Throwing the cloth on the ground he looked at a large book made of leather. He opened it and found drawings. "It's a comic book," he said to the officer and tossed it back into the trunk.

When he stooped and began to cut on the third box he grunted, "Heavy," and sawed at the rope.

The three Indians looked at one another. The officer pushed them aside and walked to the soldier's side. He knelt in the dirt, tore away the cloth wrapping, and grunted as the object inside the box came to view. It was a piece of rock crystal. The sun flew out of it in a thousand beams, making him turn his head to shade his eyes.

He turned it over in his hands and said, "What is this?"

The woman said, "It is The Heart of the World."

"Ahhh, and where did you steal. . ."

A machete sliced through his neck and cut off his voice. Instead of the rest of the sentence, a whistle escaped from the wound.

The soldier dove for his rifle but one of the men grabbed the barrel. They wrestled for a moment but the machete, wielded by the grim driver, cut him down as well.

Quickly they dragged the bodies into the roadside weeds. One of the men returned to throw the head after the bodies while the second kicked dirt onto the bright pool of blood at the edge of the black asphalt. The woman quickly put the objects back into their boxes and returned them to the trunk of the car. They jumped inside and, throwing up rooster tails of dirt, screeched into the hot distance.

Chapter 5

Tom woke at daylight with Polly in his arms. In the big fir outside the bedroom window the resident Stellar's jays were already doing their Ralph and Alice Cramden act.

He lay – filled with peace. It was the definition of serenity, this feeling.

He moved his head on the pillow so he could look at the luster of the summer morning gradually working its way around and through the trees on the hillside.

Giving, taking, sharing in the physical sense opened him up to an infusion of the very soul with what we choose, so poorly, to describe as love. The sensation cannot last for more than minutes or, at best, hours, because it does not define life. Life is hard, even brutal. But love is something other. At that moment he had it and he thanked God for it.

He picked up a lock of Polly's hair and dropped it. In the magic light of dawn it seemed to fall in slow motion back to her white, fragrant neck. He raised his hand toward the ceiling and wiggled his tingling fingers as he moved his arm in a small arc. His hand left traces and flares of ghostly light behind it.

A bubble of joy rose in him. He moved the hand in a figure eight. Its faint luminescence left the lazy 8 to flare for a moment against the dark wall. This woman could raise his consciousness to another level, a level where his perceptions took on added dimensions. She gave him powers he could not know alone. She was magic.

He put his hand under the covers and on her thigh, running it up to the small protrusion of her hip bone. Her own hand came down languorously from her pillow and placed itself on the back of his own.

He moved the hands very slowly down the thigh and then back up, moving to the inside of her leg as their hands approached her pubis.

Polly rotated her hips slowly, making a light smacking sound with her lips as she spread her legs. They pushed gently down and entered her with their middle fingers. She gave a little start and gasp of pleasure. Her mouth opened and her small hand guided his—gently, slowly, up and down, in and out. Her eyes were closed but her mouth was now tense.

She whispered quickly, "Thomas . . . ahhh! . . . you'd better hurry if you want to get in on this!"

He rolled on top and entered her. Her pelvis pushed once with all the strength that was in her, taking all of him. She groaned "Now!" and they came.

———

"We need to be there by eleven o'clock," Tom said.

"How long does it take to get to the ranch?" Polly asked as she ate a spoonful of yogurt.

"It's, oh, fifteen minutes out from Bondurant, so about an hour and a half."

"What is a jackpot rodeo?"

"It's a rodeo where the public isn't invited. It's for just the locals — for pleasure and a dab of money, not for show."

"How does it work?"

"It's lined up by a stock contractor or subcontractor, maybe a rancher. It costs about twenty-five bucks to enter. There's the roping and bulldogging rodeos or there's rough stock, which is bareback, saddle bronc, and bull riding. This one's going to be rough stock — Jackie will be riding in the bareback event."

"Aren't you worried?" she asked with a little frown.

"About what?"

"That he will get hurt."

"He might get hurt. It's part of it."

"I don't understand it at all."

Tommy shrugged. "You have to be from the country to understand."

"Explain it to me."

Tommy turned his coffee cup around and around as he thought. "Well . . . I don't think it's really accessible intellectually. It's about doing, not about thinking."

"Try me."

"Polly, trust me — you have to be raised in it to understand it, to have any feel for what it means to us."

"Who's 'us'?"

" 'Us' is the people, the culture, which is being eaten up by the influx of strangers with their money, their ideas and their . . .

lack of generosity. There's damn little room left for us and the way we do things."

"Is that really so?"

"Yes, Hon, it's really so. We are living artifacts of the human past and instead of being treasured we are sniggered at and called rednecks. Except in the bars and at the tourist rodeos—then we're 'interesting.' That's why we have these private little shows, as a way of getting right down in it and letting go.

"We have our own antiquated values and seeing that our boys become men is a real part of it. Being a man in our little world still means knowing physical fear and physical pain — and knowing you can rise above it. That's something I want my son to have. 'Being a man' is something that still has value and that means something to all of us, including our women."

"You don't have to be a cowboy to be a man."

"Nope, but I don't know any men from my little corner of the world who dance around bonfires on weekends, whacking a drum with a rubber tomahawk to feel like one."

"If they weren't getting something out of it they wouldn't be doing it."

"Pol, God bless them if that's what works. What I'm saying is that this is where the things those men are searching for are still part of everyday life. We are still horsemen, herders and hunters — all of which make 'civilized' people go nuts. They can't stand the fact that we still exist — and I am not talking about those dickheads with the doilies around their necks down at the Rancher Bar on Saturday night." He paused. "But it will only be a matter of time."

"Before what?"

"Before they get their way and we're history. They'll invade every last corner of these mountains and grub us out with their money, their politics, their 'higher sensibilities' and their no-trespassing signs." He stood up. "But today, right today, we are here and we are real. Let's drive out to Bondurant and see how they used to do it."

When they turned through the gate of the ranch, Polly could see fifty or so pickups, with and without horse trailers, parked in the big yard of the ranch. Some of the vehicles were new and expensive, some were trucks in the five-hundred dollar range and most were somewhere in between.

The Little Cottonwood Ranch sat in a little valley all its own. Dell Creek, with its broad ribbon of green willows, ran near the outbuildings. The snow laced Gros Ventre Mountains stood in the background. Newly swathed hay meadows ran to the sagebrush hills with quaking aspen groves in the middle distance. It was absolutely beautiful.

When they pulled up and were looking for a parking spot Tommy grimaced and said, "There's Holiday's outfit."

"Holiday?"

"Ed Holiday. He and Beth are seeing each other, I heard."

"I'm glad Beth found someone."

"Ed's no good for her. But I guess that's none of my business now that she's my ex." He pointed at a new white Ford pickup and horse trailer with twelve-county plates. "There's Wid's truck."

"And who's Wid?"

"One of Beth's brothers. The one PRCA, professional, cowboy of the bunch but he's second or third best of the six boys."

"Why didn't the better ones become professionals?"

"Wives, babies, responsibilities. Ford is the best, bar none, and he was on his way to the top. All the cowboy songs say 'He loves that darned old rodeo more than he loves me' — but when Pattycake moved to the valley from Idaho and Ford saw her that was it for rodeo.

"Besides, the boys aren't comfortable outside the valley. Things make sense to them at home. There's a place to park — right behind Kathy Jensen." The truck bore a bug deflector with Cowboy Crazy painted on it.

"Do you know everybody's vehicle on sight?"

"Just about."

After parking the truck Tom opened the camper shell and dropped the tail gate. Millie jumped out and started smelling tires. He slid a big Coleman cooler onto the gate and then put a leather contraption on top of it.

"What's that?" Polly asked.

"My old bareback rigging... Millie! You get back here." The dog trotted back to the truck, her head down. "You stay close, dammit. I don't want no dogfights."

"Looks like that rigging has been shined up quite a bit," observed Polly.

"It's been 'treated', my dear."

"Sorry, I guess I'd better learn the lingo if I'm going to marry you. Or is it 'get hitched'?"

"Hitched."

"Hitched it is."

"You seem awful damn positive for someone who doesn't even have a ring."

She looked up at the perfect summer sky with its puffy cumulus clouds sailing east over the Gros Ventre. Her smile was serene. "You'll marry me," she said. "And I don't need a ring." "Well good then, let's practice being married." He pointed. "Tote that durn cooler over to where the women are getting the food ready and stay there till I get back."

"OK." She slid the cooler off the tail gate and started toward the cooking area.

She hollered back, "Just don't forget to bring my purse with you, along with that . . . bucking thing."

"Yes, Dear," he hollered back and grinned as he slammed the tail gate shut. She'd do.

When Tom walked to where the hamburger grills were set up he realized that he had sent Polly into a crowd of strange women. But when he found her she had her sleeves rolled up and was making hamburger patties beside the valley matriarch, Sis Mulverhill.

It was quite a contrast: Sis with her short white hair, mammoth denim pants, homemade blouse, and orthopedic shoes next to Polly who looked like nine hundred dollars. They were laughing, acting like neighbors. And the other gals were smiling too.

"Tommy!" Sis said, "Get your butt over here."

"Hi, Sis."

"Where did you find this girl?"

"She found me. About twenty years ago."

"Now, that's a damn lie! No decent girl would pick you, even out of the sorry bunch you used to run with before you married Beth. Oops!"

"It's all right Mrs. Mulverhill," Polly said. "I was lucky enough to get him after Beth had knocked the corners off him."

"And it was work enough for her, I tell you that," Sis said. She reached up and pinched Tom's cheek with her suety fingers. "But he was the prettiest boy in the country when he was cowboying around here. The girls all thought he was special. If my husband Ralph hadn't been home all the time I'da sneaked him down in the willows my own self."

"Momma!" said a graying, sun-worn redhead who had walked up holding a tray of deviled eggs.

Sis winked at Polly, nodded her head at her daughter and said, "But Jolene would know a lot more about them willows than me. Ask Tom some time."

"Momma!"

Tommy decided he'd better get the hell out of there. Women didn't give a hoot what they said, or who they said it to, when they were bunched up like that.

Jolene! That was Jolene?

This woman had very little to do with his memory of a thin, expectant and opalescent body lying in the fragrant grass of his youth, a coppery little patch of hair glinting the summer sun.

When Tom reached the chute area he picked out the Snow brothers and headed to where they were bunched with the few non-drinkers. Jackie looked up and smiled when his Uncle Doug nodded his hat brim at Tom and mouthed, 'Here comes yer Dad.'

"Hello, Son."

"I was afraid you wouldn't make it. Have a Pepsi."

Tom popped the can top and said, "Wouldn't miss it for the world. Here, this is yours," and handed the boy the bareback rigging.

"That was your riggin'."

"It was your grandpa's. Now it's yours, like the .30/.30 I gave you last year."

"Gol', Dad, thanks."

Tom put his arm over his son's shoulders and was surprised at the muscle he felt. Working on his Uncle Doug's ranch was doing the boy some good already.

"Hi, Doug. Hi Wid. Deloy. Ford. Ernest." He shook hands with each of the brothers in turn. Though none of them said anything, they all had smiles on their faces and their eyes were real friendly. That made him glad. They had been brothers to him for a lot of years.

"Look what Dad gimme," Jackie said.

Wid reached out, took the rigging and whistled as he looked at the stamp on the rigging skirt. "Jackie, this is a Pete Dixon riggin', probably made in the forties. It belongs in somebody's museum. I'll give you five hundred dollars for it right now." He reached in his pocket and took out a wad of hundreds.

Jackie's eyes got big and he looked at Tommy.

"It's yours to do with as you please," Tom said.

"Nah, Uncle Wid. It's worth a lot more than five hundred ol' dollars. This was my grandpa's . . . and my dad's." He took the rigging back from Wid. Wid smiled and winked at Tommy. The boy had passed the test. All the brothers were grinning.

"You're putting some muscle on this kid, Doug," Tommy said and squeezed the boy's triceps until he winced.

Ford reached out and grabbed the boy's hat. "Dougie, if you paid the kid once in a while he might be able to get himself a decent hat." Ford stuck his finger through a small hole in the front of the crown and the cheap felt parted like cheese. Ford added two more fingers and then punched out the whole top of the hat.

"Now look what you done, Ford," said the boy's Uncle Ernest. "You ruined the kid's hat. Shoot!" He reached into the back of the pickup he was leaning against and retrieved an expensive Panama straw cowboy hat that Tommy knew cost at least forty dollars. "Guess I'll have to give him one of mine." He took the protective plastic off the hat and handed it to the boy, whose mouth was hanging open.

"Put it on,' said Deloy, "it'll keep the sun off yer face and save you some freckles. Heck, you already look like you been walkin' behind a horse that's been eatin' bran."

Jackie put on the hat and it was a perfect fit. Tommy's eyes were wet for some reason.

"Only one thing, Jack," said Ernest.

"What?"

"You pull it down real tight so that snaky little horse don't whip it off you and get it dirty."

"I'm gonna try, Uncle Ernie."

"What horse did you draw?" asked Tom and took a swig of the cold Pepsi.

"A mare named Peterbreath," said Jackie. "What a dumb name."

Tom blew Pepsi through his nose. The uncles dropped their heads and toed the dirt. Except Uncle Wid, who was grinning like a possum eating shit because he was the one who had named the horse.

Tom closed his eyes and dropped his own head so Wid's grin wouldn't make him irrigate his sinuses again. He swallowed, wiped his nose and said, "Pretty snaky horse, huh?"

Wid's own eyes were watering when he choked out, "Yeah, she's a swivel-hipped cuss. I rode her both times I drew her, but she's a triple A bucker for sure." He took out his hanky and wiped his eyes as Jackie looked at the men, puzzled.

"What's she do?" Tom asked.

All the brothers were now serious. They leaned in and watched Wid's hands as he made the motions which illustrated his description of the horse's bucking habits.

"First, she's bad for rearing in the chute. Second, she's small enough that she'll try to bang your legs on the chute just as the gate is about to open — you gotta get your spurs up and keep 'em up once you've got your seat."

Wid was now looking right into Jackie's eyes and the boy was meeting the man's earnest look and concentrating on what was being said. He was drinking it in.

Tom leaned back and took another drink of pop. The boy was in much better hands than his own. Thank God for family.

Chapter 6

Tom was talking to Clement Meeks when he saw Ed Holiday walking toward them. The hair stood up on the back of his neck.

Ed had a can of Coors in his hand and he switched it to his left when he stuck out his right to shake. Tom took his hard hand.

"Hi, Tommy. Thought I'd come over and say 'Hi.'"

"Hi, Ed. Good to see you again."

"Hi, Clem."

"Ed."

"Tom, I'm seeing Beth. I wanted you to know that."

"I knew, Ed. Jackie told me."

"Yeah, I guess he would do that alright." Ed stared at Tom for a moment and said, "I hope this doesn't cause any hard feelings."

"It doesn't, Ed. Trust me. I'm glad that Beth has someone, she's not herself unless she has someone to do for." Tom was aware of the irony in that statement. Beth was a caretaker and people pleaser to a fare-thee-well. "Anyway, I've got someone too. As a matter of fact, that's her coming now."

Polly walked up and Tom said, "Polly, meet Clem Meeks, an old friend of mine, and Ed Holiday."

"My pleasure, gentlemen." Polly stuck out her hand and shook with the men.

Clem pinched the brim of his hat and said, "Ma'am." Holiday took his off when he shook.

"Tommy, come and get something to eat," Polly said.

"OK, Hon." Tom turned to the men and said, "See you when they get the bulls out of the way and the saddle broncs ready." The bull riding had been scheduled first because two riders had other rodeos to get to.

"Hey, Thompson." It was Ed.

"Yeah?"

"You gonna ride today?"

"Nope. Jackie's going to have to hold 'er down for the Thompsons today."

"I'm gonna be riding for one of the Thompson. Beth. Saddle bronc."

"Then you'll be riding against Deloy and Ford."

"And Wid. Don't forget Wid."

Tom felt the blood filling his face in spite of himself. He knew that Holiday was trying to get a rise out of him in front of Polly and the prick was getting it done. "Well, you got your work cut out for you. Maybe you should try bareback instead. Then only Jackie will put you in the sack."

Holiday's face went pale. He glared, took the last swig from his beer, pooched his cheeks and swallowed. Then he flipped the can between Tommy's feet.

Clem squinted, looked at Tom, looked at Holiday. "No fights. Period. Them's the rules." Clement was one of those sausage-fingered good-old-boys who meant exactly what he said and could back it up a hundred percent.

Holiday spun around and left. Tommy felt his pulse racing.

"Gonna go get himself some more of that 'spurring fluid,' I guess," said Clem. He looked at Tommy. "Go get yerself something to eat with your pretty friend, Tom. He's about a dumbhead."

"Dumb enough to think he can ride with the Snows."

"Don't write him off. Ed's a hell of a rider, drunk or sober. He may be a prick, sorry ma'am, but he does know how to ride buckin' horses."

"See you over at the chutes, Clem."

The big man pinched the brim of his hat again and walked away toward the crowd at the corrals.

Tommy looked at Polly for the first time. She was pale and she was angry.

"Sorry about that," Tommy said.

"You had to give him that dig, didn't you?"

"Yup."

"You men and your damn male strut. It was juvenile."

"Yup, you're right. Lots of juveniles around here. Littles ones, big ones, and some about this tall." He held his palm over his own hat. "That's some of what we're here for, I guess."

———

Deloy was the first cowboy to ride and he scored a seventy-six. Seventy-sixes win a lot of money, even at big shows. It takes the combination of a very good horse and a very good rider to make that score.

Two more riders came up. One got bucked off and the other scored a sixty. Wid Snow, who made a hundred thousand dollars a year as a pro cowboy, was the next rider. He made it look easy, his left hand moving up and down, giving the horse his head, but keeping the pressure on. He predicted the animal's actions through his arm, tied to the animal's muscular neck and thrashing head. And where the horse's head went the body was quick to follow.

Wid kept his knees hooked under the saddle's swells as he raked the horse's shoulders and ribs. He sawed the rope up and down as though he were playing an instrument. He scored a seventy-six, just like his older brother.

When Ed Holiday got up he was grinning like a jack-o-lantern. And he was drunk. Tommy was helping with the animals and when Holiday straddled the chute and looked into Tom's face with his spooky smile Tom could smell his breath. It reeked of alcohol.

"Keep your eye on this one, Thompson," he said as he took hold of the bucking rein.

When the gate swung open the big, powerful gray horse blew out into the arena as though he'd been levitated. His first jump ended with an insane squeal of rage, a ripping fart and the squealing, slapping sound of tortured leather. The men at the chute could hear Holiday's grunts and curses from twenty yards away.

The horse jumped again, straight in the air, and landed with all four feet in area no larger than a dishpan. Holiday's body compressed like an accordion and his hat whipped down onto the ground as the big gray vaulted back into the air and twisted himself so his front legs were almost opposite his back legs. Ed stayed in the middle, reading the animal's head. The force of the landing was still jarring enough to make the rider groan again from the shock. Ed's teeth were bared in a grimace of concentration and pain. A big bubble of mucous ballooned out of his nose then popped and flew away.

The horse spun and threw his head down. For the first time Holiday seemed to lose control. Tom thought he was going down. But Ed stabbed the horse viciously with his spurs and powered the bucking rein. The animal gave one more twisting buck and went across the arena in great bounds. The rider stroked him with the spurs and played him as though he were now a frisky stable horse and little more. The horn blew on the second bound, the pickup men took Ed off his back and it was over.

"I'll be a son-of-bitch," said one of the chute men. "If that ain't a eighty-five I'll kiss your ass till your hat flies off."

He'd been close. It was good for an eighty-one.

Tommy felt like hell. He'd goaded this man, said that his fifteen-year-old son could out-ride him. If he had inspired the ride then he kicked himself for doing it. If the man were really that good a rider then he'd made himself look like a fool. Either way, Holiday was going to come out of this on top.

He turned to Clem, who was standing beside him and said, "I guess I let my mouth overload my ass."

Clem smiled wryly and said, "Looks like. That was one helluva ride."

The next rider got dumped right in front of the gate and the horse leaped across the arena like a frolicking colt till they hazed him out.

The rider after him drew a lazy snip-nosed sorrel who made him look bad.

Then it was Ford's turn.

He had drawn a big line-back buckskin with insane eyes. As Tommy fought to control the animal's head, twisting his hands into the black mane, he could feel the animal's power. He was big and he was crazy. This was going to be real good or it was going to be real bad.

"Who is this spooky son-of-a-bitch?" he asked through clenched teeth.

"Rumrunner, a proud-cut mustang. He's a gooder," said Wid, who was working across the chute from Tom. "He'll make you money or he'll stomp a mudhole in your ass. He don't like people and that's a fact."

Tom looked at Ford's face and saw the little smile that was always there. His eyes were serene, he winked at Tom and gave a little nod. The gate flew open.

The horse put his head down, screamed and threw himself on the ground. Calmly, Ford put his boot out and gave a little push on the ground which seemed to vault both him and the animal back into the air.

As the animal came down, twisting himself into a huge knot of muscle and man, Ford reached out and ran a spur down the whole length of the animal's neck. It damn near turned the horse inside out. He rose up with another squeal of rage, almost throwing himself over backwards as he pawed at the air then flew eight feet high, almost bringing his hind hooves to his nose. The whole while Ford hooked him on one side or the other as he stroked the opposite side, driving the horse into a frenzy. Tom could see the art in it and so could all the other experienced riders.

The horse balled himself up again, this time coming away from his contact with the ground in a sideways vault. Ford lifted the bucking rein high over his head and raked the horse evenly, effortlessly while he was flying through the air at a forty-five degree angle.

When the horse landed, at the eight-second horn, he seemed to crumple in the middle. His mind had been blown. He'd been ridden and knew it. It was an 85 and a winner.

Polly had been straddling the top rail, only a few feet from the chute with Deloy and Ford's wives. They had been explaining what was going on. When Tom walked over her eyes were wide.

"I had no idea. When I used to watch you ride I was always in the grandstands. It looked . . . athletic, I guess would be the word. But over here close you can see the power, the tension . . ." She smiled a wan little smile. "I had no idea." She took his arm.

"Did you like it?"

"Honestly?"

"Honestly."

"No."

Tom stopped and looked at her in surprise. "How come?"

"Thomas, this may come as a great shock to you but there is a whole world of people out there who don't enjoy this kind of... action. It's too much, it's. . ."

"Scary?"

"That and more. It's simply too much for someone who isn't familiar with this world."

"It's the only world I ever knew, except the military."

"And that was more of the same kind of thing, wasn't it?"

"In a way, I guess."

"It's violent."

"It's real." He crooked a finger under her chin. "That's it — it's real, it makes you so much more alive."

"Well, you're welcome to it. My idea of feeling alive is a steam and a massage."

"Different strokes for different folks. Welcome to my world."

"Well, the people are nice. And honest! They all come right out and say what they're thinking, don't they?"

"Except when it wouldn't be polite." He patted her hand and said, "There's Ed and Beth. I owe him an apology. You stay here."

She gripped his arm and he felt her fingernails dig in. It hurt like hell. She muttered, "If you don't think I can handle meeting your ex-wife you are sadly fucking mistaken."

He was shocked. Polly never swore.

"Then let's go."

Ed was leaning against the fender of a pickup, not getting too far away from the beer tub or the jug of Black Velvet that the boys were passing around. It brought back a lot of memories for Tom.

Beth had her back to Tom and Polly. It was Ed who noticed them approaching. Tom saw him drop his head and say something. He saw Beth stiffen. She didn't turn around until Ed looked over her head and said, "Quite a show, huh Thompson?" He was real drunk now.

"Yeah. They rounded up some sure winners for stock."

Beth turned around. Her face was pale, even under her tan. She took off her sunglasses and her eyes crinkled as she made an attempt at a smile.

"Beth this is Polly, Polly this is Beth." The women shook hands and then both turned their eyes to Tom. Suddenly, he felt real bad inside.

"Ed, I owe you an apology. That was one hell of a ride."

"Thanks." He took a big swig of his beer and Beth grimaced, lowered her head.

There was a very awkward silence for a moment. Then Polly said, "Let's go." Simple. They turned and left.

When they were a few yards away Tom said, "Thanks."

"You know, that really embarrassed her. You do the dumbest things."

"No shit?"

"No shit."

———

What a night, Tom thought as he swept through the lazy S turns of the Hoback River canyon road. It was midnight. A big moon was washing the cliffs and trees before it dropped its light to scallop the cold river's undulating water.

And what a day, he added to himself.

He looked down at Polly's sleeping face. She had folded his jacket for a pillow, put it on his lap and been asleep before they hit the ranch gate. Her mouth was open and her breathing deep.

All the lines were gone from her face and she slept in an innocence he hadn't seen since his son had slept on his mother's lap the same way, years and years ago.

Tears came to his eyes as he looked back through the windshield at the headlit road and moonlit canyon. The memories of those lost nights when he had driven this same canyon, coming back from some rodeo event with Beth and Jackie, made his heart hurt.

He sighed and wiped his face. He laughed at himself. Things were better now than they had ever been.

He turned his mind to the little miracles of the day. He saw Jackie getting a deep seat in his grandpa's rigging. He was hanging onto the top rail of the chute with one hand, the other gripped in the handle and his thin muscles standing out in his forearms. Spurs high, his face was white as he nodded at his uncle's last minute advice on the markout rule — and then the ride.

He'd been smooth, so smooth. His genes took over. He laid back against the horse's rump, smiled and spurred the animal at will. He looked just like Ford and Ford was the best in this corner of the country. He won it. He'd won the damn thing. Tommy's throat tightened with emotion.

And then he laughed out loud as he remembered something else that had happened, the gust of laughter making Polly stir on his lap.

Tom had been standing with the whole Snow bunch and seen his dog, Millie, bristled up and growling, circling with the red heeler who belonged to Ernest. He started to holler at the dog and then he remembered that by some horrible act of fate he'd been given a half-grown dog whose name was the same as his ex-mother-in-law. And the woman was standing about three feet away from him.

"Uh, Jackie, go get that damn dog."

His son had just looked at him with those big innocent eyes, took a sip off his Pepsi and said, "Heck, Dad, why don't you just holler her name? She'll tuck her tail."

Tom had seen red, spluttered and growled then strode over to get his dog.

Score one for the kid. He knew he was going to hear that story a few times during the years he had left.

And Beth.

It had been dark and the musicians, three locals, were grinding their way through "Queen of the Silver Dollar," their pudgy platinum blonde singer giving it her all.

Tom had felt a light touch on his arm and looked down to see Beth standing next to him. She leaned around him and said, "Polly, can I borrow Tommy for a minute or two?" Polly hadn't even paused, just smiled and said, "Of course, Beth."

They'd walked out past the vehicles and stood next to the corral. The moon was rolling up over the Hoback Rim, making the new-mown hayfields turn to silver.

She'd cried and he'd held her. She was so small, so cold. He'd put his jacket over her and waited until she could speak.

"Tommy, I know now that I have a problem."

Tom said nothing. He couldn't say anything, he was praying.

"I picked Ed, he didn't pick me. I can see that now." She wiped her face with the backs of both hands. "When he found out I was seeing Ed, Jackie told me that I was getting someone who needed fixing, and someone who couldn't be fixed. He told me that I had Alanon."

Tom smiled a little smile but didn't say anything. He'd told her before that Alanon was an organization, not a disease.

"Where do I go, Tommy? God, what do I do?"

"Look in the paper for an address and go to ninety meetings in ninety days. Let those people love you till you can love yourself. And pray."

"Lord, but Ed embarrassed me. The drinking was bad enough but picking a fight with one of my own brothers. . ."

"Do you remember patching me up and taking my side even when I was more wrong than Holiday was today?"

"Oh hell yes!"

They had laughed, she'd wiped her nose on his jacket sleeve and smiled as she apologized. And then she'd broken his heart — looked up at him and said, "Come home. We need you."

The big lump came back to Tom's throat as he remembered kissing her on her wet, cold cheek and saying, "I can't. I've changed."

He picked out the Sulphur Springs bridge coming up in the headlights. They rumbled across it and broke out into the sagebrush flat across the river from Willow Creek. The moon had washed it all and made it clean.

And Tommy felt clean. He'd said the right things to Beth. He'd said the right things to his son. He'd told Mom Snow that he loved her and her children. He'd thanked her for her love all those years and she'd cried and kissed him. Then he'd danced with all the girls, Polly danced with all the men and charmed their asses loose — then the prettiest girl at the dance had gone home with him.

If he didn't have a flat tire before they reached the house the day was going to be as close to perfect as it was possible to get.

Chapter 7

Sunday morning was perfect too. Tom rose early, as always, and exercised on the deck as the first rays of sun came over the Gros Ventre Mountains. The jays swooped down on the sunflower seeds he'd piled at the edge of the deck and ate brazenly as Tom did his sit-ups less than ten feet away. Then he left on his morning run, along the trails that ran up and over the mountain behind his house.

He was reading at the breakfast counter when Polly came downstairs to pour herself a cup of the freshly ground Great Northern coffee and joined him. She took a sip of coffee then reached up to tug at his hair where it touched his neck.

"Good morning."

"Good morning." He leaned down and kissed her mouth. It opened slowly and took the kiss with lazy abandon. He moved his head back and opened his eyes. Her mouth was still open and her eyes had darkened to a cobalt blue. He shook his head. "Drink your coffee, Hotpants."

"I thought my name was Sugarbritches."

"Same thing. Drink your coffee, I've already had my exercise this morning."

She laughed, took another sip and stood to walk out on the deck. He joined her.

From the back, he reached out with one arm and put it around her chest as he drank from his own cup. "Beautiful, huh?"

The valley was full of light now, slowly breaking down the morning fog above the Snake River and outlining the tall cottonwoods which crowded its course. Green trees, green pastures, green mountains. Twenty shades of green, at least. It wasn't Ireland but it would do, for color.

Polly kissed his forearm and said, "I love this place. You done good."

He took another drink of coffee and said nothing.

She went on, "What a pair we were last spring. Me trying to nurse you from a wheelchair and the neighbor's nanny coming over to nurse me when I couldn't help myself. A real sick ward." Tom nodded. He remembered lying on the couch day after long day, recovering from his stab wounds, and looking out through the french doors as Polly did her best to nurse him. She'd been recovering from a smoke-inhalation coma.

One day he knew they were getting better when she emptied his bedpan off the deck saying, "So this is what it feels like for you guys."

When he'd asked what she meant she'd smiled and said, "I've always wanted to pee off a deck and now I've done it." It had made him laugh and then cry out from the pain that flared in the wounds. It hurt like hell but it was funny, even at this distance in time.

He put his face in her hair and kissed her ear lightly. "Did I ever say 'Thank you' enough," he asked.

"Yes . . . uh, maybe no, when I really think about it."

"Then I would like to thank you again. Over there on the couch. Now."

She smiled, tossed her coffee dregs off the deck and said, "If you feel up to it, mon gros homme d'vache."

———

At one o'clock that afternoon Tom and Polly picked up the artifact expert at the airport. Betty Mason worked for the Smithsonian. U.S. Customs had arranged for her to assess the trove in Ward's basement. Paula Clark, the textile specialist from the University of Idaho had arrived in Jackson Hole the day before.

They drove to the Snow King resort where rooms were reserved and rang Professor Clark, who turned out to be a small woman with sharp eyes and a ready smile.

"Good to see you again, Dr. Mason," she said.

Dr. Mason smiled and turned to Tom. "Dr. Clark and I have been working together for some time. Her expertise is in Peruvian coastal textiles but she is one of the very best in textiles generally."

Tommy asked, "Have you had a chance to look at the clothes Ward was wearing?"

Polly broke in. "Wouldn't we be more comfortable out by the pool?"

Dr. Clark smiled, "Yes, I was out there this morning and it's very pleasant. No kids running and screaming, just this clean mountain air and sunlight."

Once they had gathered around the table beside the blue pool, Dr. Clark turned to Mason and said, "To answer Mr. Thompson's question, yes I've looked at the clothes the victim was wearing and I'm sure that they are Mexican. The pants and shirt are of plain peasant hand manufacture and are modern, though popular only in the remote mountain areas. I would say that they were made special for the dead man because he was an anglo and very tall. Most Mexican people in the south are quite small."

"Why do you say 'south'?" Mason asked.

"He was buried in a woolen serape typical of Oaxaca state. It's black with vertical red stripes and a stylized corn plant motif in bright colors." She smiled and shaded her eyes against the bright mountain sun. "I identified the serape style only yesterday afternoon and haven't told anyone about my conclusions."

Mason explained, "But Dr. Ward is famous, or perhaps I should say 'notorious' in the literary studies of the southern Mexican cultures."

She pursed her lips and put a finger on her chin, hesitant to speak at first. Finally, she said, "Let me begin by saying that a codex is a manuscript volume, usually one from antiquity. The name comes from caudex, which indicated that they were originally written on tree bark or wood tablets. There were six known codices extant from the ancient Mixtec culture of the southern Mexican sierra, the people known as the Cloud People.

"The Mixtec is one of the major extant cultures of Mexico. Generally speaking, it is also the least appreciated of the major peoples, even though their ancient world rivaled that of the Aztecs. They were very highly respected by the Aztecs for their astronomical and astrological skills. To say nothing of the fact that their potters supplied much of the Aztec elite's pottery. Mixtec polychrome pottery was also a favorite of the later colonial Spanish."

She looked around the table and added, "They are one of the truly underappreciated ancient cultures of the western hemisphere."

She went on. "Anyway, there were six known codices extant from pre-colonial times. They were the basis of most of the literary studies, perhaps I should say 'studies of the literature,' of the Mixtec culture — until about five years ago . . . ." She paused to recollect. "When Dr. Ward revealed that he had possession of a codex he named 'Lady Eight Monkey' but is unofficially named for him — Codex Ward. It's the generational history of a line of people who appear in no other known codex. But there is internal evidence from his papers that there is at least one other codex which corroborates the line of caciques, rulers." The woman's brow knitted and her voice trailed off.

Polly had been deeply engrossed in the conversation. She leaned forward and observed, "It sounds like he did something very wrong."

Dr. Mason grimaced and said, "It's not that he did anything really wrong. It's just that he wouldn't let anyone study the codex except to have it authenticated, as to date, and that was done by a British auction house! Perhaps you are familiar with the controversy over the refusal by some biblical scholars to disseminate the Dead Sea Scrolls — well this is a like case. The difference being that Ward wasn't sharing any of the material.

"There are many scholars around the world, including myself, who would kill for the chance to examine the codex, which, incidentally, he has used as the basis of some original, and brilliant, scholarship."

It was Tommy's turn to be interested. "Did you say 'kill'?"

Dr. Mason looked surprised for a moment. "Why, I guess I did say 'kill'. And I've been talking about the man as if he were still alive. He has been murdered, hasn't he?"

"Yes. And murdered in a ritual manner, too. Does that sound like the work of an academic?"

"Only in a very, very meticulous, and poetic, way — speaking of poetic justice." She looked around the table to see if the black humor had registered but it had not. She sighed inside and said, "You said there was ritualization. How so?"

"He was knocked unconscious and then strangled with what has been described to me as a ceremonial strangling rope," Tom answered.

Dr. Mason said, "That's very interesting. Ritual strangulation and mutilation was common to most of the ancient cultures in the southern two-thirds of this hemisphere. As a matter of fact, it's reported that it still goes on among the Tiahuanaco people in the Lake Titicaca area of Bolivia-Peru and other places."

Polly gasped. "It's still going on?!"

Mason nodded. "It has been reported reliably. No one has come forward as an actual witness but it's possible that there are academic people who have witnessed it but won't report it — too controversial." She leaned back in her chair. "One has to remember that shedding blood is the oldest and most universal act of piety. From the earliest periods of Mesoamerican culture, human sacrifice was a fundamental element of worship. As a matter of fact, there are still many people whose fundamental life and customs have changed only superficially over the last thousand years. When one goes into these ancient cultures one has to be very careful about looking at what goes on through our late twentieth-century, American eyes."

Dr. Mason paused, then added, "And underline that American. Ours is doubtless the most intrusive post-colonial culture. Just like the British, French, Dutch, Portuguese and Spanish of those earlier colonial times, we will probably have to learn our lesson in turn."

Polly was interested. "What lesson is that?" she asked.

Dr. Mason answered, "That, in most instances, we should keep our values to ourselves."

"That's been my experience. I'll try to keep that in mind if I ever get out of the country again," Tommy said, thinking about Southeast Asia and his experiences there.

Dr. Mason went on. "The government has decided that my institution, the Smithsonian, will be in charge of the final assessment and report on Dr. Ward's . . . collection. We will also help in determining if there are any pieces which should be seized as national treasures of countries with which we have international agreements.

"Also, I am very interested in the Zapotec and Mazatec peoples of central-eastern Oaxaca state. They have mixed with the Mixtecs for centuries so the cultures are interbedded. I have done a lot of scholarship on this mixing and have examined those relationships as reflected in the artifacts found in the temple of Monte Alban. It's near the modern capital, Oaxaca City."

Dr. Clark said, "I have been there. And I've seen the pieces in the national museum of anthropology in Mexico City — they are spectacular!"

Mason smiled. "Yes, they rival anything the Aztec produced." She went on, "I talked to the Customs agent and a Mr. Dittus on the phone. Mr. Dittus seemed to think he had seen some of the pieces in Ward's collection in a book on Monte Alban artifacts. If that is the case we have a scandal of enormous proportions here. It would mean that someone has corrupted some very, very important officials. We are going to have to be scrupulous about any speculations on this reaching the press before I have made my determinations and forwarded them to Washington. It could seriously affect our relations with our neighbor. Mexico is very sensitive about irresponsible accusations of corruption in our press." She looked around the table and got nods of assent from everyone present.

———

They arrived at the Ward home on Monday morning. The sheriff and the feds had driven over with Dr. Clark so Dittus could talk with her some more. Tommy drove Dr. Mason.

When they had parked, Tommy asked, "Doctor, something you said yesterday has been bothering me. Do you think that anyone would actually murder Ward for the book you were talking about?"

"Not an academic type, I'm sure. However, the codex has an enormous value as an artifact. Underground collectors spend untold millions, maybe billions, each year for rare things plundered around the world. The codex is one-of-a-kind and I'm sure there is a collector whose interest includes literary items. If enough value has been ascribed to it I wouldn't be surprised at robbery. That, I don't need to tell you, can lead to murder.

"But please, Mr. Thompson, don't even mention the possibility that the codex has been stolen. I couldn't bear the thought that it has disappeared into that demimonde of the rich with too much money and too few scruples."

Tom asked, "A lot of money out there for artifacts, huh?"

Mason shook her head. "There are collectors out there who, individually, will spend more money for a few small items than my whole department's annual budget. I have heard stories of Saudis spending millions each year for items plundered from Yemen by American oil company employees. They are incorporating stelae and other absolutely priceless Sabaean pieces into their houses as decoration. Disgraceful!

"The traffic from this hemisphere and Southeast Asia, especially Kampuchea, also generates tens of millions for the middle men. And men like Ward pay the looters only a few dollars per item." She looked at Tommy and the smile was gone. "From my point of view, and that of many, many others, it is a catastrophe. More knowledge of ancient civilizations is lost in any given year than is generated at universities and government institutions, worldwide, in decades."

"You are angry about that, aren't you?"

"I'm damn mad!"

"Mad enough to kill?"

Dr. Mason's smile returned. "Not me."

"But someone else, perhaps?"

She grimaced. "I honestly don't know. It's not inconceivable that some academic with an aberrant personality might be driven over the edge by the activities of someone like Ward.

"But if I were you I'd look for someone from that underworld I spoke of a minute ago. When there is that kind of money changing hands it's realistic, I think, that men would kill."

It was Tommy's turn for a grim smile. "It doesn't have to involve millions, I know that from personal experience. Life is so precious, yet people are capable of throwing one away like a candy wrapper out a car window."

Chapter 8

Tommy finished his sit-ups on the deck and stood up to stretch. It was a wonderfully cool summer morning. Birds were filling the surrounding woods with their songs. The tanager he often saw flitting through the trees was singing his particularly beautiful melody. Tom went to the end of the deck to scan the pines for a glimpse of its brilliant black, white, orange, and red plumage.

"C'mon, Millie," he said and opened the screen for his dog. She smiled up at him and hopped across the threshold, tired from their run through the woods to Indian Point and back with Polly. Her short Australian heeler legs were a distinct disadvantage when it came to running any long distance.

In the shower he began to go over the Ward murder in his mind, having received a personal phone call from the government man in Rock Springs who'd finally been made the officer-in-charge. While the murder itself was still Tom's responsibility, all the rest of Ward's sins had become the FBI's business.

In the two days since Dr. Mason had returned to Washington a lot had been discovered and a lot more had been hinted at for which they had no real evidence. They had linked Dr. Ward's computer workstation directly to the National Security Agency's computers and it had given up its secret trove in short order. The breadth of the man's intellect, as reflected in the range of his activities, had amazed everyone. The depth of his personality defects, which caused hardly a ripple among the law enforcement types, had scandalized the academics.

Tom smiled at the remembrance of Dr. Mason's gasps as she opened drawer after drawer and box after box of Ward's "collection." Some of it had indeed been stolen from government and university archives. Most of it consisted of unique and priceless pieces unknown to any legitimate collectors. All the pieces would have been at home in fine public collections. The best rivaled and sometimes surpassed the crowning pieces of museums in both hemispheres.

Ward had recorded his business transactions, though the code for sources and customers had not yet been broken—the key to the code was probably a ledger or notebook stashed somewhere in a safety deposit box. His income from sales only hinted at the desirability of the items he'd passed on. The amounts were sometimes staggering, single items at two and three million dollars. The master file entries were simple: "#347: Pec, multi., Tol, 93.2 gold, 52.1cm X 120.4cm, 22.3cm X 38cm, 40.8 T; TMJ.7 11/9/89 450,000US/Ref METO-87 #79."

One of the cryptological experts had broken it out almost at a glance: A chest ornament with multiple elements; product of the ancient Toltec culture; 93.2 percent pure gold, measurements of the main elements in centimeters; weight in Troy ounces; code for buyer and date sold; selling price in U.S. currency and finally, a catalog number which probably stood for Mexican/Toltec collected in 1987, the seventy-ninth item received that year or the seventy-ninth Toltec, or even the seventy-ninth Toltec gold item received that year. The IRS was trying to break out the whole thing exactly so they could attach Ward's estate.

The man had also dealt in "legal" commodities, such as exotic lumber. But what with the row over tropical forests even his legitimate businesses verged on the criminal. The guy had a nose for it, alright.

But it was another secret file the NSA cryppies had broken into that pushed Tom's buttons. Ward was apparently deeply into the study of hallucinogens. He had a whole library of the literature surrounding the use and religious practices associated with them. And, of course, he had found a way of making money from his interests. He had also been a drug dealer.

Tom turned off the shower, pushed the curtain aside, and reached for a towel. As he dried himself, he smiled. Addictive personalities like himself interested Tom. He was fascinated by what drove them, how they functioned, what behavior they exhibited when whipped by their personal demons. He liked to compare them with his old self, to see how far he'd come.

Addicts are usually people given exceptional powers which they have turned against themselves. They tend to be smart, often brilliant, and always self-destructive. They make very interesting criminals .

Ward, it seemed, was a funder of research into hallucinogenic plants and animals such as toads. He funded legitimate research through a foundation in Florida which sent people all over the world to collect the agents themselves. But he also funded research into mystical practices of indigenous peoples from the Arctic to the other extremes of all continents. He had been welcomed into various rites of groups as various as Siberian Eskimos and Colombian jungle peoples. Bogus or genuine, he was a shaman.

But, again the borderline sociopath, Ward had also been involved in supporting a clandestine laboratory somewhere which created "designer" hallucinogens. Dr. Mason had made a dazzling proposal: the Peruvian mummy's pharmacopoeia might have contained spores of hallucinogenic mushrooms which could be resurrected. It was being investigated.

What with the new interest in native religions by moneyed Americans, Ward had found a way to profit from his expertise. Exotic drugs are expensive to buy, yes, but they are also very illegal in this country. The guy just couldn't help himself.

But that wasn't Tom's deal. Ward had been whacked and he'd been whacked in Tom's provenance. His murder was all that concerned Tom. The feds were welcome to all the rest of it, though what with the private air and naval fleets bearing down on the States laden with cocaine, smoke, smack, hash, crank and God-only-knows-what all else, he thought that a rich and eccentric pot stealer would have a real hard time diverting much of U.S. Customs', the DEA's, or anyone else's attention.

But Jackson Hole was a small place. Here a guy like Ward might be exotic, and apparently a genius asshole who deserved to die by some people's lights. But you couldn't kill him for free. Not here. Not yet.

———

Tom was running late when he got to the law enforcement center. He walked past the receptionist and paused. Hysterical laughter was coming from the detectives' room. He went in and found his two partners coughing from the exertion of their mirth.

"Oh no, please stop!" Lewis said and wiped his eyes with his jacket sleeve.

"What's so funny?" Tom asked.

Miles groaned, glanced slyly at Lewis and said, "Oh, we had a shoplifting at Albertson's last night."

"Yeah? So . . ."

Miles leaned forward, now looking grimly at Tom. "You see, Tommy . . . ," his hand appeared from below the desk with a bulbed tube in it, "this medical instrument was stolen with the intent to commit a crime of . . . hideous . . . passion."

Lewis started to laugh again but it seemed to get stuck in his throat. His mouth formed a tight, white *O,* his face purpled and he began to struggle with his tie. He then leaned over to grab the wastebasket with one hand, while he loosened his tie with the other. Then he began to wheeze and choke. Grasping the wastebasket with both hands, he leaned forward and vomited his morning coffee and something else. Too bad. His scant breakfast splashed onto the beautiful paisley tie he'd torn loose.

Miles was little better. He was laughing until he could barely breathe, too.

Lewis put the wastebasket down and looked at his tie mournfully, his eyes watering though they were still full of bright mirth. "You sonuvabitch, Miles, that was a fifty dollar tie."

The convulsions started again and Tom left the room. It was useless to try to get anything out of those two idiots.

He went to the reception area and saw Rhonda, one of the dispatchers. "Hey, Ronnie, what the hell is wrong with Lewis and Miles?" The sound of their laughter was still rolling down the hall.

"You haven't heard about the Harry Carey caper last night?"

"Harry Carey, the actor?"

"Yeah, Harry Carey, as in the most famous actor in the world who lives here in The Hole. Him."

"OK, OK, there's only one Harry Carey and he lives here. What happened to him?"

"Nothing happened to him, exactly. Some of him was stolen, you might say." Her eyes were beginning to show the same alarming brightness that had signaled Lewis' upchucking onto his new tie. She began to giggle. "Maybe you better ask someone else, Tom, it's kind of embarrassing." She turned away, her shoulders hunched over as she tried to stifle a laugh.

"Well, kiss my . . ." Tom turned back and started toward the detectives' office again. Just then Sheriff Harlan came in the front door.

"Hey, Sam, what the heck is all this about Harry Carey?"

Sam's face broke into a broad grin and he said, "Come in my office. It's a hoot."

Sam plopped down in his chair and said, "Sit down, this is pretty funny."

Tom sat down. He could hear Lewis and Miles going at it again. Damn.

Sheriff Harlan shook his head and said, "A couple of young gals were at the Rancher bar last night, one a local and the other a young gal from — so help me — Bone, Idaho. Their boyfriends are old buddies and the one had come over to see his pal. The guys were shooting some pool while the girls chatted and the local girl told the Idaho gal that she worked over at the sperm bank. Well, that's always good for conversation, I'm sure, but in the course of their discussion the local girl mentioned that Harry Carey was a donor . . ."

"At the sperm bank, right?"

"Right. Well, the truth is that Carey doesn't even know the place exists, but the evening goes on and they keep drinking and at some point the girl from Idaho reveals that Harry Carey is her ideal. In fact, she is so in love with Carey that she can hardly stand it."

Sam picked up a paper clip, straightened it out halfway and, still grinning, began to poke the loop end in his ear.

"So, after a few shots of tequila and a few beers the girls sneak out of the bar and go to the sperm bank to kidnap Harry Carey's potential progeny, which is in fact the undone deed of some local schmoe. But the one girl has gone too far to tell the other one the truth."

Tom was beginning to get the picture. "No shit."

"No shit."

Tom leaned forward, clasping his hands and shaking them up and down as the picture began to develop in his mind. "Don't tell me that that . . . ," he nodded down the hall at his office, "turkey baster figures in this crime."

Sam grinned. "Yeah. God only knows what goes on in the minds of drunks."

"I have a pretty good idea."

"I guess you do. But a vial of sperm and a turkey baster?!"

Now it was getting funny. A mental picture began to form in Tom's mind of a cop stopping the car after receiving a shoplifting complaint. It turns into a DWUI offense, but the driver probably thinks the stop is associated with the burglary and breaks down. The stunned cop figures out what is really going on . . . Actually, it was a very, very funny scene as it unfolded in Tommy's imagination and he began to run with it.

The Sheriff broke into Tom's thoughts. "Actually, Tom, I would appreciate it if you'd help the matron take the two girls to court. We're shorthanded today, the deputies have to qualify at the pistol range and they're all out there. Would you mind?"

Tom waved his hand at the laughter which was still rolling out of the detectives' room. "What about one of those two idiots?"

"They're supposed to be down at the sperm bank, taking statements. I'll go get them off their asses if you'll find Marianne and tell her you're going to help her."

Tom sighed. "Yeah, sure. By the way, I got a call from Failoni, the FBI agent-in-charge in Rock Springs."

The sheriff looked blank.

"The Ward murder and all that other federal stuff over in Alta."

"Oh, yeah. What's up?"

"They think they know who did it. They're going to be doing an interview of him later this morning and I'd like to be there."

"Maybe I'd better slide over there too. The papers have been splashing a lot of ink over this and I don't want to look disinterested."

As he walked to the jail to join the matron, Tom shook his head. It must be a pain in the butt, having to keep your feelers out for every little change in amplitude of public opinion. Being a law enforcement person was hard enough, having to be a politician on top of it must be a real bitch. He was glad he didn't have to carry that burden.

When Tom entered the holding area he saw the two young women waiting as Marianne finished the paperwork. She looked up, said, "Gimme two minutes, Tom," and went back to the papers. Tom looked at the prisoners. Both were in their early twenties and would have been pretty on most any other day.

One was blondish with big blue eyes, now red rimmed from crying. The other was brunette. Her face was pale and her eyes were also blue, but vacant. Small alarms went off in Tommy's head: suicide risk. This woman was falling further and further away from her memories of the night before. Tom knew the feelings from his alcoholic past—the wakening in the morning, the recollection, the shame, the retreat then a clearer recollection and burgeoning shame, finally the suicide ideation. This pretty young woman would rather die, literally, than have to face what was happening to her in this room. The contrast between this scene and the hilarity of the detectives' offices made Tom feel bad.

Tom walked up to the holding cell and said, "Hi."

The blonde girl's bottom lip began to tremble and tears welled up in her big eyes. They ran in rivulets down cheeks already streaked with eye makeup. She mouthed a 'Hi' but nothing came out.

The second girl didn't mark Tom's greeting with so much as an eyeblink.

"What's your name, Hon?" he said to the blonde.

"M-M-Melody."

"And your friend?"

"Her name's Jen." The other woman said nothing, only smacked her lips and went back to breathing through her mouth.

"You from here, or are you the one from Idaho?"

"I'm from Idaho."

Tom turned to the matron and said, "Let's talk about this, Marianne." He nodded toward the jail door.

Once outside he said, "Let's get Dr. Wright over here."

"The shrink?"

"Yeah. The dark haired one needs to see a doctor, not a judge."

"But we're supposed to be in court in," she looked at her watch, "less than fifteen minutes."

"She can be arraigned after she sees the doctor."

"What's up?"

"She's suicidal."

"How can you tell?"

Tom couldn't tell her about his own suicide attempt, the one that had shown him his bottom and pushed him into a Vet's hospital and months of treatment. All he said was, "Let's get an evaluation."

"Okay by me, but you're going to have to go to the jail administrator first."

"No problem, I'll go right down there and arrange for protective custody and a suicide watch if they won't take her at the hospital."

"You sure she's not faking it?"

Tom put his hand on Marianne's arm and said, "Trust me, this is something I know a little bit about."

"She's going to have to be arraigned before we can release her. Don't you think we should get it over with?"

Tom thought for a moment. "Okay, but let me go see the judge. Let's see if we can't get him to come over here for the arraignment. I have a suspicion that this is going to be news and I wouldn't be surprised if there were a photographer or two over at the courthouse. It could be a real bad deal if there were."

"Yeah. I heard about this in the coffee shop this morning, before I came to work. Everyone was getting a big kick out of it."

Tom said, "Can you handle this alone?"

"Sure. I'll just sit here and keep an eye on them until I hear from you."

"Great, you're a sweetie pie."

Tom left to see the jail administrator and then the judge. He realized he was poking his nose into the jail's business but he couldn't help himself. He shook his head as he walked down the hall. One thing that made his ass ache was a do-gooding liberal, and here he was . . . He sighed inside. Sheriff Harlan had once told him that there were too many grey cats in his life, that as a good law enforcement officer he had to think in black and white, good and bad. It was something he was definitely going to have to work on.

Chapter 9

When Tommy and Sheriff Harlan walked into the courthouse in Driggs they saw the stir in the building. The offices of the assessor, county clerk, clerk of court, and just about every other office were on the first floor of an old brick building typical of the rural west. It didn't take much to excite the occupants of the building and if the couple of dozen people who worked there were gathered in whispering groups then the whole town probably was too. The taking-in for questioning of the Mormon bishop's first counselor had run an electric charge through the whole community.

He was a dairy farmer who'd branched out into real estate development on what had been marginal pasture until the recent property boom. He was in his late thirties, with an impeccable reputation. If the investigation had been in the hands of the local authorities he would have been approached in the privacy of his own home and shown the respect due his position in the community. But federal agents have no sense of what is proper etiquette in small communities like those in the Teton Valley.

They had not arrested the man, give them credit for that much. But he had been escorted to the courthouse and was being prepared for a polygraph test. When the sheriff of Teton County, Idaho, saw the sheriff of Teton County, Wyoming, in the hallway he beckoned.

"Hi, Sam," he said and motioned his two guests to come into his office and sit.

"Hi, Terry. What do you think about this?" Sam waved at the small crowd outside the door.

"Oh, it's horseshit — federal horseshit. If LeRoi Metcalf is a murderer I'll kiss your ass on the courthouse lawn."

"They must think they have something."

"Well, Metcalf told Ward he would beat his brains out, but that doesn't really mean anything." He grimaced sourly. "You can't ignore the fact that he said it, but to haul him down here and disgrace him in public . . ."

Tom said, "The agent in Rock Springs said Metcalf did more than just threaten him. He said that he'd attacked Ward."

"Knocked him on his ass, alright. And did it at the pizza place in front of a dozen folks. But you have to remember that we're talking about Metcalf's daughter here. You know how Mormons are about their kids, especially their daughters."

"Was Ward messing around with her?"

"No. But she had to be taken to the hospital for a psychotic episode and LeRoi blamed Ward for that. One of the local boys had given her some LSD or something and she'd gone crazy. The boy got scared and dropped her off in the hospital at night, screaming and carrying on. When I questioned him he said that his big brother had gotten the drugs from Ward while they were backpacking together—gone out on some kind of "vision quest" thing together in the Jedediah Smith Wilderness. You know how goofy these yuppies are about that Indian stuff.

"I talked to Ward and he denied possession of anything illegal, of course. I couldn't prove anything but LeRoi didn't need any more proof than the boy's story and he was more than likely right on. He phoned Ward and threatened to kill him. A couple of times, I guess, but Ward never reported it or filed a complaint. Then LeRoi ran into him at the pizza place the same day that his daughter came home from school because of a flashback and he knocked Ward down. Then he told him that if his daughter had one more problem associated with the drugs he was going to take a baseball bat and beat him to a pulp."

"Well, someone did just about that," Tom said. "But he was buried in Mexican temple garments, so it must have been someone besides the Bishop's counselor."

Sheriff Rogers grimaced, "We're all sure Ward's wife did that. The feds tell me that it was a Mexican-type burial and she was a Mexican. Don't make fun."

Tom colored. He should have guessed that Rogers would be LDS, most officials with the confidence of the valley communities were. "I apologize, I shouldn't have said that. I didn't mean any disrespect."

Sheriff Rogers waved his hand in dismissal. "It's OK, I understand."

Non-Mormons often made fun of LDS secret ritual, out of ignorance, and it was a burden the people bore with their customary generosity, but through gritted teeth. Tommy was what was called a jack-Mormon, raised by a Baptist father and a Mormon mother. Though he didn't practice the religion he respected it and was inordinately proud of his pioneer heritage. That made him doubly ashamed of his gaffe.

"So you think this is just a lot of —"

"Horseshit, excuse my French." Sheriff Rogers finished Sheriff Harlan's sentence.

Sam stood. "Well, that's good enough for me."

Tommy stood too, and waited as the two men shook hands.

Once they were outside, Sheriff Harlan stood for a moment and pinched at his bottom lip. "Let's find Nolan," he said. "He spent quite a bit of time with Ward on rescues and in training. I want to make damn sure one of my deputies isn't ingesting psilocybin mushrooms and running around in the woods calling on Wakan Tanka or Timothy Leary to drop a celestial staircase into the Jed Smith Wilderness."

———

Nolan paled at the sheriff's questions. "Nolan, did you ever eat any of them damn mushrooms? I'm asking you straight out and don't lie to me."

The deputy's brow wrinkled and his face hardened as he looked directly at his boss. "I don't lie," he said. He then paused and nodded slowly. "Yeah, I ate one of the damn things."

Sheriff Harlan's face took on a perplexed look. Then he said in a mournful tone, "Tell me what happened, Nolan."

"Doc Ward and I went on a conditioning run and scramble — just daypacks, running shoes, shorts. We were up in Alaska Basin, taking a break, and Doc started talking about nature, native religions he was familiar with, ceremonies he had taken part in. He talked about some Indians in Mexico who run for days on end without stopping . . . Oh, he talked about a bunch of real interesting stuff that I'd never heard before. The guy had been everywhere and done just about everything." Nolan looked back out the window and Tommy knew what the young man was thinking — he was thinking that he'd never been anywhere or done anything interesting.

"Sheriff," Nolan went on, "I know that mushrooms are illegal and all that, but I also know that the Native Church over at Fort Hall and a lot of other places use the same stuff in their ceremonies." He raised his hand against Sam's objection, "And I know that I don't belong to that church so it doesn't make it right for me. I know that. But, you see, I'd been going through a real long dry spell with my church. I felt alone, isolated. My family life was falling apart because I'd quit going and was feeling cut off from life . . ." His voice trailed off.

"For whatever reason, I ate half of this nasty mushroom button that Ward had brought. He built a little fire, burnt some grass bundles he'd made, sang in some strange language and we split the damn thing and ate it. And I think I met God."

The statement seemed to echo in the car, leaving vibrations. There was a long silence, unbroken by either Sheriff Harlan or Tommy. Nolan went on.

"Something happened to me that I can't explain. You see, I'd always believed in God mostly because I was raised in the church and it was a big part of our lives. But the God I was raised with carried a very big stick. The God I met out there in Alaska Basin loved me. He flooded me with love, it was like falling into a Mississippi River of love.

"I . . . I . . . don't know how to say this, exactly. Doc was the only one I ever talked to about it and he just said that it didn't need any explanation. He said that the blessing I received would remain in my heart forever, that it was my private vision.

"You see, I thought I'd known what love was but in fact I didn't know how . . . *big* it is. I had an experience that day which has changed my whole understanding of who I am and what this world is all about. I now go to church and I can see who stands behind the men who are the authorities, the ones who supposedly know all about God and what he wants for me — and it makes them look pretty small. Sometimes I just grin, hoping that one of them will look over his shoulder and see what I saw, feel what I felt up there in the mountains. It would make his hair stand up and blow his shoes off." The young man grinned in spite of his situation.

"You see, now I know that I am loved. That afternoon with Doc Ward was exactly what I needed. It changed my life, Sam."

Sheriff Harlan shifted uncomfortably in the seat of Nolan's squad car, "You know what happened with the Metcalf girl."

Nolan's face registered real pain. "Yes. I talked to Ward and he said that Boyd Vandusen had taken the button. His little brother stole it from him and gave some to her."

Sam straightened up. "That's no excuse. I'm putting you on administrative leave starting tomorrow. I want you to come over the hill to Jackson and we'll have a meeting, try to work this out— and hope it doesn't hit the papers with too big a splash."

Tommy was momentarily shocked at the quick decision. He had been moved by Nolan's story. His own quest for spirituality had resonated with Nolan's story. His revelation — or whatever it was — showed in the man's face, though at the moment that face was very troubled. Losing a good job in Wyoming is a damn serious thing for a man with a family. Life can be very hard, still, in these mountains.

Nolan nodded. He looked at Sheriff Harlan and said, "Am I going to lose my job, Sam?"

"I don't know. I promise I'll do everything I can to find something for you with the county, somewhere, but I think you're through as a cop. The sheriff looked at his deputy and his eyes were cold, "You fucked up. Big time. This is the real world and I have to operate in it according to real world rules. You broke the law." His eyes softened a bit. "I think I understand a little of what you must have been feeling when you did what you did. But God doesn't spend a lot of time sowing love in law enforcement agencies, courts, jails, and prisons. We handle the devil's end of the business. It's our job."

———

It was hot in Huajuapan de Leon. The torch of the sun had blasted the limestone hills a glaring, dusty white. The few leaves on the trees had paled from green to a dirty gray as traffic on the mostly unfinished roads lifted the powdered limestone into the languid air—adding to the dust from the stone buildings shaken down by a moderate earthquake the week before.

On a tall hill in the center of the modern city stood an ancient pyramid of the Mixtec civilization which had flourished a thousand years ago. It had not been moved as the earth shook. It shone in the hot sun and hazy air like a beacon, a beacon which had lost its light in the modern world.

In an ordinary year regular pulses of wet air moved east from the Gulf of Mexico and, cooled by their rise on the backs of the coastal range and interior sierras, drenched the heartland with afternoon rains. The rainy season should have begun in early May. It was now the middle of June and no rain had yet fallen.

Huajuapan was a major city of Oaxaca state, lying halfway up the highlands from the plains south of Mexico City. Here it was dry, dusty, hot. Higher up in the mountains the forests of Mixtec pine and highland oak were torching in a hellish acceleration of the seasonal spot fires which cleansed the forest environment in normal years. Even this far north there was an alkaline, smoky taste mixed with the fine, hot dust.

Concha Osorio and her brother Cenovio sat on a stone wall, sharing a glass of cold horchata, a sweet rice drink, and eating little pink bananas bought with the very last of their money.

"One more tank of gas, that is all," said her brother.

"Yes."

But the money for that one last tank seemed an impossibility. Not that they believed it was impossible, given time, but they had no time. One hope was that their companion, Valerio Trujano, would be successful in borrowing from a cousin. He owned an electrical supply house and was rich by provincial standards. In fact, he was the local godfather, known as el cacique.

"I sincerely regret the death of the soldiers," Cenovio said. It was the first mention of it since the incident on the Sinaloa road.

Concha nodded and wiped her sweating face with a handkerchief. "There was nothing else to do. They would have taken our money and probably the car. But they could not take the things of the people. Dzaui lent stealth to your feet and strength to your arm."

"Perhaps, but I feel the need to repent. In the sanctuary." He looked across the street at a colonial-era chapel.

"Of course. Go." Concha was also a believer and she heartily approved of her brother's impulse. "I will wait here for Valerio. Pray for his success too."

The small woman sat in the shade of the palm awning in front of the tienda and watched the car and its precious contents. Having stepped into the endless continuum of peasant time, she thought of very little. She did not think of her lost life in the north or of her dead husband and the riches he'd owned. She was going home.

In the trunk of the car were two treasures of her people which had been taken through the use of money on two weak men. She was taking them home to the valley of her birth and to her family, who had been custodians of these powerful objects before the time of the Spanish capitanes. The theft of those objects by her husband's men, one of whom was her oldest brother, had turned the world of the Mixteca upside down. And set it on fire.

Earthquakes, fire, blood. It was another time of great calamity. But, as always, it would be followed by a long time of tranquillity. That she knew. It was the way the world worked down here. But not in el norte. There, even with all its riches, it was always a time of calamity because most of the people did not love God.

Valerio walked up to Concha and from the smile on his face she knew he'd gotten the money. "My cousin, Armando Pacheco, is generous. He has given me 125,000."

Out of habit Concha quickly figured that the pesos would be about forty dollars. She smiled. They could have made it home on a fourth of that. She held out her hand to receive the folded money, glancing around as he did. It was a lot of money in this barrio.

"Where is Cenovio?"

"He is praying, asking for absolution."

Valerio crossed himself. "Yes. And I will pray also. Now I will get my things."

He went to the big green Chevrolet and took his suitcase and a U.S. Army issue laundry bag from the rear seat. "You will go north again?" he asked.

Concha, her hand shading her eyes, shook her head. "No. I am a widow now."

Valerio sucked on his teeth in the Indian way of expressing disgust. "You are young. Just because you are back in Mexico does not mean that you have to take back all the old ways. You will find a good man."

"I am going back to Achiutla. My husband was responsible for a great wrong to all the Cloud People and I will not be looked at with respect."

"But you bring back the peoples' story. And The Heart of the World."

"I am not a man."

Valerio looked sad. "Yes. That is true." He picked up the poor suitcase and the laundry bag. "I must leave, I have found a ride to San Jeronimo. Tell Cenovio I will see him sometime at the Saturday market in Tlaxiaco. We will go north again."

Concha raised her hand over her head, motioning good-bye and thanks. He had given up much to help them bring back the people's things. The odyssey north and south again was a very brave thing to do for one's own reasons. To do it for someone outside one's community was a much braver thing.

Concha waited in the shade of the tienda for another half an hour. Although she had money, she hesitated to buy another cool drink. The money was not hers.

Finally she crossed the road, put a handkerchief on her hair and entered the chapel, nervously checking the car before she stepped through the door. She walked a few paces into the chapel, crossed herself and waited for her eyes to adjust to the dark.

Halfway to the altar her brother was kneeling in the aisle. She could see his shoulders shaking and she knew that he wept silently. He had always been the gentlest of the boys. He was the one who rescued puppies of the feral village dogs from the tortures of the other children. When their father took the rescued puppies and disappeared with them, Concha remembered seeing her brother kneeling in the dirt beside the rancho, his shoulders shaking in this same manner.

It moved her to know that this man was not above his suffering, that life had not turned him hard like most of the men of her race. Living at the margin of life and death, where the Mixtec seemed doomed to dwell, was a hard teacher.

The little woman knelt, asking for absolution from her part in the happenings of the last two weeks. After a moment, she rose and hurried back to the door. She paused before the blinding light at the chapel door, and then stepped outside.

The trunk of the big green Chevrolet yawned open. In an instant she understood. She jerked her head to the side and her eyes caught the flash of heels as they disappeared around a corner. The street urchins had been waiting for their moment ever since they had seen the American license plate on the front of the car.

She ran across to the car, her heart driving spirals through her vision. The box with The Heart was gone. She shrieked and raised her fists to the sky, then collapsed into the dirt, bottle caps, and discarded candy wrappers of the burning, filthy street.

Chapter 10

Tom set Polly's bags on the scale while she gave her ticket to the Delta attendant, a man in his forties with a handsome grey mustache and a southern accent. They then walked to the waiting area and sat down.

"I wish you could stay for the weekend," he said.

"Sorry. Business like this doesn't wait, it's a great chance for our brokerage." For two years Polly's real estate company had been working on a deal with the biggest commercial bank in Mexico and a Mexican development group. The governments of Canada, Mexico, and the U.S. had signed the free trade agreement, and now it looked like their foresight and hard work was going to pay off.

Polly's ex-husband, Ferdie Anaya, came from a family of old-time Californios who'd kept their ties with the elite of Mexico. They were "major Mexican money," as Polly put it. Anaya was not the sort of man to change and when Polly had needed room to grow in their marriage he responded by reining her more tightly. He was still very much in love with Polly and to watch him stare at her was painful, but he was also a gentleman in the Spanish style and had finally decided that what was done was done.

Tommy, as the inheritor of the romantic windfall, tried to be as generous as he could with Anaya. He was grateful to Ferdie for raising and educating Christina, Tommy's daughter, as his own for twenty years. Christina had been the fruit of a summer romance with Polly long ago. Tommy had found out about her existence the winter before and had met her only twice, once in Polly's hospital room and once in California. The meeting had been strained. She had what she thought was a perfect family — well-to-do, educated, influential, and blue-blood Californians to boot. To discover as a mature woman that her real father was a small town detective in the sticks of Wyoming had been a shock.

Like her mother, Christina was blonde, beautiful, and smart. But she had drawn a great deal from her father — stepfather — too. She was elegant and canny, with a feral instinct in business. Christina, Ferdie, and her sister, Maria (Ferdie's daughter) had put together a business deal that smelled like eventual millions, as Polly described it.

It made Tom sigh inside. One of his burdens was to wonder what he could have been if his family had money or, better, a tradition of higher education and obligatory achievement. He wondered what it must be like to have a family where each generation stood on the shoulders of the last, rather than the one common in Wyoming where each child struck out on their own down the first, or widest, path which presented itself.

Polly's hand reached up and smoothed Tom's forehead. "You get in trouble when you think, Thomas."

It made him smile. "Strong back, though."

"Yes. The back is strong and that is good." She grinned. Then her face changed and she touched his chin. "Leave yourself alone. You are a good man and I love you."

Tommy said, "Which reminds me . . ." he looked around for a clock. "When's the flight due in?"

Polly looked at her watch and said, "Twelve minutes." When she looked up Tommy was taking her small hand in his large hand and putting a ring on it.

Her face melted. Her mouth turned down, her nostrils whitened and tears flooded her face. Her nose began to run too. In an instant she looked a mess.

She raised her hand and stared at the ring.

"It's French," Tommy said.

"What's French, you poop," she squeaked. "I can't see a thing."

He took the hand, which had a dollop of something, tears or mucus, on it and read the inscription: "Vous et nul autre."

Her mouth turned down even further. She raised her face to the ceiling and a squeaky little cry came out of her mouth as more tears ran down her face and neck.

"It means 'You and no other,'" he said.

"I know what it means, Thomas," she said and she hit him so hard in the chest that it made him wince, then cover the place of impact with his hand. She then put her face on that hand and he could feel the wetness and the shaking of her body. People were beginning to notice.

"Pol!" He was looking at all the starers. "People think I've done something bad to you. They're looking at us."

"I don't care," she said into his shirt. "This is Wyoming — they don't know what a really happy woman looks like."

———

"There was someone here to see you, an officer from Mexico," the dispatcher said as Tom stood in front of his message box. "He said he'd be back at two o'clock."

"Mexico? Like in the country Mexico?"

"Like from the Attorney General of Mexico's office in the national capital of Mexico City, state of Mexico, country of Mexico our neighbor to the south," she said with one eyebrow arched. She was holding out a business card. Tom took it.

"You have every National Geographic that was ever printed, don't you?" Tom said sweetly.

"No. I'm missing the one with you and your relatives in it — the Jane Goodall issue." She turned and walked across the room, leaving Tom with the sure knowledge that he had been insulted in some obscure way, though the name Jane Goodall did ring a bell.

He looked at the card.

Rigoberto Sandez Sanchez
Oficial
Oficina de Avogado General
Mexico D.F.

Tom had taken three years of Spanish in high school, but only to spend time as close to Edie Kay Kline as he possibly could. In the meantime a basic grasp of the language had stuck.

Tom was working at his desk when Lewis stepped through the door and said, "Hey, Tom."

"Huh?"

"The chili belly is here. Want me to bring him in?"

Tom's blood pressure went through the roof. "Who?" he said through clenched teeth.

Lewis realized his mistake instantly. Having been raised in Texas he thought that everyone shared his prejudices. "Uh, sorry. I'll go get 'im."

"No! I'll go out there myself."

"OK. Have it your way." He stood aside as Tom pushed his way past.

"Sheez," Lewis said.

When Tom reached the reception area he saw no one.

"Hey Rhonda, where's the guy from Mexico?"

Before she could answer a head and shoulders appeared above the reception counter as a man stood up from the couch. But not much above the counter.

Tom walked to the gate and asked, "Mr. Sanchez?"

"Sandez. Sanchez was my mother's family name. It's kinda confusing, I know. The names are real close." He put down the magazine he'd been reading, straightened his tie, and handed Tom a well-worn wallet with a badge pinned to it. Dark-complected with thick hair parted on the side, he couldn't have been more than five-foot-three, though he was built like a wedge. Tom pushed the swinging door open and said, "C'mon back. My office is down the hall on the right." He returned the badge.

"Thanks, I appreciate it." The guy had no accent whatsoever. His English was perfect, inflected like a native American's.

Tom walked to his chair and sat down. Sandez looked suspiciously at the deep, upholstered chair across the desk from Tom. Then he spotted a folding chair leaning against the wall.

"May I?" he asked.

"Sure, lemme get it for you."

"Nah, sit down. I can get it for myself. Man, when you're as short as I am it can be a bitch. All American furniture is built for people twice my size." He gave a little sigh as he opened the chair and put it down. "But what the heck, nothing you can do about your genes. My mom was an Indian. Four foot nine. My dad was pretty tall and my sister is almost five foot ten. Ain't that a bitch? Your sister is bigger than you are." He smiled, genuinely amused at his fate. Tom liked the guy. He was confident. Even a little cocky, which can be a real asset for a good cop.

"You born in Mexico?" Tom suddenly asked, and then was embarrassed at the personal question.

"Yeah. But I went to junior high and high school in Southern California. Two of us kids were kind of adopted by some people who took us north and got us educated. My mom and dad still live in Baja, in a town called Guerrero Negro."

"Then you went back after high school."

"After college. Didn't have any choice. I wanted to stay, but the pinche migra caught up with me, us. Me and my sister. But it turned out all right because they were the ones who got me my job — introduced me to a colonel in the Mexican Federal Police."

"And what is your job?"

"And why am I here, right?"

72

Tom smiled and opened his hands, meaning "You said it, not me."

"Cenovio and Concha Osorio Espinoza."

Tom plopped back in his seat, surprised.

Sandez laughed at the expression on Tom's face. "We're pretty good at this stuff."

"What stuff."

"Murderers are high on our priority list at the Attorney General's office, but smugglers of these peoples' caliber are even higher."

"These people are wanted in Mexico too?"

"Yeah. Especially Concha. We want her real bad. She's the one who made all this possible, with her brother's help, of course. She's smart."

Tom thought of the pretty woman in sexual abandon he'd seen on the videotape. Hard to get any impression of a person's intellect in that state.

"Murder?"

"Yes. And smuggling. But I guess you know about all that."

"Well, the reports aren't even close to being finished on all the artifacts. And I have no idea where the feds are on the dope deal."

"Dope?"

"Nothing major, really. Hallucinogenic mushrooms, but it's all tied up with the artifact smuggling. I guess that's what really interests you, the artifacts?" It was more of a question than a statement.

"For sure. Some of the things that we have been missing are apparently in the collection you found at Ward's. If I can speak with your promise of confidentiality . . ."

Tom nodded. "Of course, go ahead."

"The magnitude of some of the items can only be appreciated when considered from a Mexican point of view. Corruption is, and always has been a way of life at home, but there is a limit, finally. Some of the people involved in this artifact trade have far exceeded our generous idea of what is acceptable. They have given away whole sections of our cultural foundation. Priceless is a very poor word for things which were taken by Ward and our countrymen. There are very important names and academic titles involved, on both sides of the border. There can be no breath of this made public. We will handle it in our own way, of course. But we must depend upon the discretion of all the American offices involved."

"Well," Tom said, "you can depend upon me and, if I can speak for them, the sheriff and our officers."

Sandez smiled grimly. "That will make the Attorney General, and the people he reports to, very happy." Tom guessed rightly that the only people the Attorney General reports to are the Minister of the Interior and the President of the Republic.

Sandez asked, "Do you have any preliminary stuff I can look at? We're going to have to work together on this, make this airtight. If we catch them in Mexico we are going to want to have as much information on their activities as possible. And, of course, to help you catch them if they are in the States. Then it will be a matter of extraditing them to my country."

"But first we have to catch them," Tom said. "In the meantime, I can get you what we have. The federal stuff is being handled by the FBI office in Rock Springs. The agent's name is Failoni, if you want me to contact him for you. But the evidence pertaining to the murder is yours to examine also."

"Great. Let me digest the info you have and then I'll work my way up to the federal folks. Also, is it possible to look at the scene, at Ward's place?"

"I don't see why not. How does tomorrow sound?"

"Tomorrow's Saturday."

Tom waved his hand. "No big deal. My girlfriend left town today and I don't have anything planned."

Sandez stood up, slipping to the floor from the chair. "Great. What time should I be here?"

"Where are you staying? I'll pick you up."

"I'm at the Rusty Parrot."

"Nice place."

"Yeah, it is. What time do you want to take off?"

"You like big breakfasts?"

"I may not look it but I love to eat, man."

"Good, we'll slide over to Bubba's. Pick you up at eight, how does that sound?"

"Just right. I'll be waiting."

Tom followed him to the door and watched him cross the parking lot. At a distance he didn't look as short as he did up close. But then, after the first impression Tom had forgotten about the man's height. He took up a lot of room, irrespective of his physical size.

Chapter 11

Jeff was keeping the watch on Ward's house. He got out of his patrol car and stretched as Tom and Berto drove up.

"I don't suppose you brought me any coffee?" he asked with a tired grin.

"You can have the rest of this if you want," Tom said and offered him half of the cup he'd picked up in Driggs.

Jeff waved it away. "Thanks, but I like mine hot."

Tom and Sandez got out of the car and Tom introduced the men. Jeff was six-foot-seven, blonde and blue eyed. The contrast was almost comical. But Berto, as he'd asked Tom to call him, just shook Jeff's hand and began a conversation. It was obvious that the size of other men bothered him not in the least. As Tom looked at the two men before him, he came to an understanding — Sandez could be a very scary guy when it came right down to it. A good man to have on your side.

Tom also noticed that he carried the small-frame 9-mm automatic pistol Smith & Wesson designed for women. The pistol and the holster both looked like they had seen a lot of use. Just like the man.

They stepped over the yellow plastic ribbon and entered the house. Inside the front room Berto stopped in his tracks. He shook his head and whistled in a very American way. He was impressed.

"Damn! Those are some kinda mountains." He spun around in place and took in the huge picture windows, the furniture, the decorations, "and this is one hell of a house." He sucked on his front teeth, making a sound of disapproval. "The money that went into this house would support a community in Mexico for years." Then he smiled, wryly and added, "But that's the way the tortilla crumbles, man. The rich get richer and the poor get babies."

After a quick survey of the upstairs, Tom took him downstairs to the vault. Again he whistled in appreciation as he took in the depository, its cabinetwork, the computer workstation.

"All the artifacts have been packed up and are on their way to Washington for inventory and identification. I suppose you're going out there for that," Tom said.

Berto shook his head. "People from the embassy are handling things there. I'm here for the Osorios. It sure would have been nice to see the collection for myself, though. I'm into that kind of stuff."

Tom smiled and said, "There's a guy with the Forest Service, an archaeologist, who got a bunch of pictures. The feds let him do it as a professional courtesy."

"Alright! Any chance that I could see them, just out of curiosity?"

"Lemme phone him and see if he's home."

An hour later Berto stood at Kelly Dittus's desk in the empty U.S. Forest Service building. He sucked on his teeth as Kelly laid the pictures out.

"I would say that about eighty percent of the stuff here came from my country. There's things from every major prehistoric culture." He put his finger on a picture and said, "Olmec. This one is Olmec too, and that's Toltec, Toltec, Mayan, Aztec, Zapotec, Zapotec, Aztec, Mixtec, Mixtec," he moved his hand in a rocking motion, "Mixtec/Zapotec, Mayan . . ." He shook his head. "This one, so help me, is from a culture that I'm not even sure about. It could be some kind of South American piece — or it could be from some bastard or transitional Mexican culture that hasn't even been classified yet." He looked up at Tommy and there was pain in his eyes. "This hurts," he said.

Kelly added, "When I stepped into that room I told Tom that the guy deserved to die for what he had stolen. It was unbelievable."

"You said that they had a whole inventory of the stuff in the vault plus everything that he had sold up to that point? God knows what he sold along the way."

"Well, it was all in a kind of a code but they broke out most of the entries the first day. I guess there's still some they haven't figured out. He had been dealing for a long time, several years at least.

"But there's a bright side — chances are your country will get it all back," Tom said.

Berto nodded. Then he smiled and said, "And with a lot of expert curating for free, too."

The guy was hard to keep down, Tom could see that.

On the way back to Jackson, Berto asked, "What do you know about the Osorios? Any ideas where they might be?"

"The people in Idaho and Oregon are looking for them real hard. But we have put out an alert for all the states between us and Mexico, too."

Berto shook his head and said, "You need an APB — there are a lot of Mixtec colonias in the states now."

"Colonias — colonies, right?"

Berto looked at him and smiled. "Comprendes español?" he asked.

Tommy laughed out loud, pinched his index finger and thumb together tightly and said, "Oh, I understand about that much, pardner. I took Spanish in high school but that was a helluva long time ago, believe me."

"Ah, 'sta bien, chavo."

"What does 'chavo' mean?"

"Oh, it's what working men call each other. It's kind of like your word 'guy' or 'pardner.'"

"Anyway, what were you saying about Mixtec colonies in the states?'

"It's a kind of a long story."

Tom pointed down the highway and said, "We've got a drive in front of us. Go ahead."

"You sure you're interested? It's Mexican stuff."

"I'm interested. Go."

"Well, I'm a product of this little history so I know something about it and it starts in the late fifties, early sixties sometime, when they first started growing tomatoes in Baja — across the border from California. The unions in el norte were pushing for higher wages and better conditions and the price of produce was going up and up."

Berto paused for a moment, looking out the window and the fields passing by. Then he said, passionately, "Man, if you think there's prejudice in this country you need to go to Mexico and see how they treat the Indigenos down there."

"Indihenos?"

"Indigenous people. You call 'em Indians up here."

"And we treat them the same, believe me. All this stuff about the great spirituality of the Native Americans that is being exploited in the media is just following a fashion. They make a big fuss about the American Indians' kinship with the earth but it hasn't changed the realities on the reservations. All the crystal gazers, vision questers, and the people doing all the writing about our red brothers, even taken as a whole, don't contribute as much as the guy who sells 'em affordable cars next to the reservations. He's just ripping them off a few hundred bucks. The others are ripping off their culture, debasing it by popularizing it."

Berto grinned. "Bien, tu eres simpatico, hombre."

Tom waved his hand. "Nah, the liberals just give me heartburn, that's all."

"You a redneck?"

"I came by it honestly, believe me. I'm working class from my neon neck down to my shit kicking boots."

"Anyway, they needed real cheap labor in Baja, the Mexican growers did. But all the paisanos within five hundred miles of the border were too hip to the scene to work for nothing when they could run, jump, or swim to a job that paid four, five times as much. So the labor guys went to Oaxaca, which to this day is the poorest state in the country, and recruited the people from the mountains. The Mixtec are the biggest indigenous group there and they had absolutely nothing in those days. They were glad to hire out as slaves to the growers.

"When they got to Baja they were kept down in the usual ways, mostly treated like animals. As a matter of fact, it's only been the last ten years or so that the Mixtecs have begun to gain some political power. It started with a strike in Tijuana by the women who sold food in the streets but now they're getting some real recognition. They've learned a lot about grassroots politics since they've been in the north, especially in the big colonias in California and Oregon."

"Watsonville."

"Watsonville? What's that?"

"Watsonville, Oregon. That's where the license plate was from."

"What license plate."

"Oh, I forgot to tell you. We found a license plate to a pickup owned by Cenovio Osorio at the Ward's place."

"No shit!" Berto was visibly excited. "How far is it to this place? Can we drive there?"

"Oh, it's only about a thousand miles."

"Damn."

"Well, it could have been lost when he was on a regular visit, too. We can't tie him to the murder on the strength of a dropped license plate."

Berto grinned. "In Mexico I could make it stick." Then he waved his hand, "Nah, just kidding.

78

Tom said, "You said that your history was tied up in this tomato growing deal."

"Yeah, my grandparents on my mother's side came north with one of the first groups. I was born there, in Baja, as a matter of fact. My dad was a game warden at Scammon's Lagoon, the place where the whales go to get it on." He grinned. "My mom and her family had gone down there to scavenge on Junk Beach. They heard you could sell the fishing net floats, and other stuff that landed on the beach, in Tijuana and Ensenada for some good jing. She met my dad there."

"So you were raised at Scammon's Lagoon?"

"Yeah. But it wasn't as romantic as it sounds. We lived in a shack, man. And before they built the road to the place, the only time they could get stuff to us was at low tide. We lived off the ocean a lot, and there was a bunch of us kids. Eleven."

"Not the same place now, huh?"

"Turistas, hombre. Muchas turistas and dinero. Now."

Tom laughed. "There wasn't a whole hell of a lot around here when I was growing up, either. But now, in Jackson Hole, by the end of the summer season we call them 'terrorists'. But it would be pretty cold and hungry around here without 'em. "

"Hot and hungry at Laguna Scammon, chavo."

The two men laughed together. They shared a lot, it seemed, considering the cultural chasm Tom had expected.

———

Concha and her brother stood in the garden of the big house and watched the servants come and go on their duties. She thought about the American movie called The Godfather. It had come as a great shock to her that the cacigazco system existed in the north, too. The caciques, she had thought, were needed only in poor countries where the government was no help. Or in societies where the poor needed protection from the government itself. That it existed in a country as rich as Los Estados Unidos del Norte had surprised her.

In many ways it was una desgracia, how the caciques acquired power and took advantage of that power, but life without them was sometimes impossible without them. Like now.

For instance, here she and her brother were, fugitives from two governments but only because they were on a mission to preserve the very life of their people — to defend the earth itself against the corruption that money had brought to her village. And she and her brother Demetrio had been a part of it. It had cost her her husband and the rich life she had enjoyed up north but now she suffered even more than she had when her other brother, Cenovio, had taken the life of her husband. That was when she and her brother had lost the soul of her people.

"Señor?"

The voice of the cacique's secretary jolted her back to the large patio of the big house in Huajuapan de Leon. He beckoned Cenovio and Concha to follow him through a large double door at least three meters high.

Inside it was very cool. The damp air from the lush patio garden acted as an air conditioner. The black and white tiles of the floor were cool on the bottoms of her bare feet. It felt wonderful.

'Dear God we are ever in thy hands. Keep us safe, deliver our people's fate back into our hands which are clasped in your very own,' she prayed to herself.

They entered another large doorway and passed into a pleasant room where a large man, eyes magnified by his thick glasses, sat behind a desk piled high with papers.

He stared at the two small Indians in front of him, saying nothing.

Finally, the secretary said to Cenovio, "Tell Señor Pacheco what you are here for."

The little man dropped his face and waited for Concha to speak.

"Señor Pacheco, I am from the village of San Miguel Achiutla and my name is Concha Osorio Espinoza. This is my brother Cenovio."

The large man nodded, looking at Cenovio and then back at the woman beside him. In Mexican society it is unusual for a man to defer to a woman in serious business, but certainly not unheard of.

"We have been in the north, living for some time. I myself was married to a very important gringo, a professor of great distinction who made me proud to be his wife. But something happened. Something of which we are greatly ashamed, for it has brought disaster to the whole countryside here. Earthquakes, fires. . ."

The cacique looked at his secretary, a man with a sharp, vulpine face. The man nodded.

The cacique looked back at Concha, encouraging her to continue.

"My husband is . . . was a man who gained fame as a scholar of the ancient Mixtec culture. He came to our village ten years ago, which has a famous convento and a great pyramid of the ancients which has never been excavated.

"At first we were afraid that he was there to begin an excavation, which would have disturbed our dead. But he did not. He moved into the village and talked to the people. He returned several times and went to all the houses in the village, just talking. At night we would see him writing, writing. Sometimes all the night. And then, because they admired him, people began to bring my husband, el Profesor Ward, things of the ancients. Little things at first, but then things of value."

"One moment," the big man broke in. "Please bring these people chairs, Pancracio." Concha was greatly impressed by the deep voice of the cacique.

"I can tell that this is not a short tale. And Pancracio . . ."

"Yes?"

"Bring us all some agua melon."

"Yes sir." The man moved two chairs in front of the cacique's desk and left the room.

"Please continue," said the man behind the desk, his eyes enormous behind the glasses.

Concha described how some of the people had begun to bring Nathaniel objects which had been found in the fields. At first hachas — axes, and muñecas — little dolls made of fired clay. Then small items of gold, which Nathaniel gave them money for. Those things had been found by fathers and grandfathers of the men who had sold them. And when it became known that the professor would pay enormous amounts of money for things of the ancients, people began to come in with objects which had been held in trust for many, many years by their families. Nathaniel was paying in American dollars. It was so much money for the little village and life was so very hard.

Concha told of Ward coming to the kitchen of her mother. He ate there often. Concha had been sixteen that first year Nathaniel came to the village on the big sorrel mule, speaking perfect Spanish and even a good deal of Mixtec. She had fallen in love with him immediately. He came back and spent three or four months of each year talking, writing, talking, writing. And buying things from the people.

But when her older brother, Demetrio, showed Ward the deerskin book Ward became visibly excited and wanted to purchase it. When they explained to him that it was part of the family's heritage, from the time before the capitanes, he still wanted to take the book away. He then said he did not want to give them money for the book and take it for his own. He simply wanted to take to the north and show it to his compadres at the university. But that was not acceptable to the family. Not until the following year when Nathaniel took Concha for his bride.

"Señora," said the secretary. He gave Concha and Cenovio their melonade and left the room after a dismissive wave of the hand from the cacique.

"Please go on with your story," he said.

Ward was thirty-three and rich, she was nineteen and many people told her she was beautiful. He gave her father the big sorrel mule and a blooded stud horse from the Oaxaca valley to breed. There were other things in the bride price, some of which Concha did not know. There was gossip over the whole countryside that no girl in memory had brought such a price as el Profesor Ward paid for Concha Marisol Osorio Espinoza.

The book made of deerskin with the pictures of her ancestors went to Ward as her dowry. But only as a loan for five years. He wanted nothing more. And that was good because her family had nothing more to give.

"Uh, Señora," the cacique broke in. "Could you describe to me a bit more about the book? And why the professor was so interested in it."

"Yes. I learned a great deal while I was in the north, about artifacts and such things. This book was a family history, our family's ancient history, told in pictures and symbols. It was the story of Lady Eight Deer, who was the cacica of the area of Teposcolula, long before the Spanish came to our country. She came from a great family in the Oaxaca valley."

"And this is important? This made the book very valuable, si?"

"Oh, yes. But not as valuable as The Heart of the World."

"Oh? And what is this?"

"It is the most important thing that the Mixtec people have... had. It was the personal companion of the rain god Dzaui and was kept in the cave of the spring beneath the convento. Dzaui misses it so much that he has brought this drought and has tumbled the houses of our people in his anger. We were bringing it back, but we stopped for a while and it was stolen from us. Here in Huajuapan."

"So your husband had collected this Heart of the World in addition to the book."

"Yes. One of our first cousins, Marcos Albino, took the piece and sold it to two men who then sold it to my husband. I believe that my husband sent these men to buy the crystal after he had possesion of the book."

"What makes you think that?"

"They came, knowing about The Heart of the World, even though it was a great secret, even within our village."

"He had to die!" The outburst by Cenovio brought the cacique's leonine head swinging toward Concha's brother.

"Ah, and you killed him. Your sister's husband."

"Yes. But not with a glad heart. He was mostly a good man, and he was good to my family in many ways. But to take The Heart of the World was a very great sin."

The cacique turned his enormous eyes back to Concha. "And you two," he waggled his finger at them, "you are wanted by the American police for the American's death."

"Yes."

The big man leaned back in his chair, making it squeal from his weight. He pushed his bottom lip out, took off his glasses and rubbed his eyes and forehead with a huge hand.

"When was this thing taken from your village?"

Concha replied, "Last May. The two men from Oaxaca City corrupted Marcos Albino and my brother Demetrio into selling it to them. It made Dzaui very, very angry."

The cacique nodded his head. "There were many fires in the mountains and many villages fell to the ground when the earth was shaken. This I know."

"And the country has burned continually since that time," added Concha.

The cacique agreed. "Yes. And you say that the two earthquakes are a sign of Dzaui's anger." He gestured toward a great crack which ran down the plaster wall to his left.

Concha nodded. "That is how he expresses this anger. This is known in the stories that have been told in my family since long before the capitanes."

The man leaned back on his desk, crossing his big, muscular arms. "You know that many people would think that this is all superstition — stupid indigeno superstition. And that you have killed a man for nothing."

"Three men!" Cenovio's angry voice cut into the cacique's speech.

He leaned back in his chair again, and again the chair wailed in protest.

"Three." He said it simply.

"Two federales in Sinaloa tried to rob us," Cenovio said, unapologetically, as Concha put a restraining hand on her brother's arm.

"Hmmm. This is very serious. Federal agents are dead, too." He pinched his lips, staring at the two small people sitting in front of him. He then knocked loudly on the top of his desk with his knuckles. The secretary opened the door immediately.

"Yes," he said.

"Send someone for two bus tickets to Tlaxiaco. When you come back give these people some money. . ."

"We have money. Your nephew gave us 125,000 to finish our trip."

"Very well." He turned to the secretary and waved him out of the room, saying, "Tickets, tickets."

"You are very lucky, you two. I am also a descendent of the famous cacica de Teposcolula. You are my kin and I must take care of my kin, above all.

"You will be taken to a highway stop outside of Huajuapan, the federal police may be looking for you at the bus station. When the bus comes, wave it down. Once in Tlaxiaco go to the Hotel Cristobol Colon, there will be a room waiting for you. I know family who have a ranchito near Santa Catarina Tayata and they will come for you as soon as I can arrange it. Your people can contact you there; Santa Catarina is not far from San Miguel Achiutla. And as long as you are in Santa Catarina you will be under my protection. Do not leave the ranchito, for any reason."

"But what about The Heart of the World?" Concha pleaded.

The cacique waved his hand. "If street urchins have taken it, I can find them. There are only a few places where they could get money for an item such as this — let us only hope that they have not destroyed it and angered Dzaui even more."

He waved at the broken wall. "My house cannot stand much more of this."

Chapter 12

In Berkeley, Pete Villareal reached in the pouch of his hooded sweatshirt, took out a plastic bag and dropped it onto the desk of the watch commander.

"There it is. I finally scored one."

"What?"

"The Gate to Heaven."

"Looks more like The Gate to the Dog Run to me."

"That's because it's been dried."

"OK, so a dried dog turd. What are you trying to tell me?"

"This is a mushroom that was developed here in Berkeley. Supposedly from spores that were over two thousand years old. It's supposed to be the 'shroom that the royalty of the Incas used to visit the gods."

"This is the one they're feeding the soul tourists down south?"

"The same one. It's real powerful stuff. The ones who have freaked on this have freaked in a real big way. Full blown psychotic episodes, flashbacks . . ."

"Who's peddling this shit, anyway? Where did you find it?"

"A guy named Baret Froehlich. He's a typical campus freak genius — forty-one years old, has two Masters of Science degrees, one Master of Arts degree, works up at Lawrence Berkeley Lab as a computer whiz while he is working on his Ph.D. in paleomicology. You know the type."

The captain grimaced, "Yeah. Has an IQ of 190, lives with a goat and four dogs in a redwood shingle-sided tree house he designed and built himself and also did the two hundred stained glass windows. He has two women, one in her forties who's a potter and weaver and another in her twenties, a grad student who is screwing them both — another groovy little household in the hills."

"Nah. This one apparently hates women. And men too."

"So the goat's the lucky one. Tell me the rest of the story."

"The guy has a lab somewhere in Oakland and he gets his money from a foundation in Florida. He apparently developed the 'shroom by resurrecting the DNA from the remnants of the old ones, then welding them to the cells of some new ones using bacteria. Hell, don't expect me to explain all that biological stuff. At any rate, he's come up with a winner on the Nob Hill/Marin County dope scene." He pointed at the object in the bag. "Guess how much."

"For this?"

"Yeah."

"Fifty bucks."

"Lots more. Guess again."

"Five hundred bucks."

Villareal rolled his eyes to the ceiling. "You got no imagination. I'm surprised you didn't start at five bucks."

"I was going to, but I changed my mind."

"Shit, Captain." Pete picked the bag up, stared at the black object and said, "Two thousand dollars."

The commander grabbed the bag. "Gimme that!" He turned it over and looked at the other side. "Still looks like a dog turd to me. What the hell makes this thing worth that kinda money?"

"Two things. People with Ronald Reagan and Silicon Valley money who think two grand is chump change. Plus, this 'turd' will put you in a place you can't even imagine. Even the ones who freaked out say it was the most important thing that ever happened to them."

"Going nuts."

"Going to heaven."

"So now what?"

"I'm going to find the lab so we can bust it, for one. Unless I'm nuts, this beauty is going to find its way to the streets and we'll have kids flying out of dorm windows like bats out of Carlsbad Caverns. I want to stop it."

"Me too. I remember those days. I helped pick up a couple of 'em when I was a patrolman. One walked out onto the freeway and musta been hit forty times before it was over. What a mess."

Villareal picked up the mushroom. The captain reached out and snatched it back. "I gotta show this to the guys. Two thousand bucks!" He stood up. "I'll get an evidence locker going for this case. It'll be in there."

"OK. But don't even handle it. If it's as powerful as they say it is, you could go on a trip just from the spores on your hands, as old and straight as you are."

The man smiled and waved him away. "Go write your report."

"I'm not done yet. I have one more buy I have to make." Pete walked down the hall and down the stairs to the front door of the police station. He crossed the street and got into his car, a Porsche Speedster. He started the engine and let it rough-idle for a moment. He turned on the wipers to clear the condensation from the windshield. Then he reached under his sweatshirt and into the pocket of the shirt underneath. He took out another plastic bag and held it up to the lights of the passing cars. Inside was a smaller, mottled black and orange mushroom.

Pete drove down Shattuck to Channing and turned left, driving slowly past People's Park, then to frat row, and right to Dwight Way. He then turned left at the abandoned school for the deaf, drove up the hill past the student housing apartments, turned left and drove down the steep drive to the old neo-colonial Smythe House, which had been divided into two large apartments. Once upstairs, he went to the fridge and poured himself a glass of apple juice.

He crossed the large front room, his feet making comfortable slaps on the old hardwood flooring he had spent days refinishing. He opened the big French doors and went out on the verandah, sat down in his chair and looked out over the city.

Across the bay, the lights of San Francisco punctured the night and limned the dark sky above them with a pale green aureole. The orange lights of the bay bridge were draped across the dark, invisible waters between the two cities, suturing them together.

Pete sat down and put the glass of apple juice on the table. He had decided on the way from his score to the police station that he was going to keep the second mushroom. And he was going to eat it.

All his training had taught him that this was a line he should not cross. If smoking a little dope meant building a case then it was within the boundaries of good police procedure. For California anyway. But keeping a controlled substance for personal consumption was a clear transgression. He'd never had the problems shared by so many of his brothers on the force when it came to sampling the cocaine and money that turned up by the bushel basket at some of the busts. He'd been tempted not one whit. But, for some reason, on this night it was different.

He went back over the time he had spent with Oz when he'd made the buy early that evening. It had brought back a lot of memories. And a lot of feelings. Good old feelings. Old young feelings.

In college in the sixties he had felt alive. His mind had been engaged, his body healthy and strong. There were friends he would have died for — thrown himself on the barricades. He laughed aloud into the damp, brilliant night. Les Miserables all over again. He was getting sentimental.

He took the mushroom out of the plastic bag and bit the cap in half. As he'd expected it was bitter as gall and had a rank, musty taste. He picked up the apple juice and washed the taste back, swallowed.

He had gone to Oz's apartment in the hills, on Walnut Street. It had been filled with books. And '60s Fillmore posters, nicely framed. An apparition from his youth, a pretty girl with a paisley scarf wound round her head and long, straight auburn hair excused herself when Pete came in. Her hard little breasts, their nipples visible beneath the long silky dress, her Indian sandals with the leather ring around the toe, her large, stoned eyes and fixed, pretty smile; the faint odor of patchouli about her — all transported him into his past. For some people, like Oz, the past was the present. And the future too.

Oz had sat him down and given him a beer, tossed the mushrooms in Pete's lap, then reached under the easy chair and brought out a cleaning tray. As they talked, he cleaned and rolled a half dozen pin joints and laid them on the table next to him. Retrieving one, he lit it, took a big toke, and passed it to Pete. Pete took a big drag, burned the number down to a roach and passed it back. He held the smoke in his mouth for a moment and then let it slip out both corners, a trick they'd taught him at the law enforcement academy. Not getting smoke into your lungs was the idea. Too bad, too, because he could tell by the taste and smell that it was Hawaiian red bud. No wonder the girl in the bedroom had such big eyes and smile.

"I remember you, man."

Pete jerked his attention back to the room.

"Huh?"

"I remember you. You were one of the smart guys — a rad."

"Oh, the radicals. Just a lot of intellectual horseshit. I was young."

"So was I. And it was great. Never be like that again. Too bad." The old hippie's slow, deep and raspy voice told Pete he was really stoned. That time for him was slowing down and getting softer.

88

"Yeah. It was a great time to be alive."

"Alive is the word. All that action, the music, the street scene, the pussy. Heh, heh."

Pete nodded at the other room and said, "Looks like you're still doing alright."

"Nah, man, that's my daughter."

Pete felt his face flush with embarrassment.

Oz waved his hand in dismissal. "Don't worry about it, no big deal. If she wasn't mine I'd probably be strapping her on. Pretty chick. Smart, too."

"Like I was sayin', I remember you the first day I saw you. It was October 1967 and we were standing out in front of the Oakland induction center, screaming at the kids with the haircuts to join us, to not go. But, man, they just kept smiling and walking through those doors and right into hell. Good kids who had no idea what was waitin' for them on the other side of those doors — eternity. Or a long life of bad dreams."

Pete's stomach sank at the memory of all those clean, young guys striding through the doors held open by Marines, some of them surreptitiously giving the screaming crowd a very small finger because of all the news cameras around. They'd all been so damn young.

"Yeah," Oz said. "I remember you because you were the first one to make a run at the cops when their reinforcements showed up. You ran right up to this big cop, stuck your face in his, and started cussing him out. You were pigging him, cocksuckering him, telling him the truth about his mama. It was great!"

"Yeah, my head was full of big ideas and I had a mouth to go along with it."

Oz lit another of the thin joints. Pete refused it this time and took a swig of beer from the bottle.

"Well, you were smart enough to wear a hard hat. You went there knowing you were going to get the shit knocked out of you. It was beautiful, man. You gave us all the idea and when we went back on Friday we all had hardhats and old army helmet liners on. Sure did save us a lot of hair and skin!" He snickered. "Those pigs were backing up and backing up and then they turned and damn near ran. Remember?"

Villareal nodded at Oz and smiled a wan smile, remembering the cops turning tail. The picture of them in retreat inspired a whole different set of feelings in him, now that he was a cop himself. "Yeah," he said, "they booked, alright." He took a swig from his beer. "J. Edgar told Johnson that there was no way that the feds could fight the mood that was growing in the country, that they couldn't handle all the shit that was going to come down if he didn't start pulling back in Nam. Johnson quit, probably because of what those Oakland demonstrations started in the country."

Oz shook his head. "You and your intellectual prick friends at the university stirred some shit, alright. But us hippies had just as much to do with it — smoking a doob and asking the corner cop for directions to the nearest park while some stoned adolescent chick was putting her hand down your pants — that freaked 'em. Broke 'em down." He took a toke on the joint and offered it again to Pete, who waved it away again and drank his beer.

"No doubt."

"Huey blew their minds, too," Oz giggled. "The radicals, the heads, and then mouthy Maoist niggers toting shotguns and dragging their king-size nuts into Oakland City Hall — it was all so beautiful. The establishment didn't stand a chance. Too much for 'em. Too, too much, man." He dropped ash on the leg of his Levi's and rubbed it into the fabric.

Pete smiled. "But it was no revolution, not even close. When Bardacke and Rossman and those other rads crowed that there was a revolution going on, I looked around and said, 'What fucking revolution? Where's the barricades, where's all the dead people? This is a jackoff scene if there ever was one. I dropped out of the scene right there."

"What did you do then, man?"

"Split for the north. Hung in the woods, grew a little dope, then went back to school — Humboldt State."

Oz nodded. "Arcata. Pretty country up there."

"This'll make you shit."

"Try me."

Pete narrowed his eyes and watched the man carefully as he said, "I majored in Criminal Justice."

Oz snorted the smoke he'd just inhaled and went into a choking fit. He finally quit coughing and started to laugh. "Wow. Lotta good it did you."

Pete smiled and tipped his beer. He smiled a mean little smile at the old hippie and said, "Man, you'd be surprised the shit I learned. A lot of it still comes in handy."

"I bet." Oz spit a glob onto a finger, doused the roach in the blob and then popped it into his mouth. He swallowed and then stared at the wall for a second. "I knew Jim Rector. I knew him pretty good."

Pete frowned. "Too bad. Stuck his head up at the wrong time."

Oz said, "People's Park. Man it was a beautiful thing for a while. It was really beautiful, man. I was there for all of it, y'know." A tear the size of a marble welled onto his face and raced down into his beard. "Right to the fucking end . . . and then everybody came home."

"Yeah, I guess," Pete said. "The Memorial Day march of '69 was as much for Rector as it was for the dead guys in Asia. That was beautiful." He put the empty beer bottle down and stood up, putting the two mushroom bags in his pouch. "It was the last thing I did in the scene. Marched in the Memorial Day march. Then I rolled up my sleeping bag, put out my thumb and ro-o-ode away north and into the woods. Never looked back until the war was good as over and Nixon was waving good-bye in the door of that big ol' hegilopter."

"You weren't in the war either, huh?"

Pete looked at the floor. "Nah. And I still feel like shit because I skipped out on it."

Oz shook his silvery head. "Not me. Not for one fucking minute."

Pete smiled a grim smile. "And that was the difference."

"What difference?"

"Between the rads and the heads — you guys had no real conscience."

Oz's face took on a slow, beatific smile and he said, "Funny, all these years I thought it was just the other way around."

Pete had dropped the money for the 'shrooms on the coffee table next to the remaining joints, touched fingertips with Oz and left.

Pete sipped the last of the apple juice, put down the glass and stood. He walked to the low wall of the verandah and looked out at the lights again.

The old feelings came flooding back on him. The camaraderie, the clandestine meetings, the feeling of power and the possibility of changing the world. The secrets in the night.

The night, ah the night. Sweet with the scent of the big magnolia tree downhill, in the middle of the steep yard. And all the other night-blooming flowers that made it all so sweet. Sweet. Soft.

Pete stepped up onto the low wall of the verandah and looked down. The light on the wall next to the apartment door downstairs dropped a delicious cone of custardy light down onto a pair of woman's running shoes, the laces drooping in a nice languorous pile between the shoes. Luminescent blue and white shoes.

His own shoes were white and luminous too. And the scene below was taking place between the toes of those shoes.

He wondered if Courtney, the girl who owned the shoes, was downstairs with her boyfriend. Sweet Courtney with the perfect bottom.

He stepped out onto the night. There was a faint crack as his weight came down, but just the faintest little crack. He took another step and looked between his legs. Yup, the light was on in her room. She'd be studying.

He looked out over the steep, sloping yard, then over to the apartment buildings next door to the left. The kids' swings were hanging stiff and bright. The chains glinted with the dampness from the night air, the seats hung from the chains in nice little crescents. Like smiles.

To the right, the prayer flags on the roof of the Tibetan Buddhist temple were vibrant, their folds and drapes seeming to breathe in and out. Alive.

He took a few strides more and stood directly above a tulip tree with its huge fleshy flowers. Somewhere in the dark below there was jasmine, too. The scent was much stronger when you stood over the tree, the smell rising in a pillar of delicious smell.

He looked out at the city across the bay. He could see Coit and the Transamerica tower. Everything right where it was supposed to be. Pulsing. The bay and city were breathing too. Alive too.

It occurred to him that he was doing the impossible but, at the same time, anything seemed possible. This was the feeling he had wanted. This was the reason he'd known he was going to eat the mushroom the minute he'd gotten into his car at Oz's.

When he was young everything had seemed possible and he'd never been afraid. He'd felt immortal. All the doubt, the fear and the other stuff had come later.

He strode out over the hill, toward the apartment building across the street. Some students were having a little party on a fourth floor balcony, eating from huge pizzas and drinking beer. The Grateful Dead were singing, playing, singing, playing. He walked by. A young woman put a slice of pizza in her mouth and looked out into the night. Her face froze, her eyes widened. Pete smiled at her.

The next building was more apartments. Someone playing the piano, someone cooking . . . curry. Yeah, curry and fish, probably rice of some kind. International students.

Someone ironing shirts, the smell of hot starch.

A guy lying on the roof on a sleeping bag, smoking a joint and looking at the stars. He didn't even see Pete, though he walked by no more than fifteen feet above the guy's face. Probably too stoned. Or maybe he saw and it made perfect sense — a man walking by on the night.

Hey, this is pretty neat, he thought. What a perspective. What a great way to see the world in a completely new way.

The next building was dark. A university building, probably. And then the church and above the church a horse and rider.

Pete was not afraid. This was what he had come for. He'd known someone was waiting for him. The horse was white, had huge, expressive eyes and was unafraid. Just like Pete. There was a great deal of love in the horse's eyes and he was trying to communicate with Pete — something. Yes. 'Stop there,' the horse was thinking.

Pete stopped.

The rider nudged the horse with his spurs and the animal started toward Pete, prancing in the air above the intersection in front of the church. His hooves made a very soft chuff, chuff, as though he were putting his beautiful feet down in dust, or maybe sand.

The horse stopped and Pete's eyes were drawn to the silver-mounted tapadero and the silver piping that ran up the rider's pants. He focused next on the strong hands, on the reins running through strong fingers. The fingers twitched the reins and the horse made one prancing step forward and turned sideways.

Pete looked up and saw that the rider was looking down at the street below. Pete looked down also. An Asian man was standing at the corner, looking up. His mouth was open, his eyes large behind his glasses. He dropped the sack he was carrying and Chinese food cartons tumbled to the pavement. He froze in place.

Pete looked up again at the rider. The midnight blue sombrero with flashing rosettes of silver thread rose and under the hat in the blackness was a fingernail moon. It resembled a lopsided smile. There were also stars.

And the stars meant something. Something that stirred him deeply. Pete stood there for a moment and then moved his eyes away from the night face and looked at the horse. The horse turned his head, spun slowly, and began to walk away with a pasofino gait so beautiful Pete found himself weeping. He wiped his face and turned finally toward his distant house.

When he arrived back there, he saw how beautiful it was. White with red tiles. Warm windows. He stepped onto the wall of the verandah and the stucco cracked. This time the crack was loud. He hopped down, walked into the kitchen and ran a glass of water. Sweet water.

He washed his face. The water flashed and glittered, fell from his hands in gobbets of light and sound. It swished down the bowl, and fell into the drain with tinkling sounds that made him laugh aloud. He flicked water out into the room. It arced and bounced then ran, glittering and tinkling, around the floor and out under the door.

He went to the verandah and looked out into the electric night. The city was there still. And it was beautiful. Still breathing. Alive. So alive. And he knew that he had somehow, this magical night, met his destiny.

Chapter 13

Tom and Berto were sitting at Nora's Fish Creek Inn, eating the huevos rancheros, when Tom's beeper went off.

" 'scuse me," he said, and went to the pay phone outside on the porch.

"D-One. My beeper just went off."

"We've got a suicide. In the jail."

"Shit! Can't someone there handle it?"

"Uh, they said to contact you because you said that it could happen. The jail staff thought you'd be interested."

He ran his hand over his eyes and up his forehead, pushing his hat back on his head. "Not that pretty little brunette."

"Yeah, Tom. You should probably come over. Marianne found her and she's wiped out. She keeps saying that you warned everyone but the jail administrator said they couldn't afford to mount a suicide watch because of the tight budget."

"Well ain't that just special?! When are the commissioners going to get the message, anyway? Every jail in this damn state is a zillion-dollar lawsuit just waiting to happen."

"Everyone knows that."

"How in the hell did she do it, anyway?"

"They let her have some cosmetics from home. They brought them over in a plastic bag . . ."

"God, she suffocated herself?"

"Yeah. You coming?"

"Sure. I'm on my way."

He went back inside and sat down next to Berto. "I've gotta go. Let's get together later."

"What's the matter?"

"A woman killed herself. In the jail."

Berto shook his head. "I don't know why you people kill yourselves like you do, man. Us Mexicans just hang on tighter and tighter, no matter how bad it gets."

"Fue de verguenza."

"Shame? This woman died from shame?"

"Yes."

Berto wiped his plate with the last of his tortilla. Before he put it in his mouth he said, "Shame will do it, even for a tough ol' Mexican. It's the one thing that will do it for anybody. Lastima — too bad."

"Yes."

"May her soul rest in peace. I'll get the check," he said, picking it off the counter and giving it to their waitress, Erin. "See you at the hotel, come over when you're done."

"Thanks."

The paramedics had come and gone so there wasn't much to see in the jail cell, just a bunk with a blanket folded neatly on a vinyl mattress and the imprint of the slight body barely noticeable in the bed.

The jail office was something else. Marianne was still snuffling. Her makeup had run down her cheeks and her eyes were swollen and red from crying. She put her arms around Tom and smeared his shirt as she hung onto him for solace. The jail administrator and two of his staff stood around the desk. All looked sick.

Tom ran his hand over Marianne's hair and gave her a little kiss on the top of her head. "I'm sorry, Hon. I wish you hadn't had to go through this."

A whimper was all she could answer. Then she stepped back and wiped her face with her hands. "I guess I'll get used to it," she said.

Tom squeezed her shoulder. "If you start getting used to it, like some of the guys, get out of the business. You're too smart for this, anyway."

He walked to the door and one of the men let him out. He was sad, sick. It always came down to money, somehow, and there was never enough for the places which really needed it, like the jail. As he thought about it he began to get less sad and more mad. Before he knew it, he was headed for the sheriff's office.

At that moment Tom saw Sam going into his office. He followed him in.

Sam was sitting behind his desk and his face was desolate. He looked up from under his eyebrows and waggled his index finger in warning.

"Uh uh, nope. Back out that fucking door and leave your high horse out there. I am not going to take any lectures from you, Thompson!"

Tom stopped on the threshold and took a big breath. Sam was still looking out from under his eyebrows and his eyes were mean-looking. He was holding his breath. That was not a good sign.

Tommy raised his hands and walked into the office. "Don't shoot. I'm on your side."

"Sit down. And if you're on my side, don't you say one goddamn thing about that girl's death."

The room was silent except for Sheriff Harlan's breathing. Tom realized that the man was verging on hyperventilation.

"Hey, Sam," he said quietly, "watch your blood pressure."

The big man threw himself back in his chair, which rolled back and slammed into the wall. He quickly leaned forward, pulled himself back to the desk and slammed his fist down. The thick tempered glass on the desktop turned to a huge star under the blow.

Through his teeth he said, "There are five faces that keep flashing in front of my eyes. And in my mind's eye they are all dead and I have killed them. And gladly."

Tom knew that all five faces were people who, supposedly, served the county and its best interests.

"Tom, don't ever, and I mean fucking ever, ever, ever become a sheriff in this wretched, backward son-of-a-bitch state. If you dropped a quarter in the middle of the legislature there'd be dead men all over the place 'cause they'd break their damn skulls ducking for two bits at ninety miles an hour. But there damn sure wouldn't be any brain damage. Those fuckers, and their clones on the local scene, make Mississippi look progressive!"

He put his forearm on the desk and dropped his head. "They'll dump a million dollars a day into a PR campaign to bring more people to a place that is already groaning with problems caused by too damn many of the sonsabitches . . . but do you think that they'll part with enough money to bring the basic institutions up to minimum standards?" He glared at Tommy for long seconds, still breathing hard.

"Sam, I swear to God if you go for your gun I will have to go for mine."

Sam's grim face dissolved slowly into a wry grin. Then his eyes smiled. "I've thought about shooting you more than once, Thompson, but when it happens it won't be because I need a surrogate. I'll just shoot you, chat the jury up about your history in this department and they'll have me home in time for lunch."

"What's wrong with people?" Tom asked.

"Hell, be specific. I can think of a bunch right now."

"What is it with them and celebrities, with Hollywood?"

"I would guess that they think of them being so elevated mostly because they think of themselves as being so low, so anonymous."

"My anonymity saved my life," Tom protested. "When I shed some of my ego my life improved, and drastically."

"Hell, maybe that's it."

"What?"

"People who buy into that Hollywood stuff don't have egos. They've never gained enough self respect that they can think of themselves in the same terms that they think of actors or fashion models, even TV dickheads." He looked grim again. "That someone would steal the sperm of some guy who's not one damn bit different than you and me . . . and then kill herself over the deal. It is insanity."

"In jail, and then dead."

"Yeah. Maybe you're right, Tom — we have been looking up in awe at those big screens for so long we've misplaced our religions there." Sam paused, shaking his head sadly at the thought. "She probably felt like she was raiding heaven." The big man's voice was as sad as Tom had ever heard it.

"But, if we had done things here the way that things are supposed to be done she'd be alive. That's the part that's killing me. If we had mounted the suicide watch, according to the damn policy manual, and had not felt we had to chickenshit it because the damn county couldn't come up with the money for the two jail positions that I've begged them for. And now I'm gonna have to discipline my jail administrator to cover the commissioners' political asses."

Tom blanched at the political realities of Sam's job. He stood up. "Sam."

The sheriff looked up and Tom was moved at how haggard the man's sorrow had made his face in the last few moments. "What?"

"Go get drunk."

Sam grinned wearily, stood also and said, "I always try to take the advice of experts. You wanna go with me?"

Tom shook his head. He felt his heart sink and a momentary wave of genuine sorrow moved through him. Sometimes he missed the damn stuff. "Sam, I'd give you everything I have if you could guarantee me that I could go out, get drunk and have one night, and only one night, of howling at the moon."

"No sense in taking a chance. Too bad, I liked drinking with you."

"And I liked drinking with you, too. You were good company."

"I liked it because after a night of watching you make an ass out of yourself I felt like a damn paragon."

"Thanks, Sam."

"You're welcome. Get out of my office, I'm going to drive over to Big Piney and get this out of my system."

"Why Big Piney?"

"They know me over there 'cause I grew up on the Rim — and nobody will give me any shit because of who I am over here. Also, over there nobody gives a good goddamn if a man gets drunk, hugs the jukebox, and bawls his guts out — and then breaks all the damn furniture."

Tom sighed. "You sure do know how to tempt a guy."

Sheriff Harlan pushed Tom through the door, turned out the lights, put on his hat and left through the back door.

Tom almost ran after him and jumped in the car. Driving fast up the Hoback with the stereo cranking Willie Nelson and cold malty beer running down his throat sounded like more than a little bit of heaven.

Instead, he drove over to the Rusty Parrot and picked up Berto for a drive, so they could take a look at the country and talk some more. Lately he didn't enjoy the company of a lot of people but Berto was different. They had more than a little in common, the guy seemed . . . well, simpatico.

"So, Berto, what are you here for?" Tom asked as they turned off the highway and onto the Gros Ventre river road.

Berto looked at Tom, his brow wrinkled. "Huh?"

"Well, I guess what I'm asking is, what can we do for you?"

"I want to help catch these guys and take them back to Mexico. Then we'll give 'em a fair trial and shoot 'em." He grinned hugely when Tom glanced his way. "I got that from one of your movies, Tomas. You might be surprised to learn, amigo, that we actually have judges, juries, and all that stuff. Heck, we even have a supreme court!"

Tom waved his hand. "Don't put words in my mouth. You sound pretty sensitive about how Mexican justice is perceived up here."

Berto sighed. "Actually, I'm pretty sensitive about how Mexico in general is perceived up here."

Tom grinned. "Don't feel alone. America perceives the whole world in pretty much the same way — we have the franchise on rectitude. Hell, we think that ours is the only way to live and that the whole world should follow our example — and just look at us. As a country we're broke, our government is living on its credit cards, punks own the cities, half the children are being parented and fed by the school systems, a third of the country is addicted or in recovery, and most of what we believe is what we get from TV pitchmen passing as news people. Shit, Larry King has replaced Billy Graham as our model of a moral man. And yet we harp on everyone else in the world about their fiscal policies, their political morality, their treatment of the environment. . ."

Berto grinned. "I like you, we think the same." He suddenly leaned forward and exclaimed, "What happened there?"

Tom pointed out the windshield. "Half the mountain slid away and ran across the valley. The rocks right there, next to the road, used to be someplace up on the side of those mountains."

Berto shook his head. "I'm glad I wasn't standing here when it happened. Well, Tomas, to get back to why I'm here. My people want these folks just as much as you guys do. Probably more. Cenovio is one of the biggest smugglers in Oaxaca state. He's a cold son-of-a-bitch, too. Got a lot of blood on his hands.

"Plus, now that Ward is dead he, and his sister, could be the only ones who can give us some idea of what was stolen and where it went. One of our government's priorities is stemming the flow of our national heritage to other parts of the world. It's a pretty sensitive subject, anymore."

Tom nodded. "Not a month goes by that you don't read something about the richness of the Mexican prehistoric period and how advanced the early societies were. Hell, the mummy that Ward had in his case was a brain surgeon!"

"Yup. To say nothing of having invented the most accurate calendar ever made by pre-technology man. And God only knows what the Osorios and people like them have sold to crooks like Ward. It could have been something just as important as the Aztec calendar stone, for all we know."

"So they are pretty high up on Mexico's shit list, huh."

Berto smiled. "Somewhere in the top three, I'd say."

"Well, let's run through this. One, Teton County would probably not insist that we spend our money on two murder trials when you guys are willing to do it. Plus, we aren't going to welcome any political shit that might come with interfering in an international extradition. Two, our federal government seems quite interested, at the moment, in repatriating other country's national treasures so you'll probably get all the cooperation in the world there. Three, our government would probably do all it could to involve you guys in the drug stuff, hoping to learn what we can there."

"What drug stuff?" Berto seemed suddenly quite animated.

"The mushrooms and all that."

"Tell me more about the mushrooms."

"Ward was financing some pretty esoteric research on the regeneration of some hallucinogenic mushrooms and plants that the Peruvian shaman had in his pharmacy bag. The DEA thinks it could be the beginning of a whole new drug scene. I guess they've been looking at it out in California for a couple of years."

"Huh. Nobody told me anything about that."

"From the little I've heard, Ward's people have been using state-of-the-art science to clone DNA from the organic materials. It involves using living bacteria to resurrect the dead plants, I guess. The technology didn't even exist until some genius working for Ward discovered it."

Berto shook his head. "I'll give you gringos one thing."

"What's that?"

"Nobody else in the world even comes close to the perverse things you people can do with a little science."

"I guess."

"Now if we could all just figure out some way to like you guys." And he was grinning that big grin when Tom looked across the car.

"When you learn what's to like, let me know."

"You sound like you got a hard-on about something."

"Yeah. Being lied to."

"Talk to me."

"I was raised in an alcoholic home. It made me crazy in the way that it does all kids raised that way — because you never know what's real.

"Your family keeps telling you that what you're seeing and feeling isn't happening. They keep telling you that what you see going on isn't going on. They tell you that you shouldn't feel what you're feeling.

"Then you grow up and find out, at least the lucky ones do, that you knew the truth the whole while and they were lying to you about the whole scene because they were lying to themselves about it." Tom shook his head and looked grim. "Then, when I was a young man, my government did the same thing — told me something was true when it wasn't and I had to find out for myself that it was a lie. And a lot of good people died because of it." Tom gripped the steering wheel till his knuckles turned white. "Lying to me is the shortcut to my personal shit list, believe you me. I won't put up with it for one second anymore."

"Don't worry, amigo, I'm not a liar. I hate that shit myself." He leaned forward. "Hey, this place looks just like Oaxaca."

Tom looked out at the valley of the upper Gros Ventre. "Here?"

"Yeah."

"I thought Mexico was all cactus and desert."

Berto waved his hand back and forth. "No way. The border area is like that, for the most part. But Mexico is mostly mountains. And in the south it's real jungle in the low places."

"You mean mountains like these."

"Hell yes. With pine trees and the whole nine yards. Just the really big volcanoes get snow on them, but yeah, the mountains have pine forests higher up and forests of mixed pine and oak down low — looks just like this."

"Those trees aren't oaks, they're quaking aspen."

"Looks the same. Only those flat places would be fields and there'd be some guy out there guiding a plow and poking some oxen in the butt with a stick."

"I'll be darned. Learn something every day. I had no idea there were pine trees down there."

"Yep. Mixtec pine."

"Mizhtek? I've heard that word a lot the last few days."

"Named for the people down there, my mother's people. The Mixtecs."

"Never heard of them before."

"Yeah, nobody up here has. And they were one of the most famous of the ancient people — Olmec, Aztec, Toltec, Zapotec, Mixtec. The Mixtec are the only ones left, except the Maya and the Zapotec. And the Zapotec don't practice their folkways much any more. But the Mixtec do. They haven't really changed all that much since the sixteenth century, when the Spanish came."

"Not very many of them left, I guess."

"The mountains are full of 'em," Berto snorted.

Tom noticed more than a little contempt in his voice.

Chapter 14

The bus roared down a long hill, leaving the pine-forested mountains. The road branched out into the fields and small villages east of Tlaxiaco and the driver pulled the bus to the middle of the road, to avoid the people walking on the shoulder in the early morning mist.

Children waved from the doorways of the huts and blinked in the smoke from the breakfast fires. It was chilly, Concha could see. It made her want to open the window so she could savor the mountain air of her home, redolent with the pine wood smokes of a thousand breakfast fires mingled with the smell of beans and tortillas cooking. Tears welled in her eyes. She was so close to the home that she had not seen in almost five years. Today she would get word to San Miguel Achiutla that she and her brother had returned.

"It will be good to see Mama," she said to Cenovio.

"But don Armando told us that we could not see Papa and Mama until he sent word — that we would be wise to not even contact them," her brother whispered emphatically.

Concha sighed. "There must be some way that we can get word to them, to let them know that we are all right, without the authorities finding out that we have returned. It will not be hard once we are in Santa Catarina Tayata."

The bus entered the town, climbed the little hill to the main intersection, descended to the south, and turned right to the little terminal building where a dozen pickup truck taxis waited to take passengers to communities scattered among the mountains.

The brother and sister took their small bags and walked across the street to a rough-board stand. There they bought some pan sucre, sugar bread, and two cups of good, strong Mixtec coffee.

Once they'd eaten they began the gradual climb up the street toward the Hotel Cristobol Colon. They stopped at a street corner, waiting for a truck to pass from the side street into the main traffic.

When they stepped from the sidewalk they saw two policemen exit the shop on the corner. Two more appeared behind them. One of the men was huge, two meters tall at least. He was carrying a shotgun slung in his hand and wore a cruel smile.

Cenovio bolted but he moved only two steps before he was struck down by one of the policeman. He began to rise but the man stood over him with his rifle butt raised.

"Do not move again or I will break your head," he said. Cenovio slumped to the stone roadway and groaned.

They had come so far only to lose their precious cargo in Huajuapan. Then he thought of the three men who had given up their lives in his hands. All in vain.

'God forgive me, please, absolve me of my sins for I did not do them for myself but for my people.' Thus Cenovio began the preparations that he knew he must make before these men took his life. And that of his beloved sister, as they surely would.

———

When Tommy entered the building on Monday morning he noticed that something was wrong. Usually there was at least a little joking and grab-ass that went on around the coffee machine. But today it was as quiet as a Sunday.

"Morning, Rhonda."

"Morning."

"Uh, what's wrong?"

"What are you talking about?"

"It's like a hospital around here. Now what's going on?"

"Don't ask me."

"As in 'Don't ask me, but ask someone else if you want to'?"

"Go ask someone else if you want to."

"Thanks, Rhonda, and by the way. . ."

She looked up quizzically and said, "What."

"This weekend I remembered who Jane Goodall is."

A hint of a smile played on her face and she said, "You're clever, Tommy. Good work. Here's a treat." She reached into the bowl on her desk, picked a piece of candy and threw it to him.

He scratched under one arm and walked to his office.

He sat at his desk, sipping his coffee and reading his messages. The door opened and Lewis stuck his crewcut head inside.

"Can I come in?"

Tom waved at the chair across the desk and said, "Sit."

"Nah, that's OK. I was just wonderin' if you'd been in to check on Sam."

"No. Why?"

"You haven't heard, huh?"

"Lewis, you know damn good and well I haven't heard or you wouldn't be in here. You're just faunchin' to tell me something juicy. What is it?"

"Sam got tossed in jail over in Piney this weekend."

Tom's mouth fell open and coffee ran onto his chin. He wiped it away with the back of his hand and said, "What the hell are you talking about?"

"He got in a fight over there, in a bar. They took his ass to jail and made him spend the night."

"Did they book him?" Tom asked instantly.

Lewis waved his hand, "Nah. The chief there knew it would mean the end of Sam if there was any public record of him being arrested. They just put him in the tank and let him sober up and cool down."

"Has anybody talked to him yet?"

"Who's gonna take that chance?"

"Is he in his office."

"Yup." Lewis smiled. "But I don't think they're allowin' any visitors." He grinned a big, wide grin. "I guess it took every cop in that part of the county to get him cuffed and stuffed. He's still a horse, you bet."

"I wouldn't pee on his leg," Tom said and grinned too.

The phone rang and Tom picked it up. "Thompson."

"Get your ass in here." It was the sheriff.

"Be right in, Sam."

Lewis leaped to his feet. "Gotta go." He went to the door and opened it. Before he left he put his thumb and little finger to the side of his face, pantomiming a phone call later.

Tom just looked at him.

"Sheez," Lewis said and left.

When Tom knocked on the door Sam hollered, "Come in, dammit!"

Tom looked at Rhonda and she looked back at him. Her eyes were wide and her face was pale. Then she mouthed, 'Good luck!'

Tom opened the door and stepped in, trying to think of what could have inspired the summons.

Sam had his boots on the desk, a cup of coffee in his hand, a raccoon eye that defined what one should look like, and a big grin on his face.

"Siddown, Tom, siddown. How you doing, anyway?"

"Uh, I'm fine," he flicked a finger at Sam's huge shiner, "but how does that feel?"

"You know Tom, it feels real good."

"I bet it does."

"No, I mean it. I haven't felt this good in years."

"Got the shit out of your system, huh?"

"Yeah. I did."

"What's the other guy look like?"

"Oh, probably about the same. We always did end up about even."

"You tangled with this guy before?"

"Yup. Both of 'em. Started when we were kids out on the Rim."

"There were two?"

"My twin cousins. Aunt Rhea's kids."

Tom felt a smile growing on his face. "Tell me about it."

"Oh, I stopped at the Green River Bar in Daniel and visited with some folks I knew. Hadn't seem 'em in years. Then I stopped at Waterhole #3 in Marbleton and had a few. When I got to the Silver Spur I was feeling no pain." He took a sip from his cup of coffee and his face softened at the memory of the moment. "It was perfect. I walked in and there they sat, Pat and Mike."

"Pat and Mike."

"Yup, big ol' Pat and bigger ol' Mike. They never saw me coming."

"Just sitting there minding their own business, having a quiet beer. . ."

"Yeah, it was great. They had no idea I was even in the room till I popped them two big ol' heads together. Shit, Tom, it was beautiful. Pat spit his beer all over the bartender, Mike's false teeth popped out on the bar and bounced into the ice bin. It couldn't have been more perfect. Now I know that there really is a God and that he loves me, just like you keep saying."

"I assume they didn't just take it as a joke."

Sam smiled and the swollen eye winked like a black mule's ass. "Oh hell no. They both hate me, always have. Their mom liked me more than she ever did either one of those big dumb bastards."

"And then the fight was on," Tom prompted.

"It was a beauty. Pat's the smallest of the three of us and he weighs about two-ten. We broke every damn thing in the place before the cops got there."

"Just the kind of nightmare every cop dreads."

"Yeah, a family fight. Nothing like it."

106

"Well, I'm glad you had a good time."

"Couldn't have been better. It's gonna be expensive, but what the hell. Now I'm in the mood to drag those commissioners' asses through the fire. We're going to have the two jail positions I've been sniveling about and while I'm at it I'm going to wring some other things out of them that I've wanted for a long time."

"Like what?"

"None of your damn business. Don't you have any work to do?"

"Hell, Sam, you're the one who invited me."

"And now I'm the one who's dis-inviting you. Get out of my office."

"Sheez," Tom said with a grin and got up out of the chair. "You know, I haven't seen an eye like that for years."

Sam touched the swollen eye and winced. Then he smiled again. "Ol' Pat's got two of 'em — he never did learn how to counter the punch behind the jab. You know, I think I'll take Rhonda out to lunch today."

Tom left the office. When he closed the door there were half a dozen people standing nonchalantly in the reception area, all eyes on him. Rhonda raised her eyebrows in question. Tom drew his mouth down in a look of horror and shook his head. Everyone in the place split except poor Rhonda. Tom left her staring at Sam's door with a look of dread on her face.

————

"Hey, Pete. What you up to? Come in." Oz opened the door and stood aside.

"I didn't know how to get in touch with the company you work for and I didn't have your phone number so I thought I'd drop by."

"That's cool. The company isn't in the book and neither am I. You want some coffee?"

"Nah, I'm about coffeed out."

"This is some Jamaican that you've never tasted before. It's the best, it'll knock your socks down on your shoes."

"Sounds more like a description of some new kind of smoke."

"Heh, heh," Oz wheezed, "you're not far wrong. Caffeine is the drug of the nineties — that's why we got into it."

"You're growing coffee?"

"We're hybridizing it, making it more flavorful and stronger. This is some of the first crop."

"You're always right in the middle of the scene, aren't you?"

"It's not hard to see where things are going. This coffee thing was as predictable as sunrise."

Pete followed him into the kitchen. The coffee brewer was spluttering its last gasps of steam and the fresh coffee smelled wonderful, especially after the stale Safeway house brand he'd been drinking down at the police station.

"Hey, that does smell like some good stuff. Maybe I will try a cup."

Oz opened the cupboard and took down another cup. It had a picture of an art nouveau girl and the black script under the graphic said that she was Ozma of Oz. Pete turned the old hippie's cup around and saw a picture of the Wizard himself.

"Cute."

Oz grinned as he poured the fragrant brew. "I got the whole set — there's a dozen altogether."

Pete picked up his cup and breathed in the aroma. "Hmmm, you're right. This doesn't smell like anything I've ever drunk before." He took a small sip and let it run slowly down his throat. "This is . . . not sweet, but it's something like that. I don't know how to describe it."

"It's more alkaline, the opposite of acidic. Easy on the stomach too."

"It's got a kick. You're right."

"Come on in the front room — I just rolled one."

Pete smiled to himself. The Life. Oz was going to live it right to the end. And why not. Obviously it worked for him and he was happy with it. Too bad Pete was here to put an end to it if he could. He liked the guy but what he was doing was dangerous to folks with lower tolerances — which was probably the whole rest of the world. Anyone who did the quantities of dope that this guy did and still be functional had to be a world-class something.

Oz licked the number, fired it up and took a big toke. He offered it with a little gesture toward Pete, holding the smoke deep in his lungs.

Pete waved it away. "Too early for me." He smiled in genuine admiration at the guy's stamina.

Oz shrugged, let out the toke and said, "You want to do some business?"

"Yeah. I want to make this Mexico scene that you were talking about."

"The solstice gig."

"It sounds like something I'd like to try." He looked out the apartment window at the San Francisco Bay Bridge, now a lacy grey over the blue waters. "I ate one of those 'shrooms." His voice trailed off.

Oz's eyes twinkled. He was holding in another toke so he just raised his eyebrows, pantomiming a question mark.

Pete shook his head and his voice was full of awe when spoke. "I never experienced anything like it. And I've eaten some kick-ass vegetables in my time."

"The Gate to Heaven. Did anyone else share your trip?"

Pete's heart missed a beat. "You mean it wasn't part of the hallucination?"

"Nope. And it wasn't a hallucination. What happened?"

"I walked on air, man, I walked right out onto the freaking air. And I met a . . . some guy riding a white horse. And two people saw the same things I saw — a chick with pizza hanging out of her mouth and a guy who dropped his groceries."

Oz leaned forward. "You walked out in the air and some people saw you do it?"

"I swear."

Oz leaned back in his chair and smiled beatifically. "Congratulations. You had the primo trip. I've only heard of two other people making that trip." He shook his head in admiration. "You're a real advanced soul, Pedro. Almost everybody else drops."

"Drops?"

"Falls."

"People think they can walk on air and can't, and they fall."

"The big drop with the sudden stop. I should have warned you but, honestly, I thought you would have one of the garden variety of experiences — riding your body music, seeing into people, stuff like that."

"Body music?"

"Yeah. Everyone's a symphony, man. Hearing your own composition, the unique music that is God's signature . . . maybe it'll happen for you next time. It'll wring your heart, man. It'll make you whole, just like being born again — fresh from God's garden."

"I wouldn't believe you if I hadn't walked."

"You surprise me, Pedro, you really do. On the outside you seem like . . . oh, a narc even." He raised his hand as if to ward off any protest. "I don't mean an actual narc-type narc. I mean you came across as someone who wouldn't catch the train."

"Catch the train?"

"Take the big trip. Walking out onto the ether is the big trip. That's where you meet the messengers."

"Messengers."

"Yup. The folks with the messages."

"What messages?"

"From the future."

Pete's scalp tightened and goose flesh stood the hairs on his arms. "He didn't talk to me, he didn't say anything."

"They don't talk. What did he look like?"

"He was wearing a sombrero, one of those ornate ones with silver embroidery . . ."

"No, not the man. The animal."

"The horse?"

"Yeah. The messenger is always the animal, the man was the message."

"But no one said anything, there couldn't have been a message."

"Think."

"There was the horse and rider waiting for me. The horse pranced up and stopped, the guy looked up and instead of a face . . ."

"Yeah."

"There was a night sky — stars, a fingernail moon. A night sky."

"Was there a constellation?"

"None that I recognized."

"You need to remember the configuration of the stars and moon. I'll bet that that's the message, man. You gotta get that down."

Pete let out a deep breath he had been holding. "When do we leave?"

"Huh?"

"When does the group leave for Mexico?"

"Full up." Oz doused the number and popped the roach back.

"What do you mean, 'full up'?"

"We booked the last person a couple of days ago."

"Hell, I'll be glad to pay extra if that's what it takes."

"You'd make thirteen, Pedro. We can't go down there with thirteen."

"Book another one, that'd make fourteen."

"I hate to disappoint you but it ain't gonna happen. We got the group we need. You see, not just anyone can go. We weed 'em real careful — no nuts, no narcs, no nothings."

"Nothings?"

"People with no personalities who are looking for a personality — they freak every time."

110

"I guess they would. I damn near freaked myself when I came down and thought about what had happened."

"Maybe next time, Pedro. Sorry." Oz stood up.

Pete walked with him to the door. "Oz, I gotta go. I got this feeling that I should be there. In Mexico."

Oz put his big paw on Pete's shoulder and looked deep in his eyes. Pete felt as if he were looking into the eyes of a vital mummy. He smelled like a thousand years of smoke and dust. And darkness

"If you're supposed to go, you'll go."

"How?"

"If you're supposed to be down there, you'll be there." He paused. "The horse will see that it happens."

Chapter 15

Tom phoned Polly in California just before his lunch hour. Christina, his daughter, took the phone call for her mother.

"Mr. Thompson, this is Christina Anaya."

A lump came to his throat. This was the daughter he had always wanted, yet had never known. And it looked like he never would. She kept an enormous emotional distance between them. Tom might be her biological father but that had little or nothing to do with her relationship to the man who had raised her, Ferdie Anaya. It was hard.

His whole life he had looked at little girls, especially the three-and four-year-olds, and ached for one to hold. He loved his son as much as he loved anyone or anything. But having a little girl to hold, and to receive the special kind of trust they can give, was one thing he had always longed for.

"Is your mom there?"

"Yes, she is."

"May I speak to her?"

"She's in a meeting right now, an important one. I just stepped out to get a file or the receptionist would have told you to phone her at home tonight. Try about ten coast time."

"No way that I could just talk to her for a minute, huh?"

"Mr. Thompson, we have people here from Mexico at the moment. Very important people. We will be talking business until early evening and then my father . . . my father, my sister and I will be hosting them at dinner. You can expect her to be back home around ten." Polly now had her own place and Tom could tell that it hurt them.

"But you'll be sure to tell her I phoned?"

There was a moment's silence and then she said, frostily, "Of course I will."

"Thank you."

"You're welcome." Rattle, clunk.

Tom felt his face flush with anger. He knew that Christina —
and her sister no doubt — had good reason to resent him but
having to deal with their displeasure was painful.

Then he remembered the ring. Polly was certainly wearing
it and that probably served to remind them of his intrusion into
their life. Oh well, they could like it or lump it. Polly was his and
he didn't care if it hare-lipped every sheep in Lincoln County.

He left his office, pulled the door shut. When he turned
around he saw Sheriff Harlan talking to Berto, who was waiting
to have lunch with Tom.

When he walked up to the two he had to smile, just a little
bit. Berto, at five-three was dwarfed by Sam's six-five. Sam was
wide-shouldered and lean, Berto looked like a fire plug. Yet the
two men stood as equals, one could see from their stances.

"You going to have lunch with us, Sam?"

"Can't. Gotta go to a Rotary meeting. Wish I could, though,
we're having another talk by some expert on limiting growth. If it
was me, I'd give the developers five years to build anything they
wanted and then cut 'em off at the ankles — tell 'em to go back to
where they came from. I wish we could get this whole damn thing
over with, I'm tired of listening to it."

"You're not the only one. They're going to shit this nest right
to the brim, just like they did wherever they came from. It's
inevitable."

Sam rubbed his thumb back and forth across the tips of his
fingers. "Money."

Tom nodded. "Money."

Berto smiled. "Doesn't matter where you go, it's always the
same. . ."

"The rich get richer and the poor get babies," Tom finished
for him.

"You got it. Where we going to eat?"

"Let's go to Bubba's and see if we can get in."

Miraculously, there was an empty table waiting when they
got there, an unlikely event. The place was doubtless the most
popular one in town.

"You like a lot of meat?" Tom asked.

"Yes."

"Then have the rib dinner."

"Sounds good to me."

When the waitress had taken their order Tom asked, "What
did you and Sam talk about?"

"More of the same stuff that you and I have talked about — how to catch the Osorios." He went on, "I gotta tell you, this waiting is getting real old. I thought they'd be picked up by now."

Tom shrugged and took a sip of his coffee. "They could be in Mexico by now."

Berto shook his head. "You'd think that as hard as it's getting to cross the border there'd be a real slim chance of them being missed. There's thousands of cops between here and there."

Tom smiled. "Yeah, but no one's trying to stop anyone from heading back."

He saw from the sour look on Berto's face that he'd interpreted the statement as a slam but he decided to let it stand. The truth was the truth.

"If I thought they had gone back I'd be down there. My guess is that they've gone underground up here. And I'll bet they're in Oregon, or maybe California."

"I've checked with the agencies in both those places and I've done it every day. Heck, you've been in my office just about every time I've phoned."

The little man sighed. "Yeah, yeah. But I hate sitting around like this."

They'd finished their meal and were standing in front of the restaurant picking their teeth when Tom saw Sheriff's Harlan's car pull in. He waved them toward the car and then said, "Get in."

Tom opened the front door for Berto and then climbed in the back.

Sam pulled out into the traffic and drove toward Wilson, not saying anything for several minutes. Finally he said, "I don't like secrets."

Tom waited for him to go on.

"I got pulled out of my Rotary meeting to answer a call from Senator Buckley. He was afraid that what he had to say might be sensitive. He asked me to keep it under my hat until he could smooth things out with the folks at the Mexican Embassy in Washington. I told him that Mr. Sanchez . . . "

"Sandez."

" . . . Sandez was here and waiting. He said he thought that it would be better if I didn't say anything for the moment."

"But you aren't going to do that."

"No."

"What's the deal?"

"Doctor Nathaniel Ward was the nephew, the favorite nephew and namesake, of the Honorable 'Nat' Ward."

"Congressman from Virginia," Tom added.

"Well, he's an ex-congressman. He just retired. But he still has a lot of stroke in Washington. As a matter of fact, he's one of Ed's long-time friends."

"So?"

"So, until now we have had an understanding, an informal understanding, with Mr. Sandez, that we would not pursue the murder charges against the Osorios — that we would not stand in the way of an extradition request from the Mexican Attorney General's office."

"And Ed wants us to press."

"Yes. The murder charge supersedes any other processes — smuggling, trafficking in controlled substances, anything. And Congressman Ward wants them to face the music in the states."

Berto became agitated. "But they are citizens of Mexico."

"And they killed an American citizen," Sam said emphatically. "And it looks like they killed one who had a hell of a lot of influence in the centers of power here. His family, I guess, is related to just about everybody who came over on the Mayflower."

Tom leaned forward in the seat and said, "We think that they may have killed an American citizen. The evidence is only circumstantial."

"I have some other news for you."

"What?"

"Jeff just phoned from Alta and we're headed over there. We have a witness."

———

The policemen led Concha and Cenovio up the hill to the Municipio building then through the central courtyard to the offices of the regional police.

The commander, a white-haired man with the gringo name Riley, dismissed all but one of the men — the giant with the cruel eyes and the shotgun.

"You are Cenovio Osorio Espinoza."

Concha's brother said nothing until the giant put the muzzle of the shotgun gently behind his ear.

"I am Cenovio Osorio, yes."

The man was looking at a piece of paper in front of him. "And you are Concha Osorio Ward, the wife of a man who was murdered in Los Estados Unidos."

"I am Concha Osorio Espinoza."

"And you are from San Miguel Achiutla?"

"Yes," Concha answered.

The policeman looked at Cenovio, his face flushing. "If you do not find your tongue, Señor Osorio, we will find it for you."

"I am Cenovio Osorio Espinoza from San Miguel Achiutla."

"You are a bloody one, Osorio. From this information that I have here, I know that you have killed three men." The commandante looked up from under his eyebrows. "And this is true?"

Cenovio's face was pale. If he admitted to the killings he was a dead man. If he did not answer he was in mortal danger from the huge dog with the shotgun.

"Uh, Commandante?" Concha ventured.

The man turned his flushed face to her. "Yes."

"May we have a lawyer before we answer any more questions?"

The man leaned back in his chair and stared at her for a moment. "Señora Ward, you are no longer in the north. Down here we deal in the truth, not in the handiwork of law-mongers. I will decide when, and if, you talk to a lawyer."

"But sir, surely you would want my brother to give you the truth willingly and from a good heart."

"You mean that if he had a lawyer, then he would tell the truth?"

"Yes, certainly."

"But, as I have just said, lawyers do not deal in the truth — they deal in law, in words."

"And are not they the same, the law and truth?"

The man smiled. "Either you are naive or being coy with me." He picked up the piece of paper from his desk. "I am interested if what is written here is true. If it is, your brother is the murderer of three men. Or more. At this moment I am interested only in the truth of that matter."

Concha looked at the paper which the man was dangling. Curiously, she thought, it was handwritten. It occurred to her that if it had been an official report it would have come from a machine of some kind. When the policeman spoke again her attention was brought back to the room.

"But then, this report has nothing to do with you personally. For that reason I am letting you go."

"What?"

"You may go." He nodded to the huge man against the office wall. He leaned over and opened the door.

"But I would like to stay with my brother."

The man behind the desk looked sinister. "Believe me, you would not like to stay with your brother. You would not like it at all, I think. He appears to be a stubborn man."

Concha looked at her brother. The look on his face was flat and devoid of emotion. "Cenovio."

He didn't look at her.

"Cenovio . . ." She felt hot tears run down her face.

He looked at her and his eyes said "Go. Save yourself."

Concha felt the huge man's hand on her shoulder. She knew that she must leave while she had the chance. Once in the jail, in the basement below her feet, there was a real chance that she would never be seen again. And she must be the one to go for help.

She picked up the two plastic sacks which held all that she now owned and left. The huge wooden door slammed with great force. The giant was warming to his work.

———

Sheriff Harlan pulled into the driveway and up to the garage of a large house which sat across the county road from Ward's house. Jeff's patrol car was parked in front of the other garage door.

Jeff met them at the door and took them to the rear of the house, to the maid's quarters. A woman in casual but expensive clothes stood waiting. Sitting next to her in a chair was a small latina. She was a plain woman in her mid-twenties.

The moment they stepped into the room Berto began a torrent of Spanish directed at the woman. He walked toward her and began, obviously, to interrogate her. The effect was startling. She fell back into her chair, her eyes widened, and her legs began to tremble. She looked as if she might loose control of her body functions.

"Whoa, whoa, wait just a damn minute." Sheriff Harlan protested.

Berto looked up at Sam, looking as if he planned to stand his ground. But he suddenly smiled his disarming smile and said, "Lost my head. For a moment I thought I was in charge, like I would be back home." He shrugged. "Do you want me to translate?"

"Does she speak English?" Sheriff Harlan asked the owner of the house.

"Yes, her English is good. At least it is when she's not scared to death."

Sam turned to the little woman and said, "Don't worry, no one is going to do anything to you. I am the sheriff of Teton County. You can trust me."

The woman looked at Berto, not saying a word.

Sam glanced at the Mexican officer and said. "Señor Sandez is an officer of the Mexican Attorney General's office in Mexico City. He is here to help us." He saw that the words were doing little to reassure her.

"Jeff, what did she tell you?"

Jeff looked at his notebook and said, "Apparently she had a boyfriend who worked around here as a farmhand. He was a friend of Ward's brother-in-law. He used to come here to visit her and sometimes, when he was in town and over at the Ward place, she used to go over to see him. Also, she was a friend of Ward's wife."

"Concha, she was my fren'," she now offered.

"What was the name of your other friend, the man?" Sam asked.

"His name Valerio Trujano," she said.

"Tell me, what do you know about the murder of Doctor Ward?"

"It was in the night, after I do dishes from supper. I know that Valerio is at the house because Concha phone and tell me that he is want to see me when I am done with my working.

"So I am walk across the road and going across field to the house. And the door is go open with broking, breaking window..."

Jeff explained, "It was the side door to the living room, it opens onto the side yard where we found the piece of firewood with the stuff on it."

Sheriff Harlan shook his head at the deputy, "Let her go on. You can us fill in later."

The woman looked back and forth at the men.

"Please, go on."

"El Profesor Ward is come out of the house and he fall down. He is hold his head and is making bad noises — he is like . . ."

"Crying?" Sam asked.

The woman shook her head. "Is different, not crying."

"Moaning. She told me that he was moaning," the owner said.

"Go on," Sam said, gently.

"He is get up and walk funny. . ."

"Staggering," the employer interpolated.

"Then is coming out of the house Cenovio and Valerio. Cenovio is have some firewood in his hands and he run to el profesor Ward and push him. He is fall down on his knees."

"Ward," Sam said.

"Si. Then Cenovio is shout to el profesor, but he is only moan and hold his head. Then he fall down and do nothing."

"Then what happened?"

"Cenovio is cry. He shake el profesor Ward and shake him. He say, 'Wake up, wake up!' Then Valerio say, 'Oh, Cenovio you have kill him, ha' muerto.' and Cenovio say 'No, no, he is not dead he is only . . . inconsciente."

Sam turned to Berto.

"Unconscious," he supplied.

"Then what happened," Sam asked.

"They pull on him and go back into the house. It was taking them long time. And then I leave."

"And did they know that you were watching them while this was going on?"

She shook her head emphatically. "No, Señor."

"Why didn't you tell us this before?"

The little woman looked at her mistress who said, "She told me she was afraid of the police. She was afraid that she would have to go to jail."

"Well, you are not going to jail. What I want, though, is for her to tape-record her statement. Jeff, can you do that for me?"

"Sure, Sheriff. Be glad to."

"Thank you very much, ma'am," Sam said. "And thank you too," he added to the employer.

"You are quite welcome. I hope it helps."

"When and if we catch them it will help a great deal toward getting a conviction."

"If you don't catch them it will be just as well."

"Why do you say that?"

"Doctor Ward was not our idea of a desirable neighbor."

"How so?"

She shrugged. "Stories."

"Stories?"

"Yes. Rituals, drug use . . . and other things. He was not a nice man."

"What about his wife?"

"Oh, she was sweet. I enjoyed it when she visited. But she was not his wife, you know."

"No?"

"She was a bartered bride."

"What's that?"

"It means that he didn't marry her, Sheriff. He bought her."

Pete Villareal was sitting in the Cafe Med, drinking coffee and reading the *Berkeley Barb*. In it there were always clues to illegal activities of the local populace — personal ads that alluded to sexual activities across the spectrum. Also, there were outright ads for products that flagged businesses as likely hubs for trafficking in just about every substance and item that governments feel compelled to control. It was the source of some of his best intelligence.

He had put the paper down at his table and gone to the counter for a refill when he felt a hand on his shoulder. He turned and looked into the mysterious gaze of Oz Gardner.

"The horse is looking out for you."

"Huh?"

"You're going. We had a cancellation."

"The horse said I could go, huh?" Pete said, lightly, and retrieved his coffee.

Oz stared at Pete for a moment. Then he said, carefully, "Don't joke. If you don't recognize and respect what is going on then maybe you shouldn't be with us. This is serious business, this is your soul and its progress we are concerned with."

"Uh, sorry. It's just that this all real new to me. Hell, I've never been involved in anything like this outside of reading a book or two for amusement."

Oz walked back to Pete's table with him. When Pete sat down Oz leaned forward, his hands on the table, and whispered in his smoky voice, "This is not for amusement. It is not for pleasure, it is not a pastime or a hobby."

"C'mon Oz, you make it sound like a life-or-death deal."

Oz pushed his weight from the table and smiled mysteriously. "Nothing so trivial, my man. This is larger than either life or death."

Pete watched the man walk out the door and into the slanting afternoon light. The smoke-grimed windows gave the effect of a disappearance into the light. For the second time that day he felt the hair on his arms rise and his scalp tighten.

Tom was reading a book and petting Millie when the phone rang. When he heard Polly's voice he snapped his finger and waved Millie from the bed. Polly didn't like the dog on the collector's quilt she'd picked out.

"Sorry I couldn't phone sooner, I know it's late there," Polly said.

Tom glanced at the clock. It was ten after eleven, mountain time. "No biggie. How are you?"

"I'm fine, but a little tired. Long day. How are you?"

"A little tired, too. Busy, huh?"

"Yes, this development deal with the Mexican group is really quite complicated. And with the passage of NAFTA we have had to renegotiate."

"Why renegotiate?"

"Because they want to try to improve their position, now that the peso and the Mexican stock market has fallen so far. We might be able to help them a bit, but we're not going to give much."

"How so?"

"Ugh, please don't let's talk business. Talk about us."

"What's to talk?"

"Are we going to be married, Thomas? Or is this ring just your way of trying to get in my panties?"

"Hon, in case you haven't noticed, all that commotion in your panties for the last year was caused by me. I have been in your panties so many times I get breathless just thinking about it."

"Only breathless, Thomas?"

"If you keep talking like this you are going to have to let me take a break — phone me back in ten minutes, OK?"

"Don't you dare. Breathless is good enough."

"That's why I want to come back next time as a whale."

"A whale?"

"Yeah, can you imagine me with a tongue four feet long and able to breathe through the top of my head?"

"I didn't think they could improve the old model but I guess it's possible after all," she giggled. "But seriously, how have you been?"

"Oh this Alta thing took an interesting turn this afternoon."

"Uh-huh, go on. Oooh that feels good."

"Get your hands on top of the covers and keep them there!"

"I was kicking off my shoes. Go on."

"Senator Buckley phoned and said that the victim was the favorite nephew of Nat Ward."

"The congressman from Virginia."

"Well, ex-congressman but he still swings a big dick in Washington, apparently."

"And what did the senator want?"

"He wants us to get hot on the case and bring the felons to the bar for their punishment as quickly as possible. I guess this made major news back east. Ward was rich, a famous scholar and a yuppie prince with a permanent niche on the social register. All in all, a potent amalgamation of influence."

"Do you have any clues as to where they might be?"

"Berto — he's the guy I told you about when I phoned you Sunday — thinks that they are here in the states. Personally, I think that they're back across the border."

"What makes you think that?"

"Nothing more than a hunch, really. But let's not talk about my business either. Let's talk about your panties some more."

"Let's talk about a wedding."

"Simple. I meet you in Vegas, we get hitched at the *Chapel Chez Bugsy,* then do it standing up in the Caesar's Palace fountain."

"Sounds like fun but we're getting married in the Chapel of the Transfiguration in Grand Teton Park, we'll honeymoon at Lake Hotel in Yellowstone and once we're married we do it once a month — and that in our snug bed between comfortable flannel sheets while wearing sensible flannel night clothes."

"With the lights off, no doubt."

"Of course. It's the way decent people comport themselves."

"We're going to quit doing it and begin comporting. Sounds safe enough."

"Safe sex — it's the rage."

"Californians have a way of perverting everything, even perversion. You people have a genius for it."

She laughed the effervescent laugh that he loved and they talked for more than an hour.

———

When the phone rang again Tom was startled out of a dead sleep. The large phosphorescent numbers on the clock radio read 4:11.

"Thompson here."

"Hey, chavo, you awake?"

"Berto, what the hell's up? Don't you know it's four o'clock in the damn morning?"

"I just got a call from Mexico. I'll be leaving on the first plane south."

"What's happening?"

"You were right."

"About what?"

"Cenovio Osorio."

"What about him?"

"He scooted back across the border with the sister and the other guy, the one who helped him with Ward."

"Where is he?"

"Jail. Place called Tlaxiaco, down in Oaxaca state."

"What about the sister?"

"Looks like she's dead, man."

Chapter 16

Once awakened by Berto's phone call, Tom decided to stay up. He made coffee and did his exercises on the deck in the crisp June dawn. Then he went for a short jog up the hill above the house.

When Polly first set up his exercise regimen he'd bitched and complained, ragged her about California-izing him and his house, what with the exercises and running, the collector's quilts and the wildflowers all around the house.

However, once he'd fallen into a regular routine the exercises had made him feel better, physically, than he had in years. He also felt better when he walked into the bedroom and saw the antique Dresden Plate quilt dominating the decorating scheme. She'd even gone to Tom's mother and dug up old family pictures taken in 1870s Utah, had them copied and enlarged, then framed them for the walls. It was a real personal, and thoughtful, touch.

At six o'clock he'd gone to Nora's for breakfast, then decided to go for a drive before work. The sun was up and lighting the dew-sparked fields. He decided to take a turn down the back road between Teton Village and Moose, then make the loop back to town. The road was mostly in the park and had not changed all that much over the years. It was one of the few places left which had retained a bit of the valley's earlier character.

Once he was on the dirt portion of the road, memories of his childhood came flooding back: fishing trips, camping trips, the special rhythms and motions of an old western backway. The new, powerful road building equipment made possible wide roads and gentle grades. In the old days of horse-drawn scrapers and hand tools, the roads had been mostly a modest widening of the original wagon trails. In the first third of the century when this road was built, the equipment was motor-driven, though primitive. The engineers had designed roads that were within the capacities of the machines. This narrow, switch-backed byway that originally accommodated Model A's and their like had grown barely wide enough to accommodate two slow-moving automobiles. The bridges were still narrow enough that a car had to slow down and give way to any larger vehicle.

One of the largely intact, but unnoticed, artifacts of the period was the bridge that crossed Spring Creek near the south side of the present highway to Wilson. Tom often glanced at it and remembered the days when his father had yielded to approaching trucks, which had the right of way to cross that bridge first. It, and Hog Island Bridge south of town told the tales of a more measured time. A bygone time.

The old road sent gravel pinging off the wheel wells and dusted the interior of Tom's car as he drove with the window down. When the surface changed to macadam the song of the tires spoke of the changes that came after World War II, when the new prosperity of America reached its fingers even into places as remote as Jackson Hole was then. But little had changed on this road since that time. It still wound leisurely along the hillsides and through the trees. Now, on weekends, the wider cars driven by a new generation of impatient people had to stop and wait for one another to negotiate sharp turns, causing minor traffic jams and blaring horns. It all spoke of change. Impatience was a major mark of the new Jackson Hole.

Tom shook his shoulders, not wanting to fall into the chain of thought that usually followed his consideration of what the 1980s and 1990s had brought to his home. Change was the only real given in the world. Everything was subject to swoops, turns, accelerations and, inevitably, stalls. But it kept right on coming, in spite of all the wishing in the world.

Tom turned his thoughts to business, reminded by the increasing traffic coming over his radio as the troops checked in on their way back from night patrols.

This morning he had to finalize his part of the suicide report. He shook his head at the unnecessary loss that event had meant to everyone, inside the department and out. But it was one of the prices you paid in this business, and all too often.

Second, he had to close three cases the judge had disposed of during the past week. Three burglaries, all done by teenage males paying for their drug habits — more shades of the larger America falling over the little towns in the western mountains. And everywhere else.

Third, he had better let Sam know about the arrest of the Osorio guy and the death of the sister. Hmmm, what about the third guy with the Chevrolet? He'd have to try to catch Berto and find out before he left for Mexico. The first flight out was about ten o'clock so he had time. Besides, he wanted to see the prickly little guy before he left. Tom liked him.

What else? Oh, he had to phone his son Jackie and tell him that he'd rented the canoe for their fishing trip on Murphy Lake this weekend.

"Dee-One this is Jackson. Do you read me?"

Tom picked up the mic and said, "Jackson, Dee-One. Read you five-by."

"Dee-One please come to the center, Tee-One wants to see you. Stat."

"Roger." Tom looked at his watch. "Give me fifteen, uh make that twenty."

"Roger, roger. Over."

"Over."

Tom pushed a little more gas to the big engine. There had been no one on the road so far so it probably wouldn't hurt to pick it up a little, though there was always the chance that a National Park Service ranger might be patrolling, taking a quiet morning drive of his own. He hoped that he didn't get a ticket — no professional courtesies extended by the gimlet-eyed guys and gals in green and grey. No way, José.

———

When Concha walked out of the Municipio building and crossed the plaza mayor, she was stopped by two men. They told her firmly, but politely, to come with them and then pulled her into a taxi.

Once on the highway, going toward Boca de Perro, they explained that don Armando, the cacique, had sent them to pick her up and take her to Santa Catarina Tayata and the ranchito which had been her original destination. When she had protested that she was on her way to her own village, which was only a few kilometers further down the road past Santa Catarina, they told her that was not possible. Period.

Once at the little ranch, just west of the jacaranda-shaded town, she was shown the little room where she was expected to stay until don Armando sent word that it would be different. The man and woman who owned the place were nice, simple people. The man ordered to stay behind while the other returned the taxi was not nice. He told her in no uncertain terms what he expected and she had no doubt that he meant every syllable of it.

126

She could see he was a man who followed orders but did not hesitate to take what he could for himself.

When she dissolved into tears at the news that she would not be allowed to contact her parents, though they were close and she had not seen them for five whole years, he was unmoved. Don Armando would be told of her feelings. When he said it was alright to contact her parents she would be allowed to do so.

"We will stay here," the man explained, "until don Armando finds the things that were lost. In the meantime he expects that there will be federal police looking for you all over San Miguel and if even a rumor of your whereabouts is known, you will be arrested. He cannot protect you from some people, despite his power."

"But el commandante knows that I am here."

"Yes, but he thinks that you have returned to San Miguel. Here, you are close to your home but under the protection of the most powerful cacique in the Mixteca Alta. And you will be safe as long as you do what don Armando tells you to do." She knew that, in reality, she was their prisoner.

Now she was sitting in the morning sun next to a brilliant bougainvillea and drinking a cup of the local coffee. She looked at the mountains to the east and was comforted that she was so close to the valley of her birth, but she was troubled by the thick haze of smoke which hung in the valley. It obscured the view of her home mountains. Even as she watched, she could see a flare of flame on the side of one of the hills not more than a couple of kilometers away.

Cenovio had told her of the fires but she had not guessed how widespread they were. On the way between Huajuapan and Tlaxiaco they had never been out of sight of fire for more than ten or fifteen minutes. And since she had been here in Santa Catarina the ground had jerked and shuddered, sending a thrill of dread through her. When the ground itself was restless it left nowhere to go. Nowhere to feel safe.

Now she understood the urgency of her brother's plea for the return of The Heart of the World. Now she understood why her normally gentle brother had turned into a man pitiless as el tigre, the jaguar, when Nathaniel had pushed him away from the crystal that night. He had pushed her brother through the door of the photo studio and onto the floor outside the room, shouting that the artifact was his now.

"It's bought and paid for — and the money is in the hands of the Osorios, thief that your brother Demetrio is," Nathaniel had shouted. She understood now that it was probably that insult to the name of her family that had cost Nathaniel his life.

A-e-e-e-e, it had been a terrible night. Her mind turned from those thoughts in reflex. Instead, she sought comfort in memories of better times, and one time when she had been little more than a girl.

From where she sat she could see the mountain called Nindo Tocosho. Nathaniel had been so interested in it and she and her brother, Demetrio, had led him to the summit to search for the old astronomical observatory. When they found it with its foundation stones barely visible in the little meadow on top of the mountain, he had become very excited. They sat on the stones and he told them stories of Achiutla in the days of the ancient ones. Stories she had never heard before. A young girl of fourteen, she was mesmerized by the gringo who knew so much about her people, even about her own village. She had assumed then that these stories had been lost to her own people, and to her family. Only later did she find out how much her people knew. And the secrets they kept from all outsiders.

———

Sam was waiting when Tom arrived at the law enforcement center. "Morning, Tom, where's Berto?"

"He's over at the Rusty Parrot, packed and waiting."

"Have you talked to him?"

"Yes."

"He wants to leave today, right?" asked Sam. It sounded more like a statement than a question.

"Yeah, how did you know?"

"I got a phone call from someone who told me that our felons had been arrested in Mexico and I assume that he is going to be heading that way."

"Who phoned you?"

"You don't need to know that," said Sam.

"Why not?"

"Tom, you don't have a need to know."

Tom understood instantly. 'Need to know' was a cover word of sorts taken from the vocabulary of the intelligence community. Tom had been a member of that community in the military and so had Sam, during his turn in the Korean war. It meant 'shut up and don't ask questions.'

"OK Sam, I understand."

"Good. Now, these folks have been picked up down there and it brings us back to where we were the other day — Senator Buckley's friend wants them brought back here. They are doing everything they can back in Washington to make that happen. In the meantime, I want you to go down there to keep an eye on things. Try and make sure that those folks stay healthy until we can get them back to the States for trial. Especially the wife — or whatever she was.

"Congressman Ward was apparently very fond of the woman and believes that she had no part in the murder, that it was her brother and his friend who whacked Ward and then forced her to return to Mexico with them."

"Sam, I hate to tell you this but when Berto phoned me this morning and told me that she was dead. He sounded sure of it."

Sam frowned. "My understanding was that the two of them had been picked up. I'll have to call back and have the source in Mexico check the facts. In the meantime, get your stuff ready."

"You want me to head for Mexico," he glanced at his watch, "with two hours' notice?"

"No one's leaving today, you'll have time enough."

"How do you know he's not leaving? He told me that he was flying out today."

Sam smiled. "His reservation got canceled. He'll be leaving tomorrow, and you'll be sitting in the seat next to him."

Tom smiled. "Well, at least I'll have time to pack. What about a passport? I don't have one."

"Don't need one. Just take your driver's license and your department ID and badge. You'll get a tourist visa on the plane."

"Gun?"

"Deputy Smiley at the airport substation will handle all that with the airline and with Mexican customs."

"So, Sam, what am I going to be doing? Be specific."

"You and this guy get along pretty well, don't you?"

"Yeah, I like him and I think he likes me. We get along."

"Well, keep it light and friendly but keep your eyes open, too. You speak Spanish, don't you?"

Tom waggled his hand in front of him. "So-so. It comes back to me after a bit."

"Well, play dumb and keep your ears open. Phone me when you can get away, let me know what's going on until we can get you some backup down there."

"I'm going to need backup?" Tom asked, and felt a flutter run through his chest.

———

Pete walked into the office of Jaguar Travelers and looked around. There was no one behind the receptionist's desk so he sat down and picked up a copy of *Shaman* magazine.

From the articles and ads in the magazine, it appeared that magical mystery tourism was a pretty good business. As he browsed the contents it became apparent that the two most important elements of a "tour" were a destination purported to hold mystical powers and a person, an adept, who had gained spiritual powers, either through some extraordinary experience or through long and arcane study. When those two things were combined with an American company like Jaguar Travelers and customers with a Diner's Club card, you had the promise of a sure ticket to enlightenment. It struck Pete as being very American — another shortcut, this time to heaven, helped by the salve of money.

He was musing on Oz's warning yesterday about the danger of bringing any cynicism to the trip when a voice broke into this thoughts.

"Are you Mr. Villareal?"

He looked up and saw a blonde woman in her thirties. She was wearing a vest covered with exquisite cut-glass beadwork. The motif of the design was lizards, or salamanders, Pete wasn't sure which. Somewhere in the back of his mind he remembered that salamanders were a component in some old mystical tradition.

"Yes I am."

"Padrino Gardner said that you would be in to pay for your journey. Cash or credit card?"

"Credit card. How much is it going to be?"

"Eleven thousand dollars."

"For ten days?!"

Cripes, the city accountant was going to shit his pants when he got this one, Pete thought, even though it would be financed by confiscated drug money.

"That's a very reasonable price, given what you will be privileged to experience," the woman said with a frown.

"No, I was surprised that it was that cheap. Really."

The smile returned to her face. "Yes, the business is attracting some real rip artists and frauds," she said as she ran his card through her magnetic strip reader and waited for the approval and receipt.

She returned his card and looked up at him. "Your wife doesn't mind your going alone?" she asked, cautiously.

"I'm not married."

"Oh," she said in a small, pleased voice.

———

Tom phoned Los Angeles while he packed. When the receptionist tried to stonewall him he had to bully her into getting Polly to the phone.

Her voice sounded worried when she answered. "Is something wrong?" were her first words.

"I'm sorry, Pol, about breaking you out of your meeting but I'm going to be leaving tomorrow for Mexico. Something important came up and I wanted to make sure I got in touch with you before I left. Are you going to be home tonight?"

"This is so strange."

"What's strange?"

"Something came up down here, too. I'm leaving for Mexico this evening. I was looking at my watch, trying to figure out what would be the best time to phone you, when Marta broke in on the meeting."

"Where are you going?"

"Mexico City and then a place on the Pacific coast called Huatulco."

"I'm going to a place called Tlaxiaco, down in Oaxaca state."

"Thomas!"

"What?"

"Huatulco is in Oaxaca, too!"

"How weird. I wonder how far it is from Tlaxiaco."

"How do you spell it? I'm going to look it up," she said.

"T-l-a-x-i-c-o, but it's pronounced 'Ta la kee ah ko'. How long are you going to be down there?"

"I'm not sure, it's one of those last-minute deals. But if we can arrange it, I'll meet you."

"Where will you be staying?"

"Our condominium project is on a hill above the beach and the new Sheraton. I'll be staying there, at the hotel."

"Is Ferdie going?"

"Yes."

Tom paused for a moment, giving Polly time enough to say, softly, "Thomas?"

"Huh?"

"I love you, I'm wearing your ring."

That made him feel good way down deep inside, in the place where only two women had ever been.

"Yes ma'am. I apologize."

"The girls are going to be there, too. It would be nice if we could all get together."

"Well, I trust your judgment. If you think it's a good idea then it's a good idea."

"It is just going to take a little time, that's all. You are a decent man and they are good and generous young women. Give them time."

"Sure. But I don't even know if it's going to be possible for me to see you. I don't have the slightest idea what's going to happen once I'm down there."

Chapter 17

"How long will it take us to get to this town?" Tom asked Berto when the plane had leveled out and the seatbelt sign gone off.

Berto stared at the magazine he was holding. For a moment, Tom thought that he might not answer the question. It had been like this since Tom showed up at the Rusty Parrot yesterday and told him he was going to have company.

"We'll change planes at Mexico City then fly to Oaxaca City and spend the night there. I know a nice little hotel right by the first-class bus terminal. Tomorrow we'll take the bus to Tlaxiaco. That ride is about three hours."

"You're not going to stop in Mexico City and talk to your people at the A.G.'s office?"

Berto had a sour look on his face when he answered, "I don't have to check in. I've been phoning in my reports every evening. Besides, I'm a field agent and my boss will be waiting when we get to Tlaxiaco. And he is going to be one unhappy dude when he gets a load of you."

Tom took the in-flight magazine from the pocket in front of him. It looked like it was going to be a real long trip.

Suddenly, Berto's voice broke into the conversational void.

"You know, this is just a damn good example!"

"Of what?"

"How you Americans operate — how you elbow everyone around like you own the whole damn world. You just walk into my room, tell me that you are coming to my country to commandeer the arrest of a felon who is a priority prisoner wanted for multiple crimes in Mexico, then smile and say, 'Where do you want to go for breakfast?' Who in the hell do you people think you are?!"

Tom could see his point. But he had his job to do also. Sam had put him in a real tight place with this guy, and the man's agency as well. This was not going to be a picnic unless he found a way to make peace with Berto. His mind turned to the controversy over the FBI's kidnapping of a doctor who had subsequently been convicted for assisting in the murder of an American DEA agent. It had caused a major rip in Mexican-American diplomatic relations. If the folks who were pressuring the Mexican government weren't damn careful they were flirting with another incident and Tom would be right in the middle of it. He did not want to go down to Mexico and work with that kind of onus on him.

"Hey, Berto, let's try to be friends. I got called into the office and had a plane ticket shoved into my hand. I assume that the same kind of thing happened to you when you were sent up here and had to walk into my office cold.

"Not to mention that you had the advantage of having been pretty much raised in the States while I've only been to a couple of border towns and on one fishing trip to Baja. I'm going to have to throw myself on your hospitality while I'm down there because I know diddly squat about the realities of your country. I'm just doing what I've been ordered to do and I have no choice."

Berto looked Tom directly in the eyes and said, "OK, you have a point. Just tell me, what is it you were told to do. Be honest with me."

Tom nodded and said, "Sam told me that I was to go with you and keep my eyes open but my mouth shut. The muckety-mucks in Washington are working on your diplomats there, trying to get them to concede to an extradition. If it works I assume that I am to escort any prisoners back. If it doesn't work, then I suppose I get a free vacation on the money. Which, come to think of it, ain't such a bad deal, really."

Berto finally smiled that big smile of his. "Yeah, I got to have a nice little break in Jackson Hole and now you get one in Oaxaca. Maybe this is a good little deal for both of us. As long as you do like your boss said — eyes open, mouth shut."

Then he nudged Tom and added, "Hey, what a country-y-y!"

———

Pete met Oz and the rest of the group at the Oakland airport. From what he could pick up from the introductions and conversations as they waited, the other people were entrepreneurial business types or old San Francisco bay money. He made himself known as a man of independent means, talking vaguely about his interests rather than where his money came from: another rich skid, a California type that should go mostly unremarked in this group.

Oz and the blonde from the office, Olga, were the conductors for the group and there was some excited talk about a man they would be meeting in Mexico named Gorostiza. "Padrino," as the group called Oz, called the man 'Viejo,' which was an affectionate Spanish term for any older man who deserved respect. He was to be their spiritual guide once they were in the southern mountains. Apparently the man was famous in the circles where these people ran.

"How you doin', Pedro?" Oz said as he eventually circulated to Pete.

"Fine. This is quite a group you got here."

"Nice people. Only one or two, besides you, have any real business on this trip but that's about average for one of these things."

"How do you mean that?"

"Oh, most of them think that they are on a genuine spiritual quest but they have no real aptitude for it. It takes a special kind of person."

"In what way?"

"You know how the blacks talk of someone having 'soul'?"

"Yeah."

"Pretty much the same thing. They saw it in their churches — recognized the people who really had the capacity to receive what the Christians call the Holy Ghost. They are the ones who find themselves moved mightily, even what is called 'slain in the spirit.' That's when someone is struck to the floor by the force. Unfortunately, that sort of thing is all too often faked, but the people discriminate between the ones who fake it and the ones who make it by saying that the genuine recipients have 'soul.' You are one of the three here who have soul by our lights, Pedro."

"Because I could see the man and the horse?"

"Yes. And some other things I have noticed about you."

"Like what?"

Oz just gave Pete what he'd come to think of as the man's 'mummy stare' and walked away.

Once Pete boarded and found his seat, next to the window, he saw Olga walking down the aisle counting heads and handing out some sort of reading material. She finally made her way to Pete's aisle and handed him a brochure with the words *Jaguar Travelers* printed across the top. Then she sat down next to him and put on her seat belt.

Pete returned her smile and put on his belt as well. Up close he saw that she was pretty in the way that women in their thirties are if they take care of themselves. Her skin looked healthy even under the light makeup and she smelled very, very good. Like jungle flowers.

———

In Los Angeles, the Anayas made themselves comfortable in the First Class section of the plane. The stewardesses bustled efficiently, flitting through the aisles as they prepared for takeoff. The low electric hum of the airplane bespoke efficiency as well.

Maria saw that her father had set up his little office in the seat next to the window, his briefcase in his lap so he could take out his laptop computer the instant it was permitted.

She saw him staring out the window, deep in thought. She knew that look. And it hurt.

Maria closed the overhead luggage compartment, having to stand on the seat to do it because of her short height. Then she lowered herself into the big, comfortable seat and clasped the belt.

She retrieved her copy of *Mirabella* and leaned back. After a moment, she glanced again at her father's troubled face, then moved her gaze across the aisle.

Her mother had her hand on Christina's arm, and was talking to her in a low voice. Maria knew the subject of the conversation. It was Tom Thompson who was, unimaginably, Christina's real father.

That was the reason for the weary and depressed look on her father's face. He had hoped, just as the girls had hoped, that this thing with the man in Wyoming was only a passing, painful episode in their lives. It didn't seem possible that their parents were divorced in some genuinely irrevocable way. Through the whole process of the dissolution of the marriage there had been hope in their hearts. That hope had not been shared by their mother, however. She had gone to this place called Jackson Hole, somewhere in Wyoming of all places, and run into this man Thompson — and now she was going to marry him.

Maria studied her sister's face. The resolute look was set there. That meant she had dug in her heels and was not about to be budged. Maria had learned to recognize it from the same look on their mother's face. It brooked no compromise and promised no peace until she had her way.

As she gazed at the two, Maria was conscious of the symbolism that the wide aisle represented. On the one side sat

Ferdie and Maria, who were Latin to the core, who loved to put on parties, eat in restaurants, see their pictures in the L.A. Times Lifestyle section.

Polly and Christina had been happiest when their home had appeared in Sunset magazine. And there hadn't even been a picture of any of the family in the whole article! Just the house and the gardens. Maria hadn't seen the point.

The Times was going to do another article on the Anayas when they returned from their trip to Huatulco. This time it would be as a feature on the people who had been smart enough to position themselves to take advantage of the NAFTA agreement. Their project had been in the works for more than two years and they had invested almost a quarter million dollars in the preparatory phase. If NAFTA had failed they would have had to accept the loss and write it off. As it was, they had an almost three-year lead on nearly all their competitors in the real estate development field.

It was a major business coup and Maria had made sure that their favorite staff writer at the huge and influential newspaper had been kept up to speed on the project. But Polly had demurred on appearing in the article. While she was recuperating from a murder attempt the previous summer, she had said that she was going to begin a gradual simplification of her life. Keeping a lower social profile was part of her plan.

The fact that she'd almost lost her mother frightened Maria, even now. Polly had nearly died because of her relationship with Thompson — and now she was intent on reconciling Christina with the man!

Shifting her attention between the two blondes and her father's troubled face again confirmed the distance between the two halves of what had once been a tight, and happy, family.

Chapter 18

Ildegardo Osorio was making pottery on his wheel when his wife, Lilia, called to him. "Ildegardo, I see José Gorostiza coming this way. He has his sons with him."

"Eh, what brings him to this side of the barranca and up this steep hill? His spindly legs will fail him if he is not careful." He chuckled and rose to wash his hands of the clay. He loved to banter with the old man, friend of his childhood and poet who would starve except for the labor of his wife and strong sons. The boys' blood had come from their mother, thanks to God, or José would have starved among his papers and pen long ago.

Ildegardo walked around his hut and looked down the hill at the approaching men. He waited for them to near but it took some time as the boys had to support their father every five meters or so. Only the natural reserve of the people of the mountains kept him from shouting teasing insults at his friend. He could wait.

Only after the men had sat together a few moments did Ildegardo say, gently, "Surely, José, you taunt the devil when you strain your heart with a visit to me. You must be more careful, viejo, for you might burst something if you do more than push that pen of yours across the table or lap at your bowl of pulque."

"A-e-e-e, cabron, you insult me when I come with news of your daughter, Concha. You are shameless."

At his daughter's name Ildegardo froze. Lilia gave a little cry and came to the door of the hut, wiping flour from her hands onto her dress.

"You have news?"

"Yes. Socratio, my son that stands before you, saw her. She is in Santa Catarina Tayata and it is said that she is a prisoner there."

Lilia gave a cry and put her face in her hands to hide her emotion.

"A prisoner, you say," Ildegardo said, his voice full of genuine bewilderment. "A prisoner of whom, José. Who is holding my daughter?"

"A powerful cacique, it is said."

"A cacique? What cacique?"

"The godfather of Huajuapan de Leon."

Ildegardo's wife gave a gasp. Ildegardo stifled his own only at the last moment. This was more than a mystery, this was incomprehensible. And coming on the heels of the federal police's search of the village the day before, it was also a shock.

The stunning news startled all of them into silence. It was surely a mystery of great proportion.

Finally, Ildegardo asked, "How long has she been there?"

Socratio said, "Since yesterday. She is guarded by one man only."

"And how did you come by this news?"

He motioned at his brother, Plato, and said, "We were waiting for a ride in Santa Catarina when we remembered that it was getting time for tomatoes and that the Mendezes had the best ones in the valley. We walked down there to see when the tomatoes would be ripe, thinking that we might be able to get some for the market in Tlaxiaco — the Mendezes are old and we knew that we could take their tomatoes to the market for shares.

When we approached the house we saw Concha sitting under the ramada. But when we hailed her, saying only 'Good Morning' because we were not sure it was her, a man came out of the house and beckoned her inside. She stared at us and her eyes spoke to us, though she said nothing."

"This man had been shaving so had his shirt off. He was wearing a gun," Plato added.

Ildegardo nodded. "Surely then, she is a prisoner. Surely." He rubbed his hands on his pants and said, "How do you know that she is the cacique's prisoner?" he asked Socratio.

"We know that Mrs. Mendez has one friend who tells her everything that happens in the village. After we had inquired about the tomatoes we went to la soltera and asked her what she knew. She told us that Concha was being held for the godfather of Huajuapan, and none other. I have heard of this don Armando Pacheco."

Ildegardo turned to the hut, where his wife had gone. Inside he could hear her cries and little squeaks as she tried to hold in her fear.

Turning back to the other men he said, "I do not understand why she was brought so near to San Miguel to be kept a prisoner. If they meant to harm her, surely they would have done it in some other place and not brought her to Santa Catarina. A-i-e-e-e, there are many things here which my poor mind can make no sense of."

He ran the backs of his fingers over the silver stubble of his strong jaw, making a heavy scratching sound. "What should we do? What can we do?"

"Simple. We go get her! We can do nothing less," said José the poet, in an iron voice.

All the men turned toward him and were startled by the fire in his sunken eyes.

"Go get her," said Ildegardo. "Of course. There is only one man to stop us, so we could take her, surely."

José raised his hand. "But he is armed and we must not lose anyone to his gun. It must be done at night."

His sons nodded, watching their father carefully. Thinking was not their strong suit, but they were not known for their cowardice. They were as brave as the fighting cocks they bred, cocks whose fame had spread the names of the brothers throughout the mountains of the Mixteca Alta and beyond.

José turned to the young men and said, "Go to Santa Catarina and find out if the man is still alone. One of you wait for us at the tienda where the bus stops. When we arrive tell us if more guards have arrived. If there are more of them I will go to my brother for help."

He stood on his rickety legs and put out an arm for one of his sons. Plato offered his thick shoulder and the old man grasped it. "Now I go to dig up my cuarenta-cinco, my .45 automatic. It has lain mute these many years, since the days of my father and the Revolution. I have cleaned and oiled it every year for all this time. Now it must pay its keep. But, espero a Dios, I hope to God, that it will not have to speak in its strong voice, for in the hands of my father it spoke the names of many men who are still in Hell and cursing his name since those bloody times."

He reached out one hand and clasped the arm of his old friend. "Ildegardo, come down with us and we will call our friends together, the men of the Sociedad de Las Animas Ancianas. We must make our plans."

Ildegardo went inside the hut and patted his weeping wife on the shoulder, to comfort her. Then he picked up his machete, slung it over his shoulder, and left.

140

The four men were perhaps a hundred meters down the path when José stopped and glanced up the hill toward the Osorios' ranchito. He said, "I did not want to upset my cousin, Lilia, with it, but I have other news. It is not so good either."

"And what is this news, amigo?"

"Cenovio is in the jail in Tlaxiaco. They have arrested him for the murder of two federales in Culiacan."

Ildegardo felt the news like a blow to his chest. He grew dizzy. José saw him shudder at the words and reached out to steady him.

"Two of my children are prisoners. How can this be?" He turned his eyes to the smoky heavens and said, "Please, my God, spare my children. My eldest, Demetrio, is disgraced and my other two are prisoners. I pray, Lord, that you will set them free, in the name of all that is holy."

José put his hand on Ildegardo's shoulder and said, "Ah, mi compadre, it is useless to keep the rest from you."

"More?!"

"I am afraid so. It is rumored that El Profesor Ward is dead and I am afraid that it is possible that his death came at the hands of Cenovio. He is being held for the murders of three men, no less."

This time Ildegardo walked a short distance to the shade of a pine tree and let himself down slowly into the soft duff at its base.

The three Gorostiza men watched him, waiting. After a moment Ildegardo waved them down the path to the village.

"Go," he said. "I will join you later. My heart cannot bear these burdens and support my legs too. I will join you when I have regained my strength." Tears were coursing down his weathered and whiskery face.

———

When the Aeromexico flight made its turn onto the last leg over the Oaxaca airport Berto pointed out the window and said, "Monte Alban."

Tom leaned over him and looked down. He saw a big hill, flat on top, and on the hill were many buildings and pyramids.

"Whoa, what is that?"

"Monte Alban, I said. It was the major city of the Zapotec and Mixtec people, long before the Spaniards came. It was the major trade and religious center of this whole area for hundreds of years.

Some of the greatest treasures of Mexico were discovered there in the 1930s.

"Practically no one in the States knows of the Mixtec people but scholars suspect that they taught the Aztecs how to write. Certainly they were the most famous astronomers and astrologers of those times. There is a story that Moctezuma the Second was carried on a litter from Tenochtitlan, Mexico City, to consult with the Mixtecs. He hoped that they could tell him what the future held, hoping that it would guide him in devising some way of dealing with the capitanes.

"The Mixtecs, the Maya and the Zapotecs are the only intact survivors of the calamity that fell on us from Europe."

Tom thought for a moment, considering carefully before he said anything. Finally he said, "You know, sometimes I hear deep respect in your voice when you speak of your people . . . but other times I seem to hear contempt. It puzzles me."

Berto stared out the window for a long moment before he said, "It puzzles me too. I am not sure how I feel about my blood, about the genes that made me this short and my face this broad. I don't know if it's something to be ashamed of or something to be proud of."

There was another long silence and then he added, "It's the same thing with your minorities in the states. "You hear them speaking of Black Power, Black Pride and Red Power, Red Pride. But there is a terrible ambivalence in all the rhetoric."

He sighed. "I feel one way half the time and another way half the time. You see, down here it is little different than up there in the north. The general Mexican populace often speaks with pride of its indigenous peoples — look at the Ballet Folklorico and all the artists' groups which celebrate those traditions — but in the daily practice of their lives they look down on anyone with indigenous blood. We're the 'niggers' of Mexico, to put it plain and simple. There is prejudice everywhere." There was a deep, deep bitterness in his voice.

The airport, Tom saw as they taxied to the terminal, was small but modern and quite nice. The landscaping was beautifully done, the people competent and friendly. They collected their baggage and took it out to a taxi. Berto told the driver to take them to the Hotel Veracruz.

It was early evening as they drove into the city. Tom saw that it was a mix of old and new, the new reminiscent of the nice parts of Denver or Omaha. The old part of the city, though, was exciting.

142

It reminded him, in a way, of the old colonial parts of Saigon. It spoke of real culture and a long urban history.

The hotel was clean and modern with a restaurant next to the lobby. Tom stepped out to the sidewalk while Berto arranged for rooms and an old, one-eyed man walked up to him, with a beautiful rug woven in browns and beiges.

"Buenas noches, Señor. You would like a rug, perhaps? I am live in that village where it is made. Very real, very good, very good price."

"I'm sorry but I don't have any pesos," Tom said, patting his wallet.

The old man smiled, "Ah Señor, dollars even better. I give you special price for you give me American dollars. No problem."

Suddenly Berto was at Tom's side. He waved his hand at the old man and said, "Fuera, gusano. No somos turistas."

The old man looked hopefully at Tom, until Berto waved his hand again and said, "Andale, andale," then muttered "chingaso." The old man left, his head down and his face neutral. He had recognized something in Berto that made him respond in a very careful way. Tom guessed he had suddenly smelled that they were cops. Some things didn't change, no matter where in the world you were. Especially in places where cops had arbitrary, summary powers.

He sighed inside, then said, "What about dinner?"

Berto smiled. "I know a place that will blow your socks down. It's in the boutique-ey part of town near the Zocalo. It's called Cebolla y Ajo."

Tom pursed his lips and searched his memory. He suddenly smiled and said, "You have to be kidding, no one would name a restaurant 'The Onion and the Garlic'!"

"Hey, chavo, that's good. Real good!" There was genuine delight on the man's face that Tom had been able to pick the Spanish equivalents out of his brain. "But it's true, 'The Onion and the Garlic.' But don't worry, the food is great. We'll get a taxi just as soon as we put the luggage in the rooms."

"How far is it?"

Berto frowned. "Hmmm. I'd say it would take about fifteen minutes to walk there."

"Hell, let's walk."

"Why?" Berto's voice was genuinely puzzled.

Tom looked around. "I haven't been out of the States for a real long time and I like the feel of this." He waved his hand up and down the street call el Avenida Heroes de Chapultepec.

"OK, amigo, if you want to walk, we'll walk."

"Great," Tom said. He looked up and down, listened to the conversations of the people passing on the street. It had a . . . magical feeling to it. A whole new set of impressions, a whole new way of seeing and feeling things. This was going to be a real good time.

An hour later they were sitting in the restaurant, drinking coffee and waiting for their food, when a group of tourists came through the door.

Tom nodded at the people and said, "Oaxaca must be a major tourist town."

Berto nodded. "Yeah, Monte Alban is one of the primo tourist attractions in Mexico. That's what most of them come here to see. Also, Oaxaca is famous for its rugs, pottery. I think I told you that the Aztec royalty ate exclusively off Mixtec Polychrome dishware. It's beautiful stuff."

"For a cop you sure seem to know a lot about Mexican archaeology."

Berto shrugged, "It was my minor in college. I had a real good professor."

Tom nodded his head. "Same with me, only my favorite prof taught lithology." He smiled at the questioning look on Berto's face and added, "It's a specialty in the study of geology — the study of rocks themselves, how they form, what they do under pressure. That kind of stuff."

"Sounds boring to me."

"Yeah, you'd think so but it was fascinating to me." He toyed with his spoon, tipping its blade and rocking its handle up and down. "You know, being a cop was the last thing that ever crossed my mind as a profession when I was a kid."

"How'd you get into it?"

"The military. I ran out of money for college and had to go back to work. When I knew that I was going to get drafted for the war I decided to volunteer. Draftees were mostly rocket fodder so I thought I'd have a chance of sorts if I joined." He laughed a dry little laugh. "It didn't keep me out of the war but I only had to spend a little time in the boonies."

"You an MP, in the military police?"

Tom nodded. "Yeah, you could say that. It was a special kind of urban duty, but I learned to be a cop there. And when I got out it just seemed like the thing to do — get a job, get married."

Berto was surprised. "You're married?"

"Nah. Divorced." He flicked a finger at the door of the restaurant. "Look at that guy."

A big man, dressed in white, with a green and black sash tied around his waist, stood in the door with a younger Hispanic man and a green-eyed blonde woman. He wore huaraches on his feet, his hair was drawn back in a silver pony tail. A very conspicous guy, a charismatic type. They looked around the restaurant for a moment and then the maitre d' approached them. The big man spoke in fluent Spanish and the maitre d' smiled, then lead them to the back. There they joined the group of tourists who'd come through the door earlier.

"Californios," Berto offered.

"How do you know?"

Berto shrugged. "Just a guess. But after a while you get where you can pick them out by the clothes they wear, the way they act. Remember, I lived there for a long time."

Tom smiled. "You know, we're actually quite a bit alike. That's one of the little games we play in Jackson Hole, too — 'Name the Tourist.' The ones from the midwest are easiest because the men are mostly wearing hats with the names of farm machinery or grain companies on them and the women are always snapping the elastic on their underwear. On a hot day a crowd of them sounds like a popcorn popper."

Chapter 19

It was late when Plato saw the lights of the pickup coming from San Miguel Achiutla. The driver parked the truck across the street from the tienda, the little store that sold items from chicle gum to Panadol headache pills and batteries. The truck belonged to Patricio Gorostiza, brother to José and the past president of the ejido. A very respected man. And un hombre muy macho. He was known, like his brother, for his intelligence but he was not the drinker José was.

In the front of the truck Plato saw Ildegardo Osorio. In the back, with Plato's brother, Socratio, were his primos — his first cousins — Juan and Raul. They were famosos — men famous for their willfulness. Most believed them to be bad men, even banditos. Some said they were narcotraficantes, but no one knew for sure.

They had never done anything to draw the attention of the local law, but they disappeared for weeks at a time and always returned with money. It was believed that they were bandits but no one was going to ask them and no one was going to ask the law to find out as long as they caused no trouble locally.

But there were two things that everyone knew about Juan and Raul. They were fearless and they had good guns, American made. Also, they had been initiated into the Sociedad de las Animas Ancianas. Their discretion was, therefore, unquestionable.

Patricio got out of the truck and crossed the street to his waiting nephew.

"What news, Plato?"

"The man is still alone. Concha sleeps between the two old people, so they will know if she tries to get up. The guy sleeps on the other side of the room, near the door."

"Good," Patricio said, nodding his head. "And they are sleeping now?"

"The guy was still up when I left, sitting by the fire." Plato smiled. "But he was drinking las lagrimas de Dios. He should be asleep by now if he has kept lapping at 'the tears of God' since I left."

Patricio smiled, "Yes, pulque is good for sweet dreams."

"But it makes a man feel like a stallion, too. We should hurry."

"Hmmm. If he has taken liberties with Concha it will mean his life, I swear to you. Come on."

They abandoned the pickup about a kilometer from the Mendez ranchito. Ildegardo and José were left with the vehicle. Then Patricio led his four nephews quietly through the dim moonlight. Though the waning moon was less than half-full, the smoky air had dimmed its light. But the fires had been burning for so long that few any longer noticed the smoke and the pulsing red beds of embers that glowed on the hills where groves of trees had been.

The men sneaked to within a hundred meters of the little ranch and watched for half an hour. Suddenly a man appeared in the doorway, bracing himself against the frame. He carefully undid his pants and relieved himself, once having to support his weight against the frame of the door.

In the nearby field there was a pool of smiles, the white teeth of all the men showing in the dim moonlight.

They waited for another half an hour, smoking their handmade cigarettes and saying nothing. Then Patricio motioned their heads together.

"Juan and Raul, you will come with me inside. Socratio you will wait beside the door with your machete. If he comes through the door, kill him. He must not escape. Plato, you go to the door next to the hearth and oven. If he comes out there, you do the same."

Socratio sucked on his teeth, making the sound for disgust or contempt. "He will not escape."

"He has a gun. If he is alert and knows how to use it, the three of us could be killed. So be careful with this man, take nothing for granted. Vamonos."

The five men made their way carefully to the wattle and daub casita and arrayed themselves at its openings. Patricio and his two nephews squatted near the door, listening. Raul pointed at the wall to indicate that he had located the man by his light snoring.

Patricio nodded, then reached under his shirt and took out the venerable Colt .45 which had belonged to his father. Raul also drew his gun, while Juan, the largest of the three men, left his in its holster. In his hand was a leather thong.

Patricio entered first. After a moment he appeared in the doorway and described, with his hands, the location of the man and the direction in which his head was lying.

Once all three men were inside they moved to the sleeping guard's side. Patricio at his head.

"Who is there?!" old man Mendez cried out loudly from the other side of the room.

Instantly awake, the guard pulled his gun from the holster beside the blanket which served as his pillow. The little house filled up with the blast of the gun, its flash lighting the faces of the people for a millisecond.

At that instant, Raul reached out and placed his thumb over the hammer of the pistol so it would be harder to pull the trigger.

The guard yelled in pain and his gave up his grip on the gun. He cried out again, just before Raul brought the barrel of the pistol down across his face. "Stop, for the love of God, stop! Please!"

Raul's voice, low and tense, said, "Cabron, I will let go but if you move a muscle I will shoot you. Believe me!"

"Yes, yes. Oh, yes-s-s." The man's voice trailed off in relief.

"Roll over on your face, piojoso," said Juan. The man obeyed, and the light slap of the leather thong could be heard in the dark as Juan secured the man's wrists.

"Not so tight," the man protested, between his gritted teeth.

"You shoot me in the face and then ask for pity?" Raul growled in the man's ear.

"Are you hit?" asked Patricio.

"Not badly. I can talk, so my jaw must not be broken — but my face is burned. It was a close one, I tell you."

"Hey, Mendez! "Juan said, then repeated himself. "Old man!"

"Yes?"

"Light a lantern, we need light!"

"Who are you?"

"We are from San Miguel, you are safe with us."

"Yes, yes." They heard the old man rise and get down his lantern from a roof beam.

In a moment there was light in the room. Light enough to see Plato and Socratio's tense faces thrust through the door. And to see Concha sitting against the wall, old woman Mendez cowering beside her. In Concha's hand was a long, wicked-looking butcher knife, and her eyes were as calm as if she were watching a sunrise rather than the lamp being lit.

"Concha! It is me, Patricio Gorostiza."

"Yes, I know."

"Ah, good. You can put the knife down, we are here to take you home."

"I knew as much. When I saw Juan and Raul pretend they did not know me, I knew that you would come for me. Thank you." She stood and put the knife on a little table, then she helped old woman Mendez to her feet. "What are you going to do with him?" Concha asked, gesturing to the trussed man.

Raul smiled. "I think we have done enough to him!" He turned to Plato and said, "You were right, the pulque had made him like a stallion — but it gave me one great handle with which to make him beg. Did you hear him?" Then, in mimicry, he cried out in an agonized voice, "Stop! Please!" And the men roared with laughter, clapping one another on the back. But it was relief, not cruelty, at the heart of their mirth. They felt strong and clever — feelings not common to the peasants of the hills, men and women more used to being victimized than victorious. It was a very good feeling. For all of them.

———

Pete turned out the light and laid his head on the big feather pillow. The hotel they were staying in, the Señorial, was an old Belle Époque building on the main plaza, the Zocalo, of Oaxaca City. The wood was dark and well-polished, the furnishings heavy and ornate, and the bed too soft. Like the huge pillows.

He folded the pillow in half to reduce it to a size that might not smother him in the night, then lay back to consider the day.

Most of it had been spent wandering through the city-block-square Mercado, which was the major city market, and the smaller Mercado de Artesanias. Everyone had loaded up on stuff, though Pete had listened to Olga and put off his shopping for the return trip. No sense in lugging it down to Tamazulapan, over to Tlaxiaco and then back. Instead of shopping he had spent the day just looking around the old town. Olga had gone with him in the afternoon, taking him to some out-of-the-way places like the Tamayo Museum and the old aqueduct up the hill. They had enjoyed one another's company. And, he remembered with a flush, at one point he had put his hand on her shoulders as she stood in front of him and seen her quiver at his touch.

At the restaurant that night she had made a point of sitting beside him, insisting that one of the group move down a place to accommodate her. Hmmm.

The meal had been very good, but heavier than he was accustomed to and there had been a lot of good Chilean wine. He closed his eyes, feeling the wine way down deep in his body, pooling in little burgundy puddles. Which began to slowly widen into a pond and then a lake. Expanding, expanding. He looked down and he was standing up to his ankles in the deep-red wine.

The top of a pine tree began to come up out of the lake, bringing with it a rock and then a meadow. The lake was replaced gradually by the meadow. He was left standing in a wine-red alpine meadow with dark green pines and a deep blue sky trembling with stars.

A moon rose above the trees, a white sliver of a moon shaped like the smile of a Cheshire cat rising in the sky. Like something buoyant released from the bottom of a pond. It caused a bubble of laughter to rise up in Pete's chest and he heard himself laugh.

Across the meadow and in the edge of the enamel-green trees another sliver of white drew his attention away from the midnight blue spanse above him.

The sliver grew larger, seemed to bend at its middle with a regular rhythm. Then he recognized the object as it grew larger. It was the white horse again, illuminated from one side like the fingernail moon above. It was riderless and cantering toward him.

He watched it approach until it was about fifty yards away and then it shied, dancing on its back hooves, and spun away from the trees at the near edge of the meadow. It came down on all four legs, hunching its back as if in pain. Suddenly, Pete was aware that unnoticed, an animal had sprung from the trees and was now eclipsing the top of the white horse's broad body.

The beautiful animal stood, transfixed by the feline animal's strength. It was a lion of some kind, a leopard. A jaguar.

The big, muscular cat's talons dug into the animal's flanks and shoulders, though no blood was drawn. The beautiful white horse seemed to be in no pain, but its eyes spoke of helplessness.

'Help me,' it said to Pete with its eyes. 'Help me.' It moved its hooves up and down in place and they made a thock, thock sound as they came down. A soft thock, thock, thock in the wine-red meadow.

Pete woke from the dream with an explosion of breath. He felt his heart pounding and there was sweat on his hot face.

Knock, knock. Knock.

Pete strained to return to his senses, trying to remember where he was.

Knock, knock, knock. It came again.

And then he remembered where he was. He realized that someone was knocking softly at his hotel room door.

When he opened it, Olga stepped quickly inside to the darkness of his room. Before she pushed the door shut, he saw that she was dressed in a robe and slippers.

In the sudden darkness he heard the robe drop to the floor and she stepped to him. He felt her pubis against his leg, kneading the muscle of his thigh. Her breasts were soft and as hot as the mouth and tongue she was placing, again and again, against his chest. He pulled her head back by the hair and put his mouth on hers, swallowing her breath like a drowning man.

He picked her up and walked till his shins met the bed and then dropped her on it with a thump. He stripped his shorts to the floor as he heard her taking off whatever night clothes she had been wearing. He drank in the verdant smell of her, entering her body as he covered her writhing form, hearing her gurgle deep in her throat, and feeling her burning nails, first in his buttocks and then raking up his back to his shoulders.

Tommy woke at dawn, momentarily disoriented by the strange songs of foreign birds. He smiled at the sensation of being in a completely new environment. It had been way too long since he'd gone anywhere and done anything different.

He went to the window and pulled the curtains aside. Across the rooftops he could see the baroque dome of a cathedral and it reminded him of the night before, when he and Berto had strolled back to the hotel.

Berto had led him to a huge church, Santo Domingo, and they'd gone inside to look at it. It was wonderful, in the original sense of the word. Every one of the chapels had been decorated with a passion that was almost voluptuous. The mannequins were draped in vestments as opulent as the feathers of tropical birds, and gold had been used in every possible element.

Tom gazed out over the rooftops at the foreign city and had a little epiphany. The only element of passion in his life up north was Polly and the hours they spent twined together, wound around and inside one another's bodies. He looked at his watch and saw that it was a little before six o'clock and their bus didn't leave until half past seven. He decided to go for a little walk.

On the sidewalk just west of the hotel Tom saw a sidewalk vendor's stand where a woman was pouring coffee for a customer. He walked down to the stand and asked for a cup of coffee with milk and sugar. He also bought a large sweet roll which was more bread than pastry, but sweet and cinnamony.

He continued west until he reached a major intersection and then crossed the Avenue of the Chapultepec Heroes. He knew that Chapultepec was a fortress in Mexico City which had been defended to the death by cadets who had eventually thrown themselves from the parapets rather than surrender. Whom they had been defending the fortress against escaped his memory, but he had the uneasy feeling that it might have been American Marines. "The Halls of Montezuma" took on a very different connotation in the streets of Mexico.

Tom's thoughts turned to Polly as he walked up the street. This was a place she would love, especially in an early morning. A wide street bordered by huge trees full of birds singing exotic songs.

The traffic was almost nonexistent at this hour. In the rich, slanting morning light, the big windows of commercial buildings looked like faces blank with sleep.

This was a Mexico that Tom had never heard of — clean, peaceful, orderly, a rich blend of modern and ancient. Tommy shook his head, to clear it of the stereotypes he had brought with him. This was a new place and a new time in his life. It deserved an open mind.

Chapter 20

Concha stood beside her mother in the smoky little kitchen of the sturdy wattle-and-daub house. She formed balls of tortilla dough. She breathed the smoke from the open hearth beneath the steel sheet on which they would make the day's tortillas and closed her eyes. Memories of her childhood came back to her of the countless times she had helped her mother this way. It was so good to be home, to have the hard-packed adobe floor under her bare feet.

Her thoughts returned to Wyoming and the enormous house she had lived in. She remembered the deep snows, the bitterly cold days, the magnificent view of the Tetons out the enormous windows. And the kitchen with more appliances than many Mexican stores had in stock. Her bedroom had been the same — her and Nathaniel's clothes would have been enough to start a business in this country. So much. So much.

She glanced around the homely little house with its basic furniture. Very little more than was needed to survive. No paintings, no little tables with sculpture on them, no glass cases full of Indian muñecas worth many thousands of dollars. And no enormous secrets in the basement.

Here she was happy inside herself. In the north she had learned that happiness came to her mostly through the accumulation of things. She had used them to fill the hole in her chest that echoed with loneliness for her home. She knew that the hole in her heart had been shaped like her mother. And now it was filled.

She turned her eyes to her mother's head, bowed over the cutting board on which she was dicing chilis. Her hair was grayer than Concha remembered. She reached out and ran her fingers down her mother's nearer braid and the old woman smiled at her. Concha went back to her work, satisfied. She was home after a great adventure and here she would stay for the rest of her days. It was enough.

But, as she flattened a ball of dough, she remembered The Heart of the World and the book of her family's story. She tried to dismiss the thought, shaking her head at its persistence, but it would not go away.

The smoke from the family hearth was one thing — fresh and redolent of pine gum. The same for the pit in which her father fired his pottery. But the stale smoke from months of forest fire that hung in the air outside was something else again. The corn they'd ground for these tortillas was some of the last from their native fields. And there was no money to buy corn from places which had not been cursed by Dzaui, the rain god whose companion had been stolen.

Shame flushed her mind. She knew that she must do something to atone for the greed in her family which had prompted the selling of the people's very souls. But what? Nothing would serve in the place of the heart. And nothing would ever replace the history book of her family line, lost through the greed of her eldest brother, Demetrio, and the insatiable acquisitiveness of her husband.

A-i-e-e-e. And what of Cenovio, the brother who had tried so hard to set things right with both the family and with the gods? The brother whose fate had passed into the taking of men's lives for the sake of what was unarguably right. Oh! The unfairness of it all made her heart pound. But what could she do, a woman here in the hills? Even now she was being protected from her own government through a watch set by the men of the village to warn of the return of the policemen who had scoured the village only recently for her and her brother.

As she stood, lost in thought, automatically forming tortillas with the heel of her hand, she heard her mother say, "Oyez." Listen. Concha froze.

The neighbors' dogs were barking frantically. The dogs from down the hill, whose eyes saw all passersby, and knew strangers for what they were.

Concha's mother came out of the ranchito, carrying her shawl and a handful of tortillas. She paused for a moment, then called her husband from his wheel.

Concha followed her quick steps up the hill, on an angling path that led to the family sanctuary, the limestone cave hidden in the brush above.

154

Tom was impressed with the bus. It was better than any he had ever been in, and he had ridden in many when he was a soldier trying to live on his soldier's pay.

He had forgotten the rhythms and sounds of a powerful bus negotiating mountain roads, slingshotting out of the curves with the motor growling and the manual transmission meshing gears.

He remembered the day in the Gros Ventre River valley when Berto had said that it reminded him of the Mixteca Alta. It was true. They had driven into mountains covered by pine forests an hour northwest of Oaxaca City, and had been driving through them for two hours since.

There was something else that reminded him of home. The sun was a red disk in the smoke-laden sky and the singular smell of a burning forest took him back to the summer of 1988 when over a million acres of Yellowstone Park had burned. For five months the smoke had been thick in Jackson Hole and almost everyone suffered a sore throat and reddened eyes from the constant irritation. It had been a disaster for Wyoming then and it looked like a disaster now for this beautiful mountain country. Smoke plumes and thermal mushroom pillars could be seen in almost any direction. The pungent smell had seeped into the very fabric on the seats of the bus, for which this was a regular run.

They arrived in Tlaxiaco at half past one in the afternoon. When they stepped off the bus Tom suddenly saw the Mexico described by returning tourists. Everything spoke of poverty. Here were dirt streets, cruddy walls and litter everywhere. He could smell a sewage ditch not too far away, lacing the otherwise attractive odors that came from the many little food vendors' stands set up near the small bus stop.

As Tom stood surveying the place and its people, he heard Berto say, "Oaxaca is the poorest state in Mexico. Very little is ever done by the government down here. But things are changing."

"How's that?"

"The people are becoming very political, demanding more from the government. They learned it in the States and they are bringing it back with them."

"Really?"

"Yeah. They are organizing the indigenous people to vote, to begin transcending their allegiances to their home villages. The governing party is courting them like they never have before.

There are a lot of shit disturbers coming back from the North with new ideas."

"I guess that's good, huh?"

"Sometimes."

"When is it bad?"

"When I have to listen to shithead felons whine about their rights."

"Huh?"

"Sometimes it reminds me of the States, where everyone snivels about their rights and abandons all responsibility to the community, to the country, and to the need for order. There has to be a line drawn somewhere, before we also have a nation of armed punks who own the streets and men kissing each other on television." The jibe at the U.S. was obvious, and intended.

"Damn, Berto, what set you off? You've been in a shitty mood ever since breakfast."

"Ah, don't worry about it. Jesús is at the hotel and he's going to be nice as hell to you and roast my ass when he gets me alone."

"Does he know that I'm with you?"

"Yeah, I phoned him from Oaxaca and told him. He wasn't happy." Berto stepped to the street and waved down a taxi. "Hotel Portal," he said when the driver got out of the car to help with their baggage.

The Hotel Portal was a nineteenth-century building on a corner across the street from a main plaza distinguished by a Moorish style clock tower set in its middle. The portico of the hotel rose above the rest of the city square, commanding the view. Inside, the lobby was modern. A small restaurant across the entrance way gave off enticing smells. The courtyard, with a fountain in the center, was ringed with flower beds and potted camellia bushes heavy with flowers. Nice.

"Dos sencillos, atras, Santiago," he heard Berto say to the man at the desk inside, asking for two single rooms and addressing the clerk by his last name. Apparently he was a regular here.

"Si, Rigoberto. Quien es el gringo?"

"Policia, y entiende español." A cop who understands Spanish.

"Bueno. Numeros dies y once, bien?"

"Bien. Hey, Tomás, come and get your key. You're in number ten and I'm in eleven."

Tom stepped into the lobby and picked up his suitcase. A smiling porter took the bag from his hand. Tom followed the little man across the courtyard. Once across the patio they passed through a door and into the parking lot of a modern, two-story motel modeled after the older part of the building, the parking lot replacing the patio. It was unmistakably a motel — no charm whatsoever, but clean and adequate.

He was hanging his clothes when he heard voices in Berto's room next door.

Tom moved to the wall between the two rooms but the words, loud as they were, were unintelligible. The voice was not Berto's, so Tom assumed that it was the voice of his field supervisor, Jesús Bernalillo. Berto had given a thumbnail biography of the man during the bus ride from the city. He came from a rich family, was a polo player and pilot, vacationed in the States and Europe. His hobby, like his father's, was raising thoroughbred horses and polo ponies. It was something familiar to Tom, coming from a town which had its own horsey set. Maybe the guy would like to come to Jackson Hole and play some polo. Tom was friends with some of the folks who had made international polo competition an annual deal in Jackson. But for the moment the guy didn't sound like he was interested in socializing.

Moments later, there was a knock at the door and Tom opened it to a man in his mid-thirties dressed in Docker pants, Reeboks, and a madras shirt left outside his pants to hide his sidearm. Handsome, he looked like he'd stepped out of an L.A. Times ad for the May Company. He had a perfect smile that seemed genuine enough and he had a roguish scar on his chin.

As he stepped into the room he said, "Hi, I'm Jesús Bernalillo," he said and stuck out a hand that sported a thick, gold-link bracelet.

"Tom Thompson, glad to meet you."

"Rigoberto says that you are here to extradite Cenovio Osorio."

"No. I'm here just in case there is an extradition. Personally, I don't think it's going to happen."

"Oh? What makes you think that?"

"To be honest, I think that the Mexican Attorney General doesn't give a shit what the U.S. wants, any more. The Camarena deal has probably queered extradition between the two countries for a long time." Tom smiled disarmingly. "Also, I have promised Berto that I will keep my eyes open and my mouth shut. I will do everything I can to stay out of your road."

Bernalillo smiled. "You are frank, I must say. And I am glad that you understand things."

157

Tom shrugged his shoulders. "I try to be as open as I can be, it solves a lot of problems. I don't like secrets."

"Good, neither do I. But, just so there are no misunderstandings, I am completely loyal to my agency. If they tell me that I am supposed to be, uh . . . circumspect with you then I will do just that."

"That's more than fair. I have my loyalties as well."

"Excellent! We understand one another. This is good." He folded his well-tanned arms, "I suppose that you want to interview Cenovio Osorio."

"Well, sure. I'd like to know what happened the night that Ward was murdered."

Bernalillo opened the door and said, "Well, we have made your job real easy. He has confessed to killing Ward. It's even written down on paper." He turned in the courtyard with that model's smile on his face and said, "Your work is done. With the confession you can close the case."

They stepped outside. Tom closed and locked his door, then turned to Bernalillo and said, "Unless the trial is held in Wyoming, remote as that possibility may be."

"But the man has confessed! It is on paper!"

"No offense, but an American lawyer would probably have the confession disqualified."

"How?"

"A thousand ways. The lawyers decide how things go up North, despite any realities." Tom was being diplomatic. He knew that any good lawyer would claim duress for a confession extracted in this country, and probably make it work. This could be a real problem.

They went next door for Berto and Tom saw that the man was sullen, having had his butt dragged over the coals for something that wasn't his fault. Tom sympathized. There was little that made him madder than to have to take a raking-over for something that was beyond anyone's control. But it gave him an insight in the character of Mr. Bernalillo. The kinds of personalities who indulged themselves in scapegoating were usually insecure or incompetent. It stood in contrast to Berto's apparent cock-sureness.

Suddenly Tom remembered Berto's comment the day before about Indians being the "niggers" of Mexico and the situation made sense. Bernalillo was a member of the thin upper crust of Mexico's population, one of the rich few who either led indolent lives or skimmed the cream of the jobs. Because of their influence, they had their choice of what they wanted to do and they never started at the bottom. On their first day at any given job they were usually supervising people with years of practical experience.

It was no wonder Berto had fretted about their meeting with his boss. He was in a lose-lose situation every day with this guy, no doubt. And too bad, Berto was a good cop with good instincts. He was a pain in the ass in many ways, but independent thinkers usually are. And Tom could see that being that sort of person in this relationship would be a damn hard assignment.

The three men walked out of the hotel and directly down the street, alongside the plaza. The municipal building was only two blocks away, directly across from the big templo, one of the ubiquitous sixteenth- and seventeenth-century Catholic churches that are the architectural centerpieces of every Mexican town of any size. The original priests had been nothing if not thorough, he would give them that.

The Municipio was a large, porticoed building with tall trees and park benches in front. Tom saw that there was a post office and a telegraph office on the little square, which was good to know. It was where one usually found telephones and he had to phone Sam and let him know he'd arrived.

Inside, they walked down a short hall and into a large court with cement floor and basketball hoops at either end. The back wall opened to a nice view of the west side of town and the mountains beyond. A smoky pall mostly obscured the mountains but Tom saw that they were large and covered with trees. They turned left and walked to the end of the courtyard. A sign over the doors identified the offices of the police.

Jesús walked past the uniformed clerk who concentrated his gaze on Tommy. They were not unexpected, he could see.

The commander was a man in his fifties with silver hair. His name was Riley and he spoke good English. Not the hip, Americanized English that Jesús and Berto spoke, but correct.

"Sit down, gentlemen, please sit down." He motioned at three chairs arrayed in front of his desk. They had been expected, indeed.

Jesús introduced Tom and made a polite comment about his being a visiting officer who was there to observe procedure and get some knowledge of the Mexican law enforcement system. There was no mention of extradition. Rather, he made it sound as if the case of Cenovio Osorio were a handy one to use, to illustrate what Tom had come down to learn.

Riley nodded. "Very good. I will explain about Señor Osorio.

"He and two accomplices were stopped by an anti-smuggling patrol at a roadblock in Sinaloa state. They were asked to open the trunk of their car, and when the lieutenant and a soldier on the detail discovered contraband, Señor Osorio killed the two men with a machete. Luckily, another soldier, who had been relieving himself in some trees, came back just in time to witness the murders and get the license plate number.

"The car was found abandoned in Huajuapan de Leon and officers were dispatched to the bus station and every other place they might exit the town while a search was mounted. We received notice of the murders and were told who the owner of the car was, through a computer link to the U.S. authorities. Because Mr. Osorio is known locally, we sent a large detail to his village and searched it for them.

"However, we were lucky. They might have escaped except we received a tip that they had boarded the bus from Huajuapan to Tlaxiaco at a stop outside the city. When they reached Tlaxiaco we arrested them."

Tom interrupted. "Who are we talking about?"

"Cenovio and Concha Osorio, brother and sister."

"I am curious, how did Miss Osorio die?"

Riley frowned. "Who said that she was dead? She is not dead, that I know of."

"Oh," Tom said, realizing from the withering glances Jesús and Berto were giving him that he'd broken his promise to keep his mouth shut. "Please go on, sir."

"So, the two were arrested and Señor Osorio confessed to the murders of the policemen. As to his sister, she was released as she played no part in the murders. We could have held her on federal suspicion of smuggling but we saw no point to it. If the federals wish to pursue it, then we will have to try to find her of course. But we have received no requests."

Jesús leaned forward. "And you do not know her whereabouts."

"No. We have informants in the San Miguel and there has been no word of her since she left this building. That is a bit strange, certainly, but these Indigenos have family everywhere and an aunt is the same as a mother. She could be anywhere in that valley. But if you need her, we can find her. It may take a while, but word always gets back to one of our daily patrols once we make it known what we need. A few pesos will get us anything, things being as poor as they are out there."

"Uh, Commandante?" Tom ventured, avoiding the glares of his partners.

"Yes?"

"Did Osorio say anything about a murder in the States, in Wyoming?"

Jesús stood up. "Well, thank you, I think that is all we need." He turned to Tom and said, perfunctorily, "Unless Señor Thompson can think of anything else."

"Oh, you are interested in that?"

"Yes."

"He said that he knew nothing about this, when Señor Bernalillo asked him."

Tom hesitated a heartbeat, remembering his promise, but his mouth went on even though his brain was saying 'Don't do it!'

"I'd like to talk to Mr. Osorio, if it's OK. And I'd like to talk to him alone."

The three other men looked at one another. Riley paused for a moment and then said, "Certainly. I'll get the jailer to take you down."

When they stepped out of Riley's office, Berto leaned toward Tom and hissed, "My ass is going to be in a sling now, for sure. Thanks." He left the office. Jesús walked to the door and said, "I'll be here when you come up."

Tom felt more than a little sheepish about breaking his promise. But something down deep in him had prompted the words out of his mouth.

Steep steps led down into the basement, lit only by bare light bulbs in sockets mounted to the cement walls. At the landing Tom got a smell of human excrement and urine and it got stronger the further down they went.

Once in the basement, they reached a stub wall with a barred door. A small man in a uniform sat on a chair at the door. He leaped to his feet when he saw Tommy, a puzzled look on his face.

"Abre la puerta," said the jailer and the man unlocked and opened the door, then locked it behind them.

They walked to the second door. A man was lying face down on a pad on the floor, his face pillowed on his crossed arms. In the corner was an enamel slop jar, accounting for the smell. The place was chilly, but fairly clean.

"Osorio!" said the jailer and the man on the mattress rolled over and sat up slowly, then leaned stiffly against the wall.

Tom took one look at the small man's face and saw that any confession he'd made would not stand up in an American court. Not for one minute.

Chapter 21

Concha and her mother came out of the cave after Ildegardo sent Demetrio to retrieve them from hiding. A group of village men were gathered in the little grove of trees near the hut.

José Gorostiza broke away from the group and called Concha to come with him. Patricio Gorostiza's sons Raul and Juan were in a group with José's sons, Socratio and Plato. In addition, her brother, Demetrio, and Marcos Albino were with them. This was strange because her mother had told her they had been sent away from the community, exiled for their parts in the selling of The Heart of the World. The fact that her own husband had bought the crystal had not been mentioned since she'd come back. Perhaps this was what the meeting was all about!

'Oh God! Please do not let them send me away from my home!' she prayed silently. The thought that she might be torn from her mother's side just when she had regained a measure of peace for her soul was more than she could bear. The little domestic chores she set for herself were gradually dissolving the huge knot that had formed under her breast in the cold, beautiful country of her husband's home. She still felt the pain of knowing that her husband had paid ten thousand dollars to the men who had bought The Heart of the World from Marcos and Demetrio for only two hundred American dollars. Que desgracia!

In Wyoming, when Cenovio had told her of the rain god's anger and his expressions of it, she had felt disgraced. For Marcos and Demetrio to enter the holy cave beneath the hill on which the old Catholic nunnery sat had been a sacrilege in itself. To remove the heart had been a blasphemy. For her husband to have received it, and given money for it, then locked it away in a foreign land...

As she followed José, her heart falling in her chest, she looked out over the valley and its thousand smokes. The cost was obvious, and becoming clearer. When they sent her away she would kill herself at the first opportunity.

Most of the men were sprawled on the ground beneath the trees. Concha saw the hard looks in their eyes. There would be no mercy from these men. Never. She almost burst into tears. Demetrio and Marcos stood back a bit from the group, their shame still written on their faces, though their eyes were hard too.

José took Concha's arm lightly in his soft fingers. "Concha," he said.

Her voice quavered as she said, "Yes."

"Tell us all you know of the cacique, don Armando. We want to know where his house is, what it is like on the inside, how many people are there . . . everything."

A little thrill ran through her body. "I do not understand."

"We know that he has The Heart of the World and the book of your family. We also know that he has decided that he is not going to return it to us, except for a price. If we do not pay that price — and there is no doubt that we cannot — he is going to offer it to men in Mexico City. It will be gone from our country again and we will be ruined. The lives of the Cloud People will be extinguished."

"But," Concha exclaimed, "he gave his word that the things would be returned to us. He said that he was of the family of the famous Cacica de Teposcolula, just as my family is. He promised that our holy properties would be returned as soon as he had recovered them! Again I say that I do not understand."

José shrugged. "It is the way of men in this world. He found out that The Heart is worth many thousands of American dollars and it is an opportunity he will not pass up. However, to give him credit, he has given us a chance to recover it."

"But how?" Concha exclaimed. "We have no money, no one has any money in these mountains."

José nodded and said, "That is true, there is no hope of raising the money for the return of our holy objects. And the only possibility that exists is to take them back by force. We will go to Huajuapan and tear them from this man's greedy fingers. And, if he will not give them up gladly, we will feed those fingers to the dogs of the street."

Concha smiled. She had forgotten José's florid speaking style. Then she looked at the men again and was now impressed with their sense of resolve. Her rescue had apparently inspired them with a newfound sense of competence. All too often the people of the mountains could be counted on to be passive in the face of any authority, legal or not. This explained the hardness in the eyes of the men. It also explained the presence of Marcos and Demetrio. They were being given a chance to redeem themselves with the people of Achiutla and with the rain god, Dzaui.

"So you are going to Huajuapan to take back our things," Concha observed. "But is this possible? Have you considered the dangers, do you have a plan?"

"Patricio spoke. "We have a plan for Tlaxiaco, and to rescue Cenovio. But the reason we are here is to try to work out something for Huajuapan. Only myself and my sons," he gestured at Juan and Raul, "have been to the city. And none of us knows it very well."

Concha was stunned. "You are planning to rescue Cenovio from the jail in Tlaxiaco?" She was horrified at the prospect. It would bring the police into the village thick as grasshoppers in a plague year. It was not a good idea. But she would hold her tongue for the moment.

However, a plan for Huajuapan stirred her. "I can take you to don Armando Pacheco's house, I know it. While Cenovio and I were waiting I asked to go to the bathroom and was taken through the house. I remember how it is built."

"You must make a drawing for us, then," Patricio said.

"Better. I will take you there."

She saw the men's eyes widen, though their faces remained impassive.

Patricio paused for a moment. "You are a woman."

"And what of it?" interjected José. "She has been away in the north for five years, she must have learned many things. Is it not true that those who come back from there have a knowledge, an understanding that none of us could ever hope to learn down here?"

The look in Patricio's eyes was guarded. "That I cannot dispute. A great many things can be learned in the North but bravery is not one of them, and this will take someone with an iron will. It would take someone who is not afraid to go to jail . . . or to die."

José snorted through his nose in disgust. "Did you yourself not tell me that Concha had taken a knife at the Mendez's house and was prepared to defend herself? Did you not say that you could tell from her eyes that she would have gladly cut the guts out of anyone who touched her?"

Patricio nodded, his eyes taking on a more thoughtful cast. "I did."

"And does not the blood of the famous Cacica de Teposcolula run in her veins? Are the Osorio women not famous for their intelligence?"

One could tell from Patricio's silence that he agreed this was something he might reconsider.

"Then take her with you," José said with conviction.

Patricio looked at Juan and Raul. Raul nodded and looked at his brother. Juan nodded.

Patricio looked at Concha for a long moment. He saw a woman.

But also, in that long moment, he suddenly saw something else that he had not looked for, and so had not seen. The woman was completely at ease here, at a council of men. Her eyes were confident and he could tell that it was not a false confidence that came from the need to thrust oneself forward. It was genuine.

He nodded slowly, thoughtfully. "Tell us what you think," he said to her.

———

Oz Gardner parked the van and watched in the rearview mirror as Olga parked her van behind his. Then he turned in his seat to address the passengers, one of them Pete.

"This is a holy place for me." He motioned out the windows of the van. "This is the Tamazulapan Valley and this," he pointed through the windshield, "is the Mixtec pyramid I was helping to excavate when I had my vision and received my spirit animal."

Pete looked at the large mound. It was overgrown with small trees and bushes — it looked nothing like the wonderfully engineered structures on top of Monte Alban.

So this is where the jaguar appeared, Pete said to himself. This is where the logo for Jaguar Travelers and Gate of Heaven brand mushrooms popped into Oz's head, heh, heh. A little bubble of cynicism worked its way into his head, despite his promise to the old hippie that he would take all this seriously. He was having a good time and there was no sense in ruining it with a lot of pseudo-religious bullshit. He turned in his seat to look out the back window at the other van.

Olga was engaged in a lecture that, he assumed, both guides knew by rote.

He looked again at the big mound of rubble and let himself have another private little laugh.

They all piled out after the talk and walked down a path toward the hill. A small man in a straw hat who was plowing a field nearby waved his hand and many of the group returned the wave, eliciting a big smile from him.

Oz led them to a spot at the base of the ruined pyramid. Pointing to a flat corner of a field next to a low rubble wall, he said, "I was sleeping here, beside a little fire. I was taking the place of the watchman, a local who had to be with his wife, who was having a baby.

"I was staring into the fire, my shoulders covered by a cobija, a blanket, because it was winter and, believe it or not, the nights occasionally get cold enough to freeze water. Anyway, I remember staring into the fire and it began to flare. It took on the form of an oval and the flickering began to make some sort of sense. The flames had died down to embers which had a bluish hue, then a deep bluish green. It pulsed, then pulsed again. on the second pulse it turned into a beautiful, iridescent blue and green bird. It had a longish tail and a brilliant black bead for an eye. That eye had the most intelligent look I had ever seen. It was not the facial expression, birds' faces are immobile, but the look in the animal's eye sent a thrill through me. I began to get giddy with a sense that something unusual was about to happen." Oz's voice died away to a whisper. "And that was when I received my knowledge."

The knowledge of how to turn this whole thing into a lot of money, Pete thought, then turned with a smile to look at Olga. She pursed her lips in disapproval and jerked her head at Oz, bidding Pete to return his attention to what the man was saying.

Instead, Pete glanced down at the ground near his feet and saw a potsherd. He stooped to pick it up and examined the white clay decorated with an orange design.

"Pete? Hey Pedro! Leave the pottery here. It belongs to the people."

Pete felt a little sheepish, everyone in the group was looking at him and their faces all showed signs of disapproval. Before they'd left the hotel in Tamazulapan, Olga had lectured them all on leaving anything they found right where it was. She also added something about it angering the spirits of the pyramid, he remembered. He flipped the sherd to the ground.

"OK," Oz said, "Let's walk up this way. I'll explain how the pyramid was built and tell you some anecdotes about the excavation. Then, when we get to the top, I'll tell you some of what the Quetzal told me, about the people of this valley and about my own life."

Suddenly, Pete had a thought. The jaguar, the jaguar of Jaguar Travelers! He had thought that Oz's "spirit guide" was the powerful cat of Indian myth. It had made sense that the big man with the feline eyes and manner would be guided on his spiritual odysseys by that animal. Instead, he followed a bird around, heh, heh.

They stopped about half way up the pyramid so the group could get their breath and Pete looked east. There was a walled structure about a mile away, surrounded on one side by a grove of large trees. It looked cool and inviting.

Pointing, he said, "Hey Olga, what's that over there?"

"That's a large swimming pool. It's fed by springs, the springs which were the life of the community that built this pyramid."

"Great! Let's go for a swim after we get done here. It's hot."

Olga smiled a secret little smile and whispered, "I planned to take you in there, but not in the day. It's a real sexy place at night."

Pete felt a flash of heat. He surreptitiously ran the heel of his hand down his groin, trying to quell the sudden tumescence there.

———

Commandante Riley sat in his office alone. He was thinking. After a moment, the clerk tapped on his door and then brought in the bottle of Pepsi that Riley had sent him to get. The silver-headed man put his feet up on his desk and took a long drink from the cold bottle. He loosened his uniform tie.

This was getting complicated and he hated complications.

He thought back over the chain of events that had brought him to this moment.

First, the federal police had notified him that the Osorios had killed two federals and were thought to be heading this way.

Second, don Armando had phoned and told him the Cenovios were on the bus. Then he offered Riley a business proposition. This was something momentous because Riley had been worrying that very morning about his mistress in Huamelulpan. She needed money for her kids, so he agreed to arrest Cenovio, but let the sister go.

Then Jesús Bernalillo had turned up, saying that a gringo cop was coming down from the States with Sandez. He had explained to Riley that this man's agency was seeking an extradition for Osorio and that, given the present positive political climate in the wake of the NAFTA treaty, it might happen. Bernalillo was scared silly that this gringo might get to take Osorio back to the States. He had wanted Osorio to disappear, which was stupid as well as impossible. The money Bernalillo offered

168

would have been nice, but Riley could only do so much. However, Riley had agreed not to notify the feds in Mexico City that he had Osorio in custody until Bernalillo had a chance to try to work some things out. Riley had given him two days. Jesús had paid for three. Not bad. Two pay envelopes in one week, and no taxes on either one.

And then the gringo had surprised them all by asking for an interview with the prisoner. Riley had not known what to do, for if word were to come from the Attorney General that the gringo could take Osorio he, Riley, would be in the position to catch some major political shit if the man complained that Riley had not been cooperative.

The choice had been a hard one. After all, Bernalillo was the chief field agent for the Mexican DEA's regional office. He had access to many U.S. drug interdiction dollars in their inflated, and mostly unaccounted, budget. Bernalillo had money to burn for law enforcement-related activities and he could shove it to any police official he chose. But money couldn't buy everything — a man had to use a little discretion, especially when it came to the golden goose, Uncle Sam.

Riley's father had been an American law officer, a deputy U.S. Marshal who had met his mother in Guadalajara while working a case. Riley was born in Mexico. Then his mother had followed the man to Victoria, Texas, and made him marry her. They moved to Fort Smith, Arkansas, and lived there until his father had been killed during a railroad strike.

Without the protection of the law officer father, they became "spics." Their fortunes fell until Riley's mom felt they would be better off back in Mexico, near family and away from the prejudices of the good folks in the north. But it had turned out OK, the money from the death benefits had made them prosperous compared to their neighbors.

Riley took another drink of his soda, then smiled a little smile. Bernalillo and Sandez must be sweating their asses off right now. This gringo was going to complicate their little game a whole lot, and he was going to have to watch how this all played out and be damn careful. He didn't want to get any more of it on him than he had to.

———

Tom, Berto and Jesús were sitting on the patio outside the restaurant of the Hotel Portal. They were waiting for their food and talking, and none of the conversation was in English. The two didn't even pretend to include Tom. The two men were obviously steamed about his interview with Cenovio Osorio.

But he couldn't really blame them. He had promised to keep his mouth shut and hadn't — he'd asked about Ward's wife, thinking she had been killed because Berto had told him so. Now it turns out the woman is alive and not in custody. Why the lie?

Then he had taken advantage of the situation and gone straight to Osorio. And if the two cops had known about his and Osorio's conversation they'd have been even madder.

Cenovio had agreed, gladly, to an extradition. He knew that he would be spending his life in the deepest shithole in Mexico for killing the two federals. There might not be a death penalty, as such, in Mexico but life in prison for a killer of federal cops was short indeed.

Osorio had told him that he would cooperate with Tom, make a complete confession, and describe the mitigating circumstances if Tom took him back to the states. Tom had assured him that if there were real mitigating circumstances his prison term could be as little as seven years. And he would serve half that if he kept his nose clean. The man had jumped at it.

Now Tom had to get to a phone and talk to Sam. He desperately wanted to make contact with someone at home. He felt real exposed down here. His "partners" were lying to him.

When the food came, cheeseburgers and french fries, Tom took advantage of the moment.

"Hey, Jesús, where can I make a phone call?"

Jesús stabbed a couple of french fries, stuck them in his mouth and pointed to the wall behind him. "Down the street half a block. There's a shop on the left with a phone booth right by the door. Tell the woman you want to make a call to the States and she'll get you an international operator on the line."

"Thanks."

"You're welcome."

It was Berto who couldn't stand it any longer. He glared at Tom and said, "What the hell did you think you were doing, anyway?"

Tom looked sheepish. "I know I gave my word . . ."

Berto broke in. "Yes. You did."

" . . . but I just couldn't help myself. My problem is that my mouth moves when I think."

"What the hell were you thinking about? Here we are trying to do our job and you butt in like you're in charge of the detail.

170

This is a federal murder case, a Mexican federal murder case, and you are interfering."

"I can't see how I interfered, not really. I talked to the prisoner — so kill me! All I wanted to do was try to find out how Ward got killed — and why. Hell, I have to pretend like I'm trying a little. I've got to report in to Sam and I can't tell him that I'm rocking on my nuts down here because I promised you guys I would. Give me a break, I've got to give him something."

Jesús said, "Yeah, you've got a point. But try to stay in the background. We have our job to do too." He wiped his mouth. "What did you find out from Osorio?"

Tom had known that it might come up so he was ready with his answer. It might be half an answer but it would do for the moment.

"He did it, alright. He got in an argument with Ward over some crystal and a book that has the history of his family in it. I guess it's real old and his family had loaned it to Ward. They wanted it back but he kept putting them off and putting them off.

"He had it locked up in that monster safe of his and there was no way they were ever going to be able to get it, locked behind a door that size.

"Ward had a photo studio in his basement and he used to take things out of the vault and photograph them for a little catalogue he put out for his customers. I guess that Ward's wife took him down a cup of coffee and saw that he was photographing the book and the crystal, which probably meant that he was planning to get rid of them for money.

"Well, her brother and a friend happened to be at the house and she went back upstairs and told them what was going on. The two men went down to the studio and tried to talk Ward out of the items. He got angry and they had a hell of an argument. The argument turned into a fight and the two guys knocked Ward down and grabbed the book and the crystal. He followed them upstairs and the fight got going again, this time in the front room. It ended up with Cenovio lying on the floor, the book clasped in both arms and Ward down on his knees trying to get the book back. The other guy, Valerio Trujano, grabbed a piece of firewood from the pile next to the fireplace and whacked Ward on the back and head, knocking him off Osorio.

"Apparently, he put a lot into the blow and knocked the wind completely out of Ward. So they put the book down and helped Ward's wife revive him. Well, no good deed goes unpunished — Ward woke up and immediately flew into a rage. He attacked

Cenovio, this time really kicking his ass. Ward was an Army Ranger and I guess he was putting a real hurt on the guy, but forgot his back and Trujano pushed him down. And this time Osorio picked up the club and hit Ward in the head.

"It probably gave Ward a serious concussion when he got knocked out the second time. I've read the autopsy and his brain was severely concussed three times. The third time, after Ward had fled outside, fractured his skull. Then they strangled him, he said, to offer the man to the gods.

"Osorio delivered that blow and he's a murderer, according to the State of Wyoming. But, more to the point, he is a murderer according to the Honorable Nathaniel 'Nat' Ward, congressman from the Commonwealth of Virginia."

Berto and Bernalillo looked at one another and something passed between them. Tom had no idea what it was but their faces showed real concern when they looked back at him. Something was going on with these two.

"OK," Berto said. "We'll see how it all comes out with our governments. But, don't forget, this guy is wanted for two murders down here. Unless something outrageous happens, he's not going back to stand trial for killing a man under all those mitigating circumstances. Hell, he chopped the heads off two federal policemen who were engaged in a lawful activity. No one in their right mind would think that killing Ward would take precedence over the outright assassination of two policemen. The extradition doesn't stand a chance." He leaned back in his chair and took a big swig of his Pepsi. "Why don't you relax, enjoy your stay down here. Hell, I remember something I was going to tell you. There's a rodeo coming up at the feria up in San Miguel Achiutla. You told me how you used to ride in rodeos, let's go down there and I'll show you how it's done."

"You're going to ride?" Tom asked, surprised.

"Yeah. I was good when I was young. Hell, I'm still good."

Tom looked at the cocky grin on the little guy's wide face and thought, I bet you were. I just bet you were, amigo, but time catches up with everybody. He smiled and said, "Now, I need to make that phone call." He shoved his chair back and said, "Down the street and on the left, right?"

"You got it," Bernalillo said. He looked at the check and said, "You owe about two bucks."

Tom left the money and walked out the door to the sidewalk and then down to the shop where he saw a phone booth next to the door.

"Quiero un operador internacional," he said, gesturing at the booth.

The woman behind the counter looked at a man who was sitting on a stool at the end of the counter.

"No hay servicio."

"No sirve?" Tom asked, thinking that the phone must be broken.

"No hay servicio a los Estados Unidos," the man said. No service to the U.S.

How the hell did he know I wanted to phone the States? Tom wondered to himself.

"Cuando hay?" Tom asked. When?

The man just shrugged his shoulders and looked out the door. The woman made herself busy tidying the counter.

Tom walked back out to the street and looked up and down. He would have to find another phone, there had to be more than one.

After half an hour, he found another phone. The man there also said there was no service to the U.S.

A third woman told him the same thing.

As Tom walked back up to the hotel, he was beginning to feel uneasy. He looked around at the foreign scene, with its signs in a language he was only barely competent in. Suddenly he realized just how vulnerable he was, and a vague fear began to come over him. He was a very long way from home.

———

In Tamazulapan, the sun had been down for hours before the group gathered in the little restaurant to eat. Pete was starving, not being used to eating as late as was the custom in Latin countries.

After eating his dessert, caramel flan, he pushed himself back and mentioned that he felt like a sausage. Olga had said, "Why don't we go for a walk — that should help unstuff you."

They strolled to the main square and started down a badly lit street which took them to the edge of town. They walked for fifteen minutes in the pitch dark. Olga lit the way with a little pocket flashlight. She carried two towels she'd taken from her room.

The iron door to the swimming pool had been left unlocked and when Pete wondered at it, Olga just brushed her fingers together, indicating that a little bit of money had arranged it.

Once inside, Pete could tell how large the pool was only by the number of bright stars reflected in the still, black water — a field of stars that seemed the size of a basketball court, or larger. Yes, certainly larger.

They took off their clothes and slipped into the thermal water. It was the perfect temperature, just cool enough to be refreshing but warm enough to be sensual. The only disconcerting thing was the dark night. It was impossible to see the edges of the pool until your fingers touched them. But, to Pete's delight, when he rolled over on his back, he could navigate by the pulsing night sky.

They made a game of it, swimming side by side from Pegasus to Cygnus, over to Saturn and down to Jupiter. Olga's firm wet breasts dimly flashed the starlight back up into the dark.

After leisurely crossing the pool twice, Olga led Pete to its north side, where the springs fed it from a limestone outcrop. She pushed him gently back to the rocks, flung her hair over her shoulder, wiped her face, and stepped into his arms. Her hot breasts flattened against his cool chest, her mouth opened wide, as if to swallow him and she opened her legs and lifted her thighs to embrace him. He entered her mouth and her vagina at the same time, causing her to inhale a gasp. She thrust herself upon him, gripping him as she worked more and more of him into her.

She breathed shuddering little breaths into his lungs as she worked herself slowly up and down on his shaft until she gave a little shudder and took her mouth away. She looked up at him and the pale light of the stars lit her blonde hair and pale face, turning her green eyes into black pools. Her open, wanton mouth was also a pool of dark as she breathed. Huhhh . . . huhhh . . . huhhh . . . huhhh. Occasionally she would make the erotic gurgling, panting sound deep in her throat that made Pete even harder.

Pete reached down and took her buttocks in his hand, stilling the motion of her hips. He pushed harder and harder, trying to put every last micron of himself inside her. Responding, she lay back. She gripped his wrists, her nails burning their way into him, and she thrust her globed breasts and flinty nipples up to the dark sky. Her blonde hair floated out onto the water in a large, pale aureole. Bubbles from the spring came up and mingled with the light hair and starlight. Her mouth made a dark oval and animal sounds escaped her body.

He buried himself again and again and again. At every thrust she quivered and gasped. Her vagina became looser and she felt more vulnerable to him as, he knew, she neared climax. She no longer moved her hips, just waited to receive his thrusts which were coming faster and faster. Her nails dug deeper into his arms, her legs widened, her moans became more intense.

Pete could stand no more. He gave himself up to the moment and closed his eyes so all his sensibilities were concentrated in finding the very bottom of her pelvis, the little spot that led to her center. Finally she gasped and then gave a little shriek. Her hands shook as she stilled his pelvis, holding herself rigid against the end of his shaft.

They came on the same heartbeat and her long cry turned into a pulsing yowl as it emerged from Olga's throat. It sounded as it she had been stabbed in the heart.

Chapter 22

After his abortive try to make a phone call, Tom took a walk around the mountain town. He wanted a chance to think about his situation and when he needed to think something through it was his habit to go for a walk.

He went back to the hotel, walked across the porch and turned the corner, headed up the hill. No more than two blocks on, he saw something familiar mounted on a wall next to a shuttered window. It was a small blue-and-white sign with the trademark double A of Alcoholics Anonymous. He felt a bit of relief from the knot in his gut. Tom had gone through treatment for his alcohol addiction at a Vet's hospital six years earlier. His first revelation came when a crusty old counselor had said, "You people don't have a drinking or drugging problem — you've all got a living problem." It had gotten through to him.

The second revelation didn't come as quickly but it was even more profound. All his adult life he'd felt himself a master of fear. He'd rodeoed, driven cars fast and wrecked more than one, joined the Army and gone off to a shooting war. As a cop he had entered many life-threatening situations. He thought of himself as ten feet tall and bulletproof, as they say. Especially when he was drunk. But in the hospital he discovered that, at his very center, he was still the frightened little boy cowering at his father's rages and his mother's phobias. And once he understood that fact about his personality he could find ways to deal with his terror. AA meetings were the places he went to talk about his fears — without shame.

Tom walked to the sign and read: "Tengo una problema — A — Tengo un soluccion." I have a problem but I have found a solution. That was as simple as it got. The simplicity made Tom smile. He had found God again through another of the little gifts that He gives, if we are only aware enough to perceive the loving kindnesses. He looked again and saw beneath "Horas: Lunes,

Miercoles, Viernes, 19:30." Monday, Wednesday and Fridays at seven-thirty. He'd be there tonight.

Tom looked around himself with a whole new sense of things. The little street was sunny, warm, and quaint. There was a mix of flat-roofed stucco building and log houses with pitched, shingled roofs. The latter were almost identical to the cabins sprinkled around Jackson Hole, relics of the early days in the Teton valley. It was another gift, another little reassurance that he was not as isolated and alone as he'd been feeling half an hour earlier.

He continued up the street, to a corner, and heard a familiar, buzzing sound. Turning left to follow the sound he soon found himself at a small sawmill.

His grandfather had owned a sawmill; as a matter of fact it had been the business of his mother's people since the pioneer days of 1840s Utah. The smell of freshly sawn pine and the activities of sawyers always made him nostalgic for his bucolic childhood in Wyoming. He walked down the street to the edge of town and looked at the activity.

His practiced eye saw that this was a "stud mill," specializing in two-by-fours eight feet long. By the number of bunks of the lumber he could see that someone, somewhere, was building a lot of stick-built structures. The scene was another reminder of home. Everyone was cashing out in the east and on the California coast to relocate to the mountain west. They were looking to escape all the problems they'd caused in those places, only to bring the same problems with them. The West, a historically friendly and neighborly place, was becoming as exclusive, fearful and class-conscious as any other American place. They were killing what they'd come there to be nurtured by.

As Tom looked at all the activity around the mill he wondered what had inspired it. On the way in on the bus, he remembered that he'd noticed two other sawmills on the eastern edge of the town. Come to think of it, he remembered that they were also stud mills. Indeed, someone had something going somewhere. And it wasn't small.

The smells and sounds, and the pleasant associations they brought to mind, reassured Tom. They reminded him that there was a normal world with normal people going about normal business. Not everyone had to wade around in the muck that went with his corner of this planet.

He sighed, audibly, acknowledging a minuscule impulse of the fear he'd been feeling earlier. But he smiled in spite of the reminder. He had somewhere to go tonight. That was as restorative as this nostalgic little mill.

———

Concha was riding in the back of Patricio's truck. Beside her in the back sat Marcos Albino and another man from the village. He had been brought along to watch the truck and, if they did not escape the cacique's house, take it back to Achiutla. At their feet were baskets which appeared to be full of corn, though in fact they were mostly corn husks. At the bottom of each basket were pistols and ammunition. In the front of the truck rode Patricio and his sons.

The pickup's bed had been outfitted with a pipe frame and a tarpaulin cover, making it a copy of the familiar rural taxis. The pickup bore stolen plates taken from the truck of a hapless traveler who was having new tires put on his vehicle at the Euzkadi tire store in Tlaxiaco.

As they entered Huajuapan de Leon, Concha guided them with hand signals to the neighborhood where the cacique's house sat. As they drove slowly by the big house, Concha pulled her huipil, the red, woven outer garment of the Mixtecs, up to hide the bottom of her face. But there was no one near the big door which opened on the courtyard inside.

Patricio drove the truck to a little park that the Gorostizas knew of. Everyone got out, walked to the pump, and refreshed themselves from the smoky, hot ride over the mountains.

Once they had gathered under the trees, Concha explained again the layout of the house. Now that they had all seen it, they wanted a detailed description of what they would find once they were through the door.

Concha described the location of don Armando's office in the wing where all the business of the house was conducted. They could only hope that The Heart of the World and the book of Lady Eight Monkey were being kept there. There would be only one chance to recover them and that would have to be accomplished in only a few minutes.

The plan they agreed upon was that they would get inside the door through guile, Juan and Raul posing as men seeking a favor. If that failed they would have to force their way inside. That would require Concha's going to the door and letting herself be taken inside. The cacique would not pass up an opportunity to gain control over her again. She was a witness and she knew what the cacique had in his possession.

They parked the truck farther up the street, next to a sidewalk vendor's stand, and got out. The baskets were gone, the spurious produce left with people who had been at the park and the weapons secreted on their bodies.

Juan and Raul crossed themselves and left, walking casually. The rest of the group crossed themselves too, praying with all their hearts that this would go well — that no one in their group and no one in the household would be hurt. However, they had sworn that they would do whatever they had to do to recover the objects central to the future well-being of their community and the Osorio family. If it took blood, then let it flow. They would leave with their hands full or they would die. They had sworn this.

Concha, Patricio and Marcos nibbled at their food and watched the Gorostiza boys go to the door and knock. They removed their hats and stood on the sidewalk until the door was opened. They spoke to someone the group could not see and the door closed. Juan looked up the sidewalk and gave a little motion with his hand, beckoning them to come.

When the door opened again, it was the secretary. His face was expressionless as he looked at the brothers, assaying the men and what they might want. However, his eyes bulged when he saw Patricio quickly step from the wall and point a pistol at his chest, his finger on his lips for silence.

The brothers stepped through the door and pulled their weapons from under their shirts. The secretary had a moment to understand what was happening, then he took in a great breath to shout a warning to the household. It was cut off by a stroke of Juan's heavy automatic on the side of his head.

Concha quickly crossed the patio and entered the door which led to Pacheco's office wing. The men followed on her heels as she flew down the hall toward the tall door she remembered from her last time here. As they were nearing the door it opened.

A woman was backing out the door, a tea service in her hands. Concha slammed her hands on the woman's shoulders and thrust her into the office, making the silver service fly with a great noise onto the stone floor.

The group burst into his presence and the big man with the thick glasses gaped in surprise. Another man was sitting in the upholstered chair opposite the cacique. His mouth flew open in shock as well. But while the big man registered the scene with his eyes, his hands were busy. He pulled the drawer at his right open, put his hand inside and fired his revolver as it cleared the desktop.

Concha saw the flame from the muzzle, heard the report, and saw Raul drop his gun to the floor as a bullet hit his body. Without thinking, she stooped for Raul's gun as she saw Juan leap at the cacique and bring his own pistol down on the man's thick arm. But the big man did not drop the gun, instead he brought it up again to shoot the other brother. At that moment, Concha leveled the 9mm and blew a stack of papers off the godfather's desk.

The cyclone of paper and the loud report in his ear had an immediate effect on the cacique. He dropped the pistol and raised his hands to his shoulders as he peered out the corner of his eye at the little woman with the gun held in a shooter's stance.

Nathaniel had taken Concha to the firing range and taught her how to use a pistol. Together, they had shot thousands of rounds on the pistol courses in Jackson Hole and Idaho Falls.

Patricio picked up the dropped pistol and said, in a menacing voice. "Give us our things."

"What things?" the big man said in a mollifying voice.

Concha aimed the muzzle of her gun at his face and began to pull the trigger. The man's hugely magnified eyes saw the hammer rising and, worse, saw the look on the woman's face. He knew she was beyond any bargaining or stalling. He could see she intended to blow his brains out and then look for what they'd come for.

"Over there, over there!" he said, in a strangled voice. One thick hand waved at a big carved wooden hutch standing against the wall.

Marcos Albino dashed to the cabinet and opened the door.

"That's it," Concha cried. "The cardboard box on the bottom shelf!"

Marcos took out the box and opened it, then he nodded at the group, closed the box and stood. "Let's go," he said.

Juan looked at his wounded brother and slashed his pistol down onto the cacique's skull with a sickening thunk so that the man's thick glasses flew to the floor. Don Armando sagged against his desk and groaned. The heavy gun came down again and he fell from his chair. This time no sound escaped his thick lips.

"Not me! Not me!" cried the other man, still in his chair and holding his hands over his cranium in defense. The group ran from the office and into the hallway. They saw the household

180

staff scatter in retreat, the women shrieking and the men swearing.

They all burst into the courtyard and Concha saw the man who'd guarded her at the Mendezes. He was coming from the back of the house, pulling his gun from the shoulder holster he wore. The memory of his hot hands trying to force their way between her clenched thighs came back to her and, without a thought, she fired as she ran. The bullet took the man down and they heard its flat smack over the report of the 9mm. He skidded onto his face and lay very still.

Patricio's truck was waiting at the gate, the driver's face intent as he looked out the open passenger door.

Patricio and Marcos, clutching the precious box, jumped into the front seat while Juan and Concha clambered onto the tailgate and pulled the wounded Raul into the truck. They were almost spilled back onto the street as the pickup accelerated, throwing a cloud of dust into the late afternoon air and scattering people drawn to the street by the sounds of gunfire.

———

It was an hour after the evening shift had come on at the municipal police station. José Gorostiza had reconnoitered the building, asking if would be OK to have a basketball game in the court. He told them his sons and nephews wanted to play. The man on duty at the police office looked at the schedule and approved the game. José left.

He walked to a side street across from the mercado where five men waited, all of them with gym bags.

"There is only one man in the office and probably one more downstairs in the jail. There are the two guards at the door and in the yard. Has anyone seen anyone else?"

Socratio flicked a hand for attention and said, "There's another one in the vehicle compound. He's changing a tire."

"Is he armed?"

"Not that I could see. Probably not."

"Very well. Plato, do you have the dynamite?"

Plato zipped open the gym bag at his feet so they could see the sticks of dynamite taped together. The one in the center was fused.

"Good. Take the bag inside. I have told the guard to expect us for a basketball game. Go to the office and ask the man on duty if I have been in to reserve the court. He will say yes, then you act as if you are going back outside. When we see you come back to the door, we will take out the guard at the door. Then you go upstairs to the balcony that looks down on the court and be ready. Demetrio and I will go to the office and then, God be with us."

The men, José, Plato, Socratio, Demetrio and two other men from the village, initiates into La Sociedad de las Animas Ancianas, bowed their heads for a moment then they all crossed themselves. Their souls were as prepared as they would ever be. This was the gods' work.

Plato walked past the guard and said a few words they could not hear. Then Demetrio and one of the other men walked across the small plaza and past the guard, nodding a good evening. The man with the carbine returned their greeting, though his face was alert and inquisitive. Suspicious.

"One moment," he said.

Sweat popped out on the two men's faces but Demetrio whispered, "Keep walking."

The guard said, louder, "Hey! I said to wait a minute." His voice had taken on a deadly tone. These policemen suffered nothing that smacked of disrespect from the peasants.

Demetrio and his partner turned around and met the approaching man halfway. They were joined by Plato, who was already inside.

Smiling, they waited for the man to reach them.

"Open those bags. How come all of you are carrying bags?" The fact that so many peasants could have the money for gym bags had alerted his suspicious nature.

"We're here to play basketball, Señor."

Demetrio looked over the man's shoulder and, with relief, saw José and the other man walking up behind the guard. When the guard turned toward the sound of approaching footsteps, Demetrio hit him with a leather sack full of lead shot, knocking him unconscious immediately. His carbine clattered to the cement floor.

"Close the door," José hissed. He turned to Plato and nodded his head up the stairs.

To the rest of the men he said, "Calmate, calmate!" even though his own face was bathed in sweat and he could feel his heart pounding as if it would fly from his chest.

The four men, gym bags in hand, strolled around the corner and out to the basketball court. José then led them casually toward the police watch officer and once there they stopped just outside the door. Jose said, "Sir, I think you have a problem with a broken pipe in the lavatory." He gestured to the corner of the court.

"Damn!" the man said and got up from his desk to join them.

The moment he was close, Socratio and another of the men grabbed each one of his wrists and slammed him up against the wall. José wrested his weapon from his belt.

Leveling the pistol at the man's stricken face, he said, "Take us down to the jail. We are here for Cenovio Osorio."

He nodded his terrified face. "Yes, yes."

"And, just in case there is a problem, I want you to look up there." He pointed to the balcony walk above the gym. Plato was standing high above them with a bundle of dynamite in one hand and a Bic lighter in the other. He flicked the lighter and a long orange flame hissed from it.

"OK, OK, I understand. It's down those stairs."

"I know where the jail is, you bastard," said José. "Half the people in these mountains know exactly where this jail is — and what it feels like to be in it."

Demetrio gripped the man by the neck of his uniform and followed him down the stairs of the stinking prison lit by naked bulbs that dangled from the high ceilings on long, twisted wires.

When they turned into the corridor, they saw the guard at the barred gate look up in surprise. He did not have a weapon, they knew.

"Open the gate, you son-of-a-bitch!" José roared, brandishing the watch officer's pistol.

Their captive nodded his head. "They have dynamite! Do as they say."

"Horale! Horale!" José said, his voice high-pitched with tension and fear.

Once the gate was opened they grabbed the jail guard and hustled him down to Cenovio's cell. Cenovio was waiting for them at the barred door, his face bright with amazement.

The moment the door opened he hurried through to make room for the cell's new occupants.

Clanging the door shut, José said, "I am going to wait up there. If I hear any screaming from you two, the dynamite is coming down those stairs. Do you believe me? *Do you?!*"

The two men inside the cell nodded, sick with fear.

Suddenly, a man in the cell next to Cenovio's stuck his hand out the bars, waving it for attention. "Hey! Hey! Take me with you."

José darted to the door and peered inside. "Hah! Fuck you, Dominguez. Everyone in the state knows you're right where you belong, you thieving shit!"

The men turned and ran for the stairs. Demetrio led the group, followed by his brother, Cenovio. They had no choice but to run up onto the landing, praying to God that they would not be met with a fusillade of bullets.

But there were only the pigeons coming to roost for the evening, when they ran out onto the court and past the unconscious guard. The whole rescue had taken just a few minutes, exactly as they'd planned.

There was something thrilling about their success, something larger than the almost unbearable excitement of the moment. They had planned the impossible, and done the unthinkable. But this was Mexico and they knew they could hardly escape the fury of the state.

———

Berto and Jesús were still not warming up to Tom. He had tried to ingratiate himself with them at dinner but they had been polite and little more. One thing had offered itself, however, when Berto had begun to chafe him a bit about his being a rodeo cowboy when he was young.

"You don't ride in the rodeos anymore, then?"

"Nope. I'm too out of shape for that stuff."

"You should give it a go, amigo. I am."

Tom looked at him blankly and said, "You're going to give what a go?"

"I'm going to ride a bull. I told you that I used to compete, didn't I?"

"I think I remember you saying something about it, yeah."

Berto beamed, his fifth beer glowing through the cocky smile. Tom knew that he was being challenged in a small, male way. Or maybe a small male way, he thought — another little man with little man problems. But he pushed the ungenerous thought aside. He had to get along with these guys. He was a hell of a long way from home.

Berto continued, "I rode in the local rodeos that we have on feast days. I was damn good, too." He took another drink of his beer, eyeing Tom as he drank.

"If you look around," he continued, "you'll see ads on the walls around town for a big feast day in a place called San Miguel Achiutla. . .rodeo, dance, cockfights, horse show, fireworks. Say, you think you'd like to get in a little bull riding during the feria?"

Tom winced mentally at the memories of hitting the ground, losing consciousness for a few moments and then scrambling to his feet without really knowing if he was hurt or not. Then the flash of white hot pain telling him he had a broken leg or that something else was seriously wrong.

Yeah, he thought, if there was one thing from his youth that he truly did not miss it was faking it until he got behind the chutes and then puking up his guts as the shock overtook him. "Tell you what, Berto, you go ahead and ride — I'll be perfectly happy just watching."

"Ah, I don't want to have all the fun."

Tom grinned. "Go right ahead, I guess I'll just have to let you hog it all." He looked at his watch. "I gotta go to a meeting," he said, and stood.

Berto and Jesús looked at each other and something passed between them. Something cautious.

"What kind of meeting?" Jesús asked.

"Oh, it's a kind of fraternity that I belong to."

"Fraternity?" Berto exclaimed. "Here in Mexico? You gotta be kidding, there's none of that frat rat shit down here."

Tom enjoyed the look of genuine puzzlement evident on both the men's faces. "Trust me," Tom said and left the restaurant.

The walk to the building where he had seen the AA sign earlier took only a minute. He stood on the sidewalk outside the wooden door. The strangeness of the surroundings still intimidated him.

"Can I help you, Señor?"

Tom turned and saw a man in a white shirt, tie and suit trousers standing on the sidewalk, behind him. He had a Big Book in his hand. Tom felt relief flood through him and he said, "I'm looking for the meeting."

"You are in the right place, my friend. Come with me. By the way, my name is José Francisco Garcia." He put out his hand and Tom took it.

"I'm Tom Thompson."

"And where are you from?"

"From Wyoming."

"In the United States, yes?"

"Yes."

"I think I know this place. It is very near the state of Idaho, yes?"

"Right next to it."

"I have friends from Idaho, they are coming down here to talk to us about selvacultura. . .uh, I don' know how to say it in ingles."

"It's almost the same — silvaculture. Growing trees. I have friends who work for the U.S. Forest Service, so I know a little about it. But not much."

They paused in front of a door leading to a room where Tom could see a bastard assortment of chairs in rows and a large placard on the wall with "Las 12 Tradiciones" in gothic print across the top. He could smell coffee brewing and cigarette smoke. He felt right at home.

"That is very interesting, that you know of this selvacultura. We must have dinner together and talk. Please!" He gestured for Tom to enter the room.

José took Tom about the room and introduced him to the men inside. His voice was clear and he did not drop the word endings. Tom was pleasantly surprised that he understood most of what was said.

When the meeting began, Tom began to feel more at ease with each moment. This was familiar. The rituals were almost identical, opening with a reading from the 24-Hour book of meditations, a reading of the 12 Steps and 12 Traditions, then a choir recitation of the Serenity Prayer. The prayer gave him a very solid sense of how he should be handling things. It was a blessing.

As the men around him began to share of themselves, Tom took a moment to give thanks for this place and the souls about him. A gift of understanding and acceptance. A few hours before he had been full of fear, but now he was deep into a peace that always came to him when he did what was right. Did what was right for himself, not what was right for others.

It came to him again — the understanding that there are no accidents or coincidences. Everything is exactly the way it is supposed to be and the secret to serenity is simple acceptance.

When it came his turn to share, José volunteered to translate and Tom gladly accepted his offer. He wanted to share what he was feeling, knowing that only honesty about the way he felt led to the peace he needed if he was going to stay her and do his job.

He told them how it used to be. He talked of his drinking history, beginning at 17 and ending twenty years later when he'd begun blacking out, indulging in bizarre behavior. He talked of his anger and the violence, and at this point almost all the men were shaking their heads in recognition .

Then he told them how it was now. He said that his life was full of fear, but it seldom deteriorated into anger and never, so far, into violence. He had been delivered from the fear that was at his very core, though he was not a stranger to the feeling. He described how it felt to be in a foreign country where the customs were obscure and he didn't know what was going on around him. Without being specific, he described how much at sea he was about why he was here and what was appropriate behavior under the circumstances. He added that the fact that there was no phone service to the States made it hard because he wanted to talk to his family and friends.

When he sat down next to José, the man asked him why he thought there was no phone service to the States.

"I went to three places and all of them told me that there wasn't any," Tom explained.

José frowned. "That's not true. We have satellite communication now, there's always international service. Especially to the North."

Another small alarm ran through Tom. He had more than a suspicion about the reason he'd been told there was no service. The people who provided the service had been instructed to lie to him.

José patted Tom on the arm. "But that is OK, I have a phone in my office at the sawmill. We'll go there after the meeting."

A feeling of relief warmed Tom. He thanked José and looked around the room at the men who were so unlike him on the surface. Their skins graded from olive to mahogany, their bodies ranged from his height of six feet down to men who were a full foot shorter, perhaps more. But at their cores they were identical in many, many ways. The understanding at the heart of his recovery came back to him — he was not alone.

After the meeting, José led Tom down the street that he'd walked that very afternoon. Smelling the familiar and comforting aromas of fresh heartwood, pine gums and saps brought back memories from his adolescence and the wonderful times when he had worked at his grandfather's side, his thin muscles laboring against the weight of the heavy, sticky, aromatic wood.

"Do you only produce boards for construction of houses?" Tom asked.

"Right now we are producing building material for a company in Mexico City. They have ordered almost a million board feet of lumber for one of their projects on the coast."

Tom waved at the mountains surrounding Tlaxiaco and said, "This must be national forest around here, then."

"Oh no. This is all ejidital lands here."

"Ejidital? What's that?"

"That means that it is owned by the communities organized into what is called ejidos. We buy trees from them and then harvest the wood for the mill with crews we hire."

"It is very expensive, then."

"No. Actually, the logs are quite cheap. It is the transportation which is expensive."

"If the logs are cheap then the people must not be making very much money from the deal," Tom observed.

José shrugged. "The company in Mexico makes the deals with the ejidos. And it is. . .brokered, I think is the word, by a local man."

"Then he is the one who makes the deal with Mexico City?"

"Yes," José said and this time he made a face. "Yes, and much of the time he is taking advantage of the people." He shrugged. "But, then, that is the way things are done here. The people do not trust the government and they do not trust the chilongos in Mexico City. So they do business with a local man who is, in fact, probably worse than any of the others. But they trust him more because he is of their people — a Mixteco. He is known down here as a cacique."

"Doesn't sound like they have much of a chance."

José shrugged again. "It is the way of the world. I am only a man who tries to turn trees into quality lumber with efficiency."

They were at the door to the office and Tom saw again the many bunks of wood piled about the large lumber yard.

"You say a million board feet. And all for one project?"

"Yes. The Pacific coast of Oaxaca is. . .building a boom. How do you say?"

"There's a building boom."

"Yes, yes. That is it. A building boom."

"We are having one of those in my home town also," Tom said. "It is also a resort area, but not on a coast. In the mountains."

"No building in these mountains, there is only poverty here. The government is funding a boom in Huatulco at the moment. It wants another Cancún, another Cozumel — to bring in the tourist money. They are having very big plans down there."

Tom looked at the mountains of wood again. Huatulco? Why was that same so familiar?

"Please." José was motioning to the open office door.

They went inside and the man simply dialed 09 and handed the phone to Tom. An international operator, in English, asked him for the number he was calling. He gave her the number of

Sheriff Sam Harlan's home phone and was relieved almost to tears when he heard the voice of Sam's daughter.

It did not take long for the feeling to change when he heard the note in Sam's voice.

"Tom! Where in the hell are you? Are you OK?"

"I'm in Tlaxiaco. And shouldn't I be OK?"

"Tom, Sandez isn't who he says he is!"

A shaft of dread ran into Tom's chest. "I was afraid that he wasn't. Who the hell is he?"

All I know is that there's supposedly no one by that name working for the Attorney General down there. Failoni, the FBI guy, checked it out and it looks like Berto is bogus."

"What the hell am I supposed to do?" Then Tom had a thought. "Wait a minute, I had an interview with the local chief of the regional police and he seemed to treat these guys like real cops."

"What guys?"

"Berto and another guy last name Bernalillo. Jesús Bernalillo."

"How the hell do you spell that? H-A-Y..."

"No, it's spelled like Jesus, the bible Jesus."

"That's his name? Jesus?!"

Tom had to smile in spite of himself. "Don't get upset, Sam. It's a traditional name down here."

"Takes a hell of a lot of nerve if you ask me. Now, how do you spell the last name? I'm going to see if this guy's name comes up on the A.G.'s list of officers."

Tom gave him the spelling, then asked, "What the hell do I do if they aren't cops, Sam?"

"I'm going to get you some help as soon as possible. We'll get somebody from the Attorney General's office down there ASAP. In the meantime keep your ass down so it doesn't get blown off."

"Wow, Sam, you sure say the right things. You have just scared the shit right out of me."

"You just be cool. I'll do everything I can. OK?"

"Shit, Sam!"

"You'll be alright. Just keep doing what you're doing, You sound healthy enough so you must be doing something right."

"So far so good."

There was a little laugh on the other end of the line, but it was a laugh obviously intended to comfort Tom. That made him even more uncomfortable than he was already.

"If it's of any interest," said Tom, "Osorio confessed to killing Ward."

"Well, Ward's uncle still wants the guy. But that's not important right now. An extradition is the last thing on my mind at the moment."

"Tell Congressman Dickhead that the man wants to come back real bad. He's in the shit up to his neck down here and if he gets back north he might even have a chance to live a few more years. Down here, his chances are damn small."

"Well, let's get you some backup before we worry about anything else."

"Thanks, Sam."

"Stay in touch."

"I'll try." When Tom hung up the phone the loneliness he'd been feeling before the meeting crowded back on him.

José and Tom walked outside the office and Tom thanked the man. As they were saying their good-byes, Tom was suddenly aware of a great commotion which was going on a few blocks away, in the direction of the municipal center.

"What is all that noise?" Tom wondered aloud.

"I don't know. It sounds as if it is coming from the municipio."

"Let's go see."

"Uh, Señor Thompson, in this country one does not want to go toward those kinds of sounds. It could be very dangerous."

"I'll be careful," Tom said.

But he knew better, even as he began to walk hurriedly toward the noise. There was something about the sound of things falling apart that had always beckoned him, drawn him like a bee to honey. Or a fly to blood.

Chapter 23

Tom ran down the street toward the hotel. When he reached the corner he saw Berto and Jesús jogging in the direction of the mob scene at the municipal building. He caught up with them in front of the school.

Every available police vehicle was being loaded with men. Even civilian trucks were waiting to load other groups of police standing in the square, rifles at the ready. All were talking excitedly to one another. The noise was terrific.

"What's going on?" Tom asked Berto.

"Some people broke your buddy out of jail."

"No shit?" Tom exclaimed. No wonder all the excitement. "Was anyone hurt?"

"No. A couple had their heads rung like bells, but that was all. They say the men were planning to blow the building up. Something happened and they didn't, but this is some real serious shit. This could be Chiapas all over again," he said, referring to the native uprising that had taken place in the neighboring state on the Guatemalan border.

Jesús pointed. "The sergeant who came for us is waving. Let's go down there and see what the hell is going on."

When they reached the entrance to the building the sergeant told them that Ryan wanted to talk to them.

Once inside, the comandante raised his eyebrows at Tom's presence, but then motioned them into the chairs vacated by three of his staff. The deference made Tom wonder again — who the hell are these guys, anyway?

Ryan began a torrent of Spanish directed at Berto and Jesús which Tom could not follow. But the words "El gobernador dice" kept coming through: "the governor says." He also picked out the names of two other Mexican states, Chiapas and Michoacan. The word that seemed to be repeated most often, however, was zapatistas. Tom knew that term could be applied to myriad subversive political organizations active in the indigenous areas of southern Mexico. There were dozens of organizations whose acronyms included Z's for Zapata — EZLN, OOCEZ and many others.

Although he understood that the situation was damn serious, each time Emiliano Zapata's name came up, a picture of a cross-eyed Marlon Brando popped into Tom's brain. It interfered with his concentration.

But he focused hard enough to understand that the governor of Oaxaca did not want a reprise of Chiapas, where the governor had been kidnapped and played as a major political card. And the longer the comandante talked, and the other two men offered their comments, the clearer it became that this governor was demanding caution. He wanted a sound assessment of the situation before any troops were sent in.

Tom's assessment of the conversation was that Berto and Jesús were being briefed for an intelligence foray. Goose flesh crawled across his shoulders. Once upon a time, this had been his business.

Also, Tom was impressed with a surreal sense that real insurgents were apparently readying themselves to come down out of the hills and have the heads of real oppressors. On the one hand it seemed the stuff of third-class movies, unthinkable in the political reality of the north, but here he was sitting in the middle of a planning session called to deal with it!

His paternal grandfather had been a U.S. Marshal once upon a time. Various family stories told of his disappearing into Mexico for weeks or months at a time, returning occasionally with a prisoner but more often only with proof of his catching up to them — in the form of personal belongings such as pistols, rifles or identification papers. The old cliché, "Dead or Alive," had real meaning then.

Tom was suddenly struck by the feeling that his presence in Mexico was somehow preordained, that it ran in his blood as truly as his old hunger for alcohol — something else that he had inherited from the same grandfather. The one with the gap-toothed grin and pearl-handled Colt who stared out from the family album.

Tom's attention returned to the room when Berto tapped him on the shoulder and beckoned for him to come with them.

Outside there were more than a hundred police and soldiers mustered in groups, smoking and talking. Suddenly Tom was swamped by emotion. Here were men gathered to hunt other men. Men responding to training and practice, men galvanizing themselves for the ultimate experience. He felt suddenly fearless in the face of the unthinkable. He felt a real sense of fraternity with these men gathered here in the dark and he was moved by the experience. Once Tom and the other two had passed the policemen and walked into the lighted streets, the camaraderie began to wane. He had buried all that, he reminded himself.

When they reached the porch of the Hotel Portal Tom saw the same group of American tourists he'd noticed in Oaxaca City. They were looking down the street at the crowd of police and soldiers, their faces worried. As Tom stepped through the front door of the hotel, he bumped into the big man with the silver ponytail and the Mexican peasant clothes. Behind him stood the Hispanic guy and the blonde with exotic green eyes.

"Excuse me," said the one with the ponytail. "Can you tell us what's going on over there?"

Tom said, "It's nothing for you to worry about. Some people broke into the jail and freed a local man. It's a serious thing for the police but it shouldn't effect you."

"Thanks man, I appreciate it."

"Sure," Tom answered, then walked across the patio of the hotel to the rooms in the rear.

"Come in, Tomás," Jesús said and Tom stepped in.

"Well, I hope I don't have to be the turd in the punchbowl any more. If there's no Osorio there's no extradition and I'm not going to be in the way. Can I get back on the team?"

Berto smiled and motioned for him to shut the door. "We forgive you, my gringo friend, you're back on the team." He sat down on the bed.

Jesús looked at Tom, nodded in agreement and said, "We need to make some plans. Sit down and keep quiet so we can think this out."

The two lapsed into Spanish and, again, Tom had a real hard time following what was being said. Still they obviously knew what they were doing. And the old question came back: who the hell are these guys, exactly?

––––––––

In the village of Chalcatongo de Las Cuevas, Patricio parked his pickup and turned off the lights. It was almost four in the morning. His son, Juan, went to the door of his grandfather's house and knocked, speaking lowly to identify himself. In the distance, dogs were barking.

The door to the hut opened and a tall man stepped outside. His hair was long and silver, visible even in the dark, smoky air. In his hand he carried an old Winchester lever-action rifle.

"Is everyone safe?" he asked.

"Yes, Father," Patricio answered in his raspy voice. "All but Raul. He was shot, but not badly." He turned and motioned to those getting down from the back of the pickup. "But we need some water to drink. The back roads are deep with dust and this smoke . . ." He waved his hand helplessly at the stinking night.

"Mama!" the silver-headed man called at the house.

"I know, I heard. I am not deaf," answered a woman's voice from inside. "There will be beans and tortillas in half an hour. Go to Chano's for beer, there is only a little drinking water left in the olla."

Patricio reached into his pocket and took out some pesos. "Juan, pay the driver and tell him to go with you for some beer."

"Papa," Patricio said and signaled for Concha to come to him. "This is Concha Osorio Espinoza. She is the one who has returned The Heart of the World."

The tall old man nodded at Concha in recognition. "We have heard a great deal about you, Señora," he said, choosing a term of respect. He offered his hand.

Patricio said, "My father is the man who attends the dead kings."

Concha nodded. "The dead kings of the caves. That is why the town is called Chalcatongo of the Caves. I have heard of the burial place of the Mixtec kings all my life. It is a sacred place."

The old man smiled in the dark, nodding to himself. This woman had a good mind, and an unusual appreciation for her history. "Let us take The Heart to the cave of King Three Earthquake. Dzaui will be happy to know it is being watched over by the spirits of the Mixtec kings.

"Tomorrow, if all goes well, we will take The Heart to its own home beneath the convent in San Miguel. The feria will provide enough excitement and people that we should go unnoticed."

Concha suddenly remembered her brother and the other rescue mission. "Do you know if my brother is safe?" she asked.

"Yes. All went well, no one was hurt. We have heard, though, that there is a great deal of police activity in Tlaxiaco. One of my nieces has a phone business across the street from the municipio and I have talked to her." His voice was concerned.

Concha asked, "They have not bothered our parents, have they?"

194

"No. José told me by phone that the police have only gone to Santa Catarina and San Juan — but no closer. They are stopping all vehicles and searching them but they have not so far descended on San Miguel and torn it apart, as we feared."

"Where are the ones who went to the jail?" Patricio asked.

His father nodded his head up the mountain behind Chalcatongo. "In the Cave of the Wind."

"And all are safe, then?"

"Yes, Socratio was thrown from the back of the truck when they hit a speed bump at the edge of Tlaxiaco. But it was more funny than serious. They are teasing him about it. But yes, by the grace of God, all are safe and back in the arms of their people."

He looked at Concha and even in the dark she could see the venerable old man's smile of approval. "Now let us take The Heart of the World to a safe place, the cave of our ancestor king."

Concha understood immediately that she was being included in what had always been the business of the community patriarchs. She was puzzled by the deference and respect she was being accorded. In her whole life she had never heard of a woman being given the privileges she was now given. Something she did not understand was happening.

When Patricio returned from the pickup with the box, his father sucked his teeth in disapproval.

"You have not left him a hole!"

"What hole?"

"You must always cut a hole in the sack or box when you are moving these things — so they can see." He put the box down on the table and opened its top. "There," he said with satisfaction, "that's better. Sometimes they are very ill-tempered."

"Who?" Concha asked, innocently.

The old man looked displeased, as if she should know better. "Why, the gods of course."

When Juan returned with the beer he joined Patricio, Raul, Concha, Demetrio, and Marcos Albino at a breakfast of tortillas, beans, sun-dried meat, and beer. Helping Raul, they began a slow climb up the mountain behind the hut. Soon they reached hailing distance of a large cave with an enormous roof-fall hiding most of its entrance.

"Socratio!" Patricio called.

"Yes! I see you," came the immediate answer.

"Don't shoot, it is me and the others."

"Pasale. But I will shoot all the same if you have not brought us food. We are starving."

"Food, yes. And beer."

"How is it that there is any beer left? I would think that Juan alone would have taken care of it all!" He stepped out from his sentry point and greeted each of them in turn as they entered the cave. His rough hand grasped even Concha's in the macho worker's thumb-grasp shake, another surprising show of respect.

When they reached the large room behind the roof fall, Juan put down the remaining beer and Raul, whose wound had been dressed, was helped to a corner. The men in the cave fell on the food like lions on a kill. They drank the beer with visible enjoyment, the fire casting their faces in coppery planes and angles as they exchanged excited talk about their successful sorties against the state and the caciques.

Concha went to her brother and knelt in front of him, tracing her fingers lightly over the lumps and cuts which deformed his face. He smiled shyly and said nothing, though his eyes were filled with love and thanks for her touch and her loving tears.

He tore a tortilla in half and put it in his mouth, chewing carefully.

"You are safe," she said simply.

"And you."

"By the grace of God."

"Yes. And our things — they have come too?"

"Yes, of course. Thanks to you, too. We did the easiest part. To you fell the burden." Her eyes searched his for the grief that had been there days before. It was gone.

He smiled at her carefully, his heart reading her own. "I have been absolved."

"By the priest."

"By God and the priest. God first. I fell to my knees over there," he jerked his head at a corner of the room, "and cried out for forgiveness. I was suddenly filled with love. I am at peace. I have prayed since then for your husband and his soul. And each time I have known that it is well with him." He put his hand to her face. "And so, too, with you."

His touch lifted a great weight from her heart, one she had forgotten in all that had passed in her life the last two weeks. The burden of it all was gone. And she had her loving and gentle brother back — best of all.

"Concha."

She turned and saw Patricio and his ancient father beckoning to her.

"Go," her brother said.

"To where?"

"To the Cave of the Dead Kings. I have heard them speaking of you, sister. Your name is spoken with much respect by these important men. Go."

In the light of dawn, Grandfather and Patricio led the way up a footpath that wound its way across the foot of the mountain. The old man led the way in the dim and smoky light while Patricio carried The Heart of the World and Concha followed, her heart pounding.

After a ten-minute climb they reached the foot of a limestone escarpment. They followed the scarp for a hundred meters or so, turned a corner and stood at the mouth of a cave five meters wide and less than two meters high. Stooping slightly, they entered and walked about ten meters into the mountain.

Suddenly, an enormous room opened to them and the old man turned on the Coleman hand lantern he'd brought. He flashed it to a side of the cavern where a flat piece of roof-fall sat, a couple of meters from the wall. The piece of limestone was shaped perfectly for an altar, as if it had been presented exactly for the task at hand.

The old man put the lantern down to light the top of the altar.

Someone had placed a piece of beautiful hand-loomed material on the stone. On each side of the cloth were three large beeswax candles. In front were some small clay bowls.

The anciano put a small bundle tied up in bleached homespun on the altar. Unknotting it, he removed a peach and a plastic sack containing cooked black beans and a tortilla. Two small bottles were opened and Concha recognized the smell of pulque, the fermented juice of the agave plant. The second was the distilled version, aguardiente.

He poured the drinks into two bowls, put the beans in another and added the tortillas. He reached into a jacket pocket and removed a mamey fruit, which he laid beside the peach.

"There," he said, satisfied. "He must be very hungry and thirsty by now. He has traveled a very long way."

Patricio stepped forward, placed the box on the altar, then took out The Heart of the World. Papa lit the candles of pure beeswax.

He put the crystal sculpture, an eagle and a snake, on the piece of cloth. "My brother José speaks your language but I do not," he said.

It seemed to answer in semaphore as the candle light pulsed in the cool currents which moved through the cavern. The rock crystal almost breathed in the apricot-colored light. Concha was transfixed by the effect. She stared at the eagle, his head down and wings slightly spread. The work was delicately done, the artist's hand inspired. But it was at the bottom of the piece that the sculpture lived.

The serpent, struggling to be free of the eagle, had wrapped itself around the eagle's legs. Its head was thrown up in defiance, willing to strike even though the grasp of the bird's talons had almost paralyzed it.

This is my people, she thought. One part of us is predatory, strong. The other is listo, clever. And lethal. One part of us feeds on the other, even as the other part strikes back in defense of its life. And here we are, a thousand years after the artist's life is over, still struggling with our two hearts — one against the other. At that moment, she saw the destiny of the Cloud People, described for all time by the Mixtec artist from long, long ago whose own blood could be mixed in her own. He knew then what she had come to know only in this last few moments — that the time to strike back must come. And come again.

The past two weeks had borne testimony to the continuing saga of her people. They'd recovered the rain god's companion, even at the cost of two great and dangerous journeys and the life of her husband. She and her brother had escaped captivity by the two most powerful elements of Mexican society, the caciques and the police.

It was not over, she knew. The man she had shot, dead or not, must be atoned for. The rescue of her brother, too, would have its price. But that was the story of her people. The eagle would always be upon them but they would always be ready. Listo! They might be gripped and dying, but they were ready to strike back once again. And to be willing was everything.

"Señora."

Concha turned her rapt attention away from the crystal and back to the cavern. Papa and Patricio stood watching her. "Concha, we must get back before it gets much more light. We never know who might be about and all villages have their informers."

She nodded, then turned to look again at the eagle and the snake. The light warmed it, breathing lambence into it. It pulsed. The growing daylight from the entrance to the cavern added shafts of white and pink to the yellow and apricot light of the candles. They danced with one another, twined, flew apart, melded, bloomed. It was the dance of life itself — changing and unchanged.

Chapter 24

It was in the morning's first light, when the sun gives the ocean an initial wash of color. The surf scored the shore with its slow, regular beat, rasping at the sandy edge of the continent like some tireless artisan.

Polly was on the return leg of her morning run on the beach. Her light tread left perfect impressions in the sand just inside the wash of the surf. Pebbles of abraded shell and stone rolled up and down in the wash, being worn to grains small enough to fit the matrix of the gracefully curved beach. As she jogged, she enjoyed the smells reminiscent of a childhood and youth spent next to the ocean.

But her mind was in the mountains. Tom was northwest somewhere, up in the Mixteca Alta while she ran the beaches of the Mixteca Baja. She had learned some of the area lore from a vacationing couple who worked on archaeological digs around Mexico and South America. On a map they had shown her Tlaxiaco, the last town Tom had mentioned. It was nearly sixteen hours by bus from Huatulco.

She'd thought about taking a quick trip north but it simply wasn't possible at the moment. The Mexican partners in the development venture were jockeying for a new position, wanting to restructure the agreement they had worked at so hard in California. She had to be there — otherwise her ex-husband and partner would most likely agree to an accommodation which would put them at an eventual disadvantage. The business strategy of the Mexican partners was to maximize their interests immediately with little or no eye for the long term. So she couldn't leave at the moment, as much as she trusted Christina's strong will to temper the generous natures of Ferdie and her other daughter Maria.

As her bare feet slapped lightly in the thin film of running water, Polly felt a faint sense of uneasiness. The business stuff, in spite of the Mexican partners' need to prove themselves more clever than the Americans, was not at the heart of her discomfort. It was Thomas and his penchant for taking chances, for living on the edge. He was putting himself in some kind of danger and she could feel it.

———

"OK, Tómas, today you get to see my people having a good time." Berto pointed to a poster stuck on the wall of a shop near the covered farmer's market where they had gone for morning coffee.

The coffee had been sweetened in the pot, as per the local custom, so there was no chance of getting it black. But it was good coffee all the same. Berto said it was called Plumada de Oro.

"Look," Berto continued, puffed up like a pouter pigeon. "Rodeo, dancing, horse show, folk dancing, fireworks, and cockfights. You ever been to a cockfight?"

"No, can't say that I have. They're illegal as hell, though the Bascos in Idaho still fight them in the back country."

"There's a lot to it, takes years to appreciate all the fine points."

"Some say it's a cruel sport."

Berto grinned. "Life is cruel, amigo. Especially down here in the mountains. We learn from the cocks — be fast, be brave, have no mercy. Some people think it is cruel only because they are frightened by it. And when the cruelties of life descend upon them, they do not fight because they do not know how. They are defeated by the smallest things, turn up their dainty toes to die a coward's death. But the cocks teach us where the highest planes of determination lead — victory — even in defeat, man."

"So we can flap our wings and crow, even if our asses are truly kicked."

"Yeah, even with our own heart's blood gushing from our chests, amigo."

"I guess it applies. I hope I never have to find out."

"You are right there. You better hope to hell you never have to see just how cruel it can be down here."

"I've seen a bit in my time."

"You mean the war?"

"Yes . . . amigo."

"But there are no helicopters here. Here you don't get to evacuate. You stand or die."

"Sounds more than a little melodramatic to me."

Berto grinned his infectious grin, accepting Tom's thrust with some grace.

"Well, I gotta admit, there's more than a little melodrama down here, too."

Tom stepped back from the wall till he could see the whole of a graffito spray painted on the wall next to the poster. "Fuera al gobierno, fuera al PRI — OOCEZ!" it read.

He translated it to himself: Death to the government, death to PRI. He knew that PRI was the only real political party in the country though there were others which were more fiction than fact.

"What's 'OOCEZ' stand for?" he asked.

Berto made a face, the one that signaled embarrassment. "It's a zapatista organization. Buncha shithead intellectuals and peasants. Schoolteachers mostly, and a few government employees. We know who they are."

"The zapatistas are the same ones who took over in Chiapas, aren't they?" Tom knew who they were, but he couldn't pass up the chance to make Berto squirm a little.

"Yeah, they're pretty much the same people."

"Does that mean that it could really fall to shit here too, like in Chiapas?"

"Well, the poor people are sick and tired of being kicked around and shit on by every crooked bastard with a government job or a little bit of money and influence. Too many assassinations lately. Who knows what could happen here? It's one of the things we're going to be trying to find out when we go to San Miguel."

"Hmmm," Tom said. They were crossing the main plaza and he could see a half dozen men hunched against the morning chill beneath their dirty serapes. They wore cheap straw cowboy hats and their horny, black feet were bare to the cold in worn sandals. He knew that several times over the last hundred years these same people had come down out of the hills in waves, shooting and slashing behind a peasant leader with little more than a great sense of what was right and just. It seemed implausible that things could come to that again. After all, this was a very modern society in many ways. Then again, last night he had felt something in the air. Something ponderous, something poised with a potential for great momentum.

"What time is Jesús going to get up today?" Tom asked, by way of a change of conversation.

Berto shook his head. "These chilongos lay in bed till noon, as often as not."

"Chilongo? What's that?"

"People from the capital — lazy bastards with too much money or too much social status, or both."

"We call them 'rich skids' in Jackson Hole. Too much money and zero ambition."

"Same here. And the pity is, they set the course for everyone else. All the young people can't wait to get a government job so they can go to Mexico City and do nothing but buy new clothes and strut when they come back to their villages. Famosos."

"Hmmm, sounds too familiar."

Berto grinned again. "Some things are the same, no matter where you go."

Tom shrugged, "So, I guess we wait for Jesús before we go to the feria in San Miguel, huh?"

"Yeah, he's got the car. We got no choice, amigo, he's in charge."

"Well, I guess that means I've got time to make a phone call to my son, then."

"Berto's eyebrows raised. "I thought there was no international service."

"Oh, I found a guy here who lets me use his phone."

"Yeah? Who?"

"He's the manager of the sawmill down the street from the hotel."

"Oh? His name Garcia?"

"Yeah, José Something Garcia — José Francisco Garcia."

"Too bad."

"Too bad what?"

"He's in the hospital in Oaxaca City. They were talking about it in the market this morning, the women who cook the food."

An alarm went of down deep in Tom. Again.

"What happened?"

"Some Indians beat him almost to death last night. He lost an eye. The police caught one of them and he said that the villagers had not been paid for their trees, plus the cutters took twice what the ejido had authorized them to take.

"Then they heard that the local cacique, the guy who put the deal together, was selling the lumber to a gringo company with a bad reputation. I guess they are building a thousand condos on the coast and trying to buy up every tree in the mountains. The people say that they should be using cement, that to kill so many trees for seasonal houses is a crime."

Tom, who had just had a house built, knew how wasteful the construction trades were at home. Thousands of board feet were burned at the many construction sites every day, to say nothing of what was burned at the Jackson Hole landfill.

"It sounds like some people from the north have come down with some real wasteful habits."

Berto grimaced. "Same shit, different year."

Tom sighed. "Berto, listen. I know you think that we're a bunch of wasteful people, and we are. I also know that you don't like anything about us, but I'm tired of hearing it, OK? I'm a gringo — so kill me!"

Tom expected the same old wry grin. Instead, Berto raised his hand, pointed a finger directly at Tom's forehead, cocked his thumb and softly said "Pow." Then came the grin.

The effect was genuinely frightening.

———

Pete, Oz and, Olga had a table for themselves in the hotel restaurant. The rest of the group filled all the other chairs and the one waitress looked harried, unused to so many people so early in the day.

"Who are those guys?" Pete asked, as he looked out the restaurant's door onto the plaza. He was watching Tom and Berto.

"I dunno," Oz said, taking a drink from his cup. "I talked to them for about two seconds last night, they didn't give me their autobiographies. Good coffee, I need to see who the grower is — maybe do a little business while I'm here." His gaze followed Pete's out the door. "You can find out about them from Santiago the hotel clerk."

Olga looked at Oz and said, "What time do we leave for San Miguel?"

"The feria is always a bit slow getting started so we won't miss anything if we're there by mid-afternoon. It's about an hour's drive from here and the road is pretty bad between Santa Catarina and San Miguel. But we'll get our first good look at Nindo Tocosho."

Pete turned his attention to the conversation. "What mountain?"

Oz explained. "On its summit is the old observatory of the Mixtec astronomers and astrologers. It has been a place of celestial observation and ritual for at least two thousand years. They have carbon-dated large fire scars, evidence of community ritual, to that date. But smaller pieces of evidence indicate that the site may have been used much longer than that, perhaps another thousand years."

"And still in use," Olga said with a bit of wonder in her voice. "Beautiful."

Pete said, "I take it that this is the place we are going for the solstice stuff."

"Yes," Olga said, "though it is used for other occasions too, like the spring fertility ritual." Olga's eyes seemed to dilate as Pete looked at them. At the same moment he felt her hot hand on his thigh. The woman was insatiable.

Pete broke the gaze and turned his head in time to see Oz taking in the exchange. The look was cool, appraising. Oz dropped his eyes, took a big mouthful of the coffee and held it for a moment before swallowing. Pete saw in that action what a sensualist the man was. Then, in a small moment of clarity his mind went back to the apartment in Berkeley and the pretty, stoned girl he'd seen there. Oz's daughter. Pete looked at the man's face, his delicate grip on the coffee cup, and watched his nostrils flare to inhale all the aroma from the hot, black coffee. And he understood. Even that, Pete marveled. He enjoys his own flesh. No, he added to himself, especially his own flesh.

"Pete." Olga's voice cut into his thoughts.

"Yeah?"

"There's a man here who buys local handwork from the natives. I always go to see what he has available, do you want to come?"

"Sure. Why not?"

She smiled and nodded. "Good. I think you'll like the things you see. They are exquisitely made, and the colors . . ."

"First I want to talk to Santiago, I'll be back in a minute. I want to know who those guys are." Pete got up from the table and walked to the hotel desk.

"Santiago?" Pete asked.

"Mande?"

"The men in rooms 10 and 11?"

"Yes?"

"Who are they?"

"They are policemen."

"The gringo is an American?"

"Yes. An American. I can let you see the hotel register if you like."

"Please."

Santiago reached under the counter and retrieved the register from its place. "There." He placed his finger on an entry and ran it down the next two.

Jesús Maria Bernalillo La Morena
Lista de Correos, Servicio Postal Centro
Oaxaca, Oax

Rigoberto Sandez Sanchez
Lista de Correos, Servicio Postal Centro
Oaxaca, Oax

Thomas Eugene Thompson
Box 2645
Jackson, Wyoming USA

Two general delivery addresses and one PO box. They were cops, alright.

Hmmm, I wonder what this Thompson is working on? Drugs? It had to be. Oaxacan smoke is famous for its quality and the Pacific coast was a notorious off-loading place for South American cocaine destined for the States.

But a Wyoming address? Hell, the only things in Wyoming were sagebrush, rednecks and Yellowstone Park. Pete had made the mistake of hitchhiking through in his seventies hippie period. The whole damn state had been swarming with huge volunteer barbers with hot eyes, beer breath, and bottom lips bulging with Copenhagen snuff tobacco. They'd made his life hell all the way across the unending highway that crossed the southern part of the state.

"Muchas gracias," Pete said, and laid a five-peso bill on the counter.

"And thank you very much, señor."

Pete went back to the restaurant, where the waitress was just serving their table.

"Find out who they are?" Oz asked.

"Fucking cops. I had a feeling that they were."

Oz put a small bite of omelet in his mouth and chewed carefully, his eyes on Pete the whole while. "Cops," he said. "What kind of cops?"

"I don't have the foggiest. Working the dope scene, probably."

"Well, all that has nothing to do with us," said Oz emphatically. "We are here in the interests of something universal, something larger than this," he waved his fork at the window, "poor world and its petty affairs." He poised another bite on his fork and said, "Pedro, this is going to be the experience of your life, my man. And that's a promise."

Chapter 25

In the Chalcatongo cave with its view of the valley and road below, Patricio looked at the people arrayed before him: José's sons, Socratio and Plato, his own sons, Juan and Raul, Cenovio and Demetrio Osorio, Marcos Albino and Concha Osorio. To his mind they were a ragtag — and very lucky — bunch of amateurs who had pulled off two raids on the twin citadels of the Mexican establishment.

But José, poet and politician, saw them as both heroes he could celebrate in verse and song and as brave souls who had done something unheard of in Oaxaca's recent past. Not since the Triqui Combat and Unification Movement had been put down by the state, through the assassination of its leaders; or twenty years earlier when the same had happened to Francisco Medrano, martyred by the soldiery. Or before him, Ruben Jaramillo, who rode with Zapata himself — not since these had Oaxaca seen such indigenous leaders

But José would not only raise the name of Zapata before these people, these few. He would raise the name of Zapata before the whole world, which he knew would beckon the wrath of the state. They might all be consumed by the fires of retribution. But what José saw before him was an opportunity to pull himself out of the shit and into a position of real power. Using, of course, these heroes — and maybe martyrs.

Here, with the successes of these few, José stood in a position of possible negotiation, virtually face-to-face and on equal terms, with the most powerful men of the country. Men played the game as it had been played since the birth of the party in 1929, using the strategy of "compromise and corrupt." If the state saw any stirrings of a fervid populist sentiment, they would first consider force. If they found the movement to be weak, they would destroy the dissidents. If however, they found it strong and organized, they would shower the dissident leaders with money in order to co-opt them by pulling them into the party, and the mainstream. Then the investment could eventually be withdrawn and allocated elsewhere, leaving the original constituency back in the shit. It had worked every time.

Still there was profit to be made. The balance would be delicate. José would have to convince the government, and its military, that this tiny group represented a constituency influential enough to require attention. Once they were publicly acknowledged, the money would follow.

José put his political strategies aside for the moment. First things first.

"Today begins the feria in San Miguel," he said, smiling at the people. "We are obligated to honor our saints, but we are also obligated to share our successes with the people of our pueblo. They will want to see us there.

"Also, The Heart of the World must be taken to his own place and reinstalled so that Dzaui is appeased and the rain clouds can return.

"We must be careful. The police are stationed at three places near San Miguel, stopping all traffic and asking questions. This is not an insurmountable problem; there are hundreds of vehicles going to the feria and we can disperse ourselves among them in order to go undetected.

"We are armed, but we must use force to defend ourselves only if our lives are obviously in jeopardy." He looked directly at the hotheads Demetrio and Marcos, Juan and Raul. "Only," he emphasized, "in . . . defense... of . . . our . . . lives."

———

When Jesús, Berto, and Tom reached the police checkpoint, Jesús pulled over and the three men got out. The lieutenant in charge had been in the commandante's office the night before.

Tom listened while Jesús told the officer that they were going to the feria, ostensibly to take part in the fun. However, they would also be looking for the Osorios as well as for intelligence on the rebels. Jesús claimed to have some solid informants in the village, ones he could count on.

Rebels! Tom thought. This is a little bigger than a jailbreak. And why aren't these people down in the village itself, establishing a strong presence?

He listened carefully, trying hard to get the gist of the conversation. He was surprised to learn that there were two elite army units bivouacked a few miles away, waiting for orders. Also, a man from the governor's office and some local officials had gone into San Miguel to try to establish contact with the rebels.

Apparently, there had been two very well-coordinated raids made at two distant locations, pointing to a strong leadership. This was a worry. It appeared that the political current from the neighboring state of Chiapas was lapping at the mountains of Oaxaca. They did not want it to come crashing into these valleys, given the history of indigenous unrest in this large state. There was a real need for caution.

Hell, this just might be serious, Tom thought. He remembered his days gathering intelligence in the cities of South Vietnam and a dread came over him. This had an altogether too-familiar feel to it.

Once back in the car, he asked Jesús, "What was that about two incidents?"

"Concha Osorio again. She led a raid on the most powerful cacique in the area. Apparently robbed him of a great deal of money, killed one man, and wounded some others."

"You're shitting me."

"Nah," Berto joined in. "Apparently this woman has been trained in your country as an insurrectionist. That's what everyone is saying."

"And trained by the CIA, I suppose?" Tom said sarcastically. The silence that followed gave him his answer.

Fuck me dead! he exclaimed to himself. The paranoia about one small agency of an enormous intelligence bureaucracy was unbelievable. Especially when many who worked elsewhere in the intelligence community considered CIA to be the acronym for Caught In the Act.

"Trained killer, huh?" Tom interjected with a sneer. He could not help himself. The thought was ludicrous.

"Mr. Thompson." Berto turned a very cool eye on Tom. "Six eyewitnesses confirm that this woman took a combat stance and fired one round which hit a running man in the heart, killing him instantly. She led a raid which entered a very secure compound to rob a great deal of money and some priceless art objects, then escaped after also wounding a very important man. And this is a woman. Now, I ask you, does this sound like the work of an untrained amateur?"

Tom had to admit that, on the face of it, it did not. "Doesn't sound like it. You have a point, but to give the CIA credit for her training . . . ."

"And why not the CIA?" Jesús asked, angrily.

"Because you people give them too much credit, that's why!" Tom answered. "Hell, why not blame the FTD?"

That stopped them. They both looked genuinely puzzled.

"The flower delivery company?" Berto asked, slowly.

"No! The Foreign Technology Division."

"Who's that?"

"Another member of the American intelligence community — and one which never gets any credit."

Jesús glanced at Tom again. This time there was more than hostility in his eyes, there was real paranoia. "You sure seem to know a lot about this kind of stuff."

Tom groaned aloud. "I give up. I fucking give up." It was hopeless. "Where's the damn rodeo?" he asked. "I want to be someplace where I know for sure what is going on."

———

At the blockade outside Santa Catarina the two vans of Jaguar Travelers were not prepared for the police's thorough inspection and the lengthy process of examining everyone's passports and visas. They could not recognize it for what it was — a local outbreak of CIA fever.

Once through the checkpoint, the ride into San Miguel was beautiful. The road, though it deteriorated as they came nearer to the town, snaked scenically through groves of giant Tule trees and hung above gorges. In the distance to the east they saw a range of wooded mountains nearing ten thousand feet, home to one of the few remaining virgin oak forests in the state. On the other side was the Nochixtlan valley, stripped by centuries of overpopulation.

But the centerpiece of the range was Nindo Tocoshu, home of the spirits and site of the ancients' celestial observatory. Home, too, of occasional clandestine solstice rituals. And the gathering place of a select few who engaged in one of the most powerful relict rites on the face of the earth — the propitiation of the sun and its wedding with the moon.

"There it is," Oz said, pointing. "That's the place, the summit of that tallest peak." He pointed to a wide spot in the road. "Pull over there," he told the driver.

Once the two groups were gathered he said, "That is the mountain Nindo Tocoshu. If you look carefully you'll see where a road has been built up to the pass adjacent to the peak. From there we have to walk to the site of the observatory. The walk is quite steep in places and takes over an hour; that's why everyone who makes this journey had to prove themselves to be as physically as they are spiritually fit. The way is . . . rigorous."

For some reason, Oz chose the moment to stare at Pete. It was disconcerting, as the gaze of the whole group seemed to also be turned on him.

Then Oz called their attention back to the smoky valley below.

"There you can see the beautiful sixteenth-century Dominican convent perched on that point of land. If you look carefully, you will see the ruin of a chapel across the road. Above that ruin is a large unexcavated pyramid, one of the most important artifacts of the ancient Mixtec kingdom. It is several times the size of the excavated pyramids we visited at Tamazulapan and Huamelulpan."

An appreciative murmur came from the group.

"The fires seem to have died down quite a bit," Oz observed. "But it is still quite smoky. We will stop at the convent when we go by and take a brief walk to the pyramid so you can see it clearly. The place is the center of a great deal of spiritual energy and you will feel it when you are there. There are tales of secret grottos beneath the convent, places where gold and other things are hidden. When the road was built, another rumor goes, the engineer in charge shut the job down for two days when a machine opened a tomb at the foot of the pyramid. The local people say he carried away a lot of gold objects as well as many things made of jade and other semi-precious materials. The story is very likely true."

Olga took the moment to add, "This whole valley is a vortex of great power." And, almost as if intending to underline her observation, the ground beneath their feet gave a lurch and then trembled.

Pete's stomach pitched, and he saw from some of the others' white faces that they'd been affected in the same way. The whole group was from California. They knew the feeling — and the fear.

Except Olga and Oz. Pete caught a look exchanged between the two, even as the earth shuddered. A glance of excitement, even of sexual arousal. Obviously, he thought, these two were into very big things.

———

Concha was sick to her stomach and her bowels felt loose. They were at the police blockade and some cops were nearing the pickup on which she had hitched a ride. A dozen vehicles had been waiting when they arrived. Now it was their turn and her mind was running wild with fear.

A sergeant approached the driver while two soldiers beckoned the passengers to get out.

Concha's mind flashed back to the events in Culiacan, not that many days before. In her mind's eye she saw, even seemed to smell, the officer's severed neck pulsing dark blood onto the hot pavement in powerful squirts. She felt sick at the vivid memory.

"What is your name, señorita?"

Concha's voice seemed to quaver, but she managed to say "Leonora Carmona Velasquez."

"Where are you from?"

"Chilapa de Diaz."

"Oh really? Do you know Guillermina Garcia Martinez? She's from there too!"

Concha looked at the man's eyes. They had a foxy look. He was trying to be clever.

"No. There is no one in Chilapa by that name."

The man waved his hand and said, "Pasale," motioning her through to the other side of the blockade.

Her legs shook as she waited for the others to be questioned. Her stomach flexed and sweat broke out on her face. A soldier looked her way and smiled. She smiled too, and for a moment was deathly afraid that he would mistake the smile for an invitation to make small talk.

But he did not, instead he turned back to the business at hand.

After ten minutes the truck was allowed to reload its passengers and they continued on toward San Miguel. Half a kilometer past the barricade, Concha leaned over the tailgate and vomited into the billowing dust of the road.

Chapter 26

San Miguel Achiutla normally had a population of three thousand people scattered along the foothills below Nindo Tocoshu. During the feria, however, as many as ten thousand people might be pushing through the streets, visiting their home village, people-watching, betting, drinking, dancing to the multiple bands, shouting to one another over the crowd noise, firecrackers, and street music.

Tom loved it — the vibrancy, the sense of real celebration. The Fourth of July celebration in Jackson Hole had the same sort of feel, but this seemed more heartfelt and spontaneous. Men in peasant clothes and masks grabbed well-dressed women and danced them along the street while their normally dead-jealous husbands smiled with approval.

Cacaphonous brass bands seemed to be under every other tree, the sweating men turning music and pulque into something otherworldly — rhythm and harmony at the edge of chaos.

Obviously, this feria was famous and popular. Tom asked Berto about all the cars and pickups with California, Oregon, and Idaho plates and he reminded Tom of the Mixtec colonias that had flowered in those places over the last twenty years. More than half the men in the village spent the bulk of the year in the north, returning in an annual migration for the feria.

"Here we are, Tomás," Berto said as they entered the patio of the elementary school. "San Miguel is famous for its fighting cocks, they've been breeding champions here for over two hundred years."

Three cockpits had been set up and the place was a madhouse. Men were shouting, cursing, drinking, and laughing. And big money, even for the States, was changing hands. Hundred New Peso notes, worth about thirty-five dollars U.S., were being passed between men in half-inch bundles. They were accompanied by grim looks and fervent curses directed at the shamefaced handlers of the defeated or dead cock.

"You stupid bastards!" Tom heard one say, "you just cost me two months of working like a dog in the north! You and that butt-fucking duck you passed off as a fighting rooster!" He pushed his angry way past Tom and Berto to a stand where pieces of cane about four inches tall stood displayed. The angry man picked up three of them in quick succession and drained them into his mouth.

"What's that?" Tom asked.

"Caña. Sugar cane brandy — it'll put your dick in the dirt."

"The man is not happy," Tom observed dryly.

"No, but that man is." Berto pointed his chin at the jubilant recipient of the angry man's wad. He was taking money from another dozen men as well.

"He musta bet the underdog," Tom said.

"Yeah. Some days it's chicken, some days it's feathers. But he'll be damn lucky if he leaves here with any of it."

"Some things are the same, no matter where you go."

"I've heard that before. Maybe because you keep saying it."

"Screw you, Berto." Tom was irritated.

"That's more like it." The old grin.

"To heck with the chickens, where are the bulls?"

"Nah, nah. C'mon, let's go watch the fights. You'll get a kick out of it once you get some idea of what's going on." Berto began to push through the crowd.

As they worked their way toward the cockpits, Tom asked, "Where did Jesús disappear to?"

"He's looking for an old guy, a local who gives him information. After all, we're here on business, right?"

"If you say so."

———

The Jaguar Travellers had gathered beneath a large tree. Oz gathered his group together and spoke.

"OK, this is what's going on." He raised his voice to be heard above all the brass bands and competing PA systems down in the village.

"This is the celebration of the Catholic patron saint's day. Every village has a celebration, small or large. San Miguel, because of its ancient importance as a crafts and religious center, plus the money its men bring back from the North, can afford to have one of the largest ferias in the Mixteca Alta.

214

"Because of the syncretism of Catholicism with some aspects of the ancient animistic religion, you will see a confusing mix here of spiritual practice. What makes San Miguel even more interesting is that it still has a very strong tradition of practicing the pre-Hispanic rites of the Cloud People. Select village elders, who may also hold responsible positions in the ejido and the church, have a mostly secret society, the Society of the Old Souls, which is responsible for maintaining the traditions almost exactly as they were practiced in precolonial times.

"These practices are pagan in the extreme and not acceptable to the Catholic priests, though it is impossible to think they know nothing about them."

Pete, curious, broke in with a question. "What's so objectionable to the priests?"

Again he felt swamped by a unanimous look of disapproval. It was accompanied by a pinch from Olga.

"Sorry," he said.

Oz went on. "We, Olga and myself, have been blessed by the fact that Olga's parents were the first resident anthropologists to come to San Miguel, in the early 1950s when the place was accessible only by horse or mule. They spent years here and became a part of the village's cultural fabric, so to speak. They were the first outsiders ever to be acquainted with the continuum maintained by the Society."

Pete wanted to know what a continuum was, in this context, but he thought he'd keep his mouth shut.

"Now," Oz said, wiping his forehead of smoke-grimed sweat, "go ahead and enjoy yourselves. There is a lot to see and record. Look for the things that represent the mixture of pagan and Catholic belief, like the maskers. Enjoy yourselves. Tomorrow is the solstice and we will be readying ourselves by fasting and washing. This is your chance to enjoy the world and its earthly manifestations before we purify ourselves of its influences and begin the solar cycle again, in league with the infinite."

Pete started to question Olga but she said, "I have to go with Padrino, we are meeting with our spirit guide, the shaman of the Society. Enjoy yourself, I'll find you when we are through." Pete watched as the two of them walked into the surging crowd that filled the dusty, noisy street.

———

Concha's parents' casita was on the north side of San Miguel, in the forest above the barranca. The group of raiders met on the other side of the village two miles away. All of them knew that the elder Osorios would be under some kind of scrutiny, if not by the police then surely by police informants. It was important that the rain god returned to the home grotto from which he had been stolen by Demetrio and Marcos and the rituals be observed as soon as possible. The shaking of the ground that morning and the lingering, pungent smell of recent fire reminded them that the sooner the reinstallment rite took place, the better.

But the sight of the withered milpitas, the little corn and bean fields which supported both the exterior and interior life of the community, had inspired them most. The god must be mollified, the rain must be summoned. The loss of their lives meant nothing when compared to the breaking of the eternal cycle of rain, sun, and corn. It was the matrix on which all of village life was draped.

Concha stood beside the milpita of Señora Anna Laura de la Rosa. Instead of green corn and moist clods as the field should have been, it now consisted of gray stubs of stalk and dry, cracking furrows.

She shaded her eyes and looked at the sky. Cloudless still, even though Dzaui was almost home. The big bowl of sky above her head was a hot, washed out old-denim blue instead of alive with the towering thunderheads which typified a late-June sky in the Mixteca Alta. After all, were they not known as the Cloud People?

She turned her gaze to the west, to the pyramid and its sister Dominican convent. Her eyes followed the contour of the hill to where the little stonework dam lay hidden. Beside the green pool, behind the dam, lay the hidden entrance to the grotto of the god. As a fertile woman, she would never be allowed to enter it. But she knew exactly where it was, and she had heard descriptions of its interior.

It was in that cave that the re-installation would take place this afternoon. The men were inside the house at that moment, putting on their clothes and masks for the trip through the crowded village with the sacred bundle.

She shaded her eyes and turned them up the hill, to the acacia grove where the cold spring normally ran its sweet water onto the cool stones and down the hill to this desiccated milpita. A sense of urgency came over her. She turned her tread up the path to the house. She had to help Tia Anna Laura prepare the men for their sacred work.

———

Tom and Berto stood under a dusty tree. Berto held a frosty beer and Tom a bottle of cold orange Mirinda.

Tom was thinking about what he had just witnessed. The cockfight. Something about it had touched him in a very powerful way. Superficially, he had been surprised by the frenzy of the fighting roosters. The slashing of the little curved steel spurs had sent blood flying into the crowd, spattering faces and clothes with the red spray.

The flapping, the slashing, the triumphant crows of the victors, plus the frantic exertions of the handlers, the screaming of the crowd, and the ebb and flow of cash money had been exciting, adding palpable tension to the feel of antic death. Tiny impulses, but death all the same.

That had been somewhat expected. After all, he wasn't completely ignorant of what made up the sport.

What had moved him down to the core had been the actions of a particular cock — the supposed defeated one whose chest had been pierced by a cruel spur, thin jets of reddest heart's blood shooting onto the hard-packed dirt of the pit. Tom had been close enough to the ring, pulled there by an excited Berto, to see the eye of the dying cock.

It had been golden, hard as amber, fixed on his crowing and wing-flapping triumphant foe. Tom had witnessed a final summoning of every mote of will left to the dying bird. The eye had pulsed and glowed, gathering all that was left, draining the very sheen from its luminescent feathers to aim one last kick — and drove a spur into the femoral artery of the celebrating victor. At the contact, at the piercing, Tom had seen the pupil of the prostrate cock dilate into death and the abyss.

The victor had staggered. His wings drooped, his head cocked in disbelief as he turned an eye down to his jetting ruin. A croak escaped his throat and he fell on his side, dead of shock even as his frantic owner gathered him from the floor of the ring and placed his mouth over the beak in an effort to breathe him back to life.

A great confusion arose in the crowd of sweating, screaming men. Money given up moments before was snatched back. Fists flew and bodies thumped to the ground. Knives flashed but arms were pulled back by strong, cooler hands. Tom had been glad to get out of there. Now, standing in the shade with a cold soda in his hand, he could not relieve his mind of the eye of the downed cock. Alive, hard in a way that transcended life itself. Something long buried in him had been resurrected in that moment. A memory of the will of warriors, the will to never, never give up until you were dead.

Pete decided to brave the crowd alone. He had met everyone in the group by now and, without exception, they had not been his type. Not only that but, taken individually, they made him uneasy. These were not daffy astrological types nor intellectuals who sought wisdom in the teachings of mystics like Gurdjieff — the usual run of bay area religious nuts. They were as spooky as, say, Jim Jones or David Koresh followers — New Age doctrinaire, inflexible creeps. Every one them, except Oz and Olga, left him cold.

Pete stepped into the shade of a small storefront and bought a bottle of cold Sprite. The dusty air in the winding main street had dried his throat.

He leaned in the broad doorway and three men in peasant homespun, wearing palm hats and old wooden masks jumped him. One threw a little bunch of lit firecrackers at his feet. They burst with ear-splitting pops, throwing paper bits and acrid smoke into the shop.

One of the men leaned toward Pete, displaying a small magazine conspiratorially. Pete glanced at it and saw a picture of two men engaged in anal sex.

The clown in the mask gestured at Pete's longish hair and trade bead necklace, his street gear, and pointed to the disgusting picture. It was a very pointed insult to his manhood, and for a moment his temper flared. Then he remembered stories his grandmother had told him of old traditions still practiced in Mexico. These clowns played a very old role, originating in pre-Christian celebrations. These were the levelers, the busters of inflated egos and pomposities. It was a brave bureaucrat or popular figure who ventured to a feria where he was known. The maskers descended on him like African bees, intent on filling his hide full of stingers.

Pete decided instantly to join the fun. He put down the bottle of soda and made a gesture as if to grab the masked man and kiss him. The man stepped back, his fingers flew to his face in a coy pantomime and then shook a hand in an emphatic "no, no." Then another of the three clowns turned, dropped his pants and spread the cheeks of his ass, exposing his stained anus.

The other onlookers in the shop gasped and made exclamations. The women averted their eyes. The men, Pete included, roared in amusement at the daring of the clown.

The three maskers then waved good-bye and, miming romantic farewells at Pete, disappeared into the crowd.

Grinning, Pete paid for his drink and stepped down to join the river of flesh and noise.

———

Juan, Raul, and Plato joined Socratio in the street, where he stood with the sacred bundle slung over his shoulder. The wooden masks were hot, almost suffocating with the dust and late June heat, to say nothing of the ambient smoke. A small fire had flared on a flank of Nindo Tocoshu and the smoke was drifting down on the village.

"Did you see that gringo when I shoved the picture in his face?!" Raul said.

"Hah! It was great!" Juan said. "What did he do when I showed him my asshole?"

"He was pretty good about it, just grinned. But you should have seen the women! H-i-i-j-o, hombre, they almost fainted. It was funny!"

"Let's get down to the river. This mask is suffocating me." Juan lit a string of firecrackers and threw it behind an old man lurching drunkenly through the crowd. At the beginning of the sharp little explosions, he picked up his heels and danced crazily, knocking about well-dressed men and women. For a moment they were annoyed but once they got a good look at the dancing old geezer with the silver stubble and dirty sombrero, they pointed and roared. "Viva Mexico!" someone hollered.

The four men in the masks jigged and made obscene gestures, receiving in-kind retorts with even more depraved mimicry. Juan joined his index fingers and thumbs together in a triangle, flexing them into a clear representation of a large vagina to insult a big, elegant woman dressed in gold and silk.

She shrieked in outrage and made a grab for Juan, her face contorted in rage. Her husband collapsed against a nearby wall, tears of laughter coursing down his face.

———

Pete found an eddy in the river of bodies and stepped out into a small side plaza with a large wooden corral set up in it. People crowded around its circumference. Pete edged his way through the crowd and saw that a man was getting ready to ride a bull.

The animal stood braced at the far side of the round enclosure. Two men held its head by the horns, the face and eyes covered tightly with a large piece of cloth. Another man held its tail. A rope circled the animal just behind its front legs, wound tightly in a double strand where the mounted man was forced his hands between the tight rope and the angry, quivering bull.

At a nod from the rider, the men shook the rag loose and freed the animal's tail.

Pete had seen American rodeos, so this was somewhat familiar while quite different in detail.

But the result was universal and, as usual, the bull won. The intense, stocky little Indian rider made it halfway across the arena, then found himself sticking out at a quickly widening angle and an increasingly sickening speed, as the merciless laws of physics overwhelmed his strength and skill.

The sight of the man trying to loose his hands from under the tightly twisted rope sent a pulse of empathy through Pete. At the moment of impact, empathy turned to real concern as the rider met the ground with a horrible *thump!* A jet of dirt and dried animal shit flew into the air.

"Wow!" Pete heard a gringo voice at his side exclaim.

He turned his head and recognized the guy from the plaza the day before. The Wyoming cop.

"That looked like it hurt," Pete said to the guy.

The tall, stocky man with the bright blue eyes grinned and shook his head. "It had to hurt. There's a lotta rocks out there — but I tried to tell him.

"You know the guy?"

"Yeah, he's a kind of a partner of mine."

Pete looked again. The rider was being helped from the arena, his hair hanging down onto his grimacing face. It was the man that Thompson had been walking with in the plaza. Another cop, a Mexican.

"Rodeo riders, huh?"

"Not me anymore. And not him anymore either."

"Not the same as Wyoming, is it?" Pete said, and was amused at Thompson's swift and wary reaction to his comment.

He stared at Pete, his thumb hooked under the small day pack slung over his shoulder, his eyes a hard, icy blue.

"Relax," Pete said, "I just did a little detective work back in the hotel in Tlaxiaco. I'm with the police department in Berkeley, California, and I'm working something undercover. Don't blow it for me."

Thompson's eyes warmed only a fraction. Obviously he didn't like being caught out. Pete would not have liked being put in the same situation, either. Not one bit. It couldn't help but make a man feel exposed, vulnerable — and that was the last thing any cop liked to feel.

As Tom stared at Pete, his first impression was negative. The guy's hair was too long, the beads around his neck too passé. It reminded him of a time that wouldn't pass into deserved oblivion — too many people worked too hard to keep the sixties alive for his taste. Tom was intent on staying in today and people stuck in the past made him wary. Once Pete explained his police beat, the Berkeley street scene, Tom relaxed. The guy had credentials and once they had begun to confide in one another some amazing things came to light.

Tom mentioned Nathaniel Ward's name in connection with stolen antiquities and Pete looked surprised. That same name had come up in Pete's investigation of a new hallucinogen that had hit the streets of the Bay Area recently. Comparing notes, they had made some connections that would help untangle Ward's affairs. When Tom told Pete that they had Ward's computer files, his eyes lit up like lanterns. It sounded like exactly what he needed to make his case against the guys who were synthesizing and growing the 'shrooms. Ward's files might even include info on the drug's distribution. Perfect.

Tom was glad for the company. He had felt more and more disconcerted by his relationship with Berto, most especially now that Jesús was in charge of things. He confided in Villareal the whole history of his investigation.

———

Tom and Pete found Berto at the clinic, where a doctor was casting his wrist. He looked pale, even under the dark hue of his skin. Pete, in perfect Spanish, inquired about Berto and was told he had also suffered a light concussion and would be staying the night for observation.

"He's lucky to get in early," the medico said. "By ten o'clock tonight we will be putting them on colchinetas out on the patio."

Tom and Pete retreated to the patio of the clinic. "So you don't know who these guys really are, huh?" asked Villareal.

"No. Sheriff Harlan said the Mexican Attorney General's office had denied any association, but that doesn't mean a whole lot. I've worked with U.S. intel groups and disavowal can be a routine way of keeping things compartmentalized and secret. I do think that they are cops, their training shows. But there's something not kosher with them, and that's a fact."

Pete asked, "Why didn't you hop a bus out of here when you knew Cenovio Osorio had been broken out?"

Tom looked abashed. "I've thought about that and, you know, I think that it's just the adrenaline. I'm afraid I might be working on a midlife crisis or something."

Pete smiled. "Next thing you know it'll be a red sports car and young, dumb pussy."

"Oh, I hope not. I just barely got my shit together, the little bit that shows."

Pete looked at Tom. "You want some real good advice?"

"Sure. Go."

"Get the hell out of here. You're in way over your head."

Tom nodded. "You're right. This is a fool's game."

Pete flipped his thumb at the clinic. "Your relationship with that guy seems to be the only thing that is keeping your ass from being kicked out of the country. Or worse. You're a real problem for these guys, especially if they're dirty."

"True. Things don't get done the same way down here. You should have seen Osorio's face and hands. They stomped him good, getting a confession."

Pete shrugged. "Hell, it happens every day in L.A., Chicago, Houston or Miami. Name a city and I'll get you the names of at least two guys whose specialty is confessions."

"Doesn't happen in Wyoming."

"Maybe I'm just a cynic, but I'll bet you dollars to doughnuts that you've got the same percentage of sick cops up there as in any other place."

Tom remembered a name. Ben Pobeda. Uh huh. The Jackson P.D. had one for sure. And he had his reservations about what one or two of the sheriff's deputies might do in a given situation.

Pete stood. "I'd like to spend some more time shooting the shit with you, but I've got to go find the people I'm traveling with. It's been a pleasure talking to someone who speaks the same language."

"Mind if I tag along while I look for Jesús? I need to tell him what happened with Berto and get a ride back to town so I can pack up and get out of here. It'll be a relief, to be honest with you."

"Sure, c'mon. Maybe I'll get a chance to introduce you to Olga and Oz."

"They sound like a pair."

"They're different, all right. Only in California."

The two gringos walked up the street from the clinic, moving toward the noisy bustle of the village. They passed a woman and two men walking the other way, toward the river, just pulling masks off their faces.

Tom looked a second time at the pretty Indian woman and the men. The men were hard. Their eyes recognized Tom's interest and flashed resentment. One, with a pendulous bottom lip, looked positively evil. Tom averted his eyes, warned by the man's wary, aggressive gaze.

"Friends of yours?" Pete asked as they continued to walk.

"I am glad to say that I have never seen them before in my life."

"Cute," Pete described the woman.

"And ugly as homemade sin," Tom replied, describing the men.

"So what is this Bernalillo up to?" asked Villareal.

"He's supposed to be on an intelligence run. The police want to know what is going on here. The jailbreak and a raid on the biggest godfather in the area have both been connected to San Miguel, which is supposed to be brimful of Zapatista sympathizers. They're afraid that the problem in Chiapas might give the Indians in Oaxaca some big ideas. They're scared, I think, that their record with the Indians in Oaxaca might be shoved into the international spotlight."

"Speaking of which, there is a TV camera crew in town, and they're not taking pictures of the festival."

"You saw them?"

"Yeah. They parked their Nissan 4X4 next to our vans. I saw their equipment and they had a hand-lettered sign in the window that said PRENSA."

"This place is probably news of some kind, then."

"Don't worry, it will be news. Whether there's a story is another thing altogether," Pete observed with an ironic tone.

Tom liked the guy, he liked the way he saw things. Suddenly Tom stopped in his tracks. He paused and then spun around.

"What?" Pete asked.

"That woman!"

"What woman?"

"The Indian that you said was cute."

"What about her?"

"It was Ward's wife!"

———

José Gorostiza was a busy man. He was a nervous man. He had been feeding Jesús Bernalillo disinformation when Padrino, the California adept, showed up with La Leonessa. José tried to balance his roles in his mind: poet, shaman, church functionary, ejido elder, police informant, political plotter. Now, he had an appointment with the press. He was getting too old for this, he was going to have to cut back.

He was a man in a hurry as he shuffled Jesús out the door, then set the hour for the annual pilgrimage to the ancient Mixtec astronomical observatory with Oz and Olga.

"The moon, a waning crescent, will rise about one in the morning," he said to them. "The rite will begin about two and the shedding of the blood will be precisely at two. The moon will be able to participate because she will be ten degrees above the horizon at that hour.

"As you know, the climb up the mountain takes a bit more than an hour and a half for your people. So, please, have them ready to leave the road's end by midnight. I will be waiting with the other members of the Society at the summit. We will bring all the things needed except that which is your responsibility."

"Yes, of course. We are aware of our responsibility. It is a large one," Olga said. "After the fiesta we will return to Tlaxiaco to sleep, fast and prepare ourselves. We will leave the hotel at ten, drive to the road's end, and climb the mountain." She paused, wanting reassurance. "And the Society will be prepared for any event — this one could prove difficult."

"Please do not worry," José said, and pointed to Olga's gold Rolex. "What time is it?" he asked, pointedly.

She glanced at the watch and said, "Almost five."

José stood from his chair. "Ah, I must be going. I have people to meet." In fact, he had said that he would meet the others at the grotto at seven o'clock, to lead the last of a long re-installment rite. In the meantime, he was supposed to be at a press conference in the Tule grove, and he was late.

"Yes," Oz said, and touched the fingertips of both hands together in a respectful gesture which meant nothing to the Mexican shaman. "Hasta mañana, until tomorrow."

"Until tomorrow." José waited until the two gringos were gone. Then he went to the bed, reached under the mattress and took out a homemade ski mask. He put it on and looked in the mirror. Good. After Chiapas, it was what the world expected from a mountain peasant demanding the rights of his people.

He took off the mask and put it in his bolsa, the purse-like bag carried by most in rural Mexico. I hope the people from Time magazine make it, he said to himself.

———

Concha, Demetrio, and Marcos were frightened. They had seen the two gringos stop and one pointed in their direction.

"Who are they?" Marcos asked.

"Gringos, that's all I know," said Demetrio.

"They're talking about us," Marcos said, watching the gesticulating man.

Concha said, "Cenovio said that the American from Wyoming was tall and wore a brown and gold ball cap. That describes the one on the left."

"Then they are both police, from the North." Demetrio's mouth turned down in a grimace of hate. "They are here for our brother. Bastards!"

"There they go," Marcos observed, as Tom and Pete turned to enter the village from the clinic's street.

"Jesús Bernalillo is here, too," Demetrio said.

"You saw him?" Concha asked, concern mounting in her voice.

"No. But I heard that he was in the village, strutting about in his gringo clothes and his gold chains, the chilongo prick."

"He has come back for more things. He wants even more from our village." Marcos's voice was fearful. "Because of him I will carry the marks of disgrace until the day I die." The whipping from months before had left both visible and invisible scars.

"We will deal with him later," Demetrio said, his voice thick with hate. "Right now we must go to the grotto. The others will be there."

They walked to the dry, gravel filled river channel, which fed out of the mouth of the barranca. Then they followed it to the junction with the river below the dam. They turned upstream and followed it to the toe of the limestone mountain on which sat the convent and the pyramid.

Making sure they were not being watched, they pushed their way into the thick brush below the vertical wall of limestone. Once inside the growth they found the path which had been cleared. Concha sent the two men ahead so she could shed the men's clothes she was wearing and prepare herself.

Concha's heart was beating rapidly as she removed the hat, mask, and shirt and donned a blouse and the huipil she had carried in a sack from the village. It identified her as a Mixtec woman and a resident of the village of San Miguel.

She undid her braid, then brushed and rebraided her hair with ribbon as José had instructed her. She took out a bottle of water and washed her face, hands, and feet, then put the bottle back in the sack for the men to wash themselves with.

Patricio waited at the mouth of the grotto. He had been dead set against the election of Concha to the Society at first, but his doubts had slowly gone away over the last couple of days. She had the body of a woman, that was clear for all to see. But her mind had spiritual strengths that were apparent to all who could get past their prejudices.

In Tlaxiaco there was a bath still in use called the Baño de Cacica Maria. It was named to honor the last cacica known in the area — more than three hundred years ago. Now, again, a woman with a will as strong, and a mind as acute as any man's, had appeared. Patricio was convinced it was a good sign. Everything else was turning on its head, why not the traditional roles given to members of the village? Besides, at the heart of the culture was the very pragmatic understanding that one should serve according to one's genuine abilities, not just according to one's nominal place in things.

He stood aside as the three dipped one knee to the ground in respect and entered the holy place. It was a practice integrated from the Catholic customs they'd learned as children.

The altar had been prepared. One hundred and thirteen hand-dipped candles threw golden light on the wooden santo, a representation of Saint Michael carved in the sixteenth century by a local artist and recently restored. The new paint and gilt glowed warmly, making it seem vibrant, almost alive, to their minds.

On the other side of the altar, a flat rock had been set in mortar, long ago. It was now decorated with many flowers of every imaginable color arranged around a stone head — an image of Dzaui. It was from this pedestal that The Heart of the World had been taken. The two guilty ones now knelt shirtless before the altar, their lips moving in real penitence. The stripes on Marcos's back were still purple.

Juan brought the sack with the hole in it and put it on the altar. He looked up at the benevolent santo and crossed himself three times, left to right, right to left and back again. Then he lifted the crystal and set it carefully in its old place, next to the rough hewn image of Dzaui.

There was a thump and a giddy lurch in the basement of the mountains. Dust and bat droppings fell from the roof of the grotto. Murmurs of fear escaped the mouths of all present and they steadied themselves.

Patricio advanced to where Demetrio and Marcos knelt. He gripped the rawhide quirt, which was the symbol of the authority of the elders. The volume of Demetrio and Marcos's supplications rose in anticipation as he slashed each one four times. He was careful to avoid the cicatrices on Marcos' back, moving the blow to the man's buttocks. At each of the strokes, the men shouted "Perdoname Señor!" And it was over. Dzaui had been mollified for their acts.

The two kneeling men rose and put on their shirts. Demetrio pulled his shoulders forward to try to relieve the burning stripes on his back and Marcos rubbed his buttocks. Patricio had spared nothing in the strokes. But it was a small price to pay. Their banishment from the village had been much more painful.

Two acolytes, one an old man and the other a younger man learning the rites, began to light the candles and set the altar with vessels for the food and drink on which Dzaui would feast during the next 48 hours. The rites would be finished with the shedding of blood on Nindo Tocoshu. All that was left for this day was the long chanting of the vocal ritual. That would be done by José, the only one who knew the complete text.

Chapter 27

It was dark. Tom, Pete, and Jesús had been talking for an hour. Bernalillo showed great interest in their description of Ward's wife and her companions. He wanted a detailed rendition of their appearance and the direction they had been heading. He kept leaving the table, then coming back for more particulars. Apparently he was consulting an informant in the village.

Bernalillo and Pete drank a few beers and sampled the wares of the pulque vendors who were dipping their "Tears of Christ" from plastic buckets with an incised gourd cup which everyone used in common.

Tom settled for Mirinda and Squirt, his thirst heightened in the presence of the drinking men. He had a very strong impulse to taste the pulque — just a taste, out of curiosity. But the second he raised the mild liquor to his lips a voice in his head echoed a cavernous **Don't!** at the last possible moment. He gave the gourd cup back to the vendor.

It shook him. After six years of richly rewarding sobriety, he had come within half an inch of a swift slide into his own customized hell. It was depressing.

He turned his eyes to the fireworks bursting thunderously overhead, casting the boisterous, laughing faces in various brilliant hues as the light flashed and the gunpowder roared. And he had a little celebration for himself. He said 'Thank you, God' ten times silently and to himself. Then he turned to watch the other two men descend into a part of their personalities best left dormant in him.

Pete had asked why he'd handed the cup back to the vendor and he'd answered, simply, "I quit drinking and my life got better." The remark amused the other two, but Tom felt deeply the life-changing power in that simple statement.

Tom joined the conversation only occasionally. He saw that both Pete and Jesús talked too much, revealing things they would have been silent about when sober. Pete was on assignment, in pursuit of law enforcement business. But one of his drunken revelations was that he had eaten a mushroom that was being trafficked illegally in California. He scoffed at the gulls in his group, at their being fleeced by Oz and Olga. He said their names as though he was announcing a vaudeville act. However when the good-looking blonde showed up to claim him, Pete went with her gladly enough. He said he'd see Tom and Jesús later, but Tom suspected not. The guy could not always be depended on to do what he promised, that was clear enough.

Jesús, too, said more than he meant to. He pointed out villagers, prominent and not, telling stories that only someone who had spent a lot of time trafficking with them could know. But trafficking in what? At the rate Bernalillo was putting them down, Tom waited for the man to reveal his hand. He herded two pretty muchachas to their table and asked for a bottle of the local mescal. Tom observed that it wouldn't be long before Jesús' tongue started wagging if he dipped into that stuff.

One of the girls, the one with the intoxicating floral perfume, was named Maria Cristalina. And, miracle of miracles, she was making eyes at Tom. He was flattered but had to tell her that he had a novia, that he was engaged. She smiled seductively, dragged her long fingernails lightly over the fabric of his Wranglers and galvanized an instant response which took him by surprise.

"I think I'd better go see how our friend, Berto, is doing," he said and stood up from the table.

"Well hurry back, amigo, I can't handle all this alone," said Jesús. He wagged his beaming, drunken face in a circle which took in the two pretty women with raven hair and crimson lips.

Ohhh, Tom thought, to be younger and dumber — hot, slippery mouths and hot, slippery bodies were what made him go. He had to get the hell out of this place! To say nothing of finding a place to dump all the soda he'd been putting down.

The crowd, as he pushed through it, verged on madness. Mouths were thrown open to the dark sky, shouting obscenities, exclaiming oaths of drunken happiness or penance. Eyes flashed, hands touched, arms clasped in friendship. A dozen men took Tom's hand as he pushed through the crowd, saying "America good" or some like sentiment. Or, "I am work Kentucky. Winn Dixie store. Ver' good, my fren'."

When he arrived at the clinic it was as the doc had predicted. The patio was half covered with injured or sick people and two nurses were busy monitoring these victims of fun. It was obvious that Berto's chimes had been rung real good, so Tom spent only a minute or two in the room commiserating with him.

"I'll check in before we leave for Tlaxiaco," he promised. Then he remembered the treacherous mountain road they'd driven in on. He had to get Jesús started back right now, and try to talk him out of the keys. Maybe he could suggest moving the party to Tlaxiaco. He knew Jesús was going to want to be wherever the pretty girl he'd been pawing was. Man, some people never did learn to quit following their dick around. He hitched the day pack around and looked at his watch. Not even ten-thirty yet.

On the other side of the village, Pete and Olga found their group eating at the open-air stands near the market. They were all sitting around the tables like good little girls and boys, Pete mocked to himself.

"You need some food," Olga said in a disgusted little way. She didn't drink at all, Pete remembered.

"Sure," he said and sat down in the chair she indicated.

———

In the hills above San Miguel, a mile away, José, Patricio, Juan, and Raul were holding the second press conference of the day. The Televisa crew from Mexico City had wanted a larger cast so, after the ritual in the grotto, José had gathered some supernumeraries around a table set up in a picturesque grove of trees.

Sweating under the hoods and bandanna masks, they blinked as José fulminated against the government's treatment of the indigenous mountain people. He spoke of the poor health services and schools. He spoke of the horrible conditions of the local roads and the lack of bus service of any kind. And he spoke of the revolution of 1910, of the ruling party's betrayal of principles which had inspired that bloody event. And, finally, he spoke of Emiliano Zapata and his love and understanding of the needs of the little people.

This was what the TV folks had come for. The cameraman panned to José and pulled focus on the man's masked face, zeroing in on the glittering eyes which reflected the bright lighting.

Finally, after a full minute of sound bites, any one of which would give a news director the hots, José smoothed a sheaf of papers and began to catalog the movement's demands.

The crew's director motioned her second camera to a profile angle. The man from Time and the woman from Reuters scribbled furiously.

Juan, who was listening to the fireworks in the village below and thinking of the fun he was missing, dropped his hand below the range of the cameras and gave the hand sign for "Fuck this." His brother, Raul, snorted back a laugh and threw out his fist in a revolutionary salute, punctuating perfectly José's demands. The journalists recorded it faithfully. On TV the next morning it would be this image that prompted the grim president of the country to turn to his most trusted cabinet members and say, "Get your asses down there. Fix the road, send some more doctors, buy a couple of busses, build a new market, double the electric service."

His eyes flashed, hard as obsidian in their anger. "Fix it all. And find that one," he pointed at the television, "whoever he is. Make him rich, buy him a house. Buy him a whorehouse, I don't care. I want his him back in front of the cameras as soon as possible with his bare face hanging out, praising the party."

One of the people in the room, a Norteño, said, casually, "It would be a hell of a lot cheaper to kill him."

The president turned to him and hissed, "One: This is not the North, this is the South. Two: These images are being seen by half the people in the world. Three: You don't know shit."

The man paled. He was undone. His career for the next six years, at best, would be to sit in a back country Conasupo office, checking the count of grain sacks and supervising slogan-painting crews for the PRI.

———

In San Miguel, Tom pushed through the crowd again, making his way back to the tavern where he'd left Jesús. Pete was also approaching the same place.

Tom arrived first. Jesús was gone, the table where they'd been sitting now occupied by other people.

"Shit," he muttered to himself. "Where did he go?" He glanced around then, on impulse, walked to the side of the patio and looked out into the relative darkness there. Jesús was leaning on a big tree with one hand and holding an unhappy muchacha by the wrist with the other.

Drunken dick head, Tom thought. He also thought he'd better give the girl a hand; it looked like she needed it. He started toward the couple at the edge of the noisy night.

At that same moment, Pete entered the bar and saw Tom step out into the dark. He started across the room to catch Tom and tell him he could go back to Tlaxiaco with the tour group. He could see that Jesús would not be interested in leaving.

Tom was at the rear of the building when a man in peasant's clothes stepped from behind the tree and blew Jesús' brains out into the night. The sound of the girl's scream was drowned out by a burst of fireworks overhead. She put her hands to her head and ran.

Tom's trained instinct was to go for his pistol, but it was buried in the bottom of the day pack he had slung over his shoulder.

The shooter slipped the gun's hammer down with a click, then began to walk quickly to the corner of the building. Tom stood still, rooted by the insane thought that he would go unnoticed in the dark.

But the man's hand came up like a striking snake. His eyes never left Tom's. It was the man who'd been with Concha that afternoon, the one with the drooping lip and hostile eyes. Now those eyes were murderous. The big .45 came up, Tom heard the hammer thumbed back. Tom could see the shooter's cold black eyes clearly and knew that he had decided to pull the trigger.

Tom's last sensation before the flash and the blackness was the knowledge that something hot was flooding his legs. His bladder had released in fear. He was pissing his pants.

Pete saw it from the rear door of the tavern: Jesús pawing the girl, the gunman step from behind the tree, the horrible distortion of Bernalillo's head as the bullet swept through it, the body falling behind a stack of pop bottle crates, leaving the white Reeboks exposed.

He saw Tom and the shooter facing one another and then another man slapping Tom across the back of the head with a sap of some kind. The blow collapsed Tom's legs as if he had been shot too.

Pete stepped into the shadow and watched as the two men dragged Tom into the night. The slack body made no sound as it disappeared. Then Pete heard a man hiss, "Get the backpack, Marcos!"

The man who had sapped Tom sneaked quickly back to grab the pack. Then, all Pete could see was Jesús' immaculate white running shoes winking as they reflected the fireworks crackling overhead.

Chapter 28

Tom woke in a panic. Something was crawling under his shirt, making its scuttling way through his chest hair. In the foggy outer banks of his mind, he was trying desperately to rid himself of the many-legged thing that tickled his flesh as it ran in zig-zags down to his stomach, over to his ribs and back.

"U-h-h-h-h." His traumatized brain could make his mouth form nothing more intelligible than a long, tormented grunt. He opened his eyes on a wall made of wattle and daub, the horizontal matrix of bare sticks visible through the adobe mud. A rude cupboard hung on another wall. At his feet there was a rubber tub half full of water against another wall.

"U-h-h-h-h!" He moaned, tears now running down his anguished face. He was terribly, terribly afraid. And he hated nothing more than his own fear. Nothing.

Tom swung his legs and kicked the cupboard. It fell from the crude wall with a crash, scattering its contents.

The noise helped clear his head. He realized now that his arms were bound tightly to his sides, secured together with something that ran across his back to just above his elbows. He was a captive. He screamed.

A moment later, an Indian woman with long gray braids pushed open the flimsy door. She carried a wicked-looking knife in one hand.

Tom's mind focused. "Insecto! Insecto grande en mi camisa!" he said, clenching his jaws.

The old woman hesitated for a moment, then opened Tom's shirt. She chased the insect down, cupped it in her hand, dropped it to the floor, and ground it to a paste with her bare heel. The damn thing was the size of a Bic lighter.

"Cucaracha," she said. Cockroach.

Goose flesh covered his body. Ugh!

She pulled the door shut. "Agustino!" she shouted. Tom heard the pad of her bare feet as she moved away.

He looked around. He was in a little bath house, the objects spilled from the cupboard were all toiletries of one kind or another. His eyes focused on a plastic bottle of Pert Plus which moved him to a strange laugh. The object was so . . . American it verged on the hallucinogenic, given the situation and the setting. So close and yet so far. He'd felt for days that he was a stranger in a strange land and he'd not been smart enough to take the myriad hints that he should pack his shit and git. And now this.

He moved his feet to where he could see them.

"I'll be damned," he muttered. He was wearing some old leg irons, relics of the nineteenth century. He'd seen equivalents at the old prison museum in Laramie. For some reason, it amused him. He chuckled softly and said, "Honestly, I'll never smile again."

The surreal juxtaposition of the familiar shampoo and the antique leg irons warmed a circuit in the part of his brain where irony was processed. At that moment, he heard soft footsteps hurrying toward the bath house.

The door opened and a small man peeked in. His face was wrinkled, the face of one who worked in the sun. A few white hairs shone among his wispy chin whiskers. His eyes also shone, in a gentle way that highlighted the humorous upward trend of his broken smile.

"Buenos dias," he said gently.

"And a good day to you too, amigo. Where are my pants? And shorts?" He willed his brain to work in Spanish. "Pantalones? Cortes?" He'd just realized he was naked from the waist down.

"Ahh, si. Yo lavó, secandolos." He'd washed them and they were drying.

Tom remembered the hot rush of urine down his thighs as the killer's gaze tightened a grip on the trigger.

"Tienes hambre?" The man asked, inquiring if Tom was hungry.

"No. A tengo sed," Tom answered. He was thirsty as hell, though.

"Momentito," he said, pinching his thumb and index finger together to indicate a moment of time.

In a couple of minutes he was back with a gourd full of water. He helped Tom sit and then held the gourd to Tom's lips. The water was cold and sweet. A pulse of emotion ran through him. The water was sweet as the untreated well water that came from his tap in Wyoming. For a moment he was afraid he might cry.

"Ahhh, gracias."

"Para servirle." The man was excruciatingly polite.

"Como te llamas?"

"Agustino."

"Bueno, Agustino." Tom wagged his head at the walls of the hut. "Es baño?" asking if it was a bath house.

"Si, es baño."

"Yo quiero bañarse."

"Ah, si." the little man pinched his fingers together again and left, pulling the flimsy door shut behind himself.

Minutes later he returned with Tom's pants and the old woman. In her hand she was carrying the knife, a butcher knife, sharpened over time to a wicked curve. The old woman had been the author of its form and knew how to use it, no doubt about it.

Agustino took a leather thong from around his neck and knelt at Tom's feet. There was a key on the thong. With a warning glance at Tom, and a nod at the woman, he inserted the antique key into the antique lock of one leg iron.

He struggled, twisting at the key, fighting the lock. Muttering, he tried the other lock. After a minute of twisting the key and squeezing the latch, the cuff released.

"Mohoso — oxidado," he said, as if Tom hadn't guessed the problem was rust.

"Son antigüedades," Tom observed, dryly. Antiques.

The little man smiled. "Si, si. Antiguo, muchos años tengan." He stood. Then he took the knife from the woman and stood as she brought a bucket of soapy water in from outside.

Humiliated, Tom realized that he was going to get his bath, but he wasn't going to be the one to give it.

"No, no," he tried to protest, but one moment's stare from the old woman told him he was going to get a bath whether he liked it or not. Kinda like being a kid again. Or in a VA hospital.

She bathed him thoroughly from the waist down. And it felt damn good. Then Agustino put Tom's laundered shorts and pants on him, re-cuffed the free leg and untied Tom's arms. He remembered one of his mother's maxims when he was a kid: change your shorts every day, you never know who will see them. He almost giggled as a ludicrous thought intruded — 'Sorry, Ma, they grabbed my pants and washed my dick but I was feeling guilty and ashamed the whole while. Promise.'

Grandma stripped Tom's shirt and finished the bath. Then they re-secured his arms. They'd bound him with a nylon strap and clamp fasteners. At least they wouldn't tighten and cut off the circulation to his arms, he thought.

Tom thought better of asking after his boots. But he was clean. Refreshed, Tom said, "Gracias a ustedes."

Agustino smiled. Grandma whetted the wicked-looking knife against the wood of the rickety door and pulled it shut. Tom was having a hard time liking her.

———

Not being able to find Oz and Olga, and not wanting to have to explain, Pete Villareal had taken a taxi back to Tlaxiaco. He phoned the Teton County sheriff's office as soon as he could find a phone. They had given him Sheriff Harlan's home phone number when he explained what had happened to Tom. Sam told Pete there were two men from the Mexican Attorney General's office in Tlaxiaco at the moment, sent to look out for Tom. He also said he was chartering a plane to Salt Lake City where he would make a commercial connection to Mexico as soon as he could. Pete gave him directions on how to get to Tlaxiaco and the hotel. It looked like Sam could be there by the next evening.

Pete then went to the police station and reported the murder of Jesús Bernalillo and the kidnapping of an American law enforcement officer. The effect was to electrify the command center which had been set up in the gym. The Zapatistas, it seemed, had upped the ante.

The comandante arrived, his face pale and tense. His first phone call was to the governor. The governor called the President of the Republic and the President called his Minister of the Interior, the man whose responsibilities included the maintenance of order in Mexico and responsible for more deaths than the bubonic plague. After that conversation, the minister phoned the negotiation team in Tlaxiaco.

"Yes sir, Mr. Minister?" the ranking officer said, expectantly.

"The President has given his word on the new road and the other demands. Find out why the escalation — and the price for the return of the American. The economic future of our country hangs in a delicate balance here."

The negotiator felt the weight. It was enormous. "What about the Mexican officer, Bernalillo?"

"He was involved in dishonest things, he was corrupt."

"Yes sir," the man said quietly. But he was alarmed. If death was now the price for being corrupt, two thirds of the government employees would be dead in a week. If a man couldn't steal, why go into public life at all?

Chapter 29

Sheriff Harlan phoned Polly's office in California from the airport in Mexico City and her office phoned her at the hotel in Huatulco. Polly chartered a plane to Tlaxiaco and beat Sam to the Hotel Portal by two hours.

"Sam, what the hell is going on?" Polly's usually cool composure was coming apart.

"How did you get here so soon?"

"Chartered a plane. Where is Tommy, Sam?"

"I came from Mexico City with a man from the Ministry of the Interior. Apparently Tom has been kidnapped by revolutionaries and they are contacting the guerrillas responsible."

"He's alive isn't he, Sam? Tell me that he is alive. Please."

At that moment, Pete Villareal entered the reception office.

He stuck out his hand identified himself. "Pete Villareal, you look like you might be Sheriff Harlan."

"Yes. And this is Polly Anaya, she's Tom's fiancée. She was already down here, so I thought she might as well be here too." He turned to Polly and said, "Polly, this is the man who saw Tom taken. He was good enough to phone the department and let us know what happened."

Pete had told Sam that he was working a case, so he was relieved when Sam didn't blow his cover. The man was a pro. Despite his cowboy boots he was no hick.

"What happened?" Polly asked Pete.

"I was drinking with Tom and Jesús . . ."

"Jesús?"

"The Mexican guy Tom was with, the one who was killed. I was with Tom for a couple of hours."

"Tommy doesn't drink."

"Lady, he drinks Mirinda like it's going out of style."

"Thomas does everything like it's going out of style," Polly said, her eyes softening. "I apologize for interrupting, please go on."

"I went back to get Tom so I could offer him a ride back to Tlaxiaco, it looked like he was stranded because Jesús was doing some serious drinking. I walked into the bar and asked where Tom and Jesús were and the owner said they had all gone out back.

"I walked out, stepped to the side of the building so my eyes could adjust to the dark. I saw Tom walking toward Jesús, who was pawing a young lady. I think Tom was going to do something about it. Bernalillo was pretty drunk.

"A man suddenly stepped from the back of a big tree and shot Jesús at point-blank range. Then he saw Tom and pointed the gun at him. Tom raised his hands and stepped back. Man, I thought he was dead." Pete shook his head at the memory. "Anyway, he stepped back and almost bumped into another guy I hadn't seen, and the guy slapped Tom with a sap. Tom went down, then the guy with the gun pointed it at Tom's head but the other man said, 'He's a gringo!' The shooter said, 'So what?' And the other guy said, 'He's worth money, stupid.' " Pete paused. "Then they dragged him off into the dark."

Sam said, "I'm going to get a room and then join the task force. Polly, you go back to your room and wait until I can find out what the plan is. Pete, thanks for your help, it's always refreshing when a civilian gets involved."

Sam signed the register, took the key and walked out. Polly followed him and once on the patio away from Pete she said, "Sam!"

He stopped. "What, Polly?"

"If it's money they want, I have money."

"I know that, but let's wait for them to make a move before we make any offers."

"Sam," Polly said, and her eyes were hard as sapphire, "I want Thomas back . . . safe. If it costs me all I have, I want him back and I want him back alive!" And her voice went soft and broke on the last little word.

———

Hidden in the hills above San Miguel, Patricio was beside himself. He needed time to sort out the implications of what had happened the night before. He hadn't decided whether it was a curse or a blessing.

"It's a blessing," José declared. "This is a gift, my brother, and we must receive it with care, with delicacy, with respect — as all great gifts must be received."

José always saw things in a completely different light and Patricio was almost always mystified by his brother's perspective. What was completely ambiguous to Patricio often seemed clear to José.

"Explain this to me, then," Patricio said. "I cannot see a dead officer of the Mexican Drug Enforcement Agency and a kidnapped American policeman as anything but an excuse for the army to come into these hills and leave us all in pieces for the ants."

José smiled. "If the government had any idea that we were a dozen ignorant peasants, they would already have us for dog meat. Your fears are not entirely misplaced, my brother. But if we inflate ourselves like the puffer fish, though our spines are few we can give any predator second thoughts about trying to consume us." He smiled. "And if our masquerade is discovered, so what? Better to reign one day as a lion than live long as a sheep."

Patricio hated metaphors. "First we are fish and then we are lions. You don't live in the real world, José."

"The real world stinks," the poet said, and took down a bottle of the local mezcal. "Yet, my brother, I have a plan that should sweeten the air considerably." He took a drink. "CNN is in town."

Agustino was having a hard time with the leg irons again. Tom needed to take his daily drizzly and was beginning to think he was bound for another embarrassment before the lock yielded to the key.

In an inspired moment, he remembered something. The junk pocket of his backpack included, along with other mostly useless stuff, a small spray can of WD-40.

"Agustino."

"Si, amigo."

"Donde esta mi maleta — maleta de espalda?"

"En la casita."

"Oye, hay un bote de lubricante."

"Ah, bueno."

Miraculously, the little man came back with the backpack itself rather than rummaging through it in the shack that passed for a house.

Tom's pulse rate began to climb. In the bottom of the pack, sandwiched between his sweater, rain poncho and extra shoes and socks should be his Sig P-220 and two clips of bullets.

"Pistola se fue," Agustino said with a grin, having read Tom's mind. The pistol was gone.

"Lastima," Tom said with a wry smile.

"Esta una buena." A good one. Then he added that someone named Demetrio had taken possession of it.

Oh well. Tom told Agustino how to unzip the small outside pocket which held the WD-40. Also in the pocket were a broken signal mirror, a snakebite kit, surveyor's tape, waterproof watches, a can opener and other various items. Each item mystified and then amazed the simple little peasant as he removed them one at a time and asked Tom to explain what they were.

When the little WD-40 can came out, Tom exhaled audibly. He'd had a secret little hope stashed in his mind ever since he'd remembered the lubricant.

The key on the thong around Agustino's neck revealed that the lock mechanism of the irons was a relatively simple two-plate affair. If it were lubricated well enough, the mechanism shouldn't be too hard to manipulate, if he ever got the chance. He blessed the lessons on locks he'd learned from Daddy-O, in what now seemed like years ago.

But at the moment his priority was to get to the outhouse before he had an accident. Black beans and chiles with tortillas for breakfast were making his stomach sound like storm surf on a beach — wet and powerful.

Agustino sprayed the locks liberally, as Tom directed. When he twisted the key, the mechanism clicked like it hadn't since the day it was first assembled.

"A-h-h-h, buenisima," he said. Score another one for the gringos.

Tom had been raised on a ranch so an outhouse held no mysteries for him. He knew what to expect. However, he'd forgotten the sensation of flies doing touch-and-go on his bum.

Agustino re-secured Tom's arms after he'd finished and they began their shuffle back to the bath house. Tom took a good look around while he had the chance. One thing he noticed was that there were no men visible except his escort. The village appeared to be populated by women and children. They all came out of their huts to stare when Tom was escorted by.

He also saw that they were high above the village of San Miguel. He could see the convent about three miles away to the west. He was relieved. Having some sense of where he was helped his state of mind — something the damn dogs did not.

The suspicious animals sniffed at the door and growled as Tom sat and pondered his fate. When he kicked the flimsy sticks the door was fashioned from, they growled and snarled. When Agustino took him to the bathroom the dogs barked insanely, baring their teeth and dashing at Tom's legs. Agustino screamed at them and plied a stick, which didn't seem to impress them very much.

"Gusano! Golfo! Oso! Perra!" he would yell, but the filthy things still dashed at Tom and snapped their wicked-looking teeth. It took only one trip to the crapper to give him a real hate for the animals. They were going to make any escape impossible, even if he could get out of his shackles.

In the bath house Tom felt less exposed. But now it was time for the lectures again. His mind reeled at the thought. If only his Spanish were good enough that he could explain the Chinese Water Torture to Agustino, to he might substitute that for the lectures, political observations, and rhetorical questions.

The whole morning had been spent with Agustino perched on the bath stool outside the door discoursing on the history and state of U.S./Third World affairs in the simplest of terms. Vietnam had been covered earlier.

Grenada and Panama had also been covered. The man had been kind enough to confine himself to the last forty years, though the U.S.'s incursions into Mexican affairs were implied by the whole running discourse.

The little man lectured gently and spiced his observations with a mostly rhetorical — "Es cierto? O falso?" — true or false? Occasionally he waited patiently until Tom finished a halting observation or mild objection.

He was gentle and very often acute, but it was obvious that his world view was from the lower left corner of geopolitics. Tom found himself agreeing with many of Agustino's conclusions, in spite of his being forced to these considerations by his helpless state. Funny, he thought, how being raised lower working class, even in America, forged your perception of the world, no matter how far you progressed up the social and economic ladder.

The early afternoon was spent on the U.S.'s sins against Nicaragua and Cuba. Tom would nod his head or shake it in disagreement as the noon meal came and went and the sun began its lazy arc down the afternoon sky.

Tom laid his head back against the wattle and daub wall, mouthed 'cierto' at mostly appropriate moments, inspiring a satisfied nod from his little philosopher guard. A falso from Tom would send a corrugation of perplexed flesh up the man's dark brow. Then he would purse his lips, re-frame his thought and, smiling, drive the refashioned point home again.

Tom eventually came to a very disquieting realization. He had been taken prisoner by the two most politically ruthless groups in the world — the women and the philosophers. As a redneck male born and bred, he understood that here he could expect no quarter and certainly no mercy. He was de facto guilty of everything. And he just might have to listen to this guy until he died.

Chapter 30

Concha stared down at the script José had given her to study. Although it was written in his florid hand and larded with metaphor, she finally satisfied herself that what he had written was the truth about the state of her people. There was little in it she could not say with a whole heart.

She looked at the table and two chairs that José had set up for himself and for her. The crews from Mexico's Televisa and the one from CNN were set up. There were also three reporters sitting on convenient logs. They were just down the hillside from the mouth of the cave. It was hidden from view at this point beside the little road.

José sat down and, with a nod, cued the directors of the crews, who ordered the cameras to roll. José spoke for a minute or two, identifying himself as the "subcomandante," and then gave Concha a nod. She walked to within camera range and sat down at the table. Her composed, pretty face was a startling contrast with the hooded and menacing males who had, to this point, been arrayed in front of the cameras. The cameras caught it all — her striking little figure in the brilliant Triqui huipil, her light step, the long black hair framing the handsome Indian features, her bare feet and, most of all, the fire in her eyes.

She forgot the script and began to speak from her heart. She gave a brief history of the rich cultures of Mexico's indigenous people, especially the Zapotecs and Mixtecs of Oaxaca state. She reminded them that Benito Juarez, one of Mexico's greatest reformers, was a Mixtec Indian — a man who stood with Abraham Lincoln in his belief that "justice for all" was more than a theory. It had to be put into real practice, even if it meant civil war.

She spoke of the divided soul of Mexico and illustrated it with the story of the eagle tearing at the snake and the snake looking for its opportunity to strike its tormentor — the seemingly eternal struggle of Mexico against both its past and its future, against its proud indigenous past and its progressive possibilities.

Then she spoke about the low estate of Mexico's women and the impending death of family life as America sent its poisonous, false liberalism deep into the heart of the great country. She called on the mothers of the country to both rise and nurture, a Herculean task which seemed to have defeated a country even as great as the United States. She talked of her own life in the North and what she had seen there. She warned of what was bad and described warmly what was good and worthy of emulation.

Finally, she pleaded on behalf of the indigenous people of the country. She demanded respect and equality for both men and women. The passion in her voice, the heat in her eyes, spoke of a soul on fire.

They had all been given background on this woman. They'd learned how she had led a strike against a powerful cacique and shot a man who had once tried to force himself on her. But this was their first look at her. And it would certainly not be the last.

When the cameras were turned off, Concha sat down with the print reporters, two of them women, and spent an hour talking.

It all came out, everything that she had felt and held inside for so long. The education she'd been denied by the Mexican system but had obtained from her husband, the breadth of her experience as a child of a village who had grown to be an American millionaire's wife.

The acuity of her mind shown brightly and made the journalists' work easy. José was pleased. After all, she was the sanguinary heiress of Cacica Maria, the Mixtec queen, was she not? The media people could barely contain themselves.

———

Because he didn't understand Spanish, Sam found himself frustrated by the activity at the tactical center. He had seen an impressive communications system with single-sideband radios, satellite phone/fax and other gear that he wasn't familiar with. There were men in uniforms of several kinds, police and military; older men in expensive suits and the traditional Latin short-sleeved pleated shirt; and younger men who preferred designer jeans, expensive running shoes and thick gold watches. All carried guns. This was a cop's world and Sam, with his long experience, had a real good idea what was happening. But it wasn't enough, even with his companion from the A.G.'s office, who spoke perfect American English.

Tom Thompson was his number one officer and Sam had lost him. You are supposed to keep good tabs on your inventory and personnel, and losing a guy was bad for business, in more ways than one. Losing him in a foreign country was real bad for the political side of his business — when county-level police officers get mixed up in an international mess it's, well, an international mess.

Alhough Tom Thompson had no idea of it, Sam had picked Tom as his eventual successor. The position of U.S. Marshal for Wyoming was coming up for grabs soon and Sam had his eye on it. He needed to secure a succession that would be as trouble-free as possible and Tom was competent and well liked. The pruning he had gone through when he came to the end of his drinking and his imminent marriage to a smart, personable woman made him the only man Sam felt he could pass the Stetson to, so to speak.

He had talked to the old pols who made things happen in Teton County and in the state as well. They knew Sam's choice and mostly agreed. The only hitch was that Tom hated politics. It was something Sam had planned to work on, given the time. But it occurred to Sheriff Harlan, as he left the command center with the A.G.'s man, that the politics he needed to handle at the moment were right in his lap.

"What's the deal?" Sam asked.

"The deal is that we don't know what we have for sure — but some of us think that we have been tricked."

"How so?"

"The press conference and all the Marxist rhetoric, plus the violence and all the movement of people in the San Miguel area made it seem that we had a major political incident on our hands. As you know, the Indians in the south of our country have been very restive lately. "

Sam nodded, "Chiapas."

"Yes."

"And you think that the murder of Jesús Bernalillo and Tom's kidnapping are related to all the previous activity, or not?"

"Well, now that the feria is over and everyone's gone home, we can't detect any large movements of people. Plus, we've had enough time for our intel people to conclude that there appears to be no traffic between the group which appeared on television yesterday and the well-organized groups down south."

"So these guys are bogus?"

"Yes. We are getting ready to go in. We're organizing a complete sweep of the area, a thousand army troops are ready and the operation will begin at daylight tomorrow."

"What about Tom?" Sam felt an alarm run through him. Tom may have been written off as a casualty of the coming situation. He knew that if the kidnappers saw a sweep coming they would probably kill their captive before sprinting for the mountain tops.

"Let's hope for the best." The A.G.'s man didn't look Sam in the eye when he said it.

It didn't help Sam's peace of mind to look up at that moment and see Polly standing on the porch of the hotel, her face haggard from the wait for news.

———

"You are going. Period!" Olga's face was convulsed with emotion.

"I guess maybe you don't understand, Olga. An American cop has been kidnapped!"

"I . . . don't . . . give . . . a . . . shit!"

Pete's face flushed. "But . . . I . . . do!"

Olga realized that she had underestimated Pete's feelings about this Thompson's predicament. She would have to take a different tack, she could see.

Oz saved her the maneuver by asking, "Pete, why?"

"Why what?"

"Why do you care so much? You only knew him for a few hours, what's the big attraction?"

Pete could not blow his cover now. He took a mental breath and reconsidered his position. Today was the solstice, the day when he would find out exactly what was driving this mushroom-money scene. He really did have to get back to his original priorities.

Besides, Thompson's boss was competent and had the support of the Mexican Ministry of the Interior. And another thing, the place was crawling with cops. They didn't need any more help from him except what he had already done. Pete shrugged. "Simple. I liked the guy."

Olga glanced at Oz and Pete caught the look. Something was going on between these two. They were nervous as whores in church.

———

José and Patricio knew that if they overplayed their hand they were dead men. The killing of the agent by Demetrio and Marcos, plus the kidnapped American had pushed the ante so high that there was no going back. Also, José's playing of the CNN and Time magazine cards had raised the stakes as high as they could go. Now the game was dangerous for both sides.

The government could not afford to throw fuel on the moment. A blood bath in the Oaxacan Sierra could flare the general situation out of control if the incident were large enough. But José was one of the few who knew that there were only a dozen people at the heart of the situation — a political Potemkin Village. The secret was to keep the situation inflated through the media, but not too inflated. The strategy must be to keep the action just large enough that the government would resort to its historical reflex of larding them with money, to co-opt the populist sentiment and corrupt its leaders. Corruption made the wheels go 'round and this was their chance to get on one of the wheels with everyone else. The money wheel. And if the strategy worked they were chingons, clever fuckers. If it didn't work they were chingaron — fucked completely. A dangerous game. CNN, Time, and the other media people were busy. The results of the press conference would be known soon enough, right after it hit the satellite feed.

At the moment, though, José had to turn his mind to the business at hand. The duties of the Sociedad de Las Animas Ancianas took precedence over everything else.

Patricio took down the linen-wrapped bundles from the scaffold in the back of the cave. He untied them and shook out the brilliant huipils, woven by the local women. He unrolled the silver-dressed leather belts and straps, the feathered caps, and other handmade adornments. Finally, he went to the scaffold, reached to the back and dragged out a sack that clinked musically as it moved.

He loosed the neck of the sack and gently slid the contents onto the table beside the other ritual objects. They were obsidian knives. Instruments older than memory, finely fluted by a hand whose craft secrets were lost for all time.

The blades had been given shapes that galvanized the artist in anyone with any sensibility. The handle of the first was the head and neck of Murcielago, the Bat King. His folded wings devolved into a blade which had been fluted to an edge sharp as a chef's instrument. The obsidian was gray, the color of Murcielago, and came from the volcano Popocatepetl.

The other, heavier, blade had been fashioned from the rock glass of Orizaba, another volcano home to the gods. Orizaba obsidian is green as the eyes of some rare cats. And some even rarer people. The handle of this instrument had been worked into the head and shoulders of the jaguar.

Tom had a plan.

Agustino had rehung the cabinet and replaced all the contents. Except one. A plastic toothbrush had fallen into a corner.

Tom stared at it as he listened to the little man sitting on the little bench with his back to the wall of the bath house. He was now telling stories, having worn Tom unresponsive by the political chatter. Pointing to the sky, he remarked that he'd noticed the moon was out during the day again, the drunken slut.

It seemed that, in the ancient times, the moon had only come out at night. But she had been intrigued by the sounds of song and music and by fascinating little lights that flared below on the dark earth. Also, the intoxicating smells of the pulque jars rose and made her head giddy. Hmmm, she had thought. It's the little humans celebrating their festivals.

One night she could not stand it any longer. She waited until she was very slim, like now, just the size of a fingernail clipping. She lowered herself to the earth and stole a huipil to disguise herself with. Then she had joined the villagers in their celebration.

She discovered what the people did in the dark. She sang, she took a cup of pulque, she was dragged into the circle of firelight and danced. At first she danced after the fashion of the women, demurely. Then she danced with the men and felt their hot hands and hard members pressing against her body. She drank more of the pulque and danced more with the men until, in the moonless dark, she had been coaxed to the black woods and experienced the sexual passion of the people who had seduced her down to the earth.

The next morning she woke and it was day. Father Sun was up and looking around. He saw her on her way home, abroad in the daylight. And he was very angry. She was ashamed and for a long time did not venture down to the earth, just sailed slowly above it and looked down at the lights, listened to the songs, smelled the pulque, and felt the itch.

Occasionally it was too much for her, as it was last night and the night before. Who knows, Agustino said, perhaps the moon herself had been walking the streets of San Miguel, singing, drunken, hot. Perhaps one of their own young men had been lucky enough to be the man who, in the dark wood, had mated with the moon.

Tom loved the story. It reminded him of his own youth, when most men had been storytellers and he had sat at the edge of the circle to listen to tales of soldiering, working, hunting, drinking, and women. This little story had been a generous thing for the old man to give.

Agustino had also given back to Tom the little MagLite flashlight from his pack. Stumped by the switch mechanism, which required a twist of the head, Agustino thought it was broken. Tom had promised the man to try and fix it. All Tom needed now was the little mirror from the wall, and he needed it broken. If he could get several shards of glass he could use them to fashion a key from the toothbrush that had fallen to the floor.

It wouldn't have to be all that strong, now that the mechanism of the manacles was liberally bathed in WD-40. He stared at the mirror for a long moment, galvanizing his will to do whatever it took to gain the prize. It could mean the difference between living and dying. And he wanted to live, very much.

Chapter 31

Larry King, TV personality and pundit, looked owlishly into the camera and introduced his guest, Jorge Castaneda, writer, columnist, leftist intellectual, and professor of political science at UNAM, the national university of Mexico in Mexico City.

"Didn't you recently announce the death of Marxism in Latin America?" Larry asked.

"Yes, but I did not predict the end of unrest, especially militant unrest among the indigenous peoples of Central America and Mexico. Quite the contrary."

Far to the south, in Mexico City, the president put his folded hands under his chin and his stare turned as hard as the grim line of his mouth under the impeccable mustache. He was alone in the big room, just him and the television set.

On the screen, Larry King was asking, "And who is this Concha Osorio?"

"She just might be another Rigoberta Menchu," Castaneda said, brightly.

Larry King stared into the camera and editorialized, "Professor Castaneda is referring to the Nobel Laureate of 1991, an Indian woman from Guatemala who captured the attention of the world and focused it on the plight of the native peoples of Latin America."

The president stared at the colorful box-of-bullshit and pressed the mute button on his channel selector. He sighed. Governing Mexico had turned out to be like working the bridge of an enormous oil tanker, one which grew larger and harder to guide with each passing year. It was big, ponderous, slow to respond, and had recently gained great momentum, due in large part, ironically, to his own economic reforms. To keep it off the shoals one had to steer right sometimes, and left sometimes. But the steering had to come long in advance of any measurable response.

Recently he had steered hard right, with NAFTA, in order to bring the country into the real and competitive world that lay ahead. He was intent on raising Mexico to the head of the second rank of nations, poising her for entry into the first rank. The giant economy of her neighbor on the north was run by aggressive and conservative businessmen and that model had been used to transform the northern states of Mexico. Now with the bloody unrest in the backward south, the general economy might lose its way as he steered left with the wheel of state.

The French said it best, patting their breasts right and then left: "On the right is the wallet, but on the left is the heart."

The socialist revolution of 1910 was the intellectual matrix of Mexico and its ideals were the stuff of its soul. The border with the U.S. was where the future and the flesh of a healthy economy took form. Mexico seemed, like man himself, to be condemned to an endless struggle between the soul and the flesh.

The president sighed, raised his remote control and sent Larry King and Licenciado Castaneda cascading to nothingness. He picked up his secure phone and pushed the button for his Minister of the Interior's office. It was picked up instantly.

"Yes, Mr. President."

"You've been watching CNN?"

"Yes."

"Call in the dogs."

"Sir?"

"Call in the special units, but leave everyone else on alert. The world is watching. I don't want those people harmed."

"That woman is dangerous."

"Very," the president agreed. "But she may be useful as well." He hung up.

It was time to steer left again and he just might be able to use this new "La Pasionara," as the press was styling her, to guide him. The ship responded more and more slowly as the cargo size and momentum increased. Some day, he knew, she would probably not respond in time, having grown too ponderous. A wreck was a real possibility. But God, please, not on his watch.

———

Tom was weary and on the edge of hysteria. He wanted to cry like a child, because he was so afraid. The stress had finally gotten to him.

He cursed Agustino and kicked the cabinet from the wall again. When he had the women, the children, the damn dogs and the one man together, watching him in his fit, he told them to go fuck their mothers. Chingan todas! They waited until he was through and then left politely. Except the snarling dogs. Agustino brought him a cup of excellent coffee. A beautiful little girl dressed innocently in her underpants, gold earrings and a shy smile brought him a sweet roll.

The Mexicans were great. They knew that when a man had to lose it, he had to lose it and they took no offense at his anger.

Now, if he could figure out some way to kill all those barking, snarling, pissing dogs his day would be perfect. Sunset, a cup of good coffee, a pretty smile from a little girl bearing a gift, and all the mangy dogs in Mexico dead. Perfect.

But best of all, in his mock frenzy he had managed to knock the mirror to the cement floor. It lay in shards near the wall.

———

Oz and Olga had everyone ready at the turnaround terminus of the mountain road. All the flashlights had been tested, everyone had a bottle of water.

"Remember, no food until after the ceremony!" Olga emphasized. "The Society of Ancient Souls will have everything prepared for us, including the meal after the ceremony. All you need is your flashlight, your water, and your reverence."

'And your bullshit detector in the off position,' Pete thought. His mind was on the police action in Tlaxiaco and here he was with a bunch of dickheads with no common sense, way too much money and too much time on their hands. He couldn't wait to put a big kink in all their lives when he chopped this action in the ass. His meanest cop instincts were coming to the fore.

Oz and Olga passed out the mushrooms, two apiece to everyone. Five thousand bucks worth. Pete now had them for delivery of a controlled substance, it was just a matter of proving it. But he didn't think that would be a problem, any one of the group would gladly roll over and testify against the team of Oz 'n' Olga when offered a deal by the prosecutor. Each had a hell of a lot to lose and would probably do anything to save their own asses.

Oz gave a little speech about the history of the cultivation of the monster 'shrooms — how rare they were, how privileged this group was. They were also the only people in the whole world who were going to share in this secret ritual.

Olga's voice joined Oz's in the dark. "This is a meditation walk. Use these two next hours to prepare and strengthen your minds. You will need a great reservoir of strength to participate in this ritual because it is from another time, another world. You will require all the mental and emotional power you can muster. Let us begin. Padrino will lead the way, I will come last."

Huh, Pete thought, that's not true, she usually comes before I do. Then he regretted the vile, adolescent thought. Reflexively, he remembered Oz's warning to take this more seriously.

They started up the dark mountainside, on the cusp of the dark of the moon. Their flashlights threw wan little circles of light onto the dark ground and the black trees, into the scorched night air.

———

Sam went to Polly's room, knowing that she would probably not be asleep. He knocked and she let him in.

"Relax. It's all off again." He saw a wave of relief cross her face. They had talked earlier and Sam had been brutally honest with her — Tom's chances of surviving a military operation were small. In his own mind he'd known the chances were a flat zero, but he hadn't wanted to deprive her of all hope.

"What happened?" she asked.

"The Minister of the Interior phoned and told them to stand down. It was close — ten more minutes and it would have gone off. The troops were in the trucks and ready to roll to the jumping-off points."

"Why did he call it off?"

Sam shrugged. "Who knows. Hell, I don't have the faintest notion what's going on. I don't have a clue."

He stared at the wall for a moment and added, "What the hell are we doing down here, anyway? We don't know the language, we don't know the rules and we can only see things from our own national bias."

Polly answered, "I know the language. And I know some of the rules."

"What are the rules, then?"

"The basic rule is to not do anything until you have to. After that you make it up as you go along."

"They're not big on planning, huh?"

"Only the technocrats in Mexico City and the industrialists in the North use real planning. The rest of the country either doesn't know anything about planning or actively sabotages most of what the guys up there do. This is the South."

"What makes it different down here?"

"It's always the year 1911. And Emiliano Zapata is as alive as he can be."

The first thing Demetrio Osorio did when he came into the bathhouse was order Agustino away and shine a bright flashlight in Tom's face. The second thing he did was lean down, breathe his stinking alcoholic breath in Tom's face, and curse him. The third thing he did was kick Tom in the stomach. Then he laughed and left with his friend, who had leaned in through the door to watch.

Now, lying in his puked-up sweet roll and coffee, Tom remembered his old, old vow never to kill another human being. That vow meant nothing to him at the moment. In his mind's eye he felt the pistol buck against his hand and saw shock spread over the man's face — in that moment when a man understands he has taken a mortal blow. Shock. Fear. Thoughts of his mother's refuge breast and her name comes to his lips. The fragile shucks of his manhood fall away and the little boy receives the wound. Fear unto death, then the slacking of the limbs and darkening of his eyes as the soul flies away.

Even in the dark Tom knew who the man was — he was the one with the pistol at the feria who had killed Jesús Bernalillo.

But, what goes around, comes around. The bastard's time would come and it would come at Tom's hands. He felt it. He knew it. And he could hardly wait.

———

The Society of Ancient Souls gathered around the fire at the summit of Nindo Tocoshu. Not all members were there. Some were not qualified to take place in the Rito Grande, while others had elected not to participate. All senior members were present.

José stooped to the edge of the fire and stirred the blackened clay pot simmering at the edge of the flames. He put his finger in it, testing the temperature. "A few more minutes should do it," he said, examining a cloth spread on the ground. On it were twenty-four gourd bowls, arranged in a spiral.

José pointed to the one in the very center and said, "That bowl is for the Elected One. Remember that we begin with that one because the extra ingredient takes a bit longer to have its effect. You, Patricio, will handle this part of the ritual so remember that the liquor must be poured into the bowls from the center of the arrangement out. It must be handed out in the same order — the first will come from the direct center. Do not forget."

Exasperated, Patricio said, "I have participated in the other Grand Rite during my time, remember?"

"Yes, yes. I apologize, it's just that you know how important it is that everything be done in exactly the same manner our ancestors did it. You know how important this is."

José turned and looked at the edge of the clearing, to remind himself why they were here to do what they had to do. Fallen logs were still glowing, red embers veined the sides of standing trees and the air was thick with the smell of smoke which was invisible in the faint light of the ceremonial fire.

That evening they had mounted Nindo Tocoshu to find its summit ablaze. If it had been daylight now, it would have been possible to see that half the circumference of the ceremonial glade had been consumed by the blaze, which had died to quiescence when the cooling air and night dew lowered the temperature and stilled the breeze. But the fire still lived.

They were here to bring an end to all that. The fires would be quenched, the convulsions in the bowels of the earth would be stilled. That was why they celebrated the Grand Rite, which had been called for only one other time in the almost forty years since the Gorostiza brothers had been active in the society — the other time was also when the earth had shaken and the clouds abandoned their people.

This one, of course, would be somewhat different. It would be only the second time white persons would witness the rite, the very first time one would serve as the Elected One.

The father of La Leonessa had been the only one previously invited, more than twenty-five years ago, so it was fitting that she participate. It was even better that she had offered them the elect. Surely Dzaui would appreciate the magnitude of that offer and respond with his presence, dragging his robes of rain behind him. The fires would be doused, the earth stilled, the corn and flowers resurrected. It had been so for the whole long, long history of his people, and it would be so this time. Dozing in his grotto down by the river, Dzaui would be awakened, and would rise in joy. When he smelled the blood.

Chapter 32

Polly knelt by her bed, her hands folded in prayer, begging for Tom's deliverance.

She was shaking from fear, both for him and for herself. This was all more than she could possibly bear, she felt. Having to accept this as something beyond her control was not what she was used to. Her intelligence, her beauty, her social standing, and her money had insulated her from this feeling of helplessness for a very long time. Nothing since her troubled first pregnancy had not yielded to her, once she had brought all those resources to bear on the problem.

But this night she had cursed the fates, she had cried, she had paced the floor, and taken showers. She had even sent the night watchman out to buy her a pack of cigarettes, but twisted them to powder and threw them in the trash after a second stinking, nauseating puff. How she had enjoyed them in the past was beyond her comprehension.

Surrendering, she had finally fallen to her knees in a posture of wordless supplication. And at that moment she remembered something that Tom always said, something which had mostly amused her in the past: Finally, we have absolutely no power over people, places, or things. He'd repeated it many times and she had not believed, having had power over all those things. The one word she had missed, it was clear now, was the first one: Finally.

She realized that finally meant when you have exhausted your own resources. The implication was that you would surely exhaust them eventually, and that you would have to turn to a power greater than yourself at some point. She had been raised a Christian but, as most do, had gone to church only when it pleased her.

She then remembered something else Tom had repeated in some of their most private talks: God is real and he works real miracles in our lives when invited with a whole heart. That was all too simplistic for her. She was High Church Anglican and the ritual made her feel that little glow, on the occasions when she had taken her daughters.

Now she was all alone in a foreign country, far from her church, far from her family, far from the phone which she might have used to call Father Bill. She was alone. But, if Tom was right, perhaps not so alone after all. With tears of helplessness running down her face, she raised her hands to heaven.

———

When Tom heard the footsteps in the dark he rolled over and put his manacled feet against the rickety door, hoping to keep the pistolero from entering again. He had promised himself he was going to resist in every way he could. He had been lying in the acid stench and the blackness, feeling sorry for himself. The helpless emotion had begun to corrode him at the core, threatening to collapse him and his will.

But he forced himself to halt the descent into self-pity, inspired by the sudden memory of that dying cock and its final kick. Tom saw again the golden eye, hard as amber, and the desperate flash of the deadly spur. Never, never, never, never give up, he had remembered at the cockfight. And he had remembered it again this night.

He felt the push of a hand against the door. Twice. And then a voice whispered, "Señor Tonson? Señor Tonson — is Cenovio Osorio."

Concha's brother? Tom rolled away from the door and said, quietly, "Come in."

The man pushed the door open, entered and shut the door behind him. He then turned on a dim flashlight and found Tom with its weak beam.

"Why are you here, Cenovio?"

"I am comin' because they are say to kill you."

"Who wants to kill me?"

"Marcos and Demetrio."

"Who are those two?" Tom asked, knowing that Cenovio was talking of the men who had kidnapped him, the ones who had been there half an hour earlier.

"Marcos is mi primo."

"Cousin," Tom supplied. "And who is the other one?"

"Is me brother."

"Your brother!" It was hard to believe that this big man with the drooping lip and murderous eyes shared the same bloodline as the other two.

"Yes. They are drinking mezcal with two otro malditos an' they talkin' to kill you. I am talkin' them that to killin' you only make police come for all our family."

"So there will be four of them coming?" Tom asked, and the thought frightened him. Two — maybe. Four — never.

"Four. Yes, so you mus' run 'way. Don' be go through the village, you mus' go over mountain to valley on 'nother side." The beam of light ran up the east wall of the bath house, opposite the village side. "Here are your shoes." He dropped Tom's old Nike's on the floor.

"How am I going to find the way? And what about the dogs?" Those damn barking, snarling, biting, mangy, rib-pooched skeletal dogs.

"Is campo . . ."

"Field."

"Yes, is big field there." Again the beam of light ran to the east wall.

"I've seen it. It runs to the edge of the trees. Then what?"

"In corner of field is camino . . ."

"Trail, yes. How big?"

"Is big one. You followin' it for two kilometer and is comin' 'nother camino, down from these mountain tops. This is one you are go on — is goin' over mountain an' w'en you over tops is barranca."

"Canyon."

"Si, cañon arbol."

"Wooded canyon."

"Is two caminos and you take the lef' one."

"OK. I go up this trail to where it meets another trail, one that goes over the ridge. I stay on that one until I get to the head of a wooded canyon and then I take the trail to the left. Is that correct?"

"Perfecto. This camino is go to camino de carros.

"A road for cars."

"Yes. Is road an' many carros and camionetas is going there."

"What about the dogs?"

"You mus' wait for the rains. The dogs are going inside and don't be hearin' you when is comin' these rains."

"Rains! What rains? It hasn't rained here for damn near a year and the place is burning up."

"Tonight is comin' rains."

"How do you know?"

There was a long silence and then Tom heard, "Dzaui is come to us again. The elders of village are on Nindo Tocoshu and is comin' the rain when they are sing an' they are . . ." The voice trailed off in the dark.

Tom banged his heels against the floor, making the chains on his ankles rattle. "What about these?"

The flashlight came on again and Cenovio handed it to Tom to hold. Tom almost gasped when he saw the thong and key that Agustino had worn around his neck. He had guessed that Cenovio was going to turn him loose, but the proof of rescue was enough to make him want to cry in relief.

When the chains and strap had been removed, Tom stood and stretched his arms. Oh! it felt good. But then a little voice said, not yet. Not yet.

"The dogs will go inside when the rain comes, but what if it doesn't come?"

"Is come. Seguro." The voice was so confident that Tom believed.

"And what if the malditos come before it rains?"

There was a silence in the little room, disturbed only by the buzz of the crickets outside. The confidence that Tom had felt a moment before was shattered. The idea of four men and a half dozen dogs tearing at him made his heart skip.

"Can you come with me? The dogs won't bark if you come with me."

"I mus' go down to house where they are drinkin' and try to hold them there. If I am do that until the rain is comin'. . ."

"And if they find out that you have helped me to escape?"

"They will maybe kill me, but is OK. I am dead man jus' the same."

"Why?"

"I have kill government men and that is something I cannot be helped. They will come for me, no matter. Me an' Demetrio and also Marcos. We are dead mens."

"You don't know that, not for sure."

"I have know this, in my dreams. There will be others dead mens too. Only my sister is livin' a long life." The same prophetic note could be heard in the man's voice, and Tom had no doubt this time either. He spoke the flat truth and there was no mistaking that truth. The man knew.

He heard Cenovio step to the door and open it, though the only evidence was the sound. It was as dark as the inside of a cow. Only the faint stars made any light.

"Adios, amigo," Tom said. The only answer was a thump as something dropped inside the bathhouse. Then he heard the man's bare feet padding away and a dog barking down the hill.

———

José had been chanting for two hours, raising his voice to the stinking black sky and the muddy stars, singing Dzaui up from his deep sleep. Calling his name, calling his name.

Patricio had relieved him at intervals, calling for intercession by others in the ancient Mixtec pantheon, asking for them to raise the god who had turned his face. Other elders and two ancient acolytes fed the fire and prepared the food for the meal after the ceremony. The acolytes cleaned the altar of fallen leaves and grasses which sprouted from between the stones.

One spoke to the other. "I am glad that this year we did not have to carry those turkeys all the way up the mountain. Last year I thought I was going to have a heart attack before I got up here with the damn things."

"Ah, but this year we will not have carne de pavo for our families. That is a pity. Lastima."

"Hmmm, yes. They will be disappointed that we do not come home with turkey meat. And why not? Why is it that there will be no turkeys to shed their blood for Dzaui?"

"Because Dzaui is very, very angry with the people. He would not be satisfied with the blood of turkeys, they say. That is why we are allowing the gringos to attend the ceremony. One of them is bringing to Dzaui the Elected One."

"What is it that we have done to make Dzaui so angry at us?"

"Some say it is because many are worshipping with these new people, the evangelistas."

"Hmmm, that is possible. The padres have always left us some of our fathers' religion to feed our souls but these new people, they are different. Very different. They say Jesus is all we need."

"Yes. Both my sons and one daughter worship with them. But they seem so happy, it does not seem right that Dzaui would begrudge them this happiness."

The other old man tugged a grass bunch from between the stones and shrugged. "The business of the gods is very complicated because they are very temperamental. One never knows what they will do and, besides, it is man's lot to suffer. It is the way life is."

At the lower edge of the clearing, Plato and Socratio saw the string of light coming up the trail, announcing the arrival of the gringos.

"It is very pretty, is it not?"

"Yes, like a serpent of light," Socratio agreed.

They were dressed in their ceremonial gear, feathered caps, necks hung with jade ornaments, arm bands, plumed bustles, and skirts of bleached homespun. When the group of Americans reached the edge of the glade they gasped at the effect of the apprentice priests' appearance. They looked as if they had stepped off the stelae or walls of Monte Alban, the royal city of the Zapotec and Mixtec empires.

Pete and Olga, both dressed in ceremonial robes, were the last to arrive. Pete was a bit chagrined that Olga'd had to wait patiently for him to catch his breath at many of the trail's zigs and zags. Hell, many of the group were in their fifties and even sixties, but had kept pace with Oz. This was a very unusual bunch of senior citizens, even for the fitness-goofy Bay Area.

Plato and Socratio escorted them to the fireside. As they cooled down, they saw José and Patricio standing in front of a large stone pillar. On the pillar had been set a limestone visage about the size of a large pumpkin. It must have been buried in the ground before being elevated because it was dark with absorbed water. The damp sculpture was striking for the effect that the water-darkened surface gave, reflecting the pink firelight from the matte black surface. Reflections heightened the contrasting eye sockets, wells into which the light fell and from which it did not return. The gouged mouth was open in what appeared to be a screaming grin.

The two brothers stood in front of the pillar and visage, their arms raised and their voices chanting together in a sing-song wail. The ancient songline rose and fell, turned from duet to solo and back to duet as the two sturdy-throated old men twined their voices.

The men's dress was just as striking, with plumes and ornaments of an unbelievable variety. The costumes were recognizable to anyone who had seen the codices of the ancient Mixtec civilization. Their extravagance underlined the intricate vocal celebrations. The effect was breathtaking.

Pete's hair stood on end. From the looks of the other gringos' faces, they were having the same sensation as the singers' voices spiked the night and twisted into a strong rope of undulating sound.

The group gathered at a place indicated by Oz and, after a couple of moments, the songline fell to José's solo. Patricio turned and walked regally to where a white cloth was lying on the ground with gourd cups set in a spiral. A man dressed in a lesser set of feathers, jade, and silver jewelry pieces was filling the cups halfway from a blackened clay pot.

Patricio stepped to the cloth and reached to the center of it for a cup. He turned, raised it to the smoky night, then walked to the group. Pete felt his sleeve pinched and Olga tugged him forward. The man in the stunning ceremonial dress handed him the cup.

"Drink it," Olga said. "And hurry, while it's still warm. It tastes awful when it's cold."

Pete raised the cup, sipped at the liquor. It was alcoholic, he could taste that, but except for the familiar little rush of the alcohol, it tasted like nothing in his experience. Not good, but not all that bad. He drained the cup, lumps and all, and handed it back to the priest.

Patricio handed the empty vessel to a helper and returned for another cup. He did that until each of the group of anglos had been given a portion. Then he filled the balance of the cups and passed them to the Indians.

Pete noticed that the cups were handed out from the center of a circle, the coil of vessels unwinding slowly. And as he watched the uncoiling, he distinctly saw the form of a serpent take shape on the cloth. It slowly unwound as the priest took up the cups. When the last cup was removed, the serpent slithered off the cloth and into the dark outside the fire's light. It moved sinuously toward a pile of rocks which two men had been tidying when the group arrived.

'All right!' he thought. The drink was mildly hallucinogenic. And quick. It had taken only a couple of minutes for it to take effect. He turned to Olga and looked at her.

Olga stared back at Pete and smiled. There was nothing seductive about the smile, it was more a smile of approval. And he liked that. But it was her eyes that struck him. They were a luminous green and the fire danced in the center of their large, dilated pupils. The eyes flashed back and forth: red then green, red and green, red then green.

Pete smiled, enjoying the play of light. He knew the hallucinogenic drink was at the heart of the striking effect and he let himself sink into the sensation, embracing it. He was visually oriented, color-sensitive, and when he was stoned that sense was enhanced.

My hell, he said to himself, I don't know if I want to eat mushrooms on top of this trippy stuff. A cosmic Grand Tour, yeah! But God only knows where a trip like that might take me.

When Tom squatted to explore what made the thump, he was happy to find that it was his back pack. He unzipped it and searched the inside with his hands, taking inventory. At the bottom was a light wool sweater, then the sweat pants. Alas, the pistol was not lying between them, wrapped in a lightly oiled mechanic's rag, as he'd packed it. For a moment the next item confused him, his fingers not recognizing it. Then he remembered his hunting slingshot, the one he used to run moose out of his yard or to kill grouse during hunting season. His rain poncho was packed next, and on top of that was a pint water bottle. Empty.

Oh well, he thought wryly, I won't need this if it rains the way Cenovio said it would.

Rain! The night air was dry and warm, heavy with the smell of fresh smoke from just-damped fires that had flared on the mountain above during the day. It sure as hell did not feel like rain.

He stood and stretched again, for the hundredth time since he'd been left alone. The tedium and tension of waiting was getting to him. But he knew he had to wait for Cenovio's promise, like it or not. Twice he opened the door to the bathhouse and stuck his head outside. Both times two of the emaciated mongrels growled from their beds beneath the bougainvillea at the side of the bath.

He sat down again, his hand on his pack, and tuned his ears to the sounds of the night: Crickets; a distant radio, a confused cock crowed and was answered by another some distance further away, a burro honked and wheezed for a few moments then quit his bray. In the village far below, a pack of dogs barked insanely, marking the passage of some stranger. The barking was faint, but Tom's hearing, sensitized by recent practice, could pick out the different groups of animals as they vigilantly reported the presence of anything unusual. It was an effective warning system, and one with teeth. He realized that the dogs, which during the day were little more than filthy, matted, scarred, flea-bitten lumps of flesh, filled a very real ecological niche. They ate the shit that was dropped virtually anyplace, making all night walks a tentative affair. They also gleaned the garbage of all offal and other stuff that drew flies, and they were an alarm system for each owner's property. They were ignored almost totally after they were pups and the death of a dog meant little more than food for the others, as far as the owners were concerned. No sentiment was wasted on them when they were grown, and when a dog had served his purpose he was killed and tossed as easily as corn husks are discarded. Tom smiled at the contrast with the canine darlings up north.

Suddenly, his attention was grabbed by the sounds of drunken men's voices coming from down the hill. There was shouting and cursing. He focused all his senses in that direction, trying to interpret the noise.

Only an occasional word was distinct enough to be recognized, almost all of them swear words, shouted for emphasis. The sound was universal enough. Anyone who has spent any real amount of time in bars can learn the language of drinkers. At first he had feared that the moment had come when the four malditos had decided to execute their plan. His choice in that event would be to run and risk the attacking dogs or stand and face the men. It was a lose–lose situation. But as he listened, gauging the volume for any indication that the men were heading up the hill, he understood that it was only a drunken argument that had broken out among them. The ruckus died away, leaving the music from a radio and the crickets' chirring to be heard over the noise of his own body.

His heart was pounding, his pulse raising a thunder in his ears. The only thing that kept him rooted in the shack was the promise he had heard in Cenovio's voice. He forced himself to concentrate on the rain. Surely it would come. It had to come.

———

The pilgrims' group sat on the ground, watching and listening as José sang. He stooped occasionally to take powders and liquids from various bags and clay dishes at his feet. He sang for a few minutes then bent to put his fingers into one or another of the vessels, stood and flicked them in the direction of the pillar and effigy.

Oz circulated among the group and told them to eat their mushrooms and drink their water.

Pete hesitated. He was enjoying the show, watching the firelight in electric play on the singing priest's glowing feathers, silver, and green stone. The man had turned into a pillar of meaning. The song, his body, the fire, the feathers and jewels, the night and the stela with the stone head had joined in a crucible

264

of significance that transcended thought. It was everything but thought. Also, the drink had given Pete a glow and feeling of peace, an acquiescence to every sensation, that he did not want to change. He was not afraid of the mushrooms, he was not afraid to step through The Gate to Heaven. But he was so . . . comfortable.

He was not surprised that Oz did not bid him to eat. He was relieved. He turned his eyes back to the singer and the song, to descend into the molten moment and meld his body with the music and the fire.

There was no sensation of time's passage. Pete only knew that the singer had turned and walked to the group, stooped, and taken Pete's hand to lift him to his feet. He joined his hand with Pete's and led him to the pillar. Pete gasped at what he saw when he stood up.

The moon had risen above the horizon. It was a thinnest crescent of silvery orange light, the last night of the waning moon. It sat on top of the stone visage like a celestial ornament. The trees behind the stela danced in the firelight, framed the pillar and the stone head in a feathery flow of night and heaven. Out of the dark mouth came a feeling that filled Pete's chest with a beauty he had never known before. Peace. Peace. Peace. Pete raised his hands to the bidding god. Tears flooded his face. The horseman had come back for him.

The two priests took Pete by his hands. They led him carefully to the stone pile for which Pete had known he was bound the moment he had stepped into the glade. He raised his arms again and the men removed his shirt. So beautiful.

He turned and looked at the visage again. The moon glowed above the trees, the stars made silent music and joined in a harmonic wave of love, which caused Pete's face to wash again with grateful tears.

The priests sat Pete on the low altar and motioned for him to lie down. When he did, two beautiful bird-men took his hands and held them gently, lovingly. Two others put their hands on his legs, removed his shoes and held his feet in the same loving way.

Pete turned his wet face from the starry sky and looked at the four wonderful creatures who were holding him. They had been joined by the most beautiful animal he had ever seen. Its coat was a mottled blanket of liquid gold and black. Its eyes were a deep emerald green with a resonant ruby set in each center. The red of the pupils beamed at him, transfixed his will with an exciting rush of feeling that centered in his groin. The beautiful beast rattled in its throat, flashed its teeth and slowly lashed its long tail. Pete's legs were spread by the bird-men to receive it. The cat put its paws on the stones and lithely vaulted up.

The animal's breath filled his lungs as it placed its cheek against his. The cool breath smelled of roses and wafted across his face like a freshening breeze. Then the animal put its paw on his chest and said 'I am the Jaguar.'

'Yes.'

'I am here to bring the rain. Can you feel it coming?'

'Yes.'

'I am here for the rose.'

'Yes.'

'I will take it now.'

'Yes.'

The Jaguar removed its paw from his chest and a red bloom which had been hidden under the paw began to grow. Pete was overpowered by the physical sensation of the great blossom widening its petals, welling, growing larger and larger, the red color taking on a metallic sheen in which the pink firelight ran in pulses.

Then Pete was looking down on the scene from above. The change was not surprising. It was only different. And he knew that his part was done. It was time to go.

He stared down for a moment, not surprised to see himself lying on the stone altar in the firelight, the brilliant priests holding his limbs and Olga kneeling between his legs. In one hand Olga held a glowing green blade and in the other she held a bloody heart.

He looked down at Oz and the other travellers. Most had fallen to their knees and raised their arms, their mouths open. Then suddenly, one of the men with silver hair clutched at his chest, spun and fell silently to the ground. The woman beside him grabbed her hair at the temples and her mouth gaped in a silent shriek.

The priests and anglos, Oz and the Jaguar Woman ran to the man lying at the feet of the silently shrieking woman.

Pete rose slowly in the silence and drifted into the smoky black night like a balloon. He glanced up and saw that the moon and stars were gone. He looked again at the slowly receding scene below. Oz was working on the fallen man, his shoulders hunched as he pumped with stiffened arms. Pete looked at the altar. The man lying there blinked. His eyes opened.

Pete turned to the dark, to look for his horse. His white horse with the beautiful eyes. It would be coming from the light. He knew that he should look for the light. He believed that the light would come, and with it the horse to carry him away. He waited in the perfect dark, but the shining horse did not come. Then he realized that he had made a terrible mistake. Many terrible mistakes.

Chapter 33

Tom woke when the thunder rolled. He cursed himself under his breath for having fallen asleep. He rose and stepped to the door to open it. When the lightning flashed he saw the dogs were gone from under the bougainvillea. He waited for another flash and, without any conscious decision, put his feet to work as the thunder boomed from the black sky. He stumbled on the furrows of the field but kept running in the direction of the wood he had seen illuminated by the lightning.

The thunder faded and the dark returned. The only sound was his ragged breath and the sound of his footsteps in the dusty clods. His ears were tuned for the sound of barking dogs in hot pursuit but they didn't pick up any sounds except those of his running stumble. He fell. He picked himself up, wiped his hands, and adjusted the backpack. At zenith overhead was a moon only a sigh away from invisibility. He ran awkwardly, tripping and staggering on the uneven ground and stubs of corn stalk.

The field ended and his feet felt the smooth forest floor. Then a great light flashed and he was struck down. Lying on his back, feeling the pain spread through his head, he believed he had been hit by lightning. He was afraid that he was dying, tasted blood. He raised his hand to his face, felt the sticky wetness, and knew what had happened. The lightning flashed and confirmed his guess that he had run into a tree. He rolled to his knees, waited for another flash and moved carefully in the direction of a clearing that had presented itself in the last pulse of white light.

He did not want to get too far into the woods, too far from the corner of the field. He needed to find the trail as soon as he could. Running his tongue over his split lip and wiping at the blood which ran from his nose, he turned in the direction he had come. He fingered the big knot growing on his head.

"Damn," he said and grinned in spite of his wound. He was out of the village and away from the dogs.

The lightning came and went and he saw no one crossing the field behind him. His escape was still undiscovered. It would be safe to use the flashlight.

He put his pack on the ground and rummaged in the junk pocket, where he had put the flashlight after Cenovio left the bathhouse. He turned the focusing ring and the little instrument shed its precious light. Tom turned his back to the field and pointed the lens away from the direction of the houses. Holding it as close to perpendicular as was practical, he zig-zagged the clearing until he found the trail and started up it as fast as he could go.

―――――

Concha could not sleep. She was back in Chalcatongo with Grandfather and his family, waiting for José and Patricio to negotiate with the government's team in San Miguel. It hardly seemed possible, but they'd heard that the government, in fact the President himself, had offered them amnesty and promised to accede to all the demands José had made in the original press conference. The same thing had happened in Chiapas.

But what was genuinely amazing was that the governor of Oaxaca wanted to meet with Concha herself, wanted to talk to her about what she recommended. He, too, was taking his cues from the events in the neighboring state to the south. In Chiapas the governor had been sacked, along with much of his administration, and replaced by someone more sympathetic to the needs of the Indian peoples. He had even sent word that the president of the country was interested in meeting her, if it could be arranged.

She stood outside the entrance to the cave and watched the sky. The fragile husk of the moon looked so delicate, set there among the pulsing stars.

A breeze had blown the haze from the sky. It had turned cool now and lightning flashed over the mountains to the south. After a minute or so, she heard the faint roll of thunder. The lightning danced on the summits, limning them in an instant of white light. And again, louder this time, the thunder rolled.

Ah, she thought, and took in a deep breath. Her lungs filled with the clean smell of cool air moving in from the east. Rain.

She ran her senses down from the soles of her bare feet, searching the earth itself for another sense of change for the better. Good. The ground itself felt solid again. Dzaui was content.

Concha turned her mind to the events of the last month and was amazed at how much had transpired. The death of her husband, their flight back to Mixteca, the horrible event south of Culiacan, the loss of Dzaui, and her captivity. The string of events ran through her head like a movie, ending with a mental picture of the camera lenses pointed at her and the reporters asking her questions that, amazingly, she knew all the answers to.

How had she gotten here? It was a mystery. As a child, she had been as anonymous as any person could possibly be in this world. She was raised in a dirt-poor village in the Oaxacan Sierra, one of the most poverty-stricken places on the face of the earth. Then came the unbelievable luck of being taken as a wife by a rich man and given a place of honor in an enormous house far away. She had learned a great deal while she was there. And she had seen things. Her education had not been trivial.

She pulled her shawl tighter around her shoulders and buried her hands in it. The air was growing cooler by the moment, as the lightning danced closer and closer, moving out from the summit of Nindo Tocoshu.

She walked to a tree and leaned against it, to watch the drama of the sky and wait for the first drops of the blessed, blessed rain. Her people would be happy and that made her happiest of all. Indeed, she had been a big part of the whole thing. Somehow, the dangerous task of returning The Heart of the World to the people had fallen to her. She was genuinely grateful that she had been chosen to play that role. It had brought the sweet rain, the smell of which was riding in on the freshening breeze at that very moment.

Destiny. Was there anything to all that? Was it true that each person is given a task to do, something important in the enormous scheme of things? Something that could change the world? Surely not.

That was the worst part of being human — the gods kept one so pitifully blind to all but what is needed for the moment. Understanding is given in such small pieces! One day at a time.

———

The thunder woke Polly. At first she didn't know what had brought her out of her troubled sleep. The lamp was on and she sat up. She'd fallen asleep in her clothes and her mouth tasted like an ashtray. Her body was sticky. Stripping her clothes, she went to the bathroom, turned on the water in the shower and waited for it to warm. Lightning flashed outside, flickering the window in the bathroom an opalescent blue. She stepped to the door and turned out the light, then returned to the tub.

She opened the window and breathed the air that rushed through the screen. The smoky smell was gone and the air was sweet. She opened her mouth and let the water rinse away the taste of the cigarette, then put her head into the stream and let it run down her face and over her breasts. She turned and let the water clean the stickiness from her back. As the pleasantly warm water washed over her, she took in a big breath of the fresh air. She drooped her chin to her chest, loosening the muscles in her shoulders, shaking her head slowly from side to side, relaxing.

Then she remembered Tom.

She snapped her head up, and felt the muscles in her shoulders tighten again. She put her face closer to the window, scanning the air for a sense of him. But there was nothing to comfort her. Tom was still gone, and now it was raining. Again, she felt absolutely helpless. A deep sense of depression overwhelmed her and she began to cry, her tears falling with the warm water.

———

Tom was making good time up the trail, given the fact that he was running by the light of a flashlight. His breathing was labored but he'd been running in the mountains around his house for months and was in decent shape. Thank God for Polly and her insistence that he start an exercise program. A year ago he would have been puking his guts up from the effort, but at that moment he was only breathing hard.

And then the rain hit. It began with a few big drops then quickened to a steady light rain. He decided to don the poncho, taking it from the day pack. But when he stepped back onto the trail, enough water had fallen that the track was slick with mud. The earth apparently contained a lot of clay. He would have to walk, no matter how much he wanted to maintain the fast pace of the previous fifteen minutes. At any rate, he reassured himself, he was a long way in front of any pursuit and it was still dark. Besides, from the sound of it the only ones likely to chase him were probably passed out by now. From the noise they'd been making just before he dropped off to sleep, they had been pretty damn far into the mezcal jug.

He slipped and slid on the steep trail. The rain slacked a bit but did not stop. He had to stretch his steps to stay on the rocks in the trail. It was slow going. But the new day would soon begin. There was almost enough light, in spite of the rain clouds, to turn off the flashlight.

He was prompted by thoughts of the flashlight to the two little men, Cenovio and Agustino, who had helped him as much as they could. In contrast to the two pistoleros, they were people with a heart for their fellow men. Despite the evil in this world, it seemed, there was a symmetry to it all. One evil man — one good man. From his own experience, he was convinced that every person has the choice to do good or ill. The results of good choices and willful, bad, choices are known to all. Every thing you choose to do has consequences — and the events in your life proceed from the choices you make. A universal law. Tom mouthed a prayer of thanks for the Cenovios and Agustinos of the world. He would be surely be dead without them. Tom hoped that God had noticed, and counted, the mercies of the two little Indian men.

Tom stepped off the slippery trail and into the shelter of a big pine tree. He dropped the pack and knelt to put the flashlight inside. The smell of pine needles and wet air suddenly flashed his mind back to his house in the mountains of Wyoming. For a moment he was almost overcome with a longing for home. He wanted to be in his house, with Polly. He wanted to feel safe.

He shook his head clear of the thought. He had to stay focused. The mountain was steep, the trail hard. And God only knew what awaited him.

The duff under the tree was comfortable to his knees. He put his hand down and felt its resilience, a softness he had not felt in what seemed like centuries. His butt was sore from the two days spent sitting on the cement floor of the bathhouse. He decided to take a little rest.

He put his back to the tree and stretched his legs. In his hurry to get up the trail and away from the village he had not comprehended the toll the trail was taking on his body. He was winded and hungry. His feet hurt and his legs ached.

He took off the poncho and turned it inside out to dry a bit and let the perspiration on his body dissipate. He was thirsty too. He'd lost a lot of water, hurrying under the plastic rain coat.

But I'm free, he thought. This is no time to indulge in thoughts of anger or revenge. This is enough. All he had to do was keep his mind in the "now" and stay vigilant to his surroundings.

The most important thing at the moment was to find the branching trail. Cenovio had not given him any notion of how far up the mountain the trail split, and he was worried more than a little by the possibility that he had jogged past it in the dark.

He leaned back against the tree, thankful for the opportunity to catch his breath. He looked around. In the dawning light he saw that he was on familiar ground, sitting on a steep hillside in the middle of a pine forest. He was a backpacker and a hunter so some of his fondest memories were built on his experiences in the mountains. This quiet forest, at dawn, in a light rain, was his present idea of heaven.

He looked at a tree nearby and something caught his eye. Something that looked like a pineapple perched on a limb. At first, his mind wanted it to be an owl, but there was no animal in the world that looked like this object. Having no idea what it was, he turned his eyes to the hillside itself. The more he looked, the stranger it all began to seem. There were plants that looked like nothing he'd ever seen before. Spiky, fleshy leaved. The grasses were wiry and strange to the touch. Also, though he'd been trained somewhat as a geologist, the rocks looked like nothing in any of the specimen drawers he'd ever opened. And not far from where he sat, there was a small agave plant. To his mind, an agave was a desert plant and the strange juxtaposition of a desert plant in a mountain forest set a little current of confusion running through his mind. He looked back at the thing in the tree. There were several others nearby. The closer he looked, the stranger it all became.

The rain had stopped, he noticed. Good. The trail had been verging on impossible. But wait, he needed the rain to obliterate the signs of his passage up the trail. He looked at the path and saw evidence of his flight in the inch of mud which had been dust an hour earlier — long gouges where he'd slipped on the mud, and where he hadn't, the distinctive track of his American-made running shoes. A donkey could have figured out who'd been making his way on the trail.

Damn! He quickly rolled up his poncho and stuffed it into the pack. Then he stood hurriedly, his mind racing. He would have to stay in the grass and duff beside the trail, unless it began to rain hard enough to wash out his tracks.

It was obvious that he would be following the trail, leaving it in order to hide signs of his passage but needing it for guidance. Hell, anyone with half a brain could figure that out. But he had to stay near this trail until he found the fork which led over the top of the mountain. Then he would have some idea where the pass which led to the wooded canyon was. Once in the pass he could decide whether to deviate from the trail. But even that could be dangerous. Dropping into the wrong canyon from a high ridge can lead to a lot of bad situations — the very least would mean coming out at a place far from the well-traveled road Cenovio had described. That's where he needed to be. He looked around, at the wood which was becoming weirder by the moment. He had to get the hell out of here.

He shrugged his pack on and looked around. He wanted a walking stick. They were damn handy in the mountains, not to mention on slippery grass and mud. Luckily, it only took a two-minute search to find a dead shrub which had stood long enough for the wood to be seasoned hard. He wrenched a limb from the rotting base then laid it on a rock and broke it to a convenient length. Looking back up the trail, he saw that the going would be steep, but if he took his time he could make it without having to step in the trail.

From what he could see, it would be better to walk on the down side. He stepped over the muddy trail and onto the grass and rocks. After a moment, he turned to see what kind of marks his feet were making. Very faint. It would take a good tracker to find where he'd been, and he doubted there were many of those down here.

At that moment something caught his ear. He closed his eyes in order to concentrate on what the air was carrying, what had sparked his attention. His heart began to pound in his ears as he concentrated, making it hard to hear. But the sound was unmistakable — distant, frenzied barking. Dogs. A pack of dogs.

Chapter 34

Sam and Polly were drinking coffee in Polly's room. Being familiar with the way of things in Mexico, she had brought coffee bags and a heating coil which boiled hotel water in the cup. The restaurant didn't open until seven-thirty and she didn't like the sugary coffee in the mercado. By borrowing cups from the restaurant, they could have their coffee en el estilo americano. Hot and black.

"It sure smells good out there, not so smoky," Sam said. "It musta rained pretty good for a while, there's puddles in the courtyard out there."

"The lightning and thunder woke me up. It rained real hard for ten minutes or so, but it gradually slowed to this." She waved her hand at the window, referring to the damp morning with monster gray and black clouds piling slowly up on the eastern horizon.

"When I came back from the tactical center it looked like it was going to be coming down in sheets any time now. I've seen it rain out on the plains, in the Powder River Basin, and I thought I'd seen clouds before . . ." He left the sentence unfinished, to indicate how impressed he'd been with the power of the storm.

"What's going on over there, anyway?" Polly asked. She looked terrible. Her hair was piled carelessly on her head in a damp coil and black circles made her blue eyes look washed out.

"Apparently they have made contact with the leaders and are negotiating. One of the things they want first, is to know where Tom is and if he's all right.

"All the cops and soldiers over there are mad as hell, they want to go in and break some heads. But I guess the media feeding frenzy that occurred during the Chiapas rebellion caused some major political fallout. The powers-that-be are in favor of negotiation, though the conservatives think the government gave away the store down there. They think this incident is a stickup and will encourage every little political splinter group to buy ski masks and call a press conference."

Polly frowned. "Well, if they had let the little bit of money intended to roll into the communities not roll into their own pockets, they might not be in this position. Only one peso out of twenty intended for the Indian communities ever makes it past the grasp of the police and government officials responsible for administration and distribution. It's the story of Mexican bureaucracy. They're just pissed because they're going to miss out on what they've come to think of as their share. I have no sympathy whatsoever."

"But they are right, in a way."

"What way?"

"When people only have to don hoods and carry guns to get what they want, it's not a recipe for public order. You can't stick up the government every time you please, using the media as a weapon. The police have to be free to do their job."

"Sam, if you knew what the job of the police has been down here since time immemorial, you would be shocked. This is not America, believe you me — though I must admit that things have been changing for the better lately. The federal police seem to be cleaning up their act, somewhat."

"Well, after finding out what Jesús and Berto were up to, it's easy enough to believe. They've got Berto sitting in the jail over there and it doesn't look good for him."

"What was that all about, anyway? What were they up to?"

"They were dealing in artifacts, but only world-class artifacts of the type Ward dealt in. They were using their offices as cops to get them. They were letting drug growers and transporters off the hook in exchange for the artifacts, most of which were being hidden and cared for by families who wanted to preserve their heritage.

He continued. "I guess there are a whole lot of things that date back to the days before Columbus and they are being kept by particular people in the community. Berto knew this because he's an Indian and in a typical Mixtec community. Well anyway, he told Jesús about some of the stuff he knew was hidden by particular families and others related to secret religious ceremonies. Because this is a big dope-growing state, they would barter with people they'd arrested: Lead us to major artifacts and, if they're valuable enough, we'll let you go. I guess they found some very, very important pieces that way."

"So they were robbing those families or communities of their history, their religion. And without a second thought. Nice guys. But pretty typical," Polly said.

"Yeah. But this is where it gets interesting. They were working with the late Nathaniel Ward."

"You're kidding."

"Nope. The guys from the Attorney General's office have been interrogating Berto and, you might be surprised, they are giving me everything they've gotten out of him."

"Surprise, surprise. Did this guy say what he was doing in Jackson Hole?"

"Yes. He was there to do damage control."

"What kind of damage control?"

"Find out what he could about the investigation into Ward's murder — whether he'd kept records and if they'd been compromised. Unfortunately, we shared some information with him that we probably shouldn't have. Tom told him all about the computer files the FBI was working on and that was relayed back to Jesús, apparently. We have phone records that show calls to Tlaxiaco. But there is something much bigger going on here, too."

"Like what?"

"Apparently Ward's customers had hired Bernalillo and Berto to investigate and do what they could to find out the extent of the damage. Also, Bernalillo sent Berto north to assassinate Ward's wife, knowing she knew too much — including their names and who they worked for. We almost supported a rogue operation and could have been a party to a murder, or murders.

"But then the Osorios turned up back in Mexico and I sent Tom down here with a hit man." Sam shook his head. "But, besides the little deal those two were doing on the side, they have led us to some important info on the smuggling and artifact dealing scene — a partial customer list that Jesús had in his briefcase. He wrote down some names Ward had mentioned while they were doing business."

"Why would he do that?"

Sam shrugged. "Just covering his backside. He could use it to pressure Ward, blackmail him. Or he might have been planning on cutting Ward out and marketing direct to the collectors. The list includes Germans, Swiss, Mexicans, Canadians, Americans — one of those on it is the Honorable Nathaniel "Nat" Ward."

"You are kidding!"

"Nope. And, unless I miss my guess, it was Congressman Ward's collection that inspired his young nephew's interest in archaeology. It also inspired him, unless I'm wrong as hell here too, to become a dealer in stolen artifacts. Who would be a better person to connect Doc Ward with a network of multi-millionaire collectors? Bernalillo was working for Ward, no doubt in my mind."

Polly grimaced. "So he is the one who is responsible for Thomas being down here, then."

"No. I am responsible for that. I can't point the finger at anyone but myself. We have no business being down here. We're in a foreign country where the rules are different, where the values are inverted." Sam looked out the window. "I just want to get Tom back and go home."

"Me too." And the strong woman Sam had come to know dropped her head and began to weep. Sam reached out a comforting hand and she took it, held onto it. Then she began to cry as if her heart would break.

———

Tom was running. He was not jogging, he was running. The muddy trail was impossible to travel on and he had given it up, choosing to stick to the rocks, grass and duff that bordered the track. It was slippery in places and he'd fallen so many times it all seemed like the same painful racking of his knees, shins and palms. But in the better areas he had been able to push himself to the limit. And then some.

His breathing was ragged, his chest heaved as his brain tried to stay ahead of his body, which was burning oxygen faster than he could get it in his lungs. A black border fringed his vision and great drops of perspiration dropped constantly onto his eyelids, making it even harder to see. He was falling into serious oxygen debt.

But the baying of the dogs from the village below told him his escape had been discovered. It would not have taken long to find his tracks, even if they were only half-assed trackers. He cursed himself for not thinking to stay off the muddy trail. Stupid!

But he had a lead on them that would be hard to overcome. All he had to do was keep moving at a steady pace. They would have to be practiced runners to catch him and he didn't think that anyone who had been drinking all night was any match for him. And the burros he'd seen, none of them more than four feet high, damn sure couldn't cover the ground very quickly.

Luckily he was running on the upper side of the trail when he came to the junction of the trails that Cenovio had described. He stopped, badly in need of oxygen. Gasping, he dropped the pack and opened it. He jerked out the sweat pants, dropped to one knee and put the cuff on a rock. He took another rock and pounded a hole in the pants a couple of inches above the elastic band, then put his index fingers in the hole and ripped the cuff from the pants, placing it on his head for a sweatband. It was tight, but it would do. He stuffed the pants back in the pack, threw it on his back, and looked up the trail. It was steep as hell. Also, the stratigraphy showed him that the mountain was made of sedimentary rock characterized by regular outcroppings. It would be tough going.

At that moment he heard the dog. He turned and looked down the trail. Oso was standing in the middle of the trail, looking back over his shoulder with his tongue hanging out a foot, barking maniacally. He'd seen Tom, and apparently could also see the pursuers. They might be no more than two hundred meters behind.

Tom vaulted up the trail. The brief respite had given his body the rest it needed and the rush of adrenaline the dog inspired was pumping through his body as well.

He ran, taking little steps and jabbing the sides of his feet into the now-soft soil. The first fifty meters were comparatively easy, but then he was in the first rock band and the going was bad. Rocks rolled from under his feet and the dirt which had accumulated over the dusty summer was now mud, a thin film of slippery mud which made the rocks shrug his feet away as if they were covered with grease.

He slipped. His right knee hit the rock so hard that a flash of light exploded in his eyes. But could not allow himself the time to feel pain. His whole being was concentrated on getting over the rocks to the little flat place that usually lay on top. There his body would be given a moment's rest, and it would need all it could get.

His mind worked as he scrambled. He had to concentrate on where to put his grasp and where each foot could go, looking for bare rock that afforded enough friction to support his weight. The dog was going to be on him by the time he reached the top of the rocks, he knew that. He was not going to let the bastard bite him, he promised himself. Not that arrogant son-of-a-bitch mongrel who'd made a point of pissing through the flimsy door of the bathhouse every time he walked by.

When he reached the top of the rocks, the dog was right behind him. It was barking insanely now, calling to the pursuers with a frenzy that said Tom was close.

Tom turned to face the animal. His lungs were burning, his throat raw from the exertion. In his blurred vision he saw a rock the right size for throwing. He bent to pick it up. But this was a Mexican dog, with a sixth sense for what distance any man is capable of throwing a rock accurately. He dodged back down the trail and stood at the bottom of the rocks, baying loudly. His eyes were hard, intelligent, predatory. At Tom's throw, he dodged behind a small boulder like a veteran of ten thousand assaults. If he could not hit the dog with a rock, his only alternative was to hit him with the walking stick and his pursuers would damn sure catch him if he spent any time at all flailing uselessly at this beast.

His strength was failing. His legs were numb and his chest afire. But the sensations were something he could prioritize, push down, put away. It was the physical realities that were putting a damper on him and his flight. The air was thin; he was forty-three; he'd not had anything to eat for almost ten hours. No amount of adrenaline or inspiration could make up for those facts.

He turned to face the dog again. It was almost at his heels at the turn, reaching out to take Tom's leg in his big sharp teeth. But the animal's reflexes threw him backward at the last moment, sensing that the man with the stick could reach him. He bounded back ten meters and bared his teeth in a horrible grimace.

"You . . . son . . . of . . . a . . . bitch!" he gasped, and looked around for a rock. But there was nothing more than wilted grass at hand. And the dog knew it. He turned his head to let the pursuers know he had his quarry, alternately baring his teeth at Tom and lolling his tongue to gasp for air. After a moment he turned his head around, keeping one eye on Tom, and again bayed crazily.

Tom was nearing panic. His oxygen-depleted brain would go into neutral from the fear if he did not do something about this animal. Then he remembered the hunting slingshot, the one he'd put in the day pack the last time he'd gone elk-hunting, in case he saw grouse. He dropped the pack to the ground and put his arm inside.

The dog lunged. He pulled his arm out in time to grasp the walking stick. The dog, anticipating Tom's intent, dodged back.

Tommy put his left hand in the pack, holding the stick in his right. The dog stayed ten meters or so away, his barking filling the air with raucous noise. Then Tom's hand found the slingshot and he pulled it out. He dropped it to the top of his pack and felt for the plastic sack of steel shot. When his hand closed on the sack, his lips moved in thanks.

But as soon as he put the stick down to unwrap the surgical tubing that was wound round the fork of the weapon, the dog dodged in to bite. Tom moved his hand toward the stick, the dog leaped back as Tom freed the rubber tubes. He grasped at the sack and the dog attacked again, retreating only when Tom dropped the sack.

Desperate, Tom realized that it was going to be impossible to load the slingshot without getting bitten. Gritting his teeth, he stuck out his left foot to try to keep the dog away while he manipulated his weapon.

The dog was on his foot in a heartbeat. And the pain was paralyzing. Tom shrieked at the bite, at the teeth running their full length into the sides of his foot at the instep. Snot flew from his nose and his hands shook as he tried to make his brain concentrate on loading the slingshot. He cried out again as the animal growled viciously, pulling his prey down the hill on the slick grass.

Tom put all his will into the weapon, his brain going into slow motion in order to cope with the impulses of intense pain which it was being asked to ignore while trying to concentrate on a fine motor skill. It was almost more than it could handle. Almost.

The suffering man was not aware of aiming or releasing the steel shot but his brain scored the effect of the missile. The animal was killed instantly. The small round shot, at a distance of only a meter, pierced the dog's skull. The jaws released, the body slacked and collapsed. It slid on the steep, wet slope, hit a protruding rock and stopped.

Tom glanced momentarily at the dead dog. Then he scrambled back up the slope to his backpack. The pain from his wounded foot sent a spasm rocketing through his body but threw a switch in his brain so the pain decreased to a throb. He grabbed the stick, realizing he would be have to use it more as a crutch than anything else. He turned back up the steep hill and began his flight again. Down the hill, out of sight below the rock band, he could hear the voices of panting, cursing men.

That was enough of an inspiration to send Tom flying up the slope, his feet churning on the grass and mud, his stick stabbing into the slope. He reached a little turn in the trail and it leveled out for a distance of about fifty meters. The flat place would give his body a chance to catch up with his will. Again, he was falling into oxygen debt and his sight was closing like the lens of a camera.

As he jogged along the flat section he raised his eyes for a moment and a thrill ran through him. He could see daylight through the trees! It was the ridgeline. The pass that led to the other side of the mountain range was less than a hundred meters above him. He was going to make it.

He cut almost straight uphill, leaving the trail when he saw a rib of rock that angled up the slope. It gave him solid footing, and it also gave him cover from the eyes of the men behind him. Then he remembered that he had not heard voices for some time. He stopped for a moment and took the opportunity to glance over the rock rib. There was no one in sight on the trail! He was outpacing them. They probably stopped to examine the body of the dog. Good!

His legs summoned strength where there should have been none. His lungs were on fire, the rush of air seared his throat. But he was almost there. He glanced up and saw an enormous agave plant. Even in his near-stupor he couldn't help but be impressed with the thing. It was probably four meters high and branched out to a circumference of five meters. Rust-colored pine needles were piled on the enormous fleshy leaves. It stood like some sort of extraterrestrial sentinel. And just up the hill from it, on the skyline, was a man on a mule. The man had a pistol in his hand. Shocked, Tom staggered to a stop. His chest heaved, his vision ran in and out of focus, his overloaded heart almost exploded.

The man on the mule was shouting down the hill to the other men. Above the pounding in his ears, Tom heard answering shouts. He wanted to cry, he wanted to throw himself on the ground, he wanted to kill himself. Anything but be held prisoner again. Not by these men and their dogs.

The man on the big roan mule was the one with the big lip and the murderous eyes. But now his eyes were mocking, alight with intense humor. He sat on his mule, the pistol held casually in his hand as he shouted down the hill. He was describing Tom to the others, saying how pathetic he looked. The goad of his mocking was painful, but even more painful was the sight of the pistol in the man's hand. It was Tom's own service arm.

Perhaps it was that final insult that made Tom remember: Never, never, never, never give up. He dropped his pack and raised his hands, abject. The man on the animal pursed his mouth, worked his throat, and launched a huge gobbet of spit down the hill at Tom.

Tom stooped and retrieved his backpack, unzipping it as he began a slow walk around the huge agave, putting it between himself and the mounted man.

The rider responded by jabbing the mule with his heels and riding to the other side of the agave, raising the pistol as he did. But he was in no hurry, his compadres were in sight now. The gringo was trapped and now the time to kill him had come. Demetrio was at first puzzled by what he saw. The man with the funny headband, wet and muddy clothes, the bloody shoe, had his arms raised in front of his face. Demetrio dropped the pistol, curious. The pose was so odd.

The steel shot entered his eye through the upper lid, rolling it back to expose the upper part of the orb in a flash of white. Tom knew when he released the projectile that it was going exactly where he'd willed it to go, but he was still surprised by the instantaneous effect of the impact. Demetrio didn't utter a sound, simply threw his arms over his head and fell backwards from his mount. He hit the ground, rolled swiftly to his elbows and knees, and put his hands to his face. The surprised animal ran a couple of paces and whirled to look at the fallen rider.

Then came the scream. If Tom had not been scrambling for the pistol lying in the grass, if he had not been seething with hatred, he might have even felt a twinge of pity. But he did not.

Once he had recovered his pistol he popped out the clip and checked it. It was full. He glanced at the fallen, screaming man and dismissed him for the moment. He then ran to the side of the agave and looked around it. Three men were standing down the hill, fifty meters away. They were soaked in sweat, hats in their hands and mud-splashed to their knees. One was wearing a holster and had a .45 in his hand, the other two wielded machetes. Their black eyebrows and mustaches stood out in stark contrast with their pale sweating faces.

It took a moment for them to understand what they were seeing. The gringo was pointing a gun at them. Their hearts vaulted, their legs froze.

Tom shot the man holding the gun, who spun and fell, grabbing his thigh where the bullet had pierced. The other two men dropped their machetes and ran, leaving him to drag himself to his feet and hobble down the hill for the shelter of the rocks below. To his credit, he made no sound louder than a gasp. He'd been shot before.

Tom turned swiftly to the man on the ground behind him. He was sitting now, one hand over the ruined eye. He was not screaming, but sat with gritted teeth and his one good eye on Tom. There was more hate on his face than fear. If he had shown fear Tom might have left him sitting there on the ground. But the one defiant eye moved him to smash the man's skull with his pistol. Demetrio groaned, rolled to his stomach, and grasped the top of his head with the other hand. He groaned again and dug his feet alternately into the hillside, his legs moving in spasms as his body was overwhelmed by the intense pain.

Tom stepped to the fallen man and aimed the pistol at the back of the shaggy head, which was seeping a lot of blood through the fingers of the clasping hand. But his promise to himself came back to him. Never again. Tom turned his back.

He walked to the mule, his hand out. The mule lowered his head and pricked his long roan ears but stood still. "Ho, boy," Tom said softly, "ho, boy. C'mere." Surprisingly, the animal responded to the English words. It's eyes softened, its lip pulled up in a bit of a grin and it even made a pleased little sound when Tom took the reins, then rubbed his forehead.

Tom turned and looked at the man on the ground. He was curled into a ball and groaning deeply. The men behind the rocks were not visible. Tom pointed the pistol where he saw them disappear and pulled off a round. The recoil of the gun and the sound of the ricocheting bullet gave him a feeling of deep, deep satisfaction. He was in control again.

He retrieved his backpack, mounted the long-legged mule from the uphill side and sat for a moment. His hands and arms were shaking uncontrollably. He stomach was doing vaults. His eyes were running tears and he was hiccuping. He turned the mule up the hill, rejoicing in the feel of the beast's strong, muscular strides as if it were his own renewed strength that propelled them up the hill. He was strong again. He was going to make it.

Once on the ridge line, he stopped and turned to look at the man he'd wounded. The man had not moved, was still curled in a tight ball. His muddy clothes and posture gave Tom a twinge. Not a twinge of conscience but a twinge of empathy. He could see himself curled in the bathhouse, lying in his own puke. What goes around comes around, he said to himself. There was a satisfying symmetry to it all.

———

The rain came again. This time it came in full buckets of water. It came in tubs full of water. It made so much noise on the roof and outside the window that it woke Polly from her profoundly depressed sleep.

Groggily, she rose from the bed and went to the window. She could barely make out the couple of cars in the courtyard, only twenty meters away. The rain pounded on the roofs and hoods of the autos, raising a tinny din. Rain spouts gouted water in arcs thick as a man's arm, propelled it three meters out, where it landed and turned into a splashing fountain.

Polly walked to the bed and turned on the lamp to light the darkened room. She went to the bathroom and washed her face. Looking in the mirror, she saw that her face had aged ten years. She brushed her teeth and returned to the bedroom for her hairbrush.

She stood at the window, watching the driving rain, as she brushed her hair. It felt good. She closed her eyes and counted... twelve, thirteen, fourteen, fifteen . . . it didn't help. Her head was aching.

She walked to the bed, sat down and returned to brushing. "What am I doing here?!" she said aloud suddenly. 'Why am I not with my family?' Her thoughts of Christina, Maria and Ferdie rushed into her head. 'They are worried sick, I know. I left them for no good reason. Here I have a family in California who loves me and this is how I am treating them. Ferdie is a good father to our daughters. He is brilliant, influential and cares for me deeply. Even if he is unfaithful to me, our life together has been liveable.

'Now I have left him for a man who is vulnerable, yet reckless and whose ambitions are limited. In a little over a year he has been stabbed almost to death and I have almost died with him. Now he is kidnapped deep in the mountains of Mexico and I am here alone. This relationship with Thomas Thompson will be the end of me.'

"I must be insane to be here!" she muttered to herself. She put down the brush and picked up the phone. The desk answered.

"Mande?"

"Llamame un taxi. Pronto."

"Si, Señora."

"Inmediatemente."

"Si, Señora."

Polly hurriedly packed and dressed. She grabbed her purse and left the room. She walked toward the office, heedless of the pouring rain. She had started to weep from fear and exhaustion. At the edge of the patio she stopped beside a large potted camellia.

Still crying, Polly took off her engagement ring. One last time she looked at the engraving: 'You and no other.' She gently dropped it among the freshly fallen pink petals. Then she dashed across the wet patio to the waiting taxi.

In the darkness, at the edge of the patio stood one of the kitchen girls who had witnessed the scene. After a moment, she hurried to the camellia and retrieved the ring. She held it to the light before she slipped it on her finger. It fit perfectly.

Chapter 35

Tom looked up at the dawn sky over the Nochixtlan Valley. The clouds were piling and piling as the morning light turned them a brassy gold along the edges. As he watched, the formation grew. It built and built like a tower until it outpaced his whole experience of clouds. He had seen storm clouds over the Great Plains and thought them impossible to surpass, but this was a new standard. The storm front became an immensity that staggered his perceptions of what a sky would accept.

The bottom of the formation grew black, the swollen sides turned brassier, verging on a molten red. It boiled and pumped, rising and rising and rising as it ballooned. Lightning began to snap from the bottom of the mass. It was stilll a few kilometers away, and his knowledge of that distance increased his awe at the size of the cloud mass which had crossed the line, surely, between natural and unnatural phenomena. The mule seemed to sense it also, sometimes turning his head and rolling his eyes as he took a couple of dancing steps sideways in the damp trail.

The drought would end in a battering beyond memory, the angry immensity sweeping down the heavens and blotting the earthscape from view. It was something of the gods' making, a product larger for having been held at bay so long. Nature was pouncing on the occasion with a vengeance.

The cold, wet wind came first, in a blast that frosted Tom's face. Moments later came the lightning. The first bolt landed less than fifty meters from him, blasting the top of an oak tree into sparks and splinters, its plume of evanescent smoke drowned instantly by the wet wind. The mule hunched his back and skittered, but did not try to buck. Then came a drenching rain in drops the size of grapes. Hail came right behind it, robbing Tom of his breath. He was cold to the bone in moments, in spite of the sweater and poncho he'd stopped to put on when he saw the storm front building.

The trail was soon running with water and growing softer by the moment. Travel would be impossible before too long. But the lightning was holding Tom's, and the mule's, attention. It slammed around the mountain like a Titan boxer throwing punches. One of them landed so close it was impossible to distinguish the flash from the cracking boom that literally shook the ground.

I've got to get the hell out of the open, Tom thought. Moments later he saw a small side canyon coming in from the left and he rode into the mouth of it. The place was lower than the rest of the terrain and open as well. He rode into it and dismounted by some bushes, to which he tied the mule. Large animals attract lightning and he did not want to be sitting on top of a lightning rod. Not after everything else he'd gone through. He ran his tongue over the split lip and fingered the large bump on his forehead. Hell, he'd already been hit by lightning once today.

In the inundating rain, he hunted for a place that might be safe. As if to underline just how pressing the situation was, a bolt flashed above him and rent the air with an ear-splitting crack. He saw the top of the tree it had struck blow into an aureole of splinters and needles. A vein of fire plunged down the side of the tree, exploding in a ball of sparks on the ground.

"Shit, fire!" he exclaimed and looked anxiously around. Another flash lit the canyon and thunder assaulted his ears. Finally, he chose a spot in the open and walked anxiously down to it. The place was running with a few centimeters of water but he stopped in a small, high place above the rivulet.

Just when he thought it could not get worse, the rain turned into balls of ice. It was the size of rice grains at first and then progressively the hail grew larger until he had to put his hands in the hood of his poncho to keep the pellets from striking his head. After a couple of minutes his hands were tender from the pounding. He flinched at each impact.

Damn! The rivulet had become a creek and he was standing up to his ankles in water. He knew he was at the mouth of a canyon that had been receiving huge amounts of water, small though it was. It might even be dammed by debris somewhere, getting ready to release a wall of water and logs. He decided it would be safer in the trees and began to walk toward them through the icy water.

Mercifully, the hail turned back into rain, but lightning struck nearby again and the deafening crash of sound made his heart almost jump out of his chest. The rushing water was full of ice and reached his knees. Rain still fell in sheets and billows driven by the icy wind.

My God! he thought, I don't want to die here. Not now, not like this. He was genuinely frightened by the rising water. He could be drowned, he could be struck by lightning, he could fall into hypothermia and collapse into the boiling rush of muddy water and ice. As a matter of fact he was shaking badly already.

He snatched a passing stick from the flood, used it to brace himself. Facing upstream, he moved his feet apart and put the point of the stout stick into the ground to form a tripod. It was something he had learned in U.S. Army survival school. Other things he'd learned there were turning out to be useful now. He monitored the progress of his body into hypothermia at the same time he monitored the rate of increase in the water, factoring in the odds of being hit by lightning. He focused his mind on the problem at hand, pushing his natural emotional responses as far down as he could in order to stay as calm as possible.

At last he perceived lengthening intervals between the bolts of lightning. The rain seemed to slacken with each passing minute. Would he have enough time? The water boiled at his crotch and he could feel pieces of debris banging his shins. Some of them were large enough to hurt even his numbed legs and there was a real danger of being knocked from his feet. If that happened he would never gain them again. It was time to move.

He lifted the point of the stick and poked it into the creek bottom, slid one foot to the side, and followed with the other, inching carefully across the stream. At one point his foot went into a hole and he almost lost his balance, but the water became gradually shallower until, finally, he was out of the rush and standing in ankle-deep mud.

He was shaking uncontrollably now and knew he was still in trouble. But the worse had passed. The icy front was over the mountain and the following rain was warm by comparison. He was going to need a fire.

He slogged toward the mule, which had stood hunched against the storm, responding to the lightning strikes only with a toss of its head. Thank God he had not bolted. Tom's backpack hung over the saddle horn and in that pack were waterproof matches and fire starter, part of the survival gear that all good hunters carry in snowy Wyoming. If the mule had run away he would have been a dead man.

The hunt for sticks and wood for the fire warmed him as he moved around the mouth of the canyon, gleaning pieces from under the apron of the trees. He snapped dead branches and rusty boughs of insect-kill that would kindle readily. He put the small pile under the shelter of a pine tree and placed the stick of fire-starter on it. The stuff lit at the first match and a thrill ran through him. 'I am going to make it,' he thought.

Tom piled more tinder on the fire, then added larger sticks. Even in the light drizzle falling from the tree, the fire grew with each larger piece of wood. In a matter of ten minutes his flames were half a meter tall. He raised his poncho to admit the wonderful heat. He held each hand and sodden, frozen foot in turn and let the glow work at the muddy balls they had become. His shaking lessened with each moment. 'Thank you, God,' he said silently.

He turned his back to the fire, raised the poncho to warm his back . . . and almost jumped out of his skin. A man dressed only in pants stood behind him. The specter's long black hair hung in strings over his face. The feet were bare, the eyes vacant, the skin a waxy white, without goose flesh to signal that the body was capable of recognizing itself as cold. Tom's eyes fixed on the pink, ropy weal which ran from the base of his ghostly throat down the length of his sternum.

It was Pete Villareal. And he was dying of exposure.

———

Polly sat in the waiting room of the Cristobol Colon bus station. It was crowded with Indians, some traveling but most to get in from the rain. Their conversations were about the rain which had turned the street in front to a fast moving, muddy stream.

Polly found a lone seat beside two women bundled against the cold. She raised her eyes to the flaking paint on the ceiling and then closed her eyes. She was exhausted.

'Good-bye, Thomas,' she thought. Her chest felt tight, but she had made up her mind. She would go back to Ferdie and lose herself in this development deal they had all worked on so hard and so long. A family deal in which every single one of them had contributed so much effort. They would have a family business again. They would be a family again. She and Ferdie could re-marry quickly while still in Mexico. And he would go back to his womanizing and they would go back to their separate bedrooms. She felt numb inside.

The excited conversations swirling around Polly were suddenly hushed. Polly opened her eyes and there stood Sam Harlan towering above her. The whole bus station had gone silent and all the Indians' eyes were on the enormous gringo and the rubia sitting in the plastic chair.

"Not now," Sam said. "Not 'til we know he's dead . . . or we get him back. You can leave later, but not now."

"Sam, I can't take it. I want to feel safe in my life again. I am not cut out for this sort of thing!" she cried. "I can't sit and worry constantly about Tom's safety. I am going insane with the worry!"

Huge sobs came galloping out of her chest. Sam reached down and patted her awkwardly on the shoulder. One of the Indian women stood and beckoned Sam to sit so he could give her better comfort. He sat and put his arm around her.

She grasped him as if she were drowning and began to cry, hanging onto the big man with a surprising strength. Sam continued to hold her until the storm inside her passed.

At last she released him and wiped her face on her sleeve. She rubbed her cheeks with the palms of both hands.

"Polly?"

"Yes?"

"I'm scared right now, too. I need you here. And so does Tom. You need to stay until it's over. It's the only decent thing to do."

"I know that now. If I had been going to do the right thing, I would have felt better with my decision. As it was, I could feel my heart constricting back to the small shape it was before I found Tom again." Polly attempted a smile.

Sam smiled back. "Let me get your bag," he said, looking around.

"Well, in my frightened rush I didn't take anything out of the room except my purse," Polly explained. "I'm glad you found me before the bus arrived."

"I am too. Let's go."

Polly and Sam left the bus station as the morning sunlight hit the street. They climbed into the taxi and drove back to the hotel.

When she got back to her room, she opened the door and turned on the light. The first thing she noticed was something on the bed. It was a napkin from the hotel restaurant and on it was her ring.

The missionary was a tall man with a crown of red hair and a beatific look in his eyes. He had a wife and three daughters, the smallest of whom was sitting in his lap as he puffed on a pipe.

They and a half dozen villagers were sitting around a bonfire built in front of the missionary's stone house. Tom was wrapped in a blanket, his foot elevated on a small stool.

"Still cold?" the man asked.

Tom dragged his eyes away from the fire, where he had been staring for a long time. He nodded. "I thought I'd been cold before, I was raised in some very snowy mountains, but that rainstorm just about did me in."

The man nodded. "You were in pretty bad shape. How is the foot?"

"It's OK, those Ibuprofen bombs you gave me are working. It throbs a bit but it's not too bad." Tom stared back into the fire. "Mike?"

"Yes?"

"Pete told me he was going to some kind of ritual in the mountains, to a ceremony thousands of years old where the people ate hallucinogenic mushrooms. He was investigating the drug traffic end of it, but he seemed real interested in the religion part of it. Today he told me he had been murdered, that he had seen his own ritual sacrifice. 'They killed me,' he kept saying. He died in my arms saying it.

"I guess it just seems impossible. I thought that those sorts of practices were long dead," Tommy's voice trailed off.

The man took his pipe from his mouth and said, "Hardly. There are a lot of places where shamans, witch doctors, and the like are very much a part of community life — Africa, Asia, Siberia, America . . ."

"America?"

"Sure. What do you think all this New Age stuff is? It's a reversion to the primitive, something right off the walls of Lascaux."

"Is it evil?"

The man puffed on his pipe and furrowed his forehead. The little girl on his lap turned her face up, waiting for an answer.

Finally he said, "There is a great deal of evil in the world. And, in spite of the influence of monotheistic religions, millions and milions of people still believe in the old, primitive, animistic practices of the past. They deify animals, sing, drum, and spill blood. Sometimes human blood, literally or symbolically."

The man smiled and waved out at the dark night. "It's why I'm here. Most of the people here have lost or never knew the meaning of a religion that offers them access to a loving God. Instead, they practice the old forms . . . and fall into the old follies. We sons of Abraham speak of Satan and his temptations, but it is only a useful personification of the evil that thrives where people are ignorant of love itself. It's the same old cycle."

"Which cycle?"

"The cycle of spirituality declining into religion, of faith degrading into law and ritual, of love being traded for the stuff of the world. The God part gets lost after a couple of generations and the people begin to suffer and fall away. Eventually they look into the dusty old caves of the past and are lost there. Their children find themselves in spiritual agony and begin their own seach, until they 'discover' the teachings of a man who said that God was love. Then they bring together small communities of people like themselves, and go back a simple religion that gives them great comfort and, we believe, eternal life.

"But then the children of those children begin to interest themselves in the trappings and ritual, in the superficial aspects of the spiritual experience. They begin to build bigger churches, mount bigger productions, dress their priests in grander raiment. The teachings become encrusted with more interpretations, like barnacles on a ship's bottom. Finally, the thing can't move, doesn't work, sinks. The love is lost. And the children of the ones faithful to the practices, not the spirit, again find themselves in agony. They, in their turn, disperse in search of love. Some go back into the caves to raise the moribund and fearful spirits of the old pantheon. Others find the teachings of Jesus, who said that God is love. The cycle repeats itself."

"Just goes on and on."

"We believe it will end — someday. And we look forward to that."

This was little comfort for Tom. The body of a man he had hardly known, but liked very much, was lying in a wooden box piled with ice. Who knows what they had done to him on the mountain. The mark on Pete's chest was superficial, but he had been convinced they had cut his heart out.

Tom had shared the man's last terrible hour and, if there had been any doubt in his mind before, he now fully believed it: evil was real, horrible things were practiced, and souls were lost. Today.

And then, with the background of conversational murmurs and gentle people digging aluminum foil-wrapped corn out of the fire, he thought about love.

He'd had it, lost it, been given it back only to almost lose it again, along with his life. He was tired of taking chances, riding the roller coaster. He wanted Polly and he wanted to simplify his life. He wanted what this man with the child in his lap had. He wanted peace.

"Carros."

Cars. The word broke Tom's reverie and he looked up to see three cars moving off the road into the village. Something told him the cars were there for him and a lump filled his throat. He was feeling safer by the moment.

When he saw Sam get out of the first car, he was exhilarated. When he saw Polly running up from the second car, he was stunned.

He sat near the fire, watching Mike lead her to him.

Polly approached the man in the blanket, one bandaged foot propped on a stool and she stopped. This was barely her Thomas. The face was gaunt, haunted. But the eyes were the same. She went to him and he shrugged the blanket off one shoulder to hold out his hand to her.

She walked into his grasp and felt his cold face on her body. A very long moment passed and then he looked up at her. She took his face in her hands, ran her thumbs over his temples, and said gently, "Let's go home."

Epilogue

Oz looked around the mayor of Pochutla's little office. There were pictures of his kids' christenings, a daughter's quinceañera when she turned 15. The largest picture on his desk, though, was one of the mayor and his wife with the Pope. This was a man with major influence. Excellent.

Oz looked back at the Mexican man with the Polish surname and gold teeth. And smiled. The man was placing the seven thousand dollars in his desk drawer and locking it from sight. It was the insurance policy against his and Olga's arrest. The policy had just gone into effect.

The man smiled back. "Welcome to Pochutla, Señor Jardiñero. Of course, you will in fact be living in Puerto Angel but consider Pochutla your home as well."

He rubbed his hands happily on the desk, as if stroking the bundle of money on the other side of the wood. "And welcome to the Coffee Growers and Exporters Association of Oaxaca, too."

He smiled brightly at Olga. "And, of course, you are welcome, too, Señora."

"When will the cleanup crew start renovating the hotel?" she asked.

"Tomorrow, tomorrow. No problem."

Oz took the lease papers from the man's desk and stared at them. They were his and Olga's tickets to a new life on the Costa Chica of Oaxaca. It had been for years the major Mexican off-loading area for Colombian cocaine, so all the local officials, both state and federal, had been long ago corrupted beyond redemption.

They had leased a small hotel on Panteon Beach in a picturesque and totally corrupt place called, ironically enough, Puerto Angel — Port of the Angel. Many major international players were embedded in the place: Italian Mafia, Guadalajara Mafia, New Orleans Mafia, others. Those people had spent a lot of money making sure that no one stuck their nose into the place without having it chopped off for shark bait. And he and Olga were slipping in under those people's dark aegis. Their contact man was right out of a bad action novel — a one-eyed drug running pilot from Texas with a serious nose habit.

Oz truly hated the idea of having to leave the San Francisco Bay area. Especially because of some small time cop who had killed himself, really, by panicking and running off into a storm. The combination of hallucinogens, props and the surgical sleight-of-hand Olga had learned in the Philippines had never caused them serious trouble before Pete Villareal had shown up. A couple of serious freak-outs, maybe, but nothing like this last deal.

A soul tourist dead of a heart attack was trouble enough, but a dead American cop was too much. Killing a cop was just about the last thing you couldn't do without having to pay the full price.

But, too bad, he and Olga were safe in Mexico, where money means everything. Besides, if they wanted to go home to visit all they had to do was fly to Tijuana and cross the border with the Sunday bullfight crowd. He smiled at Olga and she smiled back. No problem. And lots of new opportunity besides.

———

In Mexico, the brothers Patricio and José Gorostiza were walking, their hands behind them, into a dense thicket near a clear little stream. As they walked they talked. They spoke of their village and their duties, how it had been their whole lives. They also talked of old times, laughing about the many funny things that seemed to jump into their memories once the first tale was told. They remembered their long-dead parents. And their nephews Mario, Demetrio, Cenovio. All dead now, too.

They talked of Concha Osorio's new status as an international celebrity and of the events that had pulled them into the main current of the modern Mexican state. And they laughed at the money they had both received since their little deception. They had been given the local distributorship for Modelo canned beer and Rey bottled drinks, both products which had been peeled off the local cacique's action. They had even received a small truck for delivery of the items along their route, which was fairly large. A generous gift from the regional political leadership.

But the best part had been their elevation in the national party, PRI. They had sat at the table with the local war chiefs and, as representatives of the indigenous community, their input had seemed to be considered seriously. That was certainly something new. In the past, the local cacique had been the only Indian to sit at the privy council table.

And there they had sat, across the table from the man who had ended up having to share his business and political pies with two old farts, one of whom could barely write. He had not been a happy man, to be sure. They had even tweaked his nose publicly a couple of times, just to let him know that he was not the only rich Indian in town any more. It had been fun. The memory of it made them laugh. But mostly they laughed because a handful of Indians had made a monstrously oppressive government stumble and pause, if only for a moment.

"Okay, that's far enough."

The two chortling old men turned around, tears of laughter running down their cheeks. They faced the policemen armed with rifles who had brought them to this isolated place.

———

Tom stepped out onto the deck and looked out over the valley. He was happy. Really happy, way down deep. He had a whole new sense of things at a profound level.

His appreciation of being blessed by having been born in America at this particular time in its history was something which had begun to sprout in the aftermath of the events down south. The first thing he had done when he'd returned was turn off the TV and quit buying the paper.

Then he had gotten married and Polly had quit her partnership in California, giving her position to Christina. The wedding they had planned at the Chapel of the Transfiguration in Grand Teton National Park had devolved into a civil ceremony in Oaxaca City, Sam Harlan as best man and their daughter as a grudging bridesmaid. But, hell, nothing was perfect. Except this sparkling morning in the Wyoming mountains.

Polly was out in the yard, working in the morning sun. Bulb time. October.

He walked back inside and went to the coffee machine. He poured a cup and then stepped to the west window of the kitchen. Outside it was brilliant with the high autumn light. Polly was down on her knees at the edge of the wildflower garden she'd put in the spring before, Millie lying in the sun and watching. Polly was dividing gladiolus bulbs and sorting them with some new ones she'd bought the day before. A tendril of wheat-colored hair had fallen from her Gibson girl hairdo. A diamond stud earring beamed a needle of light at him and he grinned and shook his head.

California women! She was wearing a University of Wyoming sweatshirt, gloves, Wrangler jeans, whacked-out tennies and five thousand dollars worth of earrings.

What had he ever done to deserve her? Nothing, really. Just plain damn, dumb luck.

In the middle of his thoughts, the door opened and Polly came inside, followed by the dog.

"Hi, Millie," he said and reached down to twiddle her ears and run his finger down the top of her nose.

"Me too," Polly said and put her arms around Tom's neck. He pecked her on the forehead and reached up to pull the comb from her hair. He held a lock of her hair in his hand and stared at it. It was alive. He put his nose in it, next to her ear and drew in a breath. A tear ran unexpectedly from his face and fell onto her cheek. He had almost lost his life not long ago. And Polly with it.

She pulled her face back and looked at him. "What is it?"

"I love you."

She put her face back on his chest and kissed his shirt. "We're going to town."

"What for?"

"To buy a pumpkin. The PTA is selling them in the square downtown."

"You go."

"We are going, Thomas." There was no arguing, he could tell by the note in her voice. She reached up and wiped his cheek with her thumb. "You're leaking."

They parked in front of Stone drug, on the sunny side of the street. It was cold in the shade on the north side of the buildings. Fall was slipping away and winter was waiting somewhere up north. In the meantime the days were wondrous with their creamy light and the nights glittered with the promise of winter nights cold enough to burst trees like artillery rounds.

"I'm going to get an ice cream cone, I'll see you over there."

"Get me one too. Vanilla."

"See you in a couple." He went inside and walked to the old soda counter. It hadn't changed at all in the whole length of his life. He remembered coming in here with his sister and cousins to get ice cream after the show. They would then go to the Wort Hotel and sit on the curb to listen to the music and watch the gamblers. In the old days the bandstand had been right in front of the street entrance so the music of The Sons of the Pioneers, The Sons of the Golden West and other bands would flood the sidewalk. It pulled the tourists in like netted fish. He'd loved to look at all the interesting people that the night brought to downtown Jackson Hole. They couldn't have been more strange and exotic to Tom and the other kids if they'd been Arabians or New Guinea cannibals dressed like birds of paradise. They'd sat on the curb, licked at their cones and felt their eyes pop at the sequined shirts and silver-dressed boots that had been popular with the women in those days. The men with their piped shirts, expensive hats and glassy boots were little less impressive.

"One vanilla and one strawberry, LaDonna."

"Haven't seen you for a long time, Tommy."

"I was gone for a while. Mexico. Got married down there, then honeymooned in Ixtapa."

Her eyebrows went up. "Jeepers. Running with the fast crowd, huh?"

"Nah. A lot of it was police work."

"We paying you guys in the Sheriff's Department to go down to Mexico now?"

Tom grinned. "It's Yuppie Town."

"Hell, I guess," she said, and handed him the cones. "There you go."

"Thanks Hon." He held his hand out for the change but she winked at him and dropped it in the plastic tip jar.

"Thanks, Tom. I'm saving for a trip to Mexico," she said. It made Tommy smile.

Tom crossed the street and stepped onto the sidewalk. He stopped. In his mind's eye he saw the little Trique Indian child looking up at him, her cedar knot eyes full of anticipation, her dirty little hands outstretched. It was a memory from Tlaxiaco the summer before, so long ago. It seemed now.

'Sientase,' he said in his mind and the child sat. He handed her the ice cream bar. Strawberry. The brilliant smile cracked her grimy face again. She closed her eyes. Licked. Licked. Like one of the little native kids who used to sit on the curb and listen to the music in Jackson's primitive past.

Tom glanced into the bright park. It was teeming with people and children. He walked into the crowd. The first thing that caught his eye was a world-class mommy butt in purple Spandex. The tall blonde wearing the dermal pants, and nothing beneath, was making political conversation with a woman plain as a sparrow in a Goretex jacket, felt Bavarian clogs and granny glasses. Nouvelle Jackson Hole in a nutshell.

Tom's eye roamed the crowd. There were three tables set up with holiday cakes, cookies and candies. Thick cookies with Jack o'Lantern faces in creamy sugar frosting. He made a note to buy a half dozen. It was for the PTA, after all.

As he looked at the crowd he saw that it was made up mostly of women with toddlers and he was struck by how old many of them were. Lightly graying ex-career women in their late thirties and early forties who'd probably given up their politics and ambitions to get back to the real world before it was too late. Not very many natives he noted. Heidis and Muffys rather than LaWannas and LaDonnas. But that was just fine with him. Hell, he thought, everybody's gotta be some place.

He finally saw Polly. She was pointing to a big pumpkin and a man wearing a change apron was grinning. The pumpkin's stem drooped and was frayed into a small broom. It was wizened and cocked to one side with creases half-an-inch deep. It was ugly as hell. But she'd make it into something striking, he knew.

As he walked up to her, and the man carrying the pumpkin, he handed her the cone and said, "You always have to pick the ugly ones, don't you?"

She looked Tom dead in the eye and said, "It means some work, but they always turn out just the way I like 'em." She took a lick of the ice cream and winked.

The End